WHISPERS OF GODS AND GHOSTS

RAIN CARSWELL

SNOWCAT BOOKS

To Raven, my Fenix

FOREWORD

This book is, in a way, a part of my soul in the same way any artist pours their heart into art. It has brought comfort to me in dark moments of the time it took to pour the pieces of my heart onto these sheets of paper and I hope that one day, it may do the same for someone else.

That said, I also recognize that there may be some sensitive topics in the following pages and as an author, I believe it is my responsibility to properly address this material. Such topics include; abuse, anxiety, attempted suicide, depression, disease, death, homophobia, self-harm, transphobia, trauma and PTSD.

The characters involved in the story you are about to read are nothing more than fiction but I hope that within the mind of the reader, they may come to life.

We're all killers. We've all killed a part of ourselves to survive. We've all got blood on our hands.

   Something somewhere had to die so we could stay alive.

—m.a.w.

Prologue: Fate's Design

The Watcher

In the dark of night, the city sleeps. The dark water of the river flows calmly toward the sea in the West, tracing its banks like a black snake. A hundred boats wait in the harbour for another dawn and another day to set out, carrying goods back and forth throughout the continent. Looming over the city, a castle of stone and glass towers over nearly everything else, scraping the clouds with its twisted spires. Tonight, darkness covers the city and all is light sucked from the houses as sleep takes the people to the realm of dreams and the moon hides behind dark grey clouds. Within the walls of the city, the people of Elview rest in peace, oblivious to the darkness that lurks outside, kept away only by invisible walls built up by the protectors of their great empire.

The cathedral's stone walls match the magnificent castle in height and grandeur. Behind its walls, the Order sleeps, but the beast will not rest forever. The cathedral houses a great many warriors and soldiers, yet there is only one that holds such importance in the path of fate. He sleeps as ignorantly as the rest of the city, perhaps knowing the dangers the kingdom itself faces, but there is no knowing the darkness outside of it. Only he can change the course of the fate of this world, only he holds the power to defeat the ancient darkness.

"But he is only a child. He cannot be strong enough." The smoke-like spirit floats outside the window of that cathedral, waiting and watching.

"We will see, my dear friend." The second spirit speaks in a wistful voice. She takes the shape of a slender woman dressed in a white shift dress and a pale mask covers half of her face.

The smoke spirit snorts. "It's impossible, Airadyne. He is not his father."

"We will see," Airadyne repeats calmly.

Beyond the window, a child sleeps, tiny and vulnerable as he curls up on his side. His dark hair fans around his head like a halo and he is still fully dressed atop the covers. Beside him lies a white cat with purple horns between pointed ears, tail curled around her nose. They make a strange pair; a kid who holds the destiny of this world and a cat belonging to the wild far away from here. Yet the two of them are far more important than they know.

"Will it begin soon?" The smoke spirit asks.

"Be patient, Wolf," Airadyne chides. "He is not the first you have underestimated. Not being his father hardly means he cannot fulfil this fate. I only fear he will not like the way the threads of fate have been woven."

"Our enemy will not wait," Wolf growls. "You know that, Airadyne. We must act soon."

The pale woman nods. "Yes . . . And I will show him soon enough. Do not doubt my guidance. In time, we will have our hero."

"And if he cannot do what we need?"

"Then we die. This world will be swallowed by the darkness if he cannot stop it, and then there will be no one left to save us."

The two spirits fall silent, floating high above the ground. For only a moment, the dark clouds part and the light of the moon shines upon the sleeping boy like silvery water. In that space between the clouds, the stars shine just as bright as ever, yet Airadyne knows a day may come when they cannot shine at all.

Half a continent away, a war rages. On the docks of a white-marble city, a boy with golden hair watches the sea. There is no sound here other than the whisper of the waves against the sandy shore and the breeze ruffling his hair. Sitting on a stone wall overlooking the docks and the water beyond that, he watches as a white bird dips and dives over the bay, searching for food. Behind him, each house made of pristine white stone makes the city glow even under the dark of night, and not far away sits a cluster of towers and courtyards that make up the castle. Overhead, a thousand stars fill the clear sky, surrounding the full moon in a perfect pattern of constellations like embroidery on a black velvet curtain.

The boy looks down at the red pendant clutched in his hand, his wavy blond hair ruffled by the wind and silent tears running down his freckled cheeks. This place is not his home, but there is nowhere else to go. Everyone he knew is gone, left dead in the fire that tore apart his real home yet people keep saying "he belongs here" and "this is home now."

"There you are, dear," says a soft, kind voice. The boy turns around to see the woman they say will take care of him. She stands in the road wearing nightclothes and holding a lantern that casts a gentle light. "I was wondering where you may have gone."

He doesn't answer; he simply turns back to look at the dark water.

"Oh darling, this must be so hard for you." She sits next to him on the wall, setting the lantern beside her. "I can't imagine what it's like."

Again, her words earn no reply for a long time. They sit in silence until the woman starts to think the boy can't hear her.

"When can I go back home?" The boy whispers.

The woman tries to smile when she tells him gently, "Your home is gone, dear. I'm sorry but this is home now."

The boy nods because this is something he already knows. "But I want to go back."

She puts her arm around his shoulders and the two of them sit there, watching the sea until the lamp burns dim and the light of the moon dips toward the water. The woman watches the boy with sadness in her heart. She believes no child should lose everything, that no *person* should know the cruelty of the world as he does.

No spirits watch this scene unfold on the docks of the city of Isondale. No spirits watch the golden-haired boy as he grows older, yet they watch the boy destined to save or destroy this world not knowing that one day both will be equally important in the threads of fate. Much later, Airadyne would understand: it is far too dangerous for fate to entrust itself to a single person.

1

THE ASSEMBLY OF SPIRITS

KELLIN

None of my clothing is right. Either it isn't "proper" enough or I hate it. The ruffled collars are annoying, the sequins itch and the silk feels awful. After deliberating for longer than it should take, I yank on my jacket over top of a shirt that at least looks clean and messily tie the laces of my boots.

"You're going to be late," Taiyo observes. She stands near the door, leaning casually against the wall.

"I know, I'm going I promise," I tell her, tripping over the piles of clothing and books strewn across my tiny room. I curse in Old Alkelian as I knock a stack of paper off a shelf.

"Well, you had better hurry." Taiyo crosses her arms, clearly not intending to be of any assistance.

I kneel next to the giant white cat nearly asleep next to the window and poke her fluffy shoulder. "Sorry to disturb you, but we have to go, Fenix."

The cat blinks her violet eyes at me then yawns. She stands, arching her back, shaking her fur out, and stretching her legs sleepily. I step away and grab my sword, sheathing it across my back along with my spear. As I rush out of the room, I check that each of my daggers is in place and adjust the thin silver chain of my pocket watch. I've completely disregarded the uniform tonight, foregoing the ridiculous red and silver jacket or the armour I was told to wear. Instead, I'm wearing my usual black jacket. The only part of my outfit that indicates my role as a member of the Order is the silver pin on my lapel, embossed with the rose insignia of the Order. They should really just be grateful that I'm actually coming at all, considering my track record.

As soon as I step into the hall, with Fenix next to me and Taiyo close behind, I nearly walk right into Jyn as he suddenly appears in front of me.

"Gah, I found you," he says, almost falling over as he stops suddenly to avoid crashing into me.

"Go go go." Taiyo waves us away down the hall. "Storm is going to kill you if you're late."

Jyn starts toward the stairs and I practically have to run to keep up with him. Fenix trots along next to me with her tail flicking happily behind her. Usually, the cat is just content to be going somewhere instead of staying holed up inside.

"Can't we just not go?" I ask as we race down the stairs, passing a soldier who presses close to the wall to stay out of our way and avoid getting trampled.

"That"—Jyn glances over his shoulder to respond—"is unfortunately not how that works."

I roll my eyes. "I would rather not though."

Jyn has been my only friend for as long as I can remember, Taiyo being the second. He's older than me by a few months, but both of us are soldiers of a sort for the Order, trained to defend Alkelia as part of the Halfblood military, although I have risen to knighthood before him. Tonight, his green-blue hair is a spiky mess that sticks up in every direction in bizarre contrast to his flawless dark blue tailcoat. Unlike me, he carries no weapons, a far more reasonable choice for a court banquet.

We skid into the entrance hall of the grand cathedral. Eldric Storm, a tall man with frighteningly pale blue eyes and greying hair, waits for us, his priestly robes making him look rather like a statue. The cathedral is buzzing with activity tonight, Order members rushing back and forth as they prepare for tonight's events and civilians attempting to offer prayers but there is far too little silence for that. High Priest Eldric Storm stands out like a sore thumb, stiff and statuesque among the chaos.

When Jyn, Fenix and I appear before him, he scowls. "You're late. We intended to leave five minutes ago and we do not have time to spare so get moving."

He whirls around and practically glides out the open doors and down the stone steps to the carriage parked for us in front of the cathedral. A Sister dressed in red and silver waits for us already, her blond hair done up neatly and her robes arranged perfectly. I recognize her as Sister Naemie, a priestess of moderate power who has always been completely indifferent toward me and the chaos I bring, probably because she doesn't have the time to deal with me.

Jyn and I climb into the carriage, cramming ourselves on the bench across from the two priests with Fenix between us, and soon we're winding our way through the crowded streets of Elview. For the past few days, the city has been in a flurry of motion as people prepare for the Assembly of Spirits, an event that only happens once a year as the power of the spirits reaches its highest. Today, the streets are packed with parties and various other gatherings that make it hard to get anywhere. Traffic hardly moves in some places. It takes us nearly an hour to reach the castle when on any other occasion, it would only take perhaps half an hour.

The courtyard out front of the grand castle is a whirlwind of activity as carriages drive in and out, dropping off their respective noblemen and women. Under the light of the evening sun, the castle sparkles with rose gold and copper, and the sunlight dances off the metal trim on the many balconies, rooftops, and windows of the grand building. The expansive gardens are alive with shades of green and pops of colour; red and yellow and blue and purple, with each plant perfectly tended by the best gardeners in the kingdom. Throughout the massive courtyard, partygoers mingle in their finest with glittering jewels and expensive fabrics arranged in outfits designed to impress and sure enough, each one is more fabulous than the last.

When we step down from our carriage at the front steps, Jyn, Fenix and I fall in behind High Priest Storm and Sister Naemie, following the crowd to the doors.

"We shouldn't be here," I whisper to Jyn.

"I wish we had a choice," he mumbles back.

I sigh, running my fingers across the hilt of the dagger sheathed on my thigh. "We could just run away now."

"And get found out before we set foot outside the castle grounds?" He shakes his head. "Not going to happen."

The two-inch heels of my boots click against the stone steps as we ascend to the gold-painted doors of the castle. Guards flank the entrance, checking the invitations of everyone arriving. Here, the line of people is moving slower as people have to stop as each invitation letter is read and examined to prove its legitimacy. When we finally reach the top, I dig the crumpled piece of paper from my jacket pocket and hand it over. The guard does his best to smooth it out, his frown deepening with each word he reads. He glances at Fenix nervously, his eyes flicking back to the paper when she blinks at him with large, purple eyes.

"Kellin . . . Kane." The man reads slowly before looking up—or, rather, down at me. "The bastard heir of the North? What kind of joke is this?"

I sigh. By now, I'm used to people treating me like this. "I am a knight of the Order. It's not a joke, that's my name."

Still, the man stares at me. "Look kid, I can't be letting just anyone in here, you understand? But if you really are with the Order, I apologize for the trouble—"

"Is there a problem here?" Sister Naemie asks, appearing suddenly behind the man.

At the sight of her, the man shakes his head frantically, realizing his mistake. "No—no, Sister. I was just confirming the invitation."

"And? I presume everything is in order, then," she says firmly. "If so, we had best be on our way." She turns to me. "And this is what happens when you don't wear the uniform."

I reach out and snatch the letter back from the guard, storming past him into the castle. Behind me, the man barely glances at Jyn's invitation before waving him through without question, likely trying his best to move the line along without further trouble. Once we're all inside, we head down the long hallway, following the red and gold carpet past paintings of previous monarchs and other important figures like high priests and generals. The walls are painted a shade of off-white with gold trim along the floor and roof; the chandeliers and torches are all solid gold. At the end of the long hallway, we reach another set of gold doors. They open to reveal a ballroom full of nobles dancing and conversing in a sea of shimmering fabric and gems. The squire at the door announces our arrival but hardly anyone bothers to look up, enthralled by the enchanting music and all-out extravagance of the party.

Immediately, I steer myself toward a corner far from the centre of the room, near a window overlooking the beautiful gardens. Jyn follows me through the crowd although, with Fenix at my side, most people step out of the way to clear a path. They know well enough not to mess with someone like me. By now, the sun has nearly set, and pink and orange light shines through the patterned glass windows near the ceiling, casting rainbows across the room. Halfway to the window, a tall, dark-haired woman in a blue gown intercepts us.

"Kellin. I was wondering if we would be seeing you here. You and your ghastly cat." She speaks coldly, spitting my name like it's poison. In her dress of deep blue satin and silver embroidery, she looks like some sort of regal statue, stiff and poised for perfection. Silver jewels sparkle in her bound-up hair and around her neck like tiny stars, giving her a shining appearance despite her inky hair and the creases forming in her skin due to her age. In one blue-nailed hand, she delicately holds a champagne glass. Her other arm is linked with that of a blond man in a perfectly average blue suit with nothing remarkable about him other than the turned-up look on his face, like there's an awful smell everywhere he goes. Which I suppose is far from inaccurate, seeing as he chose to marry a woman like my mother.

"Elenore," I greet her, my stomach plummeting.

"I see you've just arrived," she notes. "Will you be partaking in the meeting this year?"

I try not to sigh too dramatically. Only generals attend the annual gathering and she knows very well that I am a knight. "No. As always."

"Hmm." She seems to stare right into my soul over the rim of her glass. "You disappear to join the Order and yet you can't even do that right. Disappointing."

Thankfully, her fool of a husband, Robert Clearwater, interjects before she can continue. "Elenore, if you wouldn't mind, I believe we should pay our respects to the other royalty, shouldn't we? People more worthy of our time?"

Elenore Clearwater only spares me one final look of ice and daggers before sweeping off into the crowd with a judgemental hum, Robert clinging to her side like a puppy. I watch as they go, my heart pounding inside my chest, hands clenched into fists. Running my fingers through my hair, I try to keep breathing, exhaling deeply. Elenore is my mother but only in that she happened to birth me and nothing else. Robert, on the other hand, is merely the man she married and thankfully has no connection to me whatsoever; my own father is a nameless man who Elenore had a brief affair with only months before her wedding. He vanished without so much as a word and certainly left behind not a hint of who he might be, so I have never met him and likely never will.

"Are you still alive in there?" Jyn asks, waving one hand in front of my face.

I nod but don't look away from the spot where they melted back into the crowd. Thankfully, none of their children seem to be present—or rather, within sight—which would have made this night far worse than it is already bound to be. "Yeah, I'm fine. I just want this to be over with so we can get out of here."

"Well it won't be too long, now," he says, trailing me as I continue toward the spot by the windows. "We only need to be here until Storm and the others get back from the meeting."

"What I don't get is why we need to be here if we aren't even allowed to join the stupid meeting." I swipe a wine glass from a passing waiter who stares at me curiously and down half of it in one go. "See, if we were needed for that, it would at least feel like there's a reason for us to be here."

He shakes his head and snatches the glass from my hand, placing it on the tray of a different waiter, half-full, and the man stares at him, somewhat disgusted. "You know they just want you here to keep an eye on you or whatever. And you shouldn't be drinking."

"Shut up, I might need a drink or three to survive tonight," I grumble.

Sure enough, it turns out to be exactly as I anticipated, hours filled with too much noise and far too many people. Honestly, I can't see how events like this appeal to anyone at all. It's just a bunch of old, formerly fancy people having stiff conversations about the weather or current affairs while a string band plays boring, lifeless music and waiters serve tiny bites of food on large plates with more decoration than food. Jyn and I hide out in our corner with little to do but watch the glittering people sway back and forth in poor attempts at what I suppose they call dancing. No one tries to talk to us, thankfully, simply ignoring our presence the second they notice two Halfbloods standing next to the windows. But of course, the spirits are the worst part.

Although it's something I've grown accustomed to over the years, the whisperings of the otherworldly spirits are a constant buzz in the back of my mind, growing louder on nights like tonight when their power reaches its apex. Sometimes they talk of nonsense, even in languages I can't understand, but they also talk of death and glory, loss and love. I couldn't really say what the spirits are, other than simply entities from a different time who transcend the bounds of the mortal plane of existence and grant Halfbloods our extraordinary abilities. They are not, however, ghosts; spirits were never dead and as far as anyone knows, cannot die. But neither can we be certain they are truly alive in the common sense of the word. Many Halfbloods have the ability to hear or see such spirits, although most simply receive only the occasional sighting. I, on the other hand, can nearly always hear them as if they live inside my head, able to speak to me whenever they please but rarely showing their physical forms.

Tonight, the voices seem louder than usual and only wish to talk of death, and although I can't make out every word said, the conversations disturb me. This talk of death is far from uncommon. In fact, it's expected at times. But when the names of those who will or already have met their maker are repeated over and over in my head along with their age, cause of death, and entire life story, I find it rather impossible for anyone to feel at ease. They also speak of monsters from another world and the end of existence for all life, apparently normal conversation topics when you're an immortal entity not entirely of this world.

Finally, after what feels like years of waiting, the golden ballroom doors open to reveal the one we've all been waiting for. Xethos, the God of Victory, stands nearly seven feet tall with a sunburst crown of gold spikes inlaid with red gems atop his light brown hair. His armour is made of gold as well, with intricate details carved into the shining plates, and he rests one gloved hand on the golden pommel of the sword sheathed at his side. A cape of gold cloth falls from his shoulders to brush against the ankles of his gold boots, shimmering in the candlelight and seeming to move on its own accord. Guards in gold armour flank him on either side, carrying long halberds with white and gold flags flowing off their shafts. The instant the god steps through those doors, the entire room falls silent to bow before him. He strides across to the dais and up the steps to sit upon his extravagant gold throne, where he can observe the crowd gathered before him. The entire room falls silent at his entrance, captivated by everything about their god as they bow before him in reverence. No one dares to look at him for longer than a glance, but those who do are left stunned by that ice-cold gaze, his eyes deeper than the sea and just as blue.

To me, the most notable thing about Xethos is his imposing, blinding aura. It instantly overtakes my consciousness. It's like walking into a room full of gold, brilliant and glorious, only to realize the gold is shaped into a hundred deadly spikes and every one of them is pointed straight at me. I keep my head bowed and avoid looking at him, but still, I feel his eyes seeking out Halfbloods in the crowd. Instinctively, I reach for his mind as well, searching for even a hint of fear like I can do with anyone else. But this time, I hit only the sharp wall of his mental defences, and a sudden pain shoots through my skull. I gasp and my head snaps up in his direction, meeting his unfeeling blue eyes before I force myself to look away.

"Good evening." When Xethos speaks, his voice echoes through the room like thunder, effortless and perfectly calm with not a single emotion behind his stoney facade. "As you are all well aware, tonight is the night the power of the spirits is at its highest. Tonight, we celebrate the rising in the strength of those who defend these lands. Halfbloods."

I frown. The Order is the main line of defence for the kingdom of Alkelia, acting both as more than half the military as well as a church of a sort, having the closest contact with both Xethos and the spirits the people worship. Due to this connection, the Halfbloods comprising the Order seem like something other than human, with incomprehensible magic and strange communications that appear to be with other worlds. Many see us as perhaps more important than humans, stronger and able to defend Alkelia along with the rest of the world in ways regular mortals cannot. I have seen people practically grovel at our feet, worshipping us far more than they should.

However, there are others, such as those from Northern Alkelia, who see Halfbloods as demons sent from the underworldly realm of Gosritaan to destroy the world and who have undermined the kingdom by brainwashing its citizens to believe they are heroes.

Most of the time, people regard the Halfbloods who look more human with more respect. If there's too many strange things about them, they might as well be demons based on how others avoid them like the plague and whisper behind their backs. At least, that's how people tend to treat me.

All across the ballroom, people gaze in awe at Xethos. He continues his speech about the brave Halfbloods who fight for Alkelia and die for their god, but all I hear is lies and half-truths. Halfbloods bow before him and tonight, they are celebrated. It makes me sick to think they could worship the one being who forged this kingdom so full of hatred for people like me. Alkelia is a kingdom of liars, hypocrites and pretenders who raise themselves up as kings on thrones made from the bodies of those they deem unworthy of living in their so-called paradise.

And I have the misfortune of hailing from such a place.

2

RUNAWAY

SENIKA

The streets of Isondale are silent in the dead of night, grave-like in the stillness of the city. I creep through the streets as quietly as I can, hurrying to reach my destination. Few soldiers patrol the streets since the majority have been sent off the fight on the war front, but at one point, I do have to duck into an alleyway to avoid being spotted before slipping back out a few minutes later. Three moons glow overhead like torches burning in the cloudless sky next to the equally bright stars above the city. A soft breeze carries the smell of the sea over the tiny white stone houses and shops, and it bends the stems of the delicate blue flowers growing outside many of the windows.

This is Isondale, the capital of the kingdom of Iolleria and renowned as a bustling port city despite the war that rages just a few hundred leagues away on the other side of the kingdom. It's a large, sprawling city and sits next to the sea as well as the mouth of the Slash with a castle of white stone atop the hill to look out over all there is to see. There are no walls around the city and very few soldiers left to guard but no one would dare attack the city through which goods headed for half the continent pass en route to their final destination.

The port that stretches around the edges of nearly the whole city is currently home to only a handful of warships while the rest belong to traders and merchants as they pass through and stay for a night or ten.

I stop walking outside a wooden door of a small white house with a clear view of the sea. My heart pounds in my chest despite the stillness of the world, and I stare at the door for a long, long time as I decide what to do.

Ten months ago, my father was killed in the war after he made up his mind to go fight. After that, they sent me off too but I was never as brave as him. For the past ten months, I have trained with other Halfbloods in preparation for the day we would have to fight for real. But when the battle came and the monsters rose up from the very earth beneath our feet, all I could do was run. And I ran right back home, a deserter with no one who knows I'm even alive. By now, a ship has probably been sent back here to tell of the battle we lost, but I was gone before the battle even started. When they gathered what they could of the dead, no one would have been able to find anything that resembled me, but they would have proclaimed me dead regardless. It's possible my mother has been notified already, a funeral on its way sometime soon.

But I'm not dead. I stand right outside her door, and if they learn of my survival, they will learn I deserted the men and women I trained with for the past ten months and left them for dead. So when I reach for the doorknob, my hand rests on the cool metal for a moment before falling back to my side.

And I turn and walk back into the night, the eyes of a cat visible in one window but no other witnesses to tell of my visit here. Guilt eats my mind like a ravenous beast as I walk toward the docks. This is the only way to avoid being sent right back to that cursed place. Even though some part of me hopes they could just let it go and let me stay here in Isondale where I don't have to fight, I know that can never happen.

The docks look strange at night with all the colours muted to shades of grey rather than the usual bright blue and yellow and red and purple and green sails that top each of the ships in the harbour. The absence of all light makes it look just as ghostly and abandoned as the rest of the city, but after some time, I find a ship with a truly black sail and gold writing on its bow. The *Vanquisher*. A man stands next to the gangplank, leaning on a stack of crates, smoking a cigar quietly. He greets me with a smile that quickly fades.

"What are you doing here, Senika?" he asks warily. "Your Mum told the Captain you were reported dead days ago."

I sigh. "Yeah . . . I ran away. And now I kind of need to get out of here before I'm sent back to fight once they realize what I've done."

He shakes his head and places the cigar between his teeth. "Alright. The Captain's out right now but I figure she'll be back soon enough. The plan was to head to Alkelia on the morrow but it wouldn't hurt to leave early, I suppose."

I follow him onto the ship and head straight to the Captain's quarters. The door squeaks open to reveal a mess of a room with a bed in one corner and a desk nearly hidden under all the paper piled on it. A trunk sits at the foot of the bed with clothing spilling out upon the scuffed wooden planks forming the floor. In the center of the room, a young man with curly red hair is asleep with his head on the cluttered table taking up the majority of the room.

The floorboards creak under my feet as I walk over to gently shake him awake. "Gendry. You alive?"

He lifts his head, blurry-eyed and half asleep. "Wha-what's happening?"

"We're going to be leaving soon," I inform him. "When your moms get back."

Finally, he notices who I am, shooting to his feet so fast he knocks his chair over backwards. "Senika! Gods, we were told you were dead! How are you here?"

"I, uh . . ." I start but he throws his arms around me in a crushing hug that knocks the air from my lungs. "Ow, too tight. Gendry, let go."

He steps back to look at me, still holding me firmly by the shoulders. Shaking his head, he laughs and grins wildly. "I have no idea how you're alive, but this is amazing. Oh gods, please let this be real."

He pulls me into a hug again, this time allowing me to breathe. "I may have run away to be here, though," I tell him. "I mean, we were attacked and I . . . just ran."

Suddenly, his overjoyed attitude is gone. "You deserted?" I nod and he continues, "So you need to get out of here, then. I mean, if they learn you aren't dead, they could throw you in prison for deserting What time is it?" He glances around the room but the ship has no clocks.

"Well past midnight, I think," I say. "Aaron told me your moms are out but they should be back soon. We'll get them to leave for Alkelia right away."

"Right, we were headed there anyway." He starts sorting through the mess on the table, rifling through maps, random drawings, lists, and reports, tossing aside an ornate dagger and shoving a few books off onto the floor. "We've been docked here for weeks now; you're lucky you got back when we can get you out fast."

As I watch him stumble across the cabin in search of something, I ask, "Gendry, are you drunk?"

He pauses, considering this. "No. Well . . . maybe. Just a little though." I sigh and he protests, "Well what else was I meant to do? I thought you were dead! Look, you're my best friend so don't go pulling another stunt like that. I can't do that again."

Before I can respond, the cabin door flies open, nearly falling right off the hinges. Both of us spin around to see Captain Kira Aliver, a woman who looks just like Gendry with that wild red hair and brilliant emerald green eyes. She throws her dark jacket on the floor and storms over to me, frowning. But instead of scolding me, she wraps her arms around me, holding me tight.

"I knew it!" she laughs. "I knew you weren't dead." She points to her wife, Emaya, who stands in the doorway, her dark hair tied up on top of her head and an only-somewhat-shocked look on her face. "Emaya didn't believe me but I knew. Aha! This is amazing!"

I carefully extract myself from her arms. "Kira, I need to come with you to Alkelia."

The pirate frowns. "Alkelia? Why would you want to go there?"

"Well . . . see I kind of ran from a battle. Which apparently resulted in everyone thinking I'm dead. But instead, I'm just a deserter," I explain yet again, this time adding, "And a coward."

"Oh no no no, there is nothing cowardly about you, Senika." Kira shakes her head adamantly. "You had best visit your mum before you go anywhere. She thinks you're dead, Senika."

Instantly, I shake my head. "No, I can't do that. I'm sorry Kira but I can't disappoint her."

She sighs heavily. "Okay. If that's what you want then I can't make you change your mind. We will take you to Alkelia and I suppose we might need somewhere to lie low for a while, too."

I smile gratefully. "Really? Thank you."

"Ah, anything for you, kid," She says, smacking my back before walking out of the cabin. Then she's off in captain mode, waking everyone on the ship and ensuring we can be off as soon as possible.

Before the sun even rises, the ship is out of the harbour, sailing on a brisk early morning breeze toward Alkelia. Once we've set off, many of the pirates head back below deck to catch a few more hours of sleep before the sun rises, leaving just Gendry and I above to watch the city disappear over the horizon.

"Are you sure about this?" Gendry asks me, breaking the silence that has enveloped the ship for so long. "It's not too late to turn around. Or jump ship."

I glance over my shoulder at him. Isondale was my home for most of my life. It feels strange to be leaving, but I know this is the right decision. "I'm sure. And I can't exactly go back now and make it before they notice I'm gone."

He shrugs. "If you flew it would be pretty fast."

"I'm not going back," I tell him. "Not until everyone forgets who I am, at least."

"What about when the ship goes back?" he questions. "Do you really want to be stranded in Alkelia?"

"I could go to Isher," I point out, looking back at the dark water.

"You don't speak Isherian," he reminds me. "And I don't think they speak anything else there, which would make it hard."

For a moment, I don't reply, thinking carefully. "Kyran then. They're close allies to Alkelia and they speak both Kyrani and Alkelian. I could go there."

"Do you really want to spend the rest of your life in a desert?"

". . . No."

For three days, we sail along the dark river, occasionally passing other boats. But mostly, we are alone on the water. This river was supposedly created by a god's sword cutting through the ground during the War of Gods five hundred years ago. It hardly counts as a river, miles wide and deep as the ocean with the banks towering cliffs in some parts. The city of Elview rises from the water on a ship's prow of ominous dark stone, its castle perched upon cliffs reaching so high, I have to crane my neck to see the top. A giant stone wall surrounds the city and cuts it off from the rest of the kingdom. It's an astounding view, a city perched atop a cliff with a bustling harbour and a glittering castle to top it all off.

"Wow," Gendry breathes. We're standing at the edge of the deck watching the water fly past as the city grows closer.

"We certainly aren't in Iolleria anymore," I say, just as stunned.

"If you're gonna run away, this place isn't a half-bad choice," he points out, brushing his wind-swept red curls out of his eyes.

I nod. "Yeah, I guess this is pretty decent."

But when I look up at the city, I can't help but feel sad for the place we left behind. Elview is not and will never be home. As the ship draws closer to the harbour, regret flickers in the back of my mind. I didn't want to run away, but the other option was to stay and face death. Sure, we all die eventually, but I would rather not die before I get a chance to live.

3

Visions of a Hero

Kellin

After Xethos arrives, hours pass before anything else noteworthy happens. Jyn and I remain in our corner, watching the party while other nobles dance and talk and celebrate. At some point, the other members of the Order disappear to hold their annual meeting with the God of Victory himself. They emerge roughly an hour later, all looking shaken and a little bit frightened. In the large crowd, I find it hard to tell exactly what they have to be afraid of, but if it's of any importance, I will know soon enough.

In addition to my ability to commune with the spirits, I can also sense the fear of anyone I encounter and make it real—at least for them. There are some, such as Storm, who are strong enough to block out those with powers over the mind, but more often than not, there is some way to take down those defences. I suppose it would be unsettling to have someone see all your fears laid out before them to use against you but this power has only been recorded one other time in history so I am thankfully safe from such a thing.

"Can we leave yet?" I ask.

"Not yet," Jyn replies. "We need to wait until Storm lets us go. But we should probably stop hiding in the corner and at least pretend to be interested in people here."

As if on cue, a dark-skinned Kyrani girl of about eighteen appears, her pale pink skirts swirling around her feet as she walks. Her hair is done up in a hundred thin braids with half of them pinned up on her head with a golden sunburst-shaped clip that has a long pin stuck through it. The golden bodice and overskirts of her dress are not of a style I recognize, combining the draped fabrics of Kyrani dresses with the more modest Alkelian fashion of flowing skirts and slender corsets. Encircling her neck and wrists are gold accessories inlaid with pink gems that sparkle in the light. Combined with the glittering makeup she wears, the girl practically glows.

"Good evening." She greets us with an accent as sweet as honey and a bow of her head. "I couldn't help but notice the two of you here and simply wished to ask who you might be. I am Princess Safiya Ancore of Kyran."

I frown, examining this girl who has the audacity to approach us like this. "I am Ser Kellin. He's Jyn. We're from the Order."

"Ah! I had thought as much." She smiles kindly. I hoped that my short answer would inform her that we are not interested in talking, but it only seems to encourage her. "There are few enough Halfbloods in Kyran, but I have certainly heard of the Order."

"So what brings you here?" Jyn asks in an attempt to spare her a conversation with me. "I mean, is there a reason you've come to Alkelia?"

At this, Safiya's smile falters a little and she sighs. "I am here to marry Prince Elias Clearwater, but we have yet to meet properly. Do you know him?"

I grit my teeth. "My half-brother. I know him. And if you ask me, you'd be best to turn around right now and never set foot in the same room as him."

She simply nods. "Yes, I can't say it's an arrangement I am all too thrilled about but it is for the sake of my kingdom so it must be done. You said he is your brother; might I inquire as to why you are with the Order rather than royalty?"

Somehow, in less than a minute, this girl has managed to learn more about me than most people ever know. I sigh. "There were . . . complications. I chose not to associate with them anymore."

"Oh," She looks crestfallen for a moment but the instant her eyes land on Fenix, she smiles again. "Might I pet your cat?"

Safiya extends one hand out to Fenix who sniffs it carefully before happily rubbing her cheek into the princess's palm. For some reason, Fenix tends to like anyone who pays her any kind of attention, and when you're a three-foot tall cat with purple spikes down your back and horns on your head, people have a habit of paying attention. Most at the Order know to leave her alone because where she goes, I go, and few of them wish to run into me.

"Is she yours, Ser?" The princess asks me, running her manicured nails through Fenix's snow-white fur.

I nod. "Yes."

Fenix meows and it turns into a yawn that shows off her deadly fangs before she starts purring again. Safiya laughs. "Well, she's beautiful. If only there were such creatures in Kyran."

When I don't say anything more, Jyn asks, "Are you enjoying the ball?"

"Certainly," The princess replies sweetly. "It's quite different from parties in Kyran but I cannot say I dislike this sort of event. Is either of you planning to dance? That . . . seems to be the thing to do."

Jyn shakes his head. "No, Kellin can't dance to save his life, and I doubt anyone would like to dance with me."

Safiya giggles. "I am certain you could find someone. There are plenty of ladies who would dance with someone like yourself."

"Would you dance with me?" he asks.

"If I were invited I would." She pauses and then adds, "Unless that was the invitation."

Jyn blinks, clearly caught off guard. "Uh . . . well it sounded like one, didn't it?"

She smiles at him again. "It certainly did. So? Shall we dance?"

When she extends her jewelled hand, he hesitates for only a moment before taking it and following her into the crowd. I watch them go with a frown, wondering what I'm supposed to do now. Fenix sits next to me, looking disappointed in the departure of her new friend but unwilling to leave my side.

I pat her on the head, sighing. "Looks like we're on our own, doesn't it?"

The cat only yawns in response.

Bored, I eventually leave the ballroom to wander through the gardens. My head hurts so the quiet gardens are a nice change from the music and outrageously loud talking, although at least all that drowned out the spirits a little bit. Out here, it's perfectly silent, and I can finally hear my thoughts.

But I can also hear the voices more clearly now, whispering away in a dozen different languages and of ten times as many things.

The nighttime air is cool and still. A soft breeze runs through my hair and offering a bit of relief from the heat of a hundred people packed into that ballroom. I close my eyes as I walk, revelling in the cool silence.

I've always found the night more peaceful than the busyness and chaos of the day, which is usually filled with running around the cathedral and stealing moments to train. Only once the sun sets, and all the people have gone to sleep, am I able to find time to hide away in the library with a book or wander the streets near the cathedral in search of something I haven't seen before. While others sleep, I am finally allowed to breathe.

Suddenly, Fenix meows. I realize I'm standing in the middle of the path—there's no one else around. In front of me stands an old stone statue of a woman holding a sword high in the air. Her carved hair flows behind her head, and her cloak billows in an invisible wind. But her clothing is surprisingly simple, a tunic and pants with boots and the scabbard for her sword at her hip. The statue is surprisingly old and unkempt, but the plaque at the woman's feet leaves no doubt of who she is. *Ophiele.* The first of the Halfbloods to serve Xethos and the one who formed the Order. Dirt cover the worn stone and her eyes have been painted black, some of it dripping down from the corner of her eyes like strange, dark tears.

The back of my neck prickles like someone's watching me. The hair on my arms stands on end. I whirl around, reaching for my sword over my shoulder, but the path behind me is empty. Beside me, Fenix growls at the hedges and her tail is puffed up like a fox's. For a moment, nothing else happens, and I think it's just the wind or my imagination, lowering my hand from the hilt of my sword.

Then the air above the path shimmers.

A young woman appears, with red hair as bright as flames, dressed in simple leather armour and twirling a fancy gold pen in one hand. Her image isn't entirely solid, like the manifestation of a spirit. She doesn't see me; she stands turned away and clearly focused on some-thing I can't see.

And just as soon as she appeared, she flickers out of view. I stumble back and squint at the spot where she supposedly stood just seconds ago until my back slams into the statue and I spin around to face it again. My heart beats like I've been running despite not having gone anywhere. A sudden, freezing wind causes fallen leaves to skitter across the stone path, sounding like the footsteps of some tiny creature. Whispers in a language I've never heard echo through the gardens, coming not from in my head but rather from the dark, shadowy path beyond the statue.

I spin around and run so fast I almost trip over my feet, heels catching on a loose stone in the path. By the time I get back to the castle, however, no sign remains of the ghostly girl, haunting whispers, or icy wind. Still, I sprint up the steps to the balcony surrounding the ballroom and race inside as fast as I can without causing a scene.

Instantly, the music is too loud, the lights too bright and the room too full. My heart is in my throat and beating so fast, I think it might be trying to escape from my body, but I force myself to breathe slower and try to remain calm. Frantically, I search the room for Jyn, desperately pushing past people to find him.

"Kellin! Kellin!" It takes me a minute to realize the name being called belongs to me and that the voice calling it is Jyn's. "Kellin, are you okay?"

I spin around to find him right behind me with Safiya next to him. "What? I'm fine."

He looks me up and down, but other than my slightly-more rum-pled clothing, there's nothing to look at. "You sure? You look kind of panicked."

Shaking my head, I repeat the lie, "I'm fine. I just want to get out of here."

"Storm left a while ago," he tells me. "Let's just leave." He starts toward the door then remembers Safiya and turns back to address her. "Um, I guess we'll see you around maybe?"

She nods and smiles. "I shall be in the city for another two months before the wedding. Perhaps we can find time to seek each other out."

"Come to the cathedral anytime," Jyn instructs. "And we'll be there."

The princess curtsies. "Of course. It has been a pleasure to make your acquaintance."

4

THE SAILOR

KELLIN

The next morning I wake just as the sun casts its first rays over the city. Fenix is fast asleep next to me and taking up far more than her share of the bed, her sleek body stretched across the entire mattress with her tail hanging off the end. I climb out of bed and cross over to the window, yawning but knowing I won't be going back to sleep. The city of Elview is still filled with the bright colours that come with festivities, but the people who crowded the streets last night are long gone. I spot only a single drunk stumbling past the cathedral doors below. As the sun rises, it stains pink the clouds trying to block it out, setting them alight with the brilliance of dawn. The silence of the city will break all too soon as the shops and markets open. The quiet perfection of the early hours of the day will be forgotten once again.

Though even now, while the rest of the city still sleeps, I can make out the tiny shapes of a handful of sailors down at the docks preparing their ship to set off.

Yawning again, I tug the curtains closed and flop back in bed next to Fenix, the cat lifting her head sleepily to look at me. The day after the Assembly is usually rather quiet around the cathedral, as the higher-up's sort through the information from the meeting the previous night and everyone else waits around on the edge of their seats for the decisions they will inevitably make. Thankfully, this means I might be left alone for a few days. And a few days to disappear is all I could ever ask for.

About an hour later, the cathedral comes to life, people stirring to begin their duties of the day. When a handful of apprentices talking far louder than necessary walk past my door, I sigh and put down the book I had been half-heartedly reading. It might be about time to start my day as well. Fenix watches me with half-asleep judgment as I search the room for my jacket and lace my boots, grabbing my sword on the way out the door.

At the top of the last set of stairs on the way down, I nearly run right into Taiyo, who is carrying a heavy stack of books in her arms. Unlike Jyn and me, Taiyo is not a Halfblood, merely a human taken in by the Order as a servant. She has a peculiar scar across her right eye that reaches all the way down to the corner of her mouth, a jagged line through her otherwise very pretty face and brilliant green eyes. Her red-brown hair is tied up messily on the top of her head, and she wears a simple blue dress with a dirty apron over top.

"Ah, so you did survive the party," she says by way of greeting. "I take it you hated every second of it."

"Wow, what a surprise," I deadpan sarcastically. "At least we got to leave a bit early."

She laughs. "Well, now it's done and you can hide away with a book and your cat for another year."

I frown. "You wouldn't have wanted to be there either if you were me."

Shrugging, she steps past me, continuing on down the hall. "Perhaps I wouldn't have. But I am me so I would have been thrilled to be there."

I sigh and keep walking with Fenix beside me. Of all the people in this cathedral, I am certainly one of the most interesting. Of course, I mean that in no way of bragging; it's something one look at me can tell you. I have coal black hair that falls all the way down to my waist and strange pointed cat-like ears on the sides of my head with feathers rather than fur. My eyes are like liquid gold with diamond pupils and my front teeth are sharpened into fangs that are also strangely reminiscent of a cat or fox. I stand hardly over five feet tall even with the heels of my armoured boots adding an extra two inches. Combined with my unusual power, just about everyone here has decided that I am not entirely like them.

Looking around the nave, the members of the Order are identifiable by their red and silver robes although many apprentices, squires or knights such as myself tend to forgo those in favour of more combat-ready attire. Every one of them is a Halfblood, sporting horns or colourful hair or claws, but the majority are of moderate powers such as pyromancy or telekinesis. There is only a handful of common folk here, a man praying in one corner, a woman offering flowers at the feet of the statue of Xethos, a young girl staring up at the awe-inspiring painted ceiling.

I turn to walk out the door, intending to join whoever is in the training yard this early in the day, but the second I step over the threshold, I smack straight into something. Disoriented, I step back, ready to say something angry to whoever was in my way, but I freeze when I see the person in front of me.

He's a Halfblood with silver hair shining like starlight under the light of the candles. He wears an eyepatch over his left eye, but he can't be any older than me. There's a tattoo of a butterfly outlined in fine black ink on the side of his neck, and strange, silvery freckles are scattered across his pale nose and cheeks. Like most Halfbloods, his ears are pointed but he doesn't possess any other typical magic qualities; no claws, wings, or tails to be seen. There's something instantly striking about him, the delicate structure of his face and even the way he moves seems oddly enchanting. A silver chain with a teardrop of red crystal hangs around his neck and he has several earrings that sparkle in the early morning sunlight but combined with his strangely pale hair, his entire being seems to glow. For a moment, I almost think he isn't real, an illusion or a spirit playing tricks with my mind, until he's suddenly speaking to me with an accent I immediately identify as Iollerian. Although, he speaks Alkelian almost flawlessly.

"Good morning." His voice, softly accented and strangely song-like, reminds me of the fae in legends of old.

"What? You're Iollerian. What are *you* doing here?" The words sound much more confrontational than the casual tone I had been going for. Fenix meows at him but the silver-haired boy doesn't seem to know what to do.

He gives me a strange look. "I'm . . . a sailor? Who are you?"

"Ah . . ." Suddenly, I seem to have forgotten how to speak. "Kellin. My name is Kellin. I work here. With the Order, I mean."

Even though I stumbled over the words, he nods and smiles. "I'm Senika. From Iolleria."

"How—how long have you been here?" I ask, trying my very best not to sound awkward. "And why are you even here?"

"Last night," he answers skeptically. "Are you from here?" He shakes his head, realizing what he said. "I mean, of course, you are. I'm sorry."

"Um, yeah. Nice to meet you." I go to walk past him, and he does the same but accidentally steps right in front of me. My face suddenly feels hot so I stare at my boots, stepping in the opposite direction just as he does.

When we almost collide again, he laughs nervously. "I'm sorry. Here, you just go."

I walk away faster than I can recall walking in my entire life. By the time I reach the training grounds, my heart is beating out of my chest. My palms are strangely sweaty.

5

INQUISITION

THE WATCHER

Night has fallen. Every window in the village is dark and every door has been bolted shut. Even the tavern is closed. The sky is dark and clouded, not a single star visible. The forest surrounding the village is like a wall of dark, dark trees. The whole area is silent, not unlike a graveyard. The main road, which passing travellers and merchants selling their wares had filled all day, is empty and abandoned. Anyone who dares to pass through now would think the place deserted.

A girl sprints through the street, her bare feet cut and bleeding from the rocks. Her long red hair flows out behind her like a flag, and she wears a simple dress with a frayed hem and holes in the sleeves. She risks a glance over her shoulder but they are nowhere to be seen. They never are.

Exhausted, she stumbles to stop in the village square, gasping for breath. She knows she can't afford to stop running but she can't run anymore. The snap of a twig makes her spin around, knowing she isn't alone anymore. Fumbling, she pulls a short dagger from her belt, clutching it in both hands and not daring to let go as if a single knife could save her now.

For a moment that lasts forever, nothing happens. Then, as if materializing from the shadows, a white horse appears, walking down the narrow road. The fog embedded in the village melts away around it, and the girl gasps when she spots the rider on the horse's back.

It's a tall woman dressed in a long, black cloak. A mask covers the top half of her face, but her ruby-red eyes are visible, glowing like embers or the fires of death. Long white hair falls down her back, and her flawless, pale skin makes her look like a ghost. All her clothing is black, from her tall boots to that flowing cloak to the gloves on her hands. A single silver ring glitters like glass on her right hand.

The rider stops at the edge of the square, silent like the phantom she is. The girl doesn't say anything, not daring to even breathe.

"State your name," the rider says after a long pause, her voice like a knife cutting through the dark.

"You won't have me alive," the girl says, determined not to give in.

"I have orders to kill you where you stand." The woman's voice remains chillingly calm and even.

The girl laughs. "You won't kill me either. I am the Halfblood Nhali, descendant of Ophelie herself! I have more power than you could imagine, Inquisitor."

"Ophelie died. Her blood spilled red on the fields and yours will do the same." The tall woman steps down from her horse elegantly, drawing a long, straight blade from her belt. "I am an Inquisitor of the Order. A single Halfblood like you will pose no threat to my sword."

Nhali grits her teeth and steps toward the Inquisitor. "You want to try that? Fine, let's go."

She lunges toward the Inquisitor, her dagger aimed straight for the Inquisitor's throat. The white-haired woman steps aside easily, circling the girl to corner her against the wall of a house. Nhali backs up away from her opponent, her dagger held out in front of her but the weapon feels horribly weak compared to the other woman's deadly sword. The Inquisitor matches each of her steps, trailing the tip of her sword against the hardened dirt road.

The Inquisitor slashes with her sword, cutting toward Nhali, but the girl steps back to dodge. Beneath her mask, the girl sees her opponent smile. She takes another slow step back, but her back slams into the stone wall of the house.

"Nowhere to run." The Inquisitor taunts. "Nhali the Halfblood, you have hit the end of your road. Set down your blade and I will end your life swiftly."

"That won't be so easy." Nhali gatherers her power, lighting the short blade of her dagger on fire in a glow that lights up the street.

"You think your pathetic power can stop me," the pale woman notes. "You are wrong. We are all mere mortals, made to serve our god. Give yourself for Xethos and you may be forgiven, girl."

Nhali slashes out, the flames on her blade creating a burning arc of fire in the sky. The Inquisitor steps back patiently as the girl attacks again and again. Their blades crash against each other in a rainbow of sparks that fly out into the night. Finally, the Inquisitor knocks the flaming blade out of Nhali's hand, and the girl staggers backwards.

"Nhali Halfblood." The Inquisitor says the name like its poison. "In the name of the one true God, I hereby sentence you to death at my blade. Do you have any last words?"

No one would ever hear the words Nhali would say next, only the Inquisitor. No matter what she said, this Inquisitor would never allow anyone else to know them. So she spits, "I am a Halfblood. We have the power of the spirits and we are not alone. There will be others who come after me, like all those before me. No matter what you and your

Order can do, there will come a Halfblood you cannot kill, one you cannot simply put an end to with your swords."

The woman stares at her for a moment and then laughs. "I was not unlike you once. You see, I am a Halfblood too. But the difference between us? I use my power to end those who stand against our god. You use yours for evil deeds like thievery and murder. One day, I will give my life for Xethos. You will die a worthless death, void of all meaning. For this, for refusing to give your pitiful life for Xethos, you shall die."

With that, she stabs forward, plunging her sword into Nhali's stomach and straight through her back. Blood flows onto the dirt beneath them as the Inquisitor pulls her blade free and Nhali falls to her knees, clutching at her stomach as if she could keep her life from spilling out onto the road even as blood turns her hands red. The girl's breath comes ragged and painful as she falls to the ground. The Inquisitor simply turns around and cleans the blood from her sword with the edge of her cloak.

Nhali closes her eyes, vision blurring, but she opens them again to see that the ground is soaked dark red with the blood from her wound. With a final breath, she goes still. Dead.

The Inquisitor climbs back onto her horse and turns to the soldier who appears behind her. "Burn everything. Put the whole town to fire."

He can only nod solemnly as she rides away.

The village becomes a vast empty plain; the dim fog transforms into snow. It falls from the sky in a flurry of white, coating my whole world in a blanket of cold, white powder.

6

Quest

Kellin

I'm on my hands and knees in the snow, dressed not for the cold but for bed. I watch in terror as the snow under me turns red with blood and tears freeze on my cheeks. It's a dream, I tell myself, this is all just a dream. But I still look over my shoulder to see my mother standing in the open doorway leading to the castle with a kitchen knife in one hand. More blood drips from the blade and in her other hand, she holds a handful of black feathers. The snow around her feet is covered in blood and feathers, black and red in the white snow.

A sob racks my body as she stares at me. "I should have done this long ago. My father always said Halfbloods were a curse, and I never believed him. Now I see you are no better than anything he ever told me, Kellin."

"Mom . . ." My voice is weak and my entire body hurts but I can't listen to her speak anymore. I bury my head in my arms and try to hide away in the snow. I haven't called her that in years, only in the dreams.

"Now leave. And don't try to come back." I hear the click of the latch as she closes and locks the door, abandoning me in the snow. I lie there for a long time, waiting for this to end, for her to come back, but she never does. Instead, I am alone in the bloody snow until it all fades away into darkness.

I wake up with tears running down my face. It was just a dream, I'm sure it was. But it felt so real. Well, the first part was a dream. I have never known a girl named Nhali and the Order is meant to protect Halfbloods, not kill them. Sure, there are Inquisitors who have been known to be ruthless killers, but it is their duty to protect this kingdom, just as it is mine.

Yet the second part . . . the second part was not a dream. It was a memory. I was nine when my mother decided she didn't want anything to do with me. Several times, she tried to make me leave, but it was that night when she dragged me from my bed and threw me out into the snow that I realized that I was not meant to have a true family. She nearly killed me.

I roll over and bury my face in my pillow, trying to forget it all. It's still dark outside, and from the look of it, morning won't come for a while. Fenix is asleep beside my bed and I don't want to move from where I am. So I just lay there, my whole body feeling distant and numb as I cry into the pillow.

Suddenly, I hear a soft knock on my window. I don't look up, thinking it must just be my imagination, but then I hear it again. When I lift my head, I see a young woman with white-blonde hair and nearly translucent skin dressed in a white dress floating on the other side of the glass. A pair of silvery horns protrude from her head and the pale mask over her eyes makes me wonder if she can see. She waves her hand shyly with a kind smile on her face. I stand up and cross the room, the stone floor cold on my bare feet. Maybe this is just another dream, I think, but after the dreams I've already had, this seems like it might be real.

I unlock the window and slide it up to see out. The girl floats down so her face is even with the opening and rests her slender hands on the metal frame.

"Hello child, I am very sorry to trouble you at such an hour." Somehow, her voice sounds familiar to me. "I am the spirit Airadyne. You may not know me but I have spoken to you before. Might I come in?"

"Um . . . Can I ask you something first?" I ask, perplexed.

"Well you already have, but I suppose you might as well ask another." She blinks her sapphire blue eyes and offers me another gentle smile.

"Yeah. Is this a dream?" This night appears to want to be as abnormal as possible—not unusual for the night of a full moon.

Airadyne laughs. "Well, of course not. I am here in person—or, rather, in spirit—to speak to you myself." She steps forward and walks straight through the wall. I guess spirits can do that. "You see, I sent a dream to you but it was far from a dream. But now I am here to give you a message from the others."

I cross my arms in front of my chest, incredibly self-conscious of the fact that I'm still wearing my nightclothes. "So that was real, then? The thing with Nhali and the Inquisitor and everything? It wasn't a dream?"

"I had forgotten how foolish mortals can be." She sighs. "Of course it was real. There would be no purpose in sending a false vision, would there? Yes, it may be hard for you to believe. Your precious Order is killing Halfbloods who stand against them, and it is by the word of Xethos himself."

"That's impossible," I snap although I will admit it makes sense. "The Order protects Halfbloods, not kills them."

"Wrong, they do as their god sees fit. And now he has gone astray, deciding the magic Halfbloods possess is too strong. Perhaps he is afraid," she muses, examining the books on my shelf. "It seems strange, but I, along with several others, have decided that you must be the one to put an end to this. There may come a time when you, Kellin Kane, are the last hope for Morsevdon. I had hoped you would understand, after all, you too have fallen victim to the Order."

I can't deny that. From the very start, I never saw the Order as 'good', only as a part of Alkelia. In the past six years, I've considered leaving more times than I can count but that was never because I thought they were evil. Part of me wants to accept her quest right away. Even then, I would be doing this first to bring down the Order; I don't care about saving lives.

Still, I shake my head.

"I think you have the wrong person, spirit lady. I'm not a hero or something and I won't be saving this shit-hole of a world." I sit back down on my bed. "I'll think about it but there isn't much I can do. Go find someone who wants your stupid quest."

"Hm. They always say that. Those who are the most worthy insist on saying they can't possibly be the right person." She glides back over to the window. "Very well, I will leave you to decide. But do know that time is running out."

With that, Airadyne disappears back through the wall, leaving me to wonder what exactly is going on here. First, a dream that was apparently a vision of some kind, ready to make me question everything I ever thought I knew about the Order. Then, a dream about my mother. Clearly the worst kind of dream. If I had only dreamed of eating pie and she happened to be in the room; even that would be better. But to top it all off, some spirit decides tonight of all nights is the perfect time to tell me I'm some sort of chosen one and that I will need to save the world one day.

There is no way I'm sleeping after this.

7

WELCOME TO ELVIEW

SENIKA

Elview is stunning, I'll grant them that, but this city is impossible to navigate. It's a maze of sidestreets, alleyways, and roads that twist and turn every which way. On top of that, so many of the buildings look nearly identical, with the exception of a handful of recognizable landmarks. Without a map, it takes Gendry and I the entirety of the first few days to learn our way around the docks and even then, I find myself lost almost every time I step off the boat.

I stand on my toes, peering over the mass of sailors and merchants that crowd the docks in search of the flag marking the *Vanquisher*. Another thing about Elview is it's bustling during every hour of sunlight as goods are exchanged and business is conducted. It's much like Isondale in that respect although, where Isondale is brimming with travellers from all over the continent, the people here all speak with accents identified as either Alkelian or Iollerian, with a few Kyrani merchants here and there.

Winding my way through the crowds, I finally spot where Kira's ship is moored. I let out a sigh of relief. The crate of fruit in my arms is growing heavier by the second. Unfortunately, between here and there a group of sailors are standing in the middle of the dock, engaged in a heated argument. They shout back and forth in Alkelian, hurling insults that grow increasingly scalding and furious.

I slow down as I approach the scene, picking out the route that will best allow me to avoid them. A merchant shoves past me on his way to attempt an intervention and I scramble to keep my precious cargo inside its box. One of the soldiers steps forward, drawing his sabre and brandishing it at a sailor who seems to be disagreeing with him. The merchant tries to step between the two but is quickly pushed aside as others draw weapons.

I press myself close to the wall, slipping into the background. More people are gathering around and the sailors are starting to sound like they've lost the original point of the argument. I try to hurry up my escape but the multiplying crowds are making it difficult to move without being jostled around or tripped over. By now, the argument has escalated into a full brawl, swords drawn as sailors push forward to join in.

Every person on the dock freezes when an arrow strikes the ground inches from the foot of some poor sailor. A second arrow follows close behind it, black and white fletching blurring through the air.

"Enough."

The voice comes from the shooter who stands on the deck of the nearest ship, speaking Alkelian. He's a young man with windswept hair, slender but strong. On his jacket, a badge shines silver, the same one that several of the sailors involved in the brawl wear, although his clothing is far more extravagant than that of any ordinary sailor. A captain.

He jumps down from his ship, pointing his bow at his crew when he lands. "I will not have my men starting pointless fights with our allies. We depart immediately. And if I hear that any one of you has done this again, I will remove you from my crew."

Instantly, the sailors step down. A few of those not belonging to the crew of the newly arrived captain, try to challenge them again by calling them cowards for retreating so easily. Whoever that captain is, he must be respected because none of his crew take the bait.

Now that the excitement is over, the crowd begins to disperse, returning to their previous tasks. Finally able to move, I melt back into the throng and hurry over to the *Vanquisher*. Kira's crew is gathered on deck, every one of them watching like hawks.

I add my box to the stack next to the gangplank. Gendry sits at the edge of the dock, peeling an orange and tossing the peels at a dog who lounges at his feet. The dog clearly has no interest in the orange.

"What was that all about?" Gendry asks in Iollerian.

"I don't know," I say. "I couldn't make out what they were arguing over."

He shrugs, popping an orange slice into his mouth. "These Alkelian sailors are always on edge. You can't say anything without pissing someone off."

Scratching the dog's floppy black ears, I sit on the sun-warmed dock next to him. "Yeah, it's best to stay out of their business. Where'd the dog come from, by the way?"

"Couldn't tell ya. He just appeared here a while ago. I'm calling him Skipper."

The dog rests his chin on my leg, looking up at me with big, brown eyes. He's clearly a stray, white-ish fur matted and dull with bones visible under his skin. Plenty of dogs like him wander around the docks, both here and back home. Gendry has always had a talent for attracting them—I don't even know how many dogs we have to say hello to in Isondale. He even names all of them but I can never remember who's who.

"Skipper." I smile at the dog. He rolls onto his back, tongue falling out of his mouth and tail wagging happily. "The name suits him."

"Senika! Gendry!" Captain Kira appears at the top of the gangplank. "Emaya and I are heading to the pub. You'll be good here?"

Gendry and I both nod.

Emaya rushes after Kira, her wife's jacket in her hand. "Kira, you have to stop leaving your stuff everywhere. We only have so much space."

The captain takes her jacket and frowns. "Why? It's my ship. I can do what I want."

"We've had this conversation before," Emaya sighs, rolling her eyes. "It's *our* ship and if you tell the rest of the crew to keep their space tidy, you better listen to your own advice."

Sometimes, it's hard to imagine Emaya being a pirate even though she grew up on the sea just like Kira. She's a kind, gentle woman with dark, curly hair and eyes the colour of caramel. Her round face is covered in freckles and her mouth has a permanent smile to it that makes her look more like a village girl than a pirate. Today, she's wearing a simple cream-coloured dress with tiny colourful flowers on it. Her hair has pale flowers braided into it in a dainty manner.

On the other hand, Kira is the perfect image of a pirate; she's loud and boisterous and likes to party and drink but loves adventure more than anything else other than Emaya. Both she and Gendry have the same wild red hair but hers is long and barely contained by her thick braid. She throws on her worn-out black jacket with a high collar and pulls her wide-brimmed hat down on her head. Everything about her screams "Captain", from that outfit to her unstoppably carefree and loud attitude.

"Now," Emaya continues, turning to Gendry and me. "Yes, we are going out. I'm not sure when we'll be back but the others should be around for the rest of the night so if you need anything, you know what to do."

Gendry groans when she ruffles his hair. "Mom, we're basically adults, you know."

"Oh, I know. But no mother ever wants her children to grow up." She smiles at the two of us. "And yes, Senika, as an honourary Aliver and crewmate, you are as much my son as you are Gisella's."

"Emaya!" Kira shouts at her from the end of the dock where she waits restlessly. "Let's get going before the pub closes."

"Right, you're in charge here," Emaya instructs. "Try not to burn down the ship and we'll be back in a few hours, alright?"

Gendry waves her away. "Yeah, yeah. Get going before Mom drags you away."

"Have fun," I add as Emaya follows Kira.

Once they're out of earshot, Gendry sighs, stuffing the last of his orange into his mouth.

"I wish they would just leave me alone," he grumbles.

"Hey, they care about you," I say. "I think it's nice."

"You're only saying that because you don't have them smothering you all the time."

"I do now."

Skipper sits up, blinking expectantly at Gendry. He holds out his hands for the dog to sniff, proving that he doesn't have any more food. Waves lap gently at the edge of the dock, adding to the now-peaceful hum of the activity around us. In a sky of perfect blue, the sun shines brilliantly, beaming down to heat the air. A silk merchant is trying to negotiate absurdly high prices with a customer who clearly has no interest in paying that much. A man pushing a cart full of fresh fish clatters past, calling out his wares. It all seems so peaceful; I find it hard to believe that this place is the same kingdom known for its ruthless military conquests.

Ears perking up, Skipper bounds away after the man selling fish.

"Oh." Gendry frowns. "I guess we weren't that interesting after all."

8

THE PRINCESS

KELLIN

"So you're saying some random spirit showed up in the middle of the night and told you this?" Jyn asks. The two of us are tucked away in the back corner of the library, hidden behind shelves overflowing with books.

From my seat on the couch by the window, I watch him carefully. "Yes . . . I promise I'm not crazy."

"I didn't say you were crazy." Jyn shakes his head, running his fingers across the spines of the books. Finally, he looks over at me. "Do you believe it?"

I nod then reconsider and shrug. Next to me, Fenix snores, fast asleep. "I don't know. I want to be sure before we do anything. I've never trusted the Order or Xethos but that doesn't mean it has to be true."

I will admit that Airadyne's offer is starting to sound more appealing, especially now that Jyn knows and I've had time to think it over. The Order saved my life but they also ruined it. They turned me into a living weapon and forced a sword into the hands of a child—children,

I was far from the only one—but they also put a roof over my head and food on my plate.

"So what's your plan?"

"I haven't had much time to make one," I say. "I don't even know if it's true or not."

He leans against the bookshelf, nodding. "Okay. I'm doing this with you, you know."

Instantly, I shake my head. "No, absolutely not. No matter how this turns out, I'll be committing treason. I'm not endangering you too, Jyn."

"And I'm not letting you do this alone," he insists. "Besides, I have my reasons to be mad about this too. I think all Halfbloods would if they knew the truth. If Xethos is killing us, there's no way I'm sitting here and letting it happen."

I sigh. "Fine, but we shouldn't risk telling anyone else. Treason is punishable by death or worse and anyone in the Order could be against us."

Jyn nods slowly. "We should tell Taiyo, too."

"Tell Taiyo what?"

Both of us jump at the voice. I'm already on my feet by the time I register Taiyo standing in the aisle between the bookshelf and the wall. She's carrying a basket of books under one arm and her hair is falling out of the messy braid she usually contains it with.

"Um . . ." I stare at her, trying to come up with an excuse. If we tell her and she doesn't buy it, she could be the one to sell us out to the High Priest.

"Well?" she asks. "If something happened, I want to hear it."

Jyn glances at me nervously and nods. I sigh, falling back onto the couch and startling Fenix awake. Measuring my words carefully, I tell her, "I had a vision."

Taiyo smirks. "Wasn't the last vision you had about some merchant scamming buyers? And he turned out to be from Anro?"

"Yeah . . ." I admit with a frown. I don't have the greatest track record when it comes to the accuracy of my visions. "This was different though. There was an Inquisitor which means it had to be Alkelia and a spirit spoke to me afterwards and said it was true." She eyes me suspiciously, waiting for me to explain what I'm even talking about. "The Order is killing Halfbloods. Xethos is trying to wipe us all out and he's making the Inquisitors do it. In the vision, it sounded like he somehow managed to convince them that any Halfblood who isn't part of the Order is plotting against him."

Taiyo lets out a deep breath, running her fingers through her tangled hair. "I have never been loyal to Xethos but this is more than I ever imagined. It sounds completely insane but I can't say it doesn't make sense." She nods decisively and stands up a little straighter. "Okay, what can I do?"

"You haven't heard anything about this before, have you?" Jyn asks.

"If I had, I wouldn't be surprised that you two stumbled into this mess," she says. "I'll keep an ear open in case something comes up, though, and I'll let you know."

Jyn smiles gratefully. "Thanks. That makes the next step forming a plan."

No one suggests anything.

"Okay . . ." Jyn says a long pause. "We need to know the truth behind this first."

"The only way to do that would be to see it for ourselves or hear it from someone like Storm." Taiyo points out, setting her basket at her feet.

Jyn frowns. "It's not like we can just go ask Storm. He'll throw us in prison without a second thought. That's not an option."

"Neither is finding an Inquisitor," Taiyo replies. "Unless we go to the Black Tower, that is."

An idea occurs to me. "So let's go to the Black Tower."

"Are you insane?" Taiyo asks. "We can't do that. If we get caught, the charges on our heads would be enough to turn the entire kingdom against us."

"Only if we get caught," I remind her. "Every mission, patrol and job has to be reported down to the tiniest, irrelevant detail and those documents are kept in the library at the Tower. If we can get in there, we'll have all the proof we need."

Both of them stare at me like I've grown an extra head. Finally, Taiyo says, "So you want to break into one of the most high-security buildings in the kingdom and find files none of us have access to? You would never get away with that."

"Maybe we couldn't but who would stop a harmless, innocent servant girl?" My eyes cut pointedly toward Taiyo.

"No way." She shakes her head. "You're going to get me killed."

I shrug. "You can learn things people would never tell either of us. It's our best bet, Taiyo. If we can, Jyn and I will go in with you but if it comes down to it, the only one of us inconspicuous enough to make this happen is you."

"You make that sound so easy," Jyn grumbles. He sighs and curses under his breath. "I can't believe I'm saying this but they're right."

Taiyo picks the basket up again and sighs. "Fine. I'll do it but I don't like this. Now, if you don't mind, I'm going back to work before you two come up with another brilliant way to get us all killed."

I can only grin as the library doors slam shut behind her.

"You look half dead," Jyn observes helpfully.

I groan. "Thanks."

After the spirit showed up, I couldn't sleep, resulting in hours of staring at the wall while Fenix slept like there was nothing wrong in the whole world. Jyn and I are still in the library, surrounded by stacks of books and dust. I lay on the overstuffed couch with a book on my face and my feet on one of the armrests, exhausted. We were originally searching through the limited collection of books we thought might help but, upon finding nothing, I've given up and left Jyn to search the shelves.

"Let's leave this alone for a while," He says, setting aside the stack of papers he was reading through. "You're exhausted and we aren't even getting anywhere."

I lift the book off my face just enough to look at him. "But I don't really want to go to sleep."

He shrugs. "No one said you have to, but you're going to fall asleep right there if you don't get up."

"It's kinda nice here though," I protest, covering my eyes with the book again. He sighs but doesn't say anything more.

Suddenly, the door creaks open, and I tilt my head back to see Princess Safiya Ancore standing in the doorway. She is dressed in a simple pale blue dress with long, flowing sleeves and a silver tiara placed on top of her dark braids. Upon seeing us in the room, her face lights up in a bright grin and she swiftly closes the heavy doors behind her.

"Oh, I had not expected to find you two here," Safiya says in greeting. "Although I suppose I should have."

"What brings you here?" Jyn asks.

The princess sighs. "I tire of the castle, and their library is somewhat lacking. I was advised to come here to read instead. Do you have any suggestions?"

"You would have to ask Kellin." Jyn points at me. "He's the one who reads."

I groan and roll onto my stomach to look at Safiya better. "What do you read? And don't say any of those stupid love stories."

She pauses before answering. "Well . . . I was going to say romance, but I do enjoy a grand adventure or epic once and a while."

Disappointed, I shake my head. "If it's romance, I can't help."

"Do you not like romance?" She asks, sounding surprised.

"Nope, I don't see any point in reading about something so ridiculous," I tell her. "And it's not like I can fall in love myself, anyway."

Safiya looks at Jyn, slightly concerned, and he explains, "If you're in the Order, you aren't allowed to get married or fall in love. It's a weird rule, but they say it's so you can fully give yourself to the kingdom."

"Oh." The princess smooths out an invisible wrinkle in her dress. "Well, I have never been given my choice in who I marry either. I just think it's nice to dream of such things."

I roll my eyes. "Yeah, well if they gave everyone a choice, no one would want to marry Elias. And they have to get rid of him somehow."

"Is he really that awful?" she inquires.

I shrug. "That would depend on how ignorant you are. When he doesn't speak, I guess he's fine, but you still have to look at his face."

She smiles before remembering who she's talking to. "I thought he was your brother, Ser. Should you really say things like that?"

"Eh, no. But no one cares," I say. "Besides, what are they going to do?"

"Yes . . . well I am still worried," she says. "I know no one here and they wish for me to marry someone so unpleasant and then live in the snow for the rest of my life. It sounds truly awful."

"You know us," Jyn points out. "And I'm sure Elias isn't all that bad."

I give him a withering look and he shrugs. "There's still the cold and the idiotic court and the not-having-a-choice part."

"Oh, forget it." Safiya waves her hand about dismissively. "Right now I need a good book and that's all. I suppose I can deal with the prince when the time comes."

We spend the next few hours in the library, searching through the endless shelves and the stacks of books that never found a spot on those shelves. Dust is everywhere, coating every surface available. Just about every time a book opens, clouds of it fill the air and leave all three of us sneezing for the next five minutes. In the far corners, all the torches are either long burned down to stubs or gone completely, so we have to stumble around for a while until we decide to look somewhere else. Under the window farthest from the door, we find a dusty piano that, upon playing, reveals itself to be so out of tune, I wouldn't be surprised if most had forgotten it was ever here.

As afternoon turns to evening, Safiya departs under the pretense that she needs to return for dinner. Jyn and I are left alone once again. As expected, no one came looking for us all day and even when we arrived in the kitchen long after dinner has finished, no one demands anything of us. Once even Jyn is asleep, I creep up to the bell tower, climbing the long, spiralling wooden stairs to reach the tiny room high above the rest of the cathedral. The trapdoor squeaks when I push it open and, climbing up the rope ladder, I step out into the cool night air.

Hardly a single cloud floats in the sky tonight, and every star glows brilliantly in the violet dusk. Of the seven moons in the night sky, three are visible, but the fourth will emerge in the next few days. Under their light, the city of grey stone looks black and white, the shadows darker than they should be. On the horizon, a storm approaches, grey clouds gathering over the plains past the city walls as the cold wind carries them closer and closer. I sit right at the very edge of the bell tower with my feet dangling over the stone lip around the tiny platform, my back to the giant copper bell.

It's the stillness of nighttime that I love, the silent perfection that few others will see. Because if I could show it to everyone, no silence would remain. I close my eyes and let the cool air wash over me, embracing the lonely night.

I was only five when the spirits granted me my powers, when they came to me in the night to bless—or curse—me with whatever magic they may hold. For a time, I loved the newfound power, but it wasn't long before I saw how it changed what others thought of me. I was the son of a princess, her bastard from a love that could never be, but for five years, that had no effect over my life. Until the day I was not like them. My mother started to claim a demon had replaced her child and would soon come for all of the Northern Court, yet that was only the start.

When I was nine, she threw me out into the snow to die.

Someone came to my rescue, and I wound up with the Order by the time I was ten, but there they saw me as royalty of a region known for their hatred of Halfbloods. So even if I was one myself, they acted as if I might harm them. I suppose none of them trusted me, but I hardly made an effort to talk to them, either. When Jyn arrived only a few months later, I can't explain what made him decide to be different from the others. Since then, he has been my best friend, although he and Taiyo and really my only friends. However, after what happened when we were eleven, it's not a surprise most of them don't trust me.

I suppose it's something of a lonely existence, but I don't mind it much. What I do mind is how the others look at me, how they change their direction to avoid me or fall silent when I walk past. And I mind how I can see that so many of them fear me.

9

THE START OF SOMETHING

KELLIN

He's here again. I watch the silver-haired Halfblood as he walks down the aisle between the pews in the cathedral, his faded silver-blue eye fixed on the beautifully painted ceiling. But when he's here, somehow I can't look at anything but him. There isn't anyone else here, only this single boy with the light of the afternoon sun shining down through the skylight making him glow golden. I sit in the last row of wooden benches watching, sitting sideways with my feet up on the bench. He doesn't seem to notice my presence, enthralled by the beauty of the cathedral. When he finally turns around to see me sitting there, he smiles, looking guilty and I turn away quickly. His smile is bright enough to light up the darkest room—and so carefree. It makes me wonder how a person can be like him, so free and joyous with that unearthly beauty.

"Hi," he says, walking over to sit backwards in the row of benches in front of me. "I didn't see you here. Do you actually live in this place?"

I nod. "Yes. It's busy."

"That's it?" He questions with a charmingly crooked smile. "Just busy? Not the most amazing building in all of Morsevdon?"

Shrugging, I point out, "It's not as cool when you live here."

"Makes sense. So what are you doing here?" he asks. "I mean, other than living."

I shrug again. "Nothing."

Somehow, no matter how I try, I can't bring myself to hate him. Maybe it's because he's so nice, or because I can see he isn't afraid of me, but with anyone else, I would simply ignore them or tell them to leave me alone. When he smiles at me, it's honest, and even though he doesn't know anything about me, there's kindness in that expression that I can't hate. I suppose I'm so used to hating people and pushing them away, I find it odd how he can be so nice to me.

He rests his head on his arms on the back of the bench. "You said your name is Kellin, right?"

I nod. "And you're Senika."

"Yup, that would be me," he answers.

"Will you go back to Iolleria again?" I ask.

He shakes his head. "Maybe one day. We're trying to stay a bit hidden for a while. Why?"

"Um, well," I stammer. "I guess . . ."

When he laughs, it sounds like music, light and cheerful enough to make me pause. "I don't really want to go back just yet. We just got here and I kind of want to see more of Alkelia."

"We're going to the Black Tower in a few days," I blurt out before I can stop myself. "Ah, do you want to . . . come with us?"

"I don't know where that is . . ." he says slowly. "And who's 'we'?"

"Me, Jyn, and Taiyo. My friends," I explain hurriedly. "It's north of here, past Edgewood. It's where most of the Halfblood military is based."

"Oh." He pauses, confused. "Why are you going there?"

I sigh. "Well, it's a bit of a long story but I suppose . . ." I start.

And to my surprise, I tell him everything. I recount the dreams, leaving out the part involving my mother, and Airadyne. I explain my connection to the spirits and the prophecy Airadyne mentioned, as brief as it was, and the discovery of Xethos's actions. When I finish, Senika stares at me, silent for a moment before he speaks again.

"That's . . . a lot," he says. "So wait, you're going to the Black Tower to get evidence if this is true or not then you're going to do what exactly?"

I shrug. "We haven't got there yet. But we'll figure it out."

"You can't convince a god to change his mind," Senika points out.

"So we kill him, then," I state simply, like it could ever be that easy. "So, are you in or no?"

I hadn't planned to tell him all this but now that I think about it, having another Halfblood on our side can't hurt. Especially when our side currently consists of three people. The fact that he's from another kingdom means he can't turn us in which makes telling him cost me nothing even if he doesn't believe it.

He doesn't answer at first, chewing on his thumbnail and furrowing his brow. "Well, people are dying because of him. It would be sick to do nothing now that I know . . . But it's also dangerous. We could all *die*. I guess, in a way, it's worth it though, since it's four of us and possibly hundreds or thousands who will die if we do nothing. And it's a bit poetic, dying to save the lives of many more. Self-sacrifice . . ."

"Supposedly, there's some prophecy about me saving the world," I remind him. "I don't believe in destiny but we've all decided we need to do this regardless of the prophecy."

"Okay, so maybe there's a prophecy," he says. "But that's against the God of *Victory*. But I want to at least give someone a chance to live so yeah, I'll come with you."

I nod. "We leave in two days then. I suggest leaving no loose ends when you go."

Under the cover of darkness, I slip into the hall of the cathedral and down the stairs silently with Fenix just behind me. I'm dressed all in black, jacket, pants, boots and corset all as dark as the night. On my back, I carry my sword and my spear as well as several daggers sheathed on my belt and in my jacket. The cathedral is silent as a graveyard, and my heartbeat feels loud enough to wake everyone in the building, but not a single sound penetrates the dark halls. Taiyo is already waiting in the front entryway, cloaked in dark green under the arched roof. Moonlight spills through the windows, but she stands just outside of its beams to remain hidden in the shadows. I nod to her by way of greeting, not daring to speak for fear of being found out.

Several minutes later, Jyn appears at the bottom of the stairs, and together we step into the dark streets of the city. A brisk wind ruffles my hair and I look back at the cathedral only once, shuddering at the way its black towers seem to watch our every move. We head straight for the docks where Senika already waits, nervously pacing in the moonlight with one hand on the winged hilt of his silver sword. The walk out of the city seems endlessly long and boring, but I jump at every tiny sound, simply waiting for guards to melt out of the shadows and drag us back to Storm.

Outside the city, we find Sister Naemi waiting in the forest, four horses in hand. Jyn had convinced her to get us horses but never told her exactly why we needed them, other than where we are headed.

"I hope you know what you're doing," she warns as we each climb into the saddle of a horse. Her voice sounds too loud after the silence of the city.

Jyn nods. "We'll be okay."

She says nothing more but shakes her head disapprovingly as she pulls up her hood and walks back to the city. I watch her with a concerned frown when she goes as I strap my spear across my horse's back.

"You're sure she won't talk?" I ask quietly.

"She won't," Jyn promises.

I continue to stare at the empty street where she vanished into the city once again. Even if she swore she wouldn't tell anyone, Storm can read minds, a power almost as rare as my own. But it hardly matters if he finds out, it's only *when* that matters. If she were to run back to the cathedral and tell him right now, he could have soldiers on us before we even reach Edgewood Forest. But if he doesn't learn of our departure until tomorrow, we will be too far gone.

After swinging into the saddle of my horse, I start off down the road through the forest. Senika follows just behind me while Jyn and Taiyo trail behind us and Fenix trots along at my side. The trees tower over our heads like statues looking down upon us with eyes we cannot see. Through their branches, stars faintly glimmer, sparkling just as brightly beyond the cover of the forest as they do in the city. I grin up at the sky and spur my horse forward. To the Black Tower.

We ride all through the night. Even as the sun breaks over the horizon, we don't stop. Thankfully, it doesn't rain, but clouds block out the sky for most of the morning and into the afternoon. Only by evening do they part to reveal the bright pink and orange light of sunset setting the entire world aflame. We reach the edge of the forest just as twilight darkens the landscape, setting our camp where the trees give way to the plains. Taiyo quickly builds a small fire and we all gather around it, exhausted from the long ride and eager for the warmth it provides.

I take the first watch, sitting at the base of a tall tree while the others sleep on the cold dirt. My eyes start to fall shut and I have to stand, pacing the edge of the forest in an effort to stay awake. Days without sleep aren't a problem for me but sneaking out of the capital of Alkelia — and my home — isn't a common occurrence. I keep my spear in hand, my sword resting at the foot of the tree and never far from my reach. As the shadows deepen and the day slips away into the night, the fire slowly burns to embers and soon the only light comes from the stars above.

"There's something strange about that forest." At the sound of his voice, I turn to see Senika sitting up and looking out at the trees. I hadn't thought he was truly asleep but it still shocks me to hear his voice in the silence of the night.

I nod slowly. "There have always been stories about how this forest grew from the body of the Goddess of the Wild. I've heard that still, her power remains to strengthen magic within the borders of the trees, but it's still odd."

He doesn't answer right away. "I can feel that my magic is stronger here. It's strange, though, like there's sudden power I never had before."

Of course, I know what he means; I can feel it too. All day as we drew closer to Edgewood, I could feel the pull of it, my magic stirring and practically begging to be set free. I've been to this forest before, so I suppose it doesn't surprise me anymore, but to him, I can imagine the confusion these woods can bring.

"You're a Halfblood. What exactly can you do anyway?" I ask, remembering.

"I'm a Shifter," he says, holding out one hand and rolling up the sleeve of his shirt. "It's not much but I can . . ."

His arm melts away into a cluster of tiny silver butterflies, each about half the size of my palm and glittering in the faint moonlight. In a small flash of light, he shifts entirely, his body replaced by tiny glowing butterflies. For a moment, it's like I'm surrounded by stars, the wings of the insects flashing silver and white all around me. I almost reach out to touch them but stop myself at the last second. A second burst of light makes each of the butterflies melt away; Senika stands in front of me once more.

He grins. "It's not exactly very powerful or anything, but I don't mind."

I shake my head. "No, it's kind of . . . pretty."

Up close, I can see his silver eyelashes, framing his uncovered eye beautifully. His skin is so pale, it's almost ghostly, but somehow it's beautiful as well, his freckles barely dark enough to be visible across the bridge of his nose, more like scattered stars. Around his neck, his red and silver pendant sparkles like stained glass. He doesn't notice my staring, looking out at the plains, but I blush and look away as quickly as I can.

"Have you always lived in Elview?" he asks after a while, oblivious.

"Only since I was twelve," I say. "Most people train with the Order in the Black City for years before getting assigned to Elview."

"What about your parents?" he asks. "What happened to them?"

I don't answer. My family is one thing I will rarely talk about. Especially to strangers, even if they are somehow different like Senika. I spent nine years of my life with them—every second was worse than the one before it.

"If you work for the Order, how is it possible that they were able to hide their true goals for so long?" he says when I don't answer, moving on from the topic more quickly than I anticipated.

I look at him gratefully and shrug. "Inquisitors and the High Priest are the highest ranking members, and they have access to information the rest of us never will. It would be easy for them to keep things hidden if they only spoke of it among themselves."

He nods thoughtfully. "This is all so strange. All I've ever heard of the Order makes them out to be heroes."

"That's why it would be so important to keep this hidden, I suppose," I say, pausing. My eyes drift back to Senika's silver hair. "What about you? Where's your family?"

He nervously shifts his gaze to the ground. "I . . . lived with my Mum in Isondale but I got sent to the army a while back. I ran away from the actual battle when it came though."

"Oh," I say. His answer isn't what I expected; he isn't built like a soldier and is certainly far too kind to actually fight. "Who did you come here with then?"

"Pirates," he says simply. "They're friends but I didn't exactly tell them where I was going when we left last night." He sighs. "My mother was a Halfblood."

I furrow my brow, confused. "Halfbloods can't have kids."

He shrugs. "Apparently it can happen. It's rare but it happens."

"So you're . . . half-Halfblood?" I ask.

"I guess so," he says casually. "I hardly remember either of them, though; they died when I was young. My Mum and Dad took me in after that so they're the only parents I've ever known."

Before I can respond, there's a flash of movement out in the trees. I drop into a defensive stance and prepare for a fight, scanning the trees for any sign of life. But the forest is still, the dark trees like a wall of black that I can't see past. Senika draws his sword with the dull rasp of metal on metal. The sword is masterfully crafted, the blade needle-thin and perfectly maintained so it shines even in the darkness. The crossguard is shaped like the wings of a butterfly, albeit thinner and sharper, and its handguard is similar to that of a rapier despite it being closer to a long sword. It's almost a shame such a blade may never be used in a proper battle.

The sharp snap of a branch breaking is quickly followed by leaves rustling. Both of us tense, ready for something to leap out at us, but I can't make anything out through the darkness of the trees. My heart is in my throat as silence follows the sound. Several beats pass before either of us has the courage to move or even speak.

"What was that?" Senika whispers.

I shake my head and reply just as quiet. I let out the breath I had been holding, hoping nothing will come of this. "I don't know. There are stories of how the magic sometimes draws in monsters, so we should be prepared for anything. But I didn't get a good look at whatever that was."

I sense fear briefly in his mind, and he draws in a deep breath. "By monsters, do you mean like the ones from Gosritaan?

"Maybe," I shrug. "No one's ever seen them."

He looks at me sideways, confused, but doesn't say anything. I lower my spear, sitting back down next to the tree, and Senika follows suit, sheathing his sword. The winged crossguard of the sword folds flat against the blade to fit perfectly in the otherwise unadorned sheath. We sit in silence for a while, watching the trees as if something might jump out at any second. But there is nothing more. Eventually, he tells me to sleep, assuring me that he will wake me if anything happens. And, too exhausted to object, I quickly fall into a deep, dreamless sleep.

10

Edgewood Forest

Kellin

The next morning we set off just after sunrise, all of us on high alert the second we set foot in the forest. Fenix follows along next to us, sometimes disappearing beneath the trees to hunt or explore. The unnerving presence of magic fills the air almost like the scent of something sweet, perhaps honey or flowers, and draws us in like moths to a flame. I doubt there is truly anything dangerous in these woods, but the feeling of someone watching us refuses to leave. I stare at the trees, waiting for something to happen.

Spirits fuel Halfblood magic; we are chosen by them and they grant us our powers. But spirits are somewhat lesser gods, immortals with the ability to manipulate the elements—and on occasion, see the future and fate woven for humanity. As such, the presence of a god, dead or alive, usually manages to affect us in ways humans never will be affected. If there truly is a god here, the bizarre rush of power coming from these trees makes perfect sense.

We stop around noon in a small clearing for a lunch of bread, salted meat, and sun-warmed cheese before riding through the afternoon. By the time we stop again, the evening is drawing close and we're all exhausted from a lack of sleep the past two nights followed by long days of travel. Dinner is just about the same as lunch; we all sit around the fire in silence eating quickly before trying to sleep.

I wake up at some point in the night, shaking and frantic but unable to remember whatever it is I may have dreamed. Complete darkness surrounds our camp, the faint light of the fire burning low. Senika is currently on watch, feeding pieces of bark and twigs to the embers, but he lifts his head when I suddenly awaken. An owl hoots, penetrating the silence of the night with the abrupt sound. I look to the trees in search of its bright eyes.

"You're awake," Senika observes softly.

I nod, standing up to stretch my arms over my head. "Yeah. You can sleep now, I'll take the watch."

"You sure?" he asks, standing up as well. "I can stay up a bit longer if you want."

"No, it's okay." I shake my head.

He steps away from the fire, laying down with his back to the flames. I sit against the thick trunk of a tree, the bark sharp in my back, and watch the fire flickering, its shadows cast upon the forest. The owl hoots again, this time sounding closer, but I still can't see it. The others are all asleep, the forest completely silent. I stare into the fire, trying to shake the feeling of wrongness this place holds.

A twig snaps loudly in the forest.

I shoot to my feet and scan the trees for the source of the sound. There's nothing there. Just like before. When nothing reveals itself, I sit back down with a heavy sigh. The instant I do, there's a person standing in front of me.

He's tall with olive skin; black and white curls fall to his shoulders. Dressed in a dark cloak, he stands with one hand outstretched in front of him so his palm faces the earth. He doesn't look at me, but rather at whatever is under his hand, although I can't see anything there. I stare at him, holding my breath as if that can hide me from him somehow. Despite standing only a few feet away, however, he doesn't notice I'm there until he suddenly looks up, not at me but rather through me. Panic briefly flashes across his face and he waves his hand through the air, disappearing as if he was never there.

I stare at the empty space in front of me, unblinking. Seconds pass, then minutes, but nothing happens. The owl hoots. I shake my head, thinking perhaps I am far more tired than I thought. Or, maybe I'm going insane. Soon, minutes turn to hours and Jyn wakes up, instructing me to sleep, but even when I lay down, exhausted, sleep does not come.

The next morning, when I wake up after only two or three hours actually spent sleeping, the forest is as normal as ever. The enhanced magic remains, of course, but otherwise, it looks like any other forest in Alkelia, tall trees with bright green leaves and sunlight that brightens the world into shades of emerald and jade. We move on quickly with few words spoken, although it's clear every one of us wants to get out of here as swiftly as possible.

After only a few hours of riding, before the sun has even reached its zenith, I stop my horse. On the path in front of us stands the same person I saw last night. In the daylight, I see him more clearly, his cloak torn at the bottom, but the rest of his clothing strangely well-kept and clean. Those robes remind me of an illustration of a necromancer from a book on lost magical arts I once read. Earlier, I would have guessed him to be in his twenties, but now I find it impossible to tell, almost as if he simply has no age. Like before, he doesn't notice me or the others. And they don't seem to see him.

"Kellin?" Jyn asks after abruptly, stopping his horse to avoid crashing into me.

"Do you see him?" I demand. "There's someone standing right in front of us, a man in a black cloak with black and white hair."

"What?" Jyn squints at the forest. "I can't see anything."

I curse under my breath and Taiyo suggests, "The forest enhances magic, right? If he's somehow watching us from somewhere else, it might be letting you see him in return."

"But why would he be watching us?" I ask, dismounting from my horse.

As I approach him, the person doesn't move. Jyn warns me that it could be dangerous, but I wave him away. Fenix stares at me, clueless as usual, but offers a concerned meow at the image of the man no one else can see. I reach out carefully, curious about what might happen. But the instant before my hand touches him, the man's head snaps toward me, and his dark eyes meet mine. My hand passes straight through his chest, and the air freezes right before the world vanishes.

At first, I stand in darkness, an endless plane of blackness where a half-inch of water covers the ground. I spin around, looking for something or someone. I call out Jyn's name, but my voice fades away like the words were never spoken. The water laps against the heels of my boots, the only sound in the strange darkness.

An icy wind rises from nowhere, tearing at my clothing, and I raise my arms to keep it out of my eyes. Slowly, I lower my arms; snow falls softly around me. I glance around, looking for the woman who always haunts my dreams, but strangely, I am alone. Usually, the snow would indicate the same dream I always have, the flashbacks and nightmares, but now it's just snow. I stare for a while, mystified, waiting for something. Yet, nothing happens. As the soft, white flakes continue to fall, my breath creates tiny clouds in the air in tiny puffs of smoke that billow from my mouth.

After an eternity, the scene transforms into the ruins of a castle I have never seen before, grey stone under a grey sky.

11

LORD OF SHADOWS

THE WATCHER

"My lord, everything is in place. Shall we begin soon?"

"Not yet. We must be patient for a while longer. In time, it will all fall into place as it is meant to be." In the shadowy ruins of a once-grand castle, the Lord of Shadows turns his back on his servant. With a gaze like daggers, he looks out over the scarred landscape of the Deadlands and remembers the days when this place was as alive as the rest of Morsevdon.

"My lord," The servant speaks again, this time far more hesitant. "Are you certain this plan will work? How can we be sure he will fall into the trap we have laid?"

Fast as lightning, the Lord of Shadows spins around and grabs the human by the throat, lifting him off the ground so his feet reach down for the stone floor but unable to touch it.

"You will not doubt me." The Lord's voice is as cold and dark as the ruins around them and sharper than any blade. Knowing better than to object again, the servant nods desperately, gasping for air as his legs kick, his fingers clawing at the hands of the Lord of Shadows. As the human starts to give up, realizing he will die if he persists, the Lord lets him fall to the ground and turns back to the window.

"Do you understand? My word is to be trusted above all else. You will not doubt me nor my plans for even an instant or you will die like so many before you. Humans are nothing but an annoyance to a god such as myself, I have no time to deal with the ones who happen to cause trouble." Pausing, the Lord of Shadows glances over his shoulder at the human. "The only one strong enough to be worth the time I have taken to deal with is that boy. He does not know of his destiny, but soon enough, the power he holds will be mine."

"Yes, of course, my lord." The servant speaks in a faint voice, still gasping for breath. "He is superior to us, but even one like him cannot compare to Your Excellency."

The Lord nods. "Yes, of course. Now leave me, you fool, and find Vendetta. I require his assistance."

Bowing, the servant disappears into the shadows of the castle, leaving the being who was once a god to look out at the ruins of his domain. This land was once a flourishing city where merchants crowded the streets, hawking their wares at all times of the day. Lavish parties could be found at stunning estates all around, surrounded by sprawling gardens. The castle once sprawled at the edge of the sea with towers rising high into the sky where the birds soared and the wind blew. Now, there are no merchants, hardly any life to be found. No birds fly, and not even a single breeze whistles through the towers of the ruined castle. Even the grass has died and given way to cracked grey dirt and stone.

Sensing a new presence, the Lord turns to see a boy dressed in the robes of a necromancer, tattered and dark. His hair is black, but near the roots, it is white as the clouds, if there could ever be another white cloud in this sky. His eyes appear black, but on closer inspection, they are such a dark purple they seem to have no pupil. Even standing before the Lord of Shadows, he does not bow nor falter. But neither does he speak.

"There you are," the old god says, with what passes for a smile. "I wish to know what you have seen, boy."

"There is nothing new, sir. Everything is progressing as we had planned." His voice is even and emotionless.

"Good. I assume we can begin soon, then?"

"Yes, it will all be ready shortly."

The Lord of Shadows nods. "Then I shall wait for the day when it is done. Go to your master, tell him we are nearly there."

The boy bows his head and turns away from the castle, heading toward the ominous tower near the edge of the city. Overhead, the sky fills with dark storm clouds seconds away from pouring rain down in the city. But he knows they won't. Clouds that have been dark and stormy for centuries aren't going to change now. The city, once full of life, is dead and deserted, weeds growing in the streets and houses crumbling. Perhaps it's a strange sight to see a city so silent, but he has been here too long to see anything but what passes as home.

The image wavers, shimmering like a reflection in water after a stone is tossed into it. For a moment, everything stands still.

12

GONE

KELLIN

The houses melt into trees before they remember they're meant to be houses and snap back into their original shape.

"...Kellin?" Jyn's voice comes from somewhere nearby, but I can't see him. "Kellin, wake up!"

Bright green leaves replace the dark sky as someone shakes my shoulder. It's as if two realities overlap to create what feels like a strange fever dream. I'm very aware that I can't see my body, and I appear to be a floating consciousness watching whatever is going on here.

"Kellin!" This voice is Senika's but it isn't the only one I hear.

"This isn't going to help," Taiyo says, her voice sounding very far away. "We need to get out of this place and then we can see if he wakes up."

The city has been fading, but now it shatters like glass, falling away to leave me back in Edgewood Forest. I'm standing frozen in the middle of the woods, right in front of the spot where I'd seen the strange person earlier. I blink, trying to get my eyes to adjust to the dark forest. Was it this dark before?

"What the hell happened?" I ask, unnerved by how my own voice sounds distant, as if it's coming from the other end of a long hallway.

"Gods, you're awake," Jyn breathes with a nervous laugh.

Senika frowns. "Sorry to say this but we don't have much time to stand here. We have to keep moving."

I nod and open my mouth to speak, but no sound escapes. At my feet, Fenix meows happily, and I reach down to touch her head right between her horns, finding comfort in that cat's presence. By now, the world has reformed into one rather than two, but the forest is even more wrong than it was before.

Taiyo climbs back onto her horse and starts off through the trees. "Senika is right, we wasted too much time here so let's move quickly now."

I start to walk back to my horse but the ground tips. I stumble forward, catching my balance again before I fall. My head spins, and my entire body shivers despite the mild weather. I hear laughter in the distance, but there's no one in this forest except for us.

"What the fuck?" I mumble in Old Alkelian, seconds before my entire body goes numb. The dirt of the forest floor rushes up as I collapse.

13

HALFBLOOD

SENIKA

I never asked to be a Halfblood. None of us did. Not a single person ever wanted the spirits to grant them powers that belong in legends. Because with that power comes the knowledge that you will always be *different*.

That fact has only become more evident since I arrived in Alkelia. Here, Halfbloods are killed by their god for nothing more than being born. Although we have yet to prove it, the possibility of such a horrific crime makes me sick. There may not be much that a few kids can do but I know we have to try.

"You okay?" Taiyo watches me from across the fire her reddish hair glowing in the flashing light. After Kellin passed out, we decided to make camp until he woke up but it's already nighttime and he hasn't stirred yet.

I nod, trying to push my thoughts away. "Yeah. There's just something unsettling about this forest."

She makes an amused sound. "I know what you mean. People avoid this place for a reason. I'm not a Halfblood but I've heard the stories of how the forest enhances magic."

"Well, it turns out the stories are true," I say. "But trust me, you don't want to feel it for yourself."

When Kellin said this place had the ability to make Halfblood magic stronger, I almost didn't believe him. But the longer we're here, the harder it is to ignore. It's as if my magic is an animal desperate to break free, restless and hungry for something I can't give it. I've never been particularly powerful which means I've never had a reason to fear my power, but this is starting to feel less and less like *my* magic.

Taiyo chuckles. "Oh, I've never wanted to be one of you. Power like that doesn't sound appealing to me. I would much rather be human. Especially after seeing what it does to Kellin."

I glance over my shoulder to where Kellin still sleeps. Fenix lies next to him, chin on her paws and her protective gaze never leaving him. After how he acted earlier, I can't say I disagree with Taiyo. The power of the spirits has been known to drive Halfbloods insane. There are countless stories of Halfbloods who suddenly lash out and murder those closest to them or spend their lives rambling on about visions and twisted prophecies given to them by the spirits. Many of us die young, used as weapons in wars we never should have fought, and none of us will ever lead an ordinary life.

There was once a time when I dreamed of growing old in a beautiful house, happily married with children and a job to occupy my time. But as I grew, I came to realize that I could never live that life. Kings want to use our power to wage war and gods want us dead.

"Do you think it's true?" I ask, turning back to Taiyo. "The whole thing about Xethos killing Halfbloods."

She shrugs. "I'm here, aren't I? My family was killed by Xethos. I've never trusted him. But I agree, we need proof before we can act."

Jyn appears next to me, dropping an armful of branches. He plops down in the dirt with a heavy sigh. "For such a massive forest you wouldn't believe how hard it is to find good, dry wood for a fire."

"Jyn, this is Alkelia," Taiyo says. "We barely know what *dry* means here."

He nods. "Good point." He glances over at Kellin worriedly. "He's still not awake."

Taiyo shakes her head. "Nope. He hasn't even moved since you went off on your search for wood."

"I guess we're spending the night here, then." Jyn picks up a twig and starts peeling its bark off.

"We could all benefit from some sleep," I say. "I'm guessing the next few days aren't going to be easy. We'll need to keep our energy up."

Jyn throws a branch into the fire. Sparks snap, flying into the air. The flames lick higher, hungry to consume anything they can. Under a sky full of stars as familiar to me as the back of my hand, I stare out at unfamiliar trees that stretch high into an unforgiving black night.

Perhaps I never asked for any of this—to be a Halfblood, to find myself fighting a war against a god—but I have learned to live with it. I place my hand on the hilt of the sword I should never have had to wield. There is no peace for people like us. I can only dream of a world where like that.

14

THROUGH THE DARK

KELLIN

I wake up in the dark. I can't remember how I got here or even where I am. For a moment, I don't even open my eyes, trying to keep my breathing even but I don't know why. My head pounds and my wrist feels like several needles are being stabbed into the joint. When I finally look up, I see the silhouettes of three people sitting around a small fire that looks like it's really just embers by now. Past them, darkness creates a black curtain of shadows. I blink, feeling oddly distant from the scene in front of me as if it were happening very far away. Squinting, I look at the figures, and it takes me a moment to realize I know them.

Everything rushes back. The forest, my vision, the monsters. Vendetta.

Frantically, I look around for the illusion of the person I saw earlier but there's nothing there. Fenix rubs her chin against my hand and I pat her head. My heart is racing and I can't shake the feeling that there's someone just behind me, watching. After a moment, Jyn notices I'm awake and grins.

"There you are," he says, his voice light but with a hint of worry underneath. "We were starting to think we lost you."

I shake my head, the tiny movement sending sharp needles of pain into my skull. "Nah, you can't get rid of me that easy." Usually, the words would be a joke but right now, I'm far too exhausted to make it even remotely funny.

Taiyo sighs. "I'm starting to think we should just turn around now, while we still can."

Jyn shoots her a look. "We're closer to the Tower than Elview now. There's no point in turning back."

I struggle to my feet, head spinning as I stand, but I push the pain away and say, "We should keep moving, whether we turn back or go forward. This forest freaks me out."

"If you think you can travel in that condition, you're a fool," Senika remarks, poking the fire with a twig.

Shrugging, I stagger over to my horse, feeling slightly drunk. "Doesn't matter if I'm a fool or not, I still have to get answers."

"Kellin, this is stupid. You know he's right," Jyn says, trying to convince me. "You fell and hit your head plus whatever happened before that. It's an incredibly bad idea to try and ride again after that."

"I'd rather die than spend any more time here, okay?" I snap. "I don't care if you come with me but I'm leaving. Now."

It takes all the effort I can muster to pull myself into the saddle of my horse. Whatever happened to my wrist doesn't make it any easier, but as soon as I do, I take off out of the small clearing. Behind me, I hear Jyn curse followed by the sound of hooves on the soft forest floor. It's dark in the forest so I ride slowly to avoid crashing into a tree. All I want is to run as fast as I can and get away from here as soon as possible. Even riding slowly manages to make me feel like someone is stabbing my head, but I keep going. Any more time here is going to drive me insane. For a brief moment, I wonder if maybe I am insane already; only an insane person would insist on riding through this cursed forest in the middle of the night in whatever sort of horrible condition I've found myself in.

"Kellin!"

I look over my shoulder to find Jyn riding a few paces behind me, Fenix plodding along beside him. Without the energy to say much, I just nod and make a sound of acknowledgement.

"Are you sure you want to do this?" Jyn shouts. "I mean this whole plan could be suicide. You can't fight a god and hope to win. I know I said I was with you but I don't want you dead."

"And you think I haven't considered that, Jyn?" I glare at the trees, too tired for this conversation. "People are dying."

He laughs. "They've always been dying, it's hardly any different now."

"Look, I'm really not in the mood for this."

"Do you really care about them, Kellin? Or is it just impossible for you to do nothing?"

I stop my horse and look back at him. "What the fuck, Jyn? Why do you have to do this? People are dying and that *fucker* is getting away with it 'cause nobody knows!"

"And you think it *isn't* stupid to deal with this yourself?"

I frown. Of course, he has a point. This is going to turn into one kid against a god, and it won't matter how powerful I am because I am still just a kid. And he will always be a god. "If I told them the truth, do you think they would listen? Do you honestly think a single person in this kingdom would believe me if I said the god they worship is killing people? No, they will always see me as a liar because to them I will always be Kellin Kane, a Halfblood. People hate me, Jyn. I'm a bastard and a Halfblood; too royal to be normal, too normal to be royal. They see you and think you're like them, but I'm just a freak, got it?"

He stares at me. "That doesn't change anything. I mean, Taiyo, Senika and me all believe you. But we aren't enough to kill a god."

"Well, maybe all I need is myself. I don't need an army." With that, I turn and storm away, wanting more than anything to be back in my bed at the cathedral and wishing that damn spirit had never shown herself to me.

Somehow, I think maybe these people killed by the Order are like me, which makes me feel a little less alone. My whole life I have been the only one like me. When I was very young, I lived with my mother and her husband and their children who were all perfectly normal. There, it always felt like I was an outcast of sorts, forgotten and pushed away. Even after joining the Order, I was the son of a princess so they treated me like I was royal, despite the fact that I could never be royal enough for my real family. The Halfbloods killed by Xethos are similar, pushed away because they could never fit in, and they deserve a chance to live. It seems pointless for Xethos to kill Halfbloods when the first Halfbloods were created to fight alongside the gods, but I'm willing to fight for the people who deserve life.

The sun has nearly risen by the time I realize just how long I've been riding. Jyn seems to have decided to stay at the back of our small group, but for some reason, Senika won't leave me alone. It isn't particularly annoying, but with my head feeling as if it's been split open with an axe—and I haven't slept properly in days—just about everything is annoying. He rides just behind me, silent apart from his horse's hooves on the forest floor, and Fenix walks next to him. Taiyo has spent the night grumbling about being tired and needing beauty sleep or whatever and complaining that all this time in the forest is ridiculous. I'm tempted to turn around and punch her in the face, but even that wouldn't shut her up. And I've been told friends aren't supposed to punch each other.

Glancing around at the trees, I slow my horse and yawn. As much as I want to keep going, I'm definitely starting to think it's going to take more than one night to get out of here. My original panic has faded a little, and I'm far too tired to stay on alert for much longer.

Senika says, "How much further do you think it is?"

"Maybe another few hours out of the forest," Jyn answers. "Plus an extra day to the Tower itself."

"Ugh. I'm starting to feel like we're going in circles." Taiyo objects. "Can't we just get there already? This damned forest is all the same."

Jyn sighs. "We might be going in circles. There's no way to know."

"You aren't very helpful, Jyn," Taiyo replies, determined to be displeased with everything anyone says.

"Well if we are going in circles, we'll end up out of the forest eventually. Maybe," Senika adds doubtfully. I'm not sure where that logic comes from but I suppose his optimism is a plus.

I close my eyes and block out their conversation, focusing on simply riding forward as quickly as I can without hurting my head too much. Holding the reins too tight hurts my wrist, so I let go with my right hand and hope I can manage with only one hand.

"What happened to your hand?" Senika's voice comes out of nowhere and I open my eyes to glare at him. At some point, the conversation about circles stopped, and Senika moved up to ride beside me.

I look at my right hand, examining the fifth finger. It's been cut off at the second joint, and various scars crisscross my skin. There are two tattoos, both plain back bands encircling my wrists, neither of which seem to have a purpose at first glance. But I have them on both arms. "It's kind of a long story."

He gives me a strange look then shrugs. "We have time for long stories, but if you don't want to tell me, that's fine."

Narrowing my eyes at him, I don't say anything, but neither does he. People always ask me questions, but answering them is usually the last thing I want to do. In fact, Jyn is the only one who truly knows what happened years ago, even if others have some sort of vague idea. It's not the kind of thing people want to hear about anyways, and definitely not what they say they care about.

Silence falls over our group for a while longer. When I feel seconds away from collapsing, the edge of the forest finally arrives. Through the towering trees, sunlight and rolling green hills, not unlike those on the other side of the forest, reveal themselves. I would almost think we really did go in circles and end up back at the start if it weren't for the cobblestone road just past the trees. The sun rests high above the horizon, but grey clouds hide most of the sky.

I speed up, wanting to escape the forest as soon as I can, but I pause at the edge to make sure no one is on the road. Just past the trees, I stop and dismount, stumbling to my feet. Fenix rubs her shoulder against my hip, and I place my hand on her head.

"Finally, we're out of that god-forsaken place." Senika sighs, flopping down in the grass and laying with his arms above his head.

I collapse on the ground beside him, and Fenix decides this is a perfect time to sniff my forehead.

Taiyo arrives a few seconds later, complaining. "If I ever have to spend another night sleeping in the dirt I might just die."

"Not everything has to look perfect, you know," Jyn tells her, earning himself a sharp scowl. "I mean, we *are* on a mission to save like, half the kingdom."

She raises her eyebrow suspiciously. "As much as I agree with you, I still don't know why any of us think this is going to go well."

"We don't," I say truthfully.

"So someone explain why we're here then," she shoots back.

I shake my head. "Apparently because we are all stupid and decided this is the only option."

Taiyo sighs. "Well, I wouldn't say you're wrong there."

The sword feels heavy and awkward in my hands. Wrapped up in layers of clothing to shield me from the cold, my movements are uncoordinated and clumsy, like a child taking its first steps. When I try to swing, the sword's weight causes me to stumble forward and it stabs the snow rather than hit my target.

"Try again," Bram encourages me.

I heft the sword over my shoulder once more, swinging it in a wild arc. This time, it nearly hits its mark. Bram steps to the side to avoid being clobbered but he grins, eyes bright.

"Good," he says. "Do you want to keep going?"

Panting, I shake my head. I hardly did anything but I'm exhausted. Bram takes the sword back from me, wielding it with enviable ease as he sheathes it.

He ruffles my hair as he walks past me. "You'll get the hang of it, kid. There will be other times to practice but for now, we should get back home. It'll be dark soon."

I pull my hood back over my head, shrinking deep within the high collar of my jacket and the soft fabric of my scarf. Afraid I might be left behind, I trudge after Bram as fast as I can without tripping in the freshly fallen snow. The footprints he leaves behind make it easier but his steps are often too far apart for me to follow them exactly. Snow continues to fall as we walk, gathering on my clothes in massive, fluffy flakes.

Only when the light begins to fade do I notice that I was too pre-occupied with following his steps to see that I had lost sight of Bram.

Picking up my pace, I scan the trees ahead of me for movement, hoping he slowed down to wait for me. Snow continues to fall around me, piling higher by the second. Before long, it becomes difficult for me to walk, thick snow banks now reaching past my knees. The light is nearly gone, too, as if night has come a bit too early and far too fast.

I stagger, falling forward into the snow. It stings my face and slips into my sleeve. Scrambling to my feet again, I gasp, brushing the snow away frantically.

I freeze when I see the cabin in front of me.

Seeming to have materialized from the woods, it stands peacefully amidst the drifting snow. Welcoming light fills its windows and smoke curls up from the chimney. I can smell Bram's favourite stew cooking over the fire, filling the air with the scent of deer meat, herbs and the last of the vegetables we were able to grow over the short summer.

I let out a sigh of relief at the sight of it. Perhaps I had lost track of time or the snow obscured the path ahead while I walked.

Despite the cold, I feel warm as I tug my collar up to my nose and push forward. The last few feet to the cabin are nothing compared to the endless trek I had anticipated. I reach for the door, more than ready to be away from the cold and the snow and to tuck myself into bed by the fire with a bowl of hot stew.

"Run."

My heart stops.

As if in a trance, I turn around, terrified.

Bram hangs from a tree branch by the rope tied around his neck. His face has already turned blue from the lack of oxygen and he no longer fights to breathe, eyes glassed over as the life fades from his body.

As I watch, the flesh begins to rot off his bones, peeling away. Bone starts to show, poking through as he becomes no more than a corpse. A scream catches in my throat, terror freezing my body in place.

The corpse moves, lifting its head as if controlled by a puppeteer.

"Run," it rasps in a voice like the scrap of metal on stone. "Run, you fool."

Powered only by fear and desperation, I whirl around, almost falling, and sprint toward the cabin. Skidding around the corner, I throw open the door to the tiny stable where Bram's horse is tied up. My hands shake as I fumble with the knot in her reins, losing precious seconds. Just when I finally yank the reins free, the sound of footsteps in the snow strikes fear into my heart once more.

The footsteps stop and I glance over my shoulder to see Elenore standing in the doorway of the stables, the kitchen knife in her hand glistening ominously. Instinctively, I reach over my shoulder for my sword, only to remember that I never carried one when my hand hits air.

The scene changes, shifting so that the door no longer leads to the stable behind Bram's cabin but rather to a kitchen, and I am the one on the outside. My mother stands framed by the light of the room behind her, a silhouette against the warm glow. Snow continues to fall around me, swirling in the frigid wind. Voices howl in my head, screaming words I can't understand, but their desperation and anger are unmistakable.

I fall to my knees in defeat, slamming my hands over my ears to block out the deafening roar of voices that only grows louder by the second. The wind picks up, creating a tornado of snow with me at its center. My mother slams the door behind her as she walks away.

This is a dream, this is a dream, this is a dream, I tell myself, begging for it to end.

The screeching voices reach an ear-shattering crescendo and the rest of the world fades away. Overwhelmed by the noise, nothing else matters anymore as I bury my head in my hands.

I scream as reality shatters and fades to black.

I wake up with tears running down my face, hands shaking, breath coming in sharp gasps. Those are the words she said. *You are not my child*. Words I will forget just as soon as I will forget every other painful detail of that night. For a long time, I lay there and stare at the stars in the sky, my eyes tracing the stars in the constellation of Doriak, the god they say came first but was banished to Gosritaan long, long ago. No one else is awake, so there isn't much else I can do but lie there. Even Fenix looks like she was hit by a boulder and flattened into the ground.

Sometimes, I wonder if she was right. Perhaps I really am the monster she said I was, sent from the depths of the Underworld to curse her. But on nights like this, I am certain that isn't true. A monster wouldn't feel hurt by those words. A monster would be able to do something to defend itself. But if there's one thing she was ever right about, it's how useless I am. Sure, I can fight, and I have power, even if it is a curse, but I can't do anything that matters. I can never be her son.

That was nearly eight years ago, I was nine when she tried to kill me. What a pitiful creature I am, monster or otherwise. Nine should be old enough to fight back, but I never did. Instead, I waited and hoped. Perhaps one day, she would love me.

All I ever wanted was for someone to love me.

15

THE BLACK CITY

KELLIN

We reach the Tower late the next afternoon after spending the last hour or two riding alongside another group of travellers heading to the city. By the time we reach its walls, the sky is growing dark. The sun sinks below the horizon, but there have been dark clouds overhead nearly all day, so there wasn't much sky in the first place. At the gates, soldiers examine our strange group before letting us pass into the city.

The streets are still busy with merchants trying to sell their goods but most people either ignore them or scowl and keep moving. Here, no one spares us a second glance, all far too busy to care about strange travellers. We part with the other group of travellers a few blocks from the Tower itself and start winding our way down the wide stone streets. This city is home mostly to Halfbloods, and the majority of the people who live here have something to do with the Order. None of us are out of place, and only Fenix earns us a few odd looks. Every soldier posted on street corners wears the red rose emblem I've become so familiar with, and we even pass an Inquisitor chatting with an ordinary baker.

When we reach the front doors of the Tower, we leave our horses and walk inside, feeling rather like we're breaking into somewhere we shouldn't be. Of course, the first person we see is Alyssa Dragonclaw, maybe my third least favourite person in Alkelia, nearly tied with Storm in annoyance level. She smirks at us and tosses her long white hair over her shoulder.

"Well, would you look who it is? Kellin Acheros Kane, what an honour it is to have you grace these halls once again, *Your Highness.*" She's sitting on a table holding a book in one hand that she makes a point of slamming shut when we appear in the doorway. I hate how she always manages to drag my royal blood into this. "I thought you said you'd never come back here, Kane, yet here you are again."

"Yeah, I'm back, but I'm not staying for long." I try to walk past her to the stairs but she slides off the table and steps into my path.

"I suppose you have a reason for dragging yourself all the way up from Elview. Are you here to see me, hmm?"

I glare at her, hating that absolutely everyone has to be taller than me. "No. This has nothing to do with you. Now get out of my way."

She laughs and places one hand on her hip, looking past me at the others. "You even brought friends. I never would have guessed that anyone other than Jyn could ever tolerate being around you. Or have you brainwashed them into following you?"

"You know I can't brainwash anyone. And if they didn't want to be here, they wouldn't be."

"Perhaps blackmail then," she taunts. "Are they *afraid* of you? Honestly, I don't get it, you just look like a freak to me."

"You want to test that?" I step forward and reach for the thin dagger strapped to my thigh.

Jyn stops me with a hand on my shoulder. "Stop it. Both of you." He turns to Alyssa. "We aren't here to cause any trouble, we only want to look for something."

Flashing him a sly smile, she says, "Why didn't you just say so? Is there anything I can help with, in that case?"

Frowning at Jyn, I grumble, "Nope, we're all good. Just leave us alone and everything will work out."

But as we head upstairs I hear Alyssa's footsteps following us up. It's been a long time since I've been here, and I have to pause at the top of the stairs to remember where I'm going. After climbing what feels like endless stairs, we reach the library and head straight to the shelves filled with documents of mission reports from various Order members.

"You aren't allowed to look at those," Alyssa reminds us as if we didn't know. "They're all classified. I'll report you and Storm will drag you right back to Elview. After that, I doubt anyone would let you anywhere near this place."

"I don't particularly care, Alyssa," I snap. "We need information and those documents are the only way we can learn what we need to know."

"And what exactly is it that you so desperately need that could bring you all the way here for documents none of you have access to?"

I frown at her. "That's not your business."

"It is actually. Depending on your answer, I may just let you in." Smiling, she adds, "Plus I'm interested in whatever might have caught the attention of the infamous Kellin Kane."

"When did it become your job to decide who reads those?" I retort, but my comment goes mostly unnoticed.

Behind me, Jyn reasons, "We don't have to tell you anything other than people will die if we don't find answers."

Alyssa's expression turns grim, her sly smile vanishing in an instant. "You know then. I knew it was only a matter of time before others started to find out, but I hadn't expected you two to have anything to do with it."

Senika raises his hand. "First, there's four of us, not just two. Second, how do you know about it if you don't expect anyone else to find out?"

"My sister is an Inquisitor. I know everything about every mission she goes on," Alyssa explains. "She was on one of the first missions to the East, but they were never told why they were being sent out until they got there."

Of course, this makes sense now. The Inquisitor in my dream had the same white hair and pale skin as Alyssa, even the same snake-like red eyes. It's not particularly rare for two siblings to become Half-bloods, but in the case of Alyssa and her sister Lisia, they were both chosen by the spirits shortly after their parents died of an unknown illness. I hadn't known Lisia had become an Inquisitor, but it's a reasonable choice given her talent with a sword.

"Does that mean we can cut this bullshit and learn what we need to know?" I ask, tired of this conversation and wanting nothing more than to get all this over with.

"What is it you want to know?" Alyssa's tone has remarkably less edge to it. "If you're looking for anything in particular I may be able to help. My sister may be an Inquisitor but I'm still a Halfblood and, unless someone can prove that there's any benefit to this slaughter, it's an injustice."

"I wanted to know if this is true," I tell her. "Now I know, so I need to know what I can do about it."

The snake-eyed girl laughs. "What you can do about it? Don't tell me you plan on actually trying to go toe-to-toe with Xethos in this.

I'd make sure I had an army at my back before even thinking about it. You're brave, I'll give you that. Or a complete idiot."

"Well I don't have an army and it's not easy to get one so we're doing this my way." This time, when I walk past her, she doesn't even try to stop me.

We spend the next few hours searching through documents and reports for any sort of pattern that might expose some weakness in the Order—or Xethos—but to no avail. The most we come across is a stack of patrol schedules from weeks ago and a report from a caravan escort from Alicante in the East. There is no mention of Inquisitors or dead Halfbloods at all. After a while, night falls outside, and Taiyo says we should probably sleep instead of spending the whole night on a wild goose hunt through piles of nothing. Alyssa tells us the Tower is half empty these days and that we can find rooms just about anywhere, so we decide to come back to our search in the morning.

Several hours after midnight, it starts to rain. I had been watching the sky all day just waiting for the grey clouds to break. The entire world is asleep, and everything seems quiet and almost lonely, but it's the time when I'm awake and standing on the balcony off the hallway housing our rooms for the night. I should be sleeping like everyone else, but my mind races and voices of the spirits won't leave me alone. Sleep would be impossible.

So I stand here and watch the downpour, soaking my clothing in the freezing rain.

"Kellin?" I turn around, ready to snap at whoever is trying to talk to me but when I see Senika standing in the doorway, I freeze. "What are you doing out here?"

I consider giving him some half-excuse, but I find that I can't come up with anything so I merely shrug and say, "I couldn't sleep."

If we are being honest, I never know how to talk to people. With Jyn, I can always just tell him the truth because I know he would never hate me, but Senika is another story. I don't know him, and he doesn't know me, even though we've ended up on this strange journey together. He doesn't know who I am or anything of my past or even of my power.

"You can't sleep so you're going to freeze yourself out here in this rain?" He gestures toward the door. "At least come back inside."

"Why did you come to Alkelia?" I ask, choosing to ignore his advice even if he's right.

With a small smile that seems almost sad, he says, "I was supposed to go to war but . . . that war killed my father and I couldn't face it. My mother said it was my duty, I had to take up my father's ship and fight in his place. I guess I left because I didn't want to see more people die because of that war."

"What are they like? Your parents, I mean." Only after the words leave my mouth do I realize that maybe it isn't the best question to ask someone whose father died in a war.

But he just gives me that same sad smile again. "The ones who raised me, they aren't my real parents. My real parents were killed when I was very young. We lived near the border and in the middle of the night, the town was attacked and just about everyone was . . . slaughtered. I don't remember them, or that town; I don't even know who they were. I was found by a sailor who took me back to Isondale where he and his wife raised me." He pauses then shakes his head before adding, "I can't fight in a war that takes so much from all of us, but running away isn't a solution either. There will be no end to this fighting, and I thought running would make it all go away, but people are dying everywhere and I can't run forever."

I look back out at the dark city and the rain pouring down on it. "This . . . this is not war. Alkelia doesn't know war, they only know how to mercilessly destroy anyone who stands in their way. At least Iolleria fights a fair battle."

"There is no such thing as fairness in war." Despair and something close to anger fill his pale silver-blue eye. His voice turns soft and distant. "There is no war in which one side does not have an advantage. Iollerians were being massacred by the hundreds and I *ran* from it. I never even tried to do anything to help. I just left."

Neither of us says anything for a very long time, standing there half-frozen in the icy rain. I never gave much thought to the Iollerian war and there is only occasionally talk of sending help that never ends up being sent. For many years there was no war at all, only a one-sided slaughter of the Iollerian people. The previous ruler only cared for himself and never reached out to assist the commoners. To him, dead Iollerians were not an issue, so he refused to do anything about it. But the enemy, of course, is not from this world.

Iolleria is at war with monsters—real monsters, from Gosritaan, the world that came before Morsevdon. The homeland of all things evil. It's a war that will last until the end of time unless someone does something about it, and Alkelia seems bent on ignoring any and all calls for help. Myria also borders the Deadlands, where the gates of Gosritaan lie, and they have sent in dragon riders, but there is only so much the tiny kingdom can do. In this matter, I understand why Senika ran away. Anyone would rather run than fight in a war that ends with inevitable death for anyone who tries to fight.

"Running does not make you wrong," I say at last. "You wanted to live. All anyone wants is to live."

"It might not make me wrong, but it makes me a coward. And no one wants a coward." In the dark, it's hard to see his face, but I can hear the sadness in his voice, and that's all I need to know.

"I don't think you're a coward," It feels like a pointless thing to say but I say it regardless. "Cowards don't worry if they're brave or not. But if wanting peace makes you a coward this world is full of cowards."

"Did you ever run? What caused you to care about the Halfbloods being killed? I realize I know nothing about you."

The sudden change in topic catches me off guard so all I can think of to say is, "I think no one really knows me."

"It doesn't help that you're so secretive. I want to know who you are." Just like that, the sadness is gone, effectively replaced with curiosity.

I shake my head. "I don't even know where to start. What about me could possibly interest you?"

"Why do you work for the Order if they're so terrible?" He asks, almost without hesitation.

I shrug. "It's just where I ended up. I would be dead otherwise, though, so I guess I have a debt to pay them. Why do you hang out with pirates?"

He smiles. "'Cause they're my friends. And they basically raised me. So I guess we both keep strange company."

"I guess so," I say quietly.

As the rain continues to pour down around us, neither of us speaks. It's cold out here and I shiver a bit, my damp jacket doing nothing to keep away the chill of the freezing rain. Lightning strikes the plains past the city walls and thunder follows an instant later, the sound echoing through the wide streets slick with rain.

"Can we go inside?" Senika looks up at the dark and cloudy sky. His face is turned away from me and his eyepatch makes it hard to discern his expression. "It's so cold out here and you're all wet now."

Since it appears he won't leave me alone otherwise, I follow him back into the Tower where the halls are nearly as dark as the balcony. Only a few torches lit along the walls. This place has always seemed like some strange, dark fortress to me, so different from the church-like appearance of the cathedral in Elview. There isn't a single sound within these walls at night, only the constant pounding of rain on the roof.

"Um . . .what now?" I ask, feeling incredibly awkward about the whole situation.

"Well, usually people sleep in the night instead of standing on balconies in the rain," Senika points out. "You should at least try to sleep."

"In that case, so should you." I push my hair out of my face in annoyance.

He shrugs. "Probably."

We stand in silence again for a while until he asks, "That girl earlier. She called you *Your Highness*. What was that about?"

I look down at the floor where my jacket is dripping rainwater onto the polished stone floor. "That's another long story."

"It seems like neither of us is going anywhere, so I'd say we have time."

This isn't anything I would expect to be telling someone who is almost a stranger, but there's something about this Halfblood sailor that makes me tell him anyway, the short version at least. "My mother is a princess—or was, at least. The Kane family rules the North, but she's married to an asshole named Robert Clearwater. My father is somebody, or maybe nobody, but he certainly isn't royal like her. Technically, I'm royalty, but I think any claim I ever had to that throne has been forgotten years ago."

He stares at me. "If you're that important, why are you just a knight in the Order and not

. . . doing royal things?"

"I don't care about any of that," I say with a nonchalant shrug. There was never a time when anyone could make me care about my royal blood or any of the duties that come with it. "None of it means anything to me, and no one wants me there anyway."

Based on the strange look he's giving me, I'm surprised he doesn't ask any more questions. Rather, he says, "You don't seem very regal, but I've never met real royalty before."

I scoff. "Yeah, well, don't expect me to be anything close to the ones in the stories. And if you start calling me Your Highness as well, I'll rip your head off, right along with Alyssa."

Not wanting to continue this conversation, I turn away and storm down the stairs back to the library, although I'm not sure what I'm expecting to find down there. I was planning to go back to bed, but now not only am I drenched, I'm also miserable. Talking about my family is evidently my least favourite thing to do, and if there was a way to make people stop asking stupid questions I don't want to answer, I would have found it by now.

In the library, I find a book about a hunter in the True North that becomes the greatest general in the kingdom after slaying a giant sea serpent. It's another book I've read before, but there are copies of it all over the place which makes it easy to find so I don't hesitate to snatch it off the shelf. I find a chair near a fireplace and add a log to the fire before lighting a lamp and abandoning my jacket on the floor near the hearth. It's nearly perfect, except Fenix isn't here. But I don't want to go all the way back up to my room to get her, and even if I did, it's unlikely she would even want to come down. She's probably fast asleep by now.

Paintings cover every inch of wall space that isn't taken over by bookshelves. They illustrate everything from animals to beautiful scenery to portraits. Some even show battles between great armies. The one above the fireplace especially intrigues me. It depicts a figure—my guess is that it's Eris, Lord of Shadows and god of the dead—in armour as black as the night standing with arms raised. A massive black gate looms over him, occupying half the frame, and the landscape is barren but painted a hundred shades of brown and grey. They say Eris was banished to Gosritaan for opening that very gate and allowing an army of horrifying monsters into our world. I assume the artist is attempting to paint the very moment before that horde invaded.

With the chilling image hanging over my head, I turn my attention to the book in my hands. I almost want to get up and take it down yet as I open the book, the heat of the fire washes over me and my eyelids fall shut, drowsy after the long day.

"Kellin." Someone shakes my shoulder.

I blink open my eyes to see Jyn standing in front of me, his hair still messy from sleep. Behind him, the fire has long burned down to nothing, and the lamp on the table extinguished as well. Looking at the sun out the nearest window, I can guess it isn't nighttime anymore but rather close to noon. The book in my hands is open to the first page—I didn't even start reading.

"What time is it? Did I fall asleep?" I groan, rubbing my eyes in hopes that it might make them adjust to the bright sunlight.

"It's past time for sleeping, that's for certain," Jyn says. "We were all going to head into the city to find some breakfast."

"Can't we eat here?" I grumble.

"We could have if we got there about two hours ago but we were all looking for you."

"For me?" I ask, still feeling a thousand miles away from the real world. "But I was right here the whole time."

"I can see that now." He seems annoyed but I can't figure out why. "We should get going while there's still food left to buy."

"Why are you so angry?"

"I'm not angry." Whenever someone is angry, they'll tell you they aren't.

"Yeah, you are actually."

Finally, Jyn sighs. "I couldn't find you and I thought you went off and did something stupid. You make me worried a lot, you know, always ending up in trouble that shouldn't have been found in the first place."

"Well, I'm sorry, but you know you don't always have to know where I am or what I'm doing." Sitting up properly, I try to fix my hair. I can tell it's a wild mess.

"Yeah, but it helps."

I pull my jacket back on and scramble around the library to find the book's shelf. Then, we're out in the city. Here, people are still celebrating the Assembly of Spirits festival even though the actual event happened over a week ago. The streets are filled with flowers and decorations while people are dancing and singing everywhere you look. Several stores we pass advertise special festival goods, and even the guards and soldiers stationed on the streets are relaxed, smiling as they enjoy the once-a-year festivities. Even though it rained last night, the skies are clear. Only a few puddles remain from the storm.

We find a bakery that isn't overly crowded and buy some pastries then head to the river that runs through the city to eat. None of us realized how hungry we are until we got there since every crumb of food vanishes within minutes.

"Mmm, that was so much better than that horrid travel food we've been eating." Taiyo grins happily. "And this city is amazing, too. I wish we didn't have to go back."

"When *are* we planning to go back to Elview?" Jyn asks. "We didn't have a very good plan with any of this."

I shrug as I finish off the last of the decadent pastry I bought with some of the silver coins we were smart enough to bring. "Not sure. Whenever we have what we need, I guess."

"Why is this place called the Black City?" Senika wonders out loud, apparently not listening to the conversation. "It's so colourful but the name sounds so . . . ominous."

"It isn't always like this," I explain. "Most of the time it's just like any other city but with more Halfbloods and *a lot* of soldiers. This is just for the Assembly of Spirits. But it will be over in a few days and everything will go back to normal."

"It's actually got a lot of military stuff going on in it," Jyn adds. "Most of the Order is based here, but for the festival, they usually send a lot of people out to other towns and cities for extra security. It's also just about the only place Halfbloods can live without being part of the Order, but most people here are."

"I've heard talk of a rebel group based in Alicante," Taiyo interjects to change the subject. "They're all Halfbloods, but they want the East to break off and become its own country." She shrugs. "They could never survive on their own."

"Well, they can't just make a new kingdom." Jyn shakes his head. "And who would be their king, anyways? The rules are that each nation must have a god, but there are only so many gods, and they can't exactly go make a new one."

Senika laughs. "Aren't we some sort of rebel group ourselves? I mean, we don't have very many of us, but we're certainly rebels."

"Are we?" Flicking some dust off her skirt, Taiyo frowns. "We haven't got much of a cause to call ourselves rebels. Besides, I think a rebellion needs more than four people fighting for it."

Glancing over at me and Jyn, Senika asks, "Have you been friends for a long time?"

Jyn shakes his head and then pauses. "Kellin and I have known each other for about six years but we only met Taiyo maybe . . . five years ago?"

I reach over to pet Fenix, who's laying flat on her back to absorb as much sun as possible. "That's kind of a long time, Jyn. We're seventeen and we've known each other for six years, almost half our lives."

"Yeah, you're right. As usual," he jokes.

"Hey, I'm wrong a lot of the time, you know," I shoot back.

It's nice to sit here on the river and just talk, not about death or war or gods but just about life. Sitting here, I feel like maybe things are on the right track. Maybe this can all work out okay in the end, even if now all four of us are armed and I've hardly let myself relax since leaving Elview days ago. I stop listening to the conversation at some point, just laying there in the warm grass, watching the celebration across the river. A jovial bard sings a lively tune that seems at odds with the band on the other side of the square but people dance and laugh all the same.

"Let's go over there," Senika says after a long period without anyone saying a word. "That looks fun."

No one seems to have a problem with the idea, so we all head back over the river to a small square where the string band is playing a cheerful song and the people dancing don't appear to care that it probably isn't a real song. Fenix instantly bounces off to chase bugs in the grass. Somehow, Jyn ends up dancing with a group of kids who are laughing at just about everything he does, but I can see him smiling and laughing as well. A young man with wild purple hair nervously asks Taiyo to dance, and she follows along as if she would rather be doing anything else.

"And that leaves us," Senika says, although that seems rather obvious from the way we linger at the edge of the square. "Um, Kellin . . . will you dance with me?"

He holds out his hand nervously and I hesitate to take it. "I'm a terrible dancer."

"Perfect, so am I." He grins when I take his hand and drags me into the middle of the dancing crowd where we attempt to dance, which is mostly just us trying to copy the people around us.

I look down at my feet, doing my best not to step on his, but I haven't the slightest clue what I'm doing. It's been years since I ever even *tried* to dance. The music seems too fast to dance properly, sounding more like an attack on the poor instruments than anything. Senika, to his credit, seems to at least have an idea of what he's doing, so I try to follow his lead through the steps. I thankfully manage to avoid stepping on his feet. I don't know why he wanted to dance with me of all people, and I doubt he would have any problem finding someone else to be his partner.

For a moment, the world fades away, leaving behind us and the ridiculous music. I let myself forget the reason we came here, all the death and bloodshed, and it's just us. It feels stupid, dancing without knowing how to dance in the middle of a tiny square in the Black City and I can hear Senika laughing.

"What are you laughing at? This is horrible." I glare at him.

"Nothing, this is just funny, I suppose." He grins—he's trying not to laugh again.

What does that mean?" I let go of his hand, worried I'm going to either trip or step on his feet.

"We're both terrible dancers and yet we're dancing in the middle of some city while on a mission to save hundreds of lives," he points out. The song ends and the next one immediately starts, a slower song this time.

"You aren't a terrible dancer," I say before I can stop myself.

He smiles. "Why thank you. I will take that as a compliment."

I roll my eyes. "Can we go back to the Tower now?" I want to ask why he asked to dance with me but there's no way I would get a straight response. "We didn't exactly come here for dancing anyways."

"Can't we stay down here for a little longer? It's so nice to dance and laugh and celebrate without a reason for any of it."

"I've never been to a festival like this," I admit. My words only manage to encourage him more.

"Well, then we can't leave yet. There's so much you're missing out on." He grabs my hand again and yanks me over to a stand selling odd little trinkets that supposedly keep away evil spirits. "Look, these are fun."

"You know they're fake right?" Sometimes I wonder how people can be stupid enough to fall for such trivialities, but I suppose not everyone can actually know spirits. "They don't actually keep any sort of spirits away, they're just for children."

"Oh shush." Of course, he's already picked out a charm, a silver coin with letters engraved in it. "It's fun, okay? Maybe having fun is what really keeps evil away. Or it's the good memories that keep them away. In either case, they are very useful."

I think about that while he pays the vendor and whisks me off to who knows where once again. Two silvers for another more useless silver with a fancy pattern on it. Spirits are everywhere, both good and evil, and it's unlikely a single coin will do anything to prevent that. Even now, I can see spirits wandering around with the people, most faceless, shapeless creatures who feed on the emotions of humans. Simply being happy doesn't make them go away, just like broken hearts don't make the rivers run backwards.

"Here, this is for you." Senika turns away from the stand and hands me the coin.

"What? Why? I don't need it."

"Look, it's a gift, and when someone gives you a gift you're expected to at least take it." He shoves it into my hand. "I don't care if you keep it, I just want to give it to you."

"Uh, thanks." The coin is silver but it's likely just iron or steel painted to shine as silver does. No one ever gives me anything so I put it in my pocket.

He shrugs. "Keep it or toss it into the river, I don't really care. But I'd rather you kept it."

By the time we actually return to the Tower, night has nearly fallen and all of us are too exhausted to continue with the search we were meant to be on all day. I immediately collapse into bed, more tired than I feel a festival should make someone. Fenix jumps up beside me and headbutts my hand. I'm clutching that stupid coin and all I can think of is Senika. There's something about him, that ridiculous smile, the way he isn't afraid of me, the way he cares about me without even knowing anything about me. Yeah, he isn't like other people.

I guess I'm used to being alone and only having Jyn and Taiyo be anything close to friends. But now Senika has appeared in my life, and he isn't like anyone I've ever met. They say people come and go from our lives for a reason, that certain people are there to help while others are there only to cause harm. I never believed that, but now . . . now everything is so different.

16

CRIMSON AND GOLD

KELLIN

Three days after arriving in the Black City, we've hardly made any progress. The stacks and stacks of reports and official documents seem endless, and it starts feeling impossible to read them all. Of course, there are years worth of missions and patrols here, most of them completely normal with only the occasional interesting event. We scan through endless mountains of books and I start to think that this whole endeavour was pointless.

"I think it's about time we consider that there isn't anything here," Taiyo says, slipping a dusty tome back onto its shelf.

Alyssa hums. Surprisingly, she has been pointing out anything that might help us and hasn't lived up to her promise of reporting us. "There's one other place you could check."

I sigh. "Will it actually help or are you leading us on a wild goose chase?"

"That depends," Alyssa says with a smirk. "Does a library where the higher-ups stash secrets they don't want anyone to learn sound useful to you?"

"And why didn't you bother to say such a thing existed earlier?" I ask, slamming the book in my hands shut and glaring at her.

She only laughs. "You made it very clear that my help was not welcome. But, if you're interested, it's this way."

Reluctantly, I follow her, casting a glance at the others over my shoulder. Alyssa leads us up a narrow metal staircase that creaks with each step and climbs steadily higher above the library. Here, the torches are burning low, casting dim light that makes it hard to make out the details of the area.

Alyssa stops abruptly at the top of the stairs. I almost walk into her before I notice the tiny landing where we have arrived. The only notable thing about it is the wooden door, padlocked and chained shut.

"It's not too late to back down, Kane," Alyssa says. Her red eyes are like those of a predator in the faint light.

"There aren't any guards here," I observe, staring at the door. There's no way she isn't up to something.

Alyssa shrugs. "That's why you have to be fast if you want to make this happen."

"So unlock it," I demand. "I assume you didn't bring us to a place even you can't get into."

Rolling up her sleeves, Alyssa produces a thin tool from her pocket and kneel down in front of the lock. I watch her every movement as she carefully twists the lockpick, wiggling it about to find the right angle to unlock the door.

"A locked door at the top of a dark staircase where we can supposedly find some hidden secret of the Order," Taiyo grumbles from behind me. "That seems trustworthy."

Before anyone else can object, the lock clicks open and the chains clatter to the ground. Alyssa slips her lockpick back into her pocket and grins victoriously as she pushes the door open. I peer past her into the dark room beyond the door, barely able to make out what looks like towering shelves.

"You first." I gesture for Alyssa to enter the room, hoping she might trigger some kind of trap. She merely sighs and steps over the threshold and into the room.

"See?" She grabs a lantern off a nearby table and lights it. "No traps. I'm not trying to kill you, Your Highness."

The light floods the space, revealing two rows of shelves along the walls of the small room. A worn carpet that gives the impression of something that used to be beautiful covers the stone floor. I step past Alyssa and reach for a book on the nearest shelf to find that it's the journal of a long-dead priest.

"Right." I look up at my friends. "Let's be quick about this then."

Reading through all of them feels strange, like something that shouldn't be done—which isn't entirely wrong. Trespassing in a place like this could get us all thrown in prison to rot. The only ones with access to these files are much higher up the ladder than we are. Usually, I would expect this part of the library to be heavily guarded which leaves me feeling like we're walking right into some kind of trap. Today, though, the only thing that keeps just anyone from getting to any of the documents is a single wooden door.

"How long does this need to take?" Alyssa asks after about an hour of searching. "Haven't you seen enough?"

"No," I say as I flip through one of the largest books I've ever seen. It happens to be filled with hundreds upon hundreds of names and locations and dates. So far, I've come across one occasion involving an Inquisitor and a dead Halfblood, but the book says that happened years ago. "I need proof of this, more than a dream—or a vision—and *your* word."

"That's ridiculous." Alyssa has done nothing to be of assistance and if she thinks it's such a stupid idea, I don't see why she's even here. "It's only a matter of time before you're caught here or realize just what a pointless task this is and go crawling back to Elview, knowing there's nothing you can do. This is just how the world is."

"I'm not leaving until I have what I need or someone makes me."

"Really?" She smiles in an amused sort of way that feels very fake. "In that case, how about I show you to the door, Your Highness?"

"How many times do I have to tell you not to call me that? I'm a knight; it's Ser to you."

"Have you told me before? Sorry, all your words sound like empty threats to me, so you can't blame me for not paying attention to anything you say."

I turn around to glare daggers at her. It's starting to feel like she finds it almost entertaining to insult me in every sentence. "Look, do you want me to throw this book at your head? 'Cause the longer you sit there and talk, the closer I am to doing that. And I promise you, I won't miss."

Alyssa laughs, unfazed or at least pretending to be. "I'm not afraid of you, Kane, and even if I was, a book is hardly the most threatening thing you could use."

"The pen is mightier than the sword, Alyssa, or have you not heard? I assume that applies to throwing books as well. If not, well, none of us here are lacking in weapons." I point to where I unceremoniously abandoned my spear on the floor. "And you know my name; why is it so hard to use it?"

"I guess it's just impossible for you two to stop arguing for *three minutes*?" Jyn always amazes me with his ability to seem perfectly calm, even now. "I get that you hate each other, but you're driving the rest of us insane."

Senika looks up as if he just realized the rest of us are here. "What's happening?"

Jyn points at us with the book in his hand, apparently deciding to ignore Senika. "Alyssa, are you planning to help or do you have something better to be doing? Kellin, no, you aren't allowed to kill anyone, whether it's with a book or a proper weapon. Now, we came here for a reason and that reason is not to murder each other."

With that, he promptly goes back to reading, and I exchange a look with a very confused Senika who just shrugs and grabs another stack of papers. Taiyo sighs and mutters something that sounds a lot like 'Halfbloods' in a rather sarcastic voice but doesn't look up.

After a few minutes, Alyssa is still determined to annoy the shit out of all of us. "Hmm, I don't suppose any of you have considered—"

I spin around and throw a knife at her head. Before it even comes close to her, Alyssa gasps and her eyes go wide. It slams into the wall next to her shoulder and no one says anything for what feels like an eternity.

"I swear to all the gods on this earth, if another word comes out of your mouth, I will kill you, you son of a bitch." I snap.

In her mind, I can see her fear, flashing by in a matter of seconds. Snakes—strangely enough—and death, but my own face is there as well. Images of me, many of them from years ago but some far newer, with the picture of me now, standing in the library with my hand extended and my eyes glowing. Alyssa, like many others, is afraid of me.

"Kellin . . ." Across the room, Senika speaks in a quiet voice, as if the quieter he talks, the sooner we can get out of here.

"*Perite*! You know nothing so stay out of this, damn pirate." I curse as I snatch up my jacket and spear before storming out of the room with Fenix close behind me.

As I go, I hear Alyssa give an annoyed *humph* while Jyn sighs and mumbles something about how exhausting this is, saying I will be back soon enough. I pass a group of kids not much older than thirteen all dressed in the dark red and silver of the Order, but every one of them falls silent and steps out of the way as I pass. Even people who hardly know me can see that I'm nothing but trouble. Outside, I find my horse and, barely pausing to make sure the saddle is on correctly, I start riding. I don't even bother trying to remember where I'm going, I just ride to get as far away from here as possible. Only once I'm out of the city and racing across the rolling green hills do I slow down.

Sometimes I feel guilty for getting mad at everyone, but I doubt they care much. It often feels like they only want me gone anyways; I'm doing them a favour by leaving. If I could leave this kingdom and away from this mess that has become my life, I would, I would take any chance to disappear. Out here, away from the city, everything is so quiet but it also feels very, very loud. Silence is loud, I suppose, when every second of it is filled with whispers that never leave you alone. But they're only in my head, the spirits talking in voices so soft I can hardly make out what they might be saying.

Eventually, I look up to see that Fenix is no longer following me and has decided to lie down in the grass. Sighing, I turn my horse around and then jump down to kneel beside her.

"Are you tired?" I ask, knowing full well that she doesn't understand a word I say but let's face it, who doesn't talk to cats? Other than Storm, of course; I'm certain the reason he seems so upset with everything anyone does is because he doesn't talk to cats. "I know, I'm tired too. Of a different thing, maybe, but still tired." The horse looks at me like I'm crazy, but I just lay down beside Fenix.

"Life is exhausting," I whisper. "At least you're a cat and no one will care if you sleep all day. But for some reason, people always care what

I do and they always say it's wrong. 'Kellin, stop that' 'You can't do that, Kellin.' I'm fucking sick of this."

Above us, the sky turns dark purple as the sun dips below the horizon, and I can see the faint shine of stars in the dark. Out here, there is only me, Fenix, this horse, and the endless hills, all a thousand miles away from anything. And of course, the spirits. Days—or rather, nights—like this always seem to attract the ones that hate me almost more than other people, the ones who talk of death and ruin. Ever since the festival nearly two weeks ago, they only seem to speak of my own death. Mostly, I can't make out real words, but occasionally, I can hear those words over and over again. Monster, demon, freak, outcast, weird, disappointment, all of them have practically become synonymous with Kellin Acheros Kane.

Acheros. My middle name means river of death, and it wasn't a name I was born with. After I became a Halfblood, my mother gave it to me, probably to forever remind me that I will always be an ailment in this world. Everything reminds me of her—my name, the scars on my body, this power I hold, and even my dreams. All are determined to remind me that I will never get away from her even by running all the way across the kingdom. If I went across the world, she would find me somehow.

I look up at the emerging stars, wondering what's up there. At this time of year, only three moons are visible, two crescents and one full moon. Supposedly there is one moon for each god, but if only three are in the sky tonight, that would mean only three gods exist right now. Which doesn't make much sense; everyone knows there are more than seven gods. They always say that those who have died earn a place in the sky, in the moons and the stars to watch over those who still live, but I've always wondered who exactly wants to be watched at all times of the day by dead people. Now I wonder who is up there watching me. Or if there's anyone at all. Perhaps it's my father. They always told me he was probably dead. Or maybe it's just a bunch of old idiots who made the world like this. Whoever it is, I'm sure they like me just as much as the people still alive.

"Do you hate me?" I ask them, just to be sure. "Do you look at me and say 'Man, what a disappointment.' Whoever you are. Are you proud of me? Are you proud that I'm a monster who fucks up everything?"

When there's no answer, I flip off the sky and laugh hysterically. Of course, they aren't proud of me. They can't hear me, and no one could ever be proud of someone like me.

Monster. Freak. Outcast. Demon. Kellin Acheros Kane.

I reach into my pocket and take out the silver coin Senika gave me. It seems like such a pointless object, a coin meant to ward off spirits that can't hurt anyone. Not physically at least. Why would he give it to me? He doesn't know me and shouldn't care about spirits hurting me, but there's something about Senika that isn't like other people. Even if he could protect me from them, it isn't the spirits I need protecting from. It's us, humans and Halfbloods. And myself.

Your Highness. I can practically hear Alyssa's voice in my ear, but she isn't here. I'm just insane. There's another word to add to the list. Insane. And perhaps while we're at it, we can throw in 'unlovable' as well, and maybe 'lonely' can follow that.

"Would it be better if I was dead?" I think out loud. Fenix sniffs my hair.

I yank my knife out of its sheath—not the one I threw at Alyssa. It's still stuck in the wall. Spinning it in my hands, I run my fingers over the edge.

They all want me dead, why not give them what they want? I hold the blade to the fragile skin below my elbow, emotionless.

For a moment, real silence takes over, like the spirits are watching and waiting to see what comes next. The dark sky is so far away and the stars are a million miles above these hills, but now they look much closer. Like I could reach up and touch them. Maybe I can; I guess I can find out for myself what happens when you die.

I hardly feel the sharp sting as the blade draws blood.

They say that when you die, your life flashes before your eyes. That doesn't happen to me. All I see are the stars, surrounded by darkness, quiet and so, so far away.

In the silence, I take a deep breath . . .

And drop the knife into the grass.

I can't do this. But I almost did.

I can't keep living either. But I am.

Closing my eyes, I lay in the grass under the dark sky with only a cat and a horse to keep me company.

This isn't the first time I've been in this position. This isn't the first time I've almost killed myself. There was a night a while after my mother tried to kill me. That's the reason I have tattoos on my wrists, to hide the scars. That time, I almost succeeded. I was eleven when that happened.

Eleven.

I am far too young for this. I curl onto my side and hug my knees to my chest, tears running down my cheeks. Fenix blinks at me, sniffing the bloody dagger in the grass next to me. I close my eyes. Slowly, darkness comes to take over, washing me away into a black sea.

". . . Kellin?" The voice is a thousand miles away, further than the stars and the sky. "Kellin, wake up, it's okay."

I blink my eyes open to see darkness. For a moment I think I've gone blind but then I realize I can see the stars. And Senika, his strangely white hair bright in the pale glow of the full moon. He looks almost like a phantom, pale and ghostly, but his hand on my arm tells me he is here. There's a strange, faint memory of a dream in the back of my mind, the kind you know has happened but can't quite remember.

I sit up and move away from his hand. "Don't . . . don't touch me . . ."

He nods. "Are you okay? What happened?"

On the ground next to him is my knife, its edge stained red with blood. My blood. I hug my knees to my chest and bury my face in my hands. He isn't meant to be here, not Senika. I can't breathe; my head is pounding. Snow and feathers and blood flash before my eyes. This isn't supposed to be happening. I don't want to be here. Anywhere but here. I don't know how this is happening.

"Kellin, it's okay." his voice is barely more than a whisper, but in the silence, it seems so loud. I realize I'm hyperventilating, my lungs refusing to draw in enough oxygen. "You need to relax, it's gonna be alright."

That's when I notice something. The spirits are gone. My head is filled only with my own thoughts. It's so strange. I've lived my whole life with them there, a constant buzz in the back of my mind, sometimes louder and sometimes quieter. But now they're all gone.

"Look at me. What happened?" His hand is on my arm again and I push him away from me, stumbling to my feet.

"Don't fucking touch me, I said!" My voice seems so loud, too loud. This is all too much. "Just leave me alone!" Then all the energy leaves my body and I fall to my knees, sobbing. "You don't understand, you're the kind of person people like. You can smile and laugh despite everything and I . . . You must hate me."

"No, Kellin I don't hate you, I—" He stops.

"You have to hate me. Everyone else does. So why should I believe you're any different?"

"Kellin, I don't hate you, I never could." He reaches for me but stops abruptly and puts his hand on the ground instead. "I don't know what happened to you and I'm not going to ask. But just know that I don't hate you. Trust me when I say that, okay?"

I nod, shakily. "You . . . you aren't like other people, Senika. I'm sorry to do this to you. You should go while you can."

"No, don't say that," He shakes his head, speaking in a comforting voice. "You don't need to apologize."

"S-sorry." No matter how hard I try, I keep apologizing. I was wrong to have dragged him into this. I can breathe now, which is nice, but my head is still far too quiet. I look down at my hands, but something catches my eye. I freeze.

Smoke. It's coming from the city, billowing up into the night sky in thick white clouds. Against the black sky, it's shockingly visible, making me wonder how I didn't notice it before. I stare at that grey and white as it curls up into the air over the dark city, stunned for a moment.

"Jyn." I'm not sure why he's the first thing that comes to my mind, but he's in the city. And the city is on fire. *Why do I care about them if they don't care about me?* But of course, I already know the answer.

Because some part of me will always hope *someone* might care.

My body reacts before I can think of any sort of real plan. In seconds, I grab my dagger and I'm on my horse, head spinning with how fast I stood and raced away without explanation. Senika curses then shifts and I'm surrounded by silver butterflies. Fenix sprints after us, caught off guard by the sudden movement. I ride fast as the wind, pushing my horse to go even faster, but I know she can't go forever. It's not fast enough. When we get close to the city, my stomach drops to my feet.

There is fire everywhere. Fire and destruction. I can't yet make out the faces of the people running around but I can see the flash of steel in the night and hear the screams. The city, so full of life just a few hours ago, has turned to ash and embers. Even the Tower, rising high up into the sky, is darker than it should be, lit only by flames that lick its windows and doorways. This is bad, very bad.

At the edge of the city, I abandon my exhausted horse and step into the ruined streets. The horrible feeling that we're too late creeps into my chest as my feet hit the charred stones. There is fire everywhere, and even if I was here earlier, I couldn't have done anything to help. The smoke is so thick here it hurts to breathe. I want to turn around and run as far away from here as I can, but I can't move—only stand there, staring in horror at what's happened. A woman runs past me, stumbling and looking frantically over her shoulder like she's expecting someone—or something—to be behind her. She doesn't even notice when Senika materializes on the road next to me.

"I'm guessing you don't have a plan." His voice is quiet amongst the snap of sparks leaping into the air as the city crumbles. He lifts one arm to shield his mouth and nose from the smoke, coughing.

"I have a plan," I tell him, although I'm not so sure of it myself. "It isn't a good plan, but it's a plan. And that's all you asked for."

Beside me, Fenix growls, turning my attention immediately to the wall of grey smoke in front of us.

In the smoke, I see a silhouette of a person wearing a long cloak that swirls around their ankles, but I can't make out much more than that until they step forward. Wild, red hair as bright as the flames around us drifts on an invisible breeze that seems so different from the chaos around us. They wear a black mask that covers their entire face, but it, along with the long black robes and the silver ring glittering on their hand, instantly labels them as an Inquisitor. Smoke curls around their ankles and parts like water when they walk toward us, tall boots silent against the stones.

"*Halfbloods.*" The person snarls in a voice that reminds me of metal scraping across stones and draws the longsword sheathed at their hip. "There you are."

There isn't a hint of mercy amongst the rage that rolls off them in waves. They won't be sparing two kids in all this destruction. Yet the hair, the colour of fire, points to their Halfblood powers. How can they stand to kill their own kind?

This night has gone from a nightmare to something far worse.

I turn to Senika. "Go find Jyn. Get out of the city. I'll stay here and buy you time."

It's a hastily constructed plan that will probably end up going the opposite of how we want, but I don't see many other options now.

"You want me to leave you here with a trained killer in a burning city? Not a chance." He draws his sword but there is hesitation in his eye.

"*I* am a trained killer, Senika," I point out. Even though I've never actually killed anyone, I know I could. It's what I've trained to do. "Go while you can. I've got this."

The Inquisitor laughs wickedly. "You are fools, I will cut down both of you where you stand. There is no escape."

Doubt flickers across Senika's face as he looks between me, the Inquisitor, and the burning Tower half a city away. Then he nods, determined. "Okay. I'll go. Try to stay alive and I promise I'll come back for you."

The Inquisitor doesn't move to stop him as Senika shifts back and disappears into the night, silver butterflies blending in perfectly with the stars overhead.

"He is not a fool." That frigid voice shakes me to the core, colder than any blizzard. "He took his chance to live but you stay knowing this could be the end." The Inquisitor laughs. "You are both brave and stupid."

"Yeah, I'm aware of that," I grab my spear and adjust my feet, waiting for the attack to come.

In a sudden flash of light, my opponent moves. A gust of wind hits me and I hardly have time to dodge before the sword slashes toward me, crashing against the shaft of my spear. They leap away again and attack before I can regain my footing. This time, the sword comes down harder, accompanied by a hurricane of wind. I manage to push them away and dance backwards, buying enough time to watch if only for a split second.

Their swordsmanship is incredible, that's undeniable, but I can't figure out just how strong they might be without knowing their power. It could be some sort of air manipulation, but the wind could be a side effect of the real ability. Sometimes, there are physical indications of power, like wind and glowing eyes for me, or that flash of light when Senika shifts. If the wind is similar, then their power could have to do with increased strength or speed, but it's impossible to know for sure.

I block another blow, but this time spot an opening under their left arm when they attack. I don't use this information yet, instead stepping back again. Fenix takes my place the second I move, clawing at the Inquisitor's robes and throwing them off guard for a moment. Smoke burns my lungs and makes me cough, but if I stop now, I die. So I ignore it and keep fighting.

My foot catches on a loose stone and I stumble. The Inquisitor's sword slashes across my shoulder before I have a chance to dodge or block. There's not enough time for me to attack even with Fenix next to me, but hopefully, I can hold them off until Senika has a chance to get out of here. I keep moving, refusing to back down.

The Inquisitor only pushes me back with attacks that come faster with every hit, each one followed by a wall of wind that knocks the breath from my chest. Soon, the clash of metal on metal is the only thing I hear, the fire a distant buzz in the background. Between attacks, I hardly have time to find my footing again, much less think of any sort of plan or gather my magic. Finally, the wind knocks my spear right out of my hand. I reach for my sword, but my hand only touches air. My stomach drops as I realize I left it back in the Tower. The only weapon I have is a dagger, and I don't stand much of a chance by bringing a knife to a sword fight.

Frantically, I look around for something—anything—that might help. I draw my dagger, but not fast enough. The sword slams into my arm, hitting my arm guard under my jacket sleeve. The blow is strong enough to make my hand go numb, but there is no time to recover before the attack comes again. There's fiery heat at my back, and I spot flames over my shoulder. There's nowhere to run.

The Inquisitor shows no signs of exhaustion or injury. I have no advantage—until I duck under a slash at my head and snatch my spear off the ground. Just like that, the battle changes directions. The Inquisitor is now the one cornered, back to the burning wall of a house with Fenix and me in the street. They don't notice until it's too late.

I raise my spear and bring it down on the stones, creating a shockwave with my power as I reach into their mind. Wind and fear push the Inquisitor to their knees, dropping their sword to the road with a clatter of steel. I spin, slashing out with my weapon. There's a final burst of magic, and the Inquisitor whispers something that sounds faintly like the Order's aphorism before I cut it off.

Silence falls.

Blood drips from the tip of my spear, landing on the stones and turning the road red. Before me lies the body of the Inquisitor, chest slashed open from hip to shoulder. Dead. Compared to the rush of battle, the burning street feels quiet, the only sounds being my breathing and the crackling fire. In the half-melted glass of the window on the building in front of me, I can see my reflection, wild-haired with my eyes glowing gold. Feeling a sudden stab of pain in my shoulder, I reach up to touch it. Blood runs down my fingers. But it's nothing compared to the body of the Inquisitor.

My head spins when what I've done actually hits me. I killed someone. And not just anyone, but a Halfblood as well. Sure, they tried to kill me first, but now I've done just what I wanted to prevent. I killed a Halfblood, an Inquisitor tasked with killing Halfbloods themself but no less a Halfblood. There's blood on my hands, and there's nothing I can do about it.

I have killed people before, but only as part of my training. Back then, I was given no choice, although I didn't have much choice here either. Those lives were taken so I could move forward but killing the Inquisitor makes me no better than my enemy. I claim to fight against them yet here I stand, the blood of a Halfblood just like me on my hands. They likely had the same training as I did, perhaps I even knew them once.

Briefly, I consider taking off their mask to see who they were but I tell myself that knowing that would only make this harder. It's easier to fight a faceless enemy.

There was a time when I trained to join the ranks of the Inquisitors. The only reason I don't wear that black mask and silver signet ring is that I failed the final test and chose knighthood instead. With power like mine, they found it fitting to turn me into a flawless killer, a weapon honed to their taste and blindingly loyal. When I was eleven, they gave me a sword and taught me to kill, but I never thought I would ever actually use that skill in battle. They said that with my skill with a blade and my magic, I could be unstoppable. I told Senika, I'm a trained killer and it's true. For the past six years, I have dedicated every day to the art of death, mastering weapons and perfecting my skills until I could win a fight completely blind but never could I have imagined the terrifying thrill of killing like this.

Now I see what Senika meant. War means people will die. But this isn't a war I started or even wanted. Yet here I am, right in the middle of it all. I wish I could lay down all these weapons and stop fighting. Learning to fight was meant to be a way to save myself from helplessness, but now the path I've laid is leading to ruin.

"You have chosen." A gentle, feminine voice speaks from behind me, soft as silk. In the middle of the destroyed city, the spirit named Airadyne stands with her white clothes and hair a stark contrast to the darkness and flames. "Good. But be warned. This is only a beginning, child."

"I didn't want to kill anyone," I whisper, but she seems to hear me anyway.

"Death comes to all mortals. It is simply the way of this world." There's something horribly unnerving about how calm she is.

I shake my head. "I don't want to be a murderer. I don't want to fight your stupid war, so go find someone else."

"That's unfortunate," She folds her hands behind her back. "You are already nearing the eye of the storm. There is nothing you can do. This is simply the progression of fate."

"*I hate you. Kill yourself with a spoon,*" I curse in Old Alkelian. Usually, I switch languages to curse at people without them knowing what I say, but this time I do not doubt that she can understand me perfectly.

"Hm, yes, if only that were possible. Spirits cannot die. I will excuse your . . . creative language, but others will not be so kind." She slowly paces across the street while she speaks, not even looking at me. Her feet glide across the ground, barely even touching the stones. "I am here to inform you that your enemies will soon be setting their plan into motion. You should move faster or prepare for the worst. They will not wait for you."

"Yeah, I gathered that." This spirit has a habit of saying the exact thing I don't want to hear, and it's starting to get on my nerves. "Tonight is all the proof I needed. Now I just need to know what comes next."

Airadyne smiles. "Good, you are not a fool. Gathering information before acting is wise, but the next step will be no easier. You must make your move before they have a chance to force your hand."

"You make it sound like this is a game."

Shrugging, she replies, "I hardly care for the lives of mere mortals, Halfbloods or otherwise. I am simply here as a messenger to inform you of the truth. If you fail, I too will die. Now, go. Before it is too late."

Before I can respond, she's gone just as fast as she arrived. Spirits have a way of speaking in cryptic prophecies and not telling the entire truth in a way that feels like they know everything but choose not to say it. They're playing games, never sharing the rules or that there even was a game in the first place. As if messages of death and ruin aren't enough.

Suddenly, the world tilts at a dangerous angle and I stumble, nearly tripping over my own feet. Nausea washes over me, and it occurs to me that it's probably the consequence of the smoke combined with the sudden rush of my magic. Staying here won't help anyone. I look back at the Tower, wondering if Senika made it and found Jyn, or if they're all dead in the fire somewhere. Reaching for Fenix, I turn away from it all and head back to the edge of the city.

There's nothing I can do now but wait for them to return.

Wait and keep walking.

17

ASH

KELLIN

Dawn finds me sitting by the river, watching the few survivors stumble out of the ruined city. Most of the fires have long ago burnt out, but smoke still rises from the charred buildings and desolate streets. Most of the people who escaped aren't Halfbloods, but there are a few who stagger out, injured but alive. I sit far away from the small group gathering at the edge of the road, watching but not approaching any of them. I could help them. But right now I don't want to talk to people, so I just watch instead.

The air still tastes like smoke even as a cool breeze pushes it away. Most of the city is only burnt wood and broken stones, all covered in blood and ash. I have no idea how many people might have died last night, but the number of survivors hardly compares to the size of the city as it was yesterday. From where I sit, I can see that most of the living are injured, nursing broken limbs or nasty-looking burns. The remaining Order members left hours ago; I watched them ride out of the city, headed for who-knows-where, some going North and some going East. I just hope they won't come looking for the person who killed one of their own.

As the sun lights up the hills, I yawn. I know I should sleep but I can't without knowing if Senika, Jyn, and Taiyo are even alive. There's been no sign of them yet, and my hope wanes as the city empties. I pick impatiently at my fingernails, trying to get the blood out from under them. Dried blood is apparently impossible to get rid of. The gash on my shoulder aches horribly and blood covers my jacket, but I've chosen to ignore that since the only medics are busy helping refugees near the road. There's no way I'm going over there.

I've taken my arm guard off my left arm to examine the purplish-green bruise and the dents in my armour left from the sword strike. Thankfully, it's just some dents and a bruise. Neither wound will last forever or be of any real consequence. My hair is filled with ash, my feathers just as messy, so I run my fingers through my hair to try and get some of it out. When that doesn't work, I shake my head, making my earrings clink together, to see if that might help. But of course, it doesn't. Sleeping next to me, Fenix's snow-white fur is practically grey from all the damn ash creating a blanket over everything.

Coughing, I ruffle the fur on her head, waking her up. "Sorry." I'm not sure why I need to apologize when she doesn't care. "You're so dirty now, though."

The cat just yawns and rests her head on my foot. Sometimes, I think Fenix is the only one who will always be there. She never leaves me. Cats don't exactly judge you for being you; they love you no matter what. Even Jyn gets mad at me, but Fenix is always here. Both of us are strange, which makes it even better—a kid with strange powers and weird ears and a cat with spikes on her back and horns on her head.

"I think those spikes are kind of pretty," I tell her, looking back at the city. And it's true, her spikes are a brilliant shade of violet with ice blue veins zigzagging through them, plus they're so clear they're almost see-through.

We sit there for a while longer until the sun is high in the sky and the worst of the smoke has cleared out. Then I stand up and slowly start walking toward the city. In one hand, I hold my spear because I don't know what's in there. Fenix creeps along beside me, her furry feet silent in the grass. When we reach the gates, I pause.

The wooden gates are practically gone, only the metal hinges and a pile of rubble remaining, but the wall around them is stone, so it managed to survive with only a few scorched bricks. Stepping through the destroyed gate, I look around the streets and then cautiously make my way through to the Tower. I walk slowly to examine everything around me, searching for signs of life. Maybe a butterfly, to indicate that Senika is alive.

As I approach the Tower, I slow down. This is where I had told Senika to find Jyn and Taiyo, but I have no idea if they even survived. If they aren't, though, I don't have the slightest clue of where I might look. I wish I had also told him where we should find each other again, but there wasn't time. I wasn't thinking straight last night. Walking beside me, Fenix doesn't seem worried or cautious, but I keep my head up and look around for any sign of movement.

The brick walls of the Tower are still smoking and the wooden roof has nearly disintegrated into ash. Most of the windows are shattered, the balconies charred into nothing more than blackened wood and stone. The whole scene looks rather like a tornado of fire went through. I am quite frankly surprised any of it is still standing. Around the Tower, the other buildings aren't exactly in much better shape, only a handful of walls and stone with the occasional pile of charred wood all through the streets. Ash covers everything—the road, the Tower, the ruined buildings. Even the air is thick with it.

I walk through the ruins, feeling like the world has just ended and I'm the last one left. Fenix wanders along behind me apparently in no hurry to get anywhere, stopping to sniff the ground and poke some fallen ash. Kicking a rock, I watch it bounce across the stones before coming to a rest near a burnt-up chair that defies all logic by even existing anymore. I consider walking over to kick it again, but it's too far out of my path. I put my hands in my pockets and keep going.

The further into the city I get, the more I start to dread what I might find. Maybe Senika did get to the others and maybe they all died in the fire. Maybe all that's left for me to find is their lifeless bodies.

Above us, the sun creeps higher into the sky, its rays pleasantly hot, a welcome change from the rain and clouds the North usually gets. Elview is typically warmer than the Black City, but even here it's practically beach weather compared to Ridgewatch where I grew up. But I'm glad it isn't cold; cold is about the worst thing there is, all snow and ice and frostbite. I hate the cold. Just thinking about it makes me want to curl up near a nice fire with Fenix and a good book to vanish for a while.

I stop walking at the steps of the Tower. The door is all but gone, giving me a perfect view of the wreckage inside. The wooden panelling on the walls and floors was incinerated along with nearly all the furniture. The building is likely about to come down on top of me, but I step inside anyway. At least it isn't on fire anymore.

The inside is dark as night with the shattered windows letting in only a few mirky beams of sunlight that create shadows on the walls with all the ash floating through the air. On the walls, a few sconces barely manage to hang on, bent and black with no torch or lamp to hold. Across the room, all that remains of the stairs are the old metal supports and a handful of nails. It's hard to imagine how, just yesterday, this place was an extravagant hall filled with life. Now it all lies in ruin like the rest of the city.

They're all dead. Shattered glass, dead butterflies. A spirit whispers in my mind.

"Shut up," I grumble aloud.

Fenix growls and I turn around to see her still standing in the doorway, fur standing on end with her eyes narrowed. That's always a bad sign. Frantically, I look around for anything that might potentially be dangerous, but there's nothing here.

"What is it?" I ask as I walk back to where she stands. Her eyes are fixed on the corner of the room under the stairs but there isn't anything there. Shaking my head, I put my hand on her back and step outside again. "Come on. We don't have to go in there. Let's go."

Reluctantly, Fenix follows me down the steps and across the street where I sit down beside the road, though it isn't much of a road anymore. She sits in front of me, still dutifully watching the door of the Tower. Maybe she sees something in there or maybe it's just some bad energy—Snowcats can sense spiritual energy far better than humans or Halfbloods, after all   but whatever it is, she refuses to let her guard down. That's what she was trained to do, after all. Protect me. But if Fenix won't let me go in, I have even less of an idea of how to find Senika.

Thankfully, I don't need an idea. Less than ten minutes after I sit down, footsteps echo from down the street. When I look up, I see Senika and Taiyo walking toward me with Jyn leaning on their shoulders and limping. The three of them are covered head to toe in black ash like the rest of the city, but they're also dripping with water. Fenix bounces over to them, instantly forgetting her vigil of watching the door to greet them, her tail flicking around happily.

"What the fuck happened to you?" I demand, choosing to skip over the part where I say hello and ask how they are.

"Well, good to see you too," Taiyo complains. "This idiot decided to drown us all and the city was on fire and we all nearly died. So yeah, a brilliant night all around."

"Okay, I didn't *drown* us." Jyn sounds exhausted and more so than the rest of us, even though we've all been awake all night. "If I didn't use magic we could have died, so stop complaining."

"Humph. You dumped an entire lake on our heads; that sounds like drowning to me," Taiyo reasons, but her tone is anything but reasonable. "It's going to take forever to dry off and in the meantime, we all get to be cold and soaking wet! I'd personally rather have dealt with that creep another way, thanks."

"Do you realize that creep was an Inquisitor who could—and would—have killed us?" Senika reminds her. "At least this way we're alive, even if we are soaked."

"An Inquisitor?" I ask. "You found another one?"

Senika nods. "Jyn summoned an entire wave of seawater on his head and knocked him out. And our heads too. We've been trying to find you but I couldn't remember where I left you so we just came back here instead."

Shrugging, I say, "We all survived the night, then. Maybe not Alyssa, but I honestly wouldn't mind if she died."

Jyn shakes his head. "Dead or not, can we find somewhere to sleep? I feel horrible. I think I broke my ankle."

Even though it's the last place I want to go, I remember, "There's a camp just outside the gates where the surviving people are gathering. We can go there but I don't know how much they can help."

"Better than nothing," Jyn says. "Off we go."

Taiyo groans. "Great, more walking."

It takes forever to reach the gates but when we do get there, the sight before us is not at all what I had expected. The ragged group of survivors is still there, but around them is another group as well, this one far more proper and bearing the blue and gold flags of House Kane. There are about half a hundred riders—which seems a little extra but leave it to my mother for that—plus two flag barriers and four heavily armoured knights. At the head of it all rides Elenore Clearwater herself, recognizable even from far away on her white stallion. But there is something very different about her attire today compared to the last time I saw her. Today, she is dressed all in white with a lace veil covering her face.

White is the colour of death, of the Underworld and of loss. It's not a colour people wear on just any day. Someone once told me the colour white is for funerals because it's a colour with all life stripped away from it.

We reach the gates and Jyn says, "Well that makes things interesting."

I turn around and walk back into the city. "Nope, I am not going out there. You can't make me." But it's useless to try and stay away; I know my mother will find me eventually.

"There's no other way out of the city," Jyn points out. "If we want to get out of here, our only option is to go past them."

"Who are they?" Senika asks. I guess I forgot that he doesn't have a clue about my family or Alkelian politics. "And what do they have to do with anything?"

Pointing to the woman seated on her horse at the head of the procession, I explain, "Mrs. Fancy-Ass over there happens to be my mother and the reason I ended up with the Order. But I have no idea what she's doing here or if she knows I'm here. There's no other reason she would drag herself out of her ice castle to a place like this so soon after the Assembly."

"I take it you two don't have the greatest of relationships." He looks out at the gathering outside the gates, watching Elenore talk to one of the survivors before she looks up, her eyes landing directly on us.

I laugh. "That would be a bit of an understatement, Senika, but yeah, my mom's a piece of royal shit."

There's no point in trying to run now that she's clearly seen us, so I turn and walk down the hill toward the procession. My mother, along with the knights she brought, ride up to meet us. We meet halfway with the eyes of every soldier and commoner gathered here, making me feel like we're actors in some play. The thought isn't entirely wrong, since every part of both my mother's and my life have been watched by just about the entire kingdom. Honestly, it's a miracle we even got here without half the continent following us.

"Kellin." Elenore's voice is just about as cold as her icy castle. "I thought I might find you here. But I can't say I fully believed that priestess who helped you."

Neamie. She told my mother. And people wonder why I don't trust anyone. "Get to the point. What are you here for?"

She turns to look at the other, glaring at them down her nose. "It looks like you managed to find some company, here. A pirate, your silly little Order friend and this . . . girl. I doubt any of them are worth your time. Three *commoners* are hardly deserving of the time and attention of any royalty."

Taiyo looks ready to shoot fireballs from her eyes which is saying something for someone without even a hint of magic, so I step forward and speak up first. It's better to offend her as little as possible; at least for them. I hardly care what happens to me, and it's not like it can get any worse. "They have nothing to do with this, so leave them out of it."

"Very well." With a sigh far more dramatic than necessary, she explains shortly, "The King of the North is dead. Your uncle and my brother, since you seem to have forgotten your place."

Now *that* is news. My uncle is a jerk who never married, has no children and cares for no one but himself. I'd be surprised if he got off his golden throne for long enough to be in a situation that could kill him, royal banquets aside of course. That man held more feasts and parties than anyone else in the kingdom.

I almost laugh. "From what? Did he choke on a plum? Or perhaps someone finally did something about their useless ruler."

"I would watch your mouth if I were you, fool. No, he had a heart attack. They are wanting a new ruler on the throne by the end of the month, and you happen to be one of his heirs, as much as everyone hates that, and the oldest too." She paused to give another dramatic sigh but I already know what is coming. "You are to be King of the North."

Fuck. I may be the oldest heir to the Northern throne, but I never thought the day would come when my mother's brother would die and I would have to go back to that stupid court but this time as a king. Sure, it seems a little strange that I, a bastard, would be ahead of Elias—my half-brother, always the perfect son. I want nothing to do with the North or being a prince or a king, yet it always seems to come around at the worst times possible. I was just starting to think I had gotten away from all that, and here it is again. As usual.

"I'm not going back there," I tell her stubbornly. "There's nothing you can do to make me come back."

"I believe I've let you run around, playing pretend with the Order for long enough. You are a royal heir, and it's high time you realize that. Come back to where you belong."

I doubt she thinks I really do belong in that horrid place. The last time I was back there, she chucked me into the snow and left me for dead. I haven't been back since.

Shaking my head, I remind her, "Last I checked, you told me to never show my face in Ridgewatch ever again. I never belonged there and everyone knows it."

Elenore's eyes are like ice blue knives trying to cut right into my soul. "I do not care where you belong, whether it's in the Underworld or Ridgewatch. You will come back North immediately or there will be consequences. You may have power and weapons but you are still a child. You will do as I say."

I want to turn and walk away, go back to Elview and never see her again, but it's starting to look like I've woken the dragon and we've passed the point of no return. Going with them will bring nothing good, but it might give me a chance to get out of the royal family once and for all. Elenore doesn't say anything else to me, just spins around and commands her escort to start back to Ridgewatch. With that, my fate is sealed.

For the first time in eight years, I'm going home. Back into the icy hell I came from.

18

THIS IS WAR

SENIKA

"You should go back to Elview," Kellin says. His mother and her procession of soldiers wait restlessly just out of earshot.

"What? No, we shouldn't split up," I protest.

He shakes his head. "You can't follow me. There is no place for outsiders in the North. Besides, this—" he gestures to the ruined city behind us. "—is all the proof I need."

Jyn sighs. "Are you really going back there?"

"I have to." There is almost no expression in Kellin's eyes. "I'll come back as soon as I can but I need you three to go back to Elview. I don't know how long I'll be so you need to continue without me. If you're still with me, that is."

"I'm with you," Jyn says. "But I don't know how you expect us to do this without you. It's a stretch to defy Xethos with four of us and even more so with only three. Plus, we don't have a plan."

Glancing over his shoulder, Kellin replies, "You'll be fine without me."

"Let me come with you," I say. "I don't know much but I don't think you should be with those people alone."

Again, he only shakes his head. "No. Just because something new came up here doesn't mean Halfbloods aren't dying anymore. This won't stop until we make it. I promise I'll be there."

"We'll be okay," Taiyo assures him, pointedly glancing at Jyn. "We might have to lie low for a while but we'll come up with something."

"Good," Kellin says. "Just don't get caught."

Jyn huffs. "We should be the ones saying that. You better be careful up there."

"Don't worry about me. I can handle this." After what I've heard, I find it hard to believe Kellin's words.

"I guess we'll see you back in Elview, then." I try to smile but it feels forced. Fenix leans her head against my leg, purring, and I scratch her ears.

"Be safe," is all he says.

With that, he turns and walks away, Fenix trotting along at his side. Every step he takes feels like a step toward his doom. My heart sinks. I hardly know anything about the North and Kellin's family but none of it sounds good. Letting him go with them sounds an awful lot like letting someone walk right through the gates of Gosritaan.

As the procession rides off over the horizon, Jyn sighs. "I guess that's it then."

Taiyo nods, tucking her hands into the pockets of her ash-covered dress. "We should get moving if we want to make it back quickly."

I nod. "Yeah, if this is really happening, we shouldn't hang around and waste too much time." I don't tell them how anxious I am to get back to Gendry, Kira and Emaya.

"Let's stay here for one more night," Jyn suggests, looking down the road at the gathering of survivors. "We don't have any food and all of us are a wreck from that."

As if on cue, my stomach grumbles. I can't reject food and rest after a night as adventurous as that. From the lack of objections, Taiyo seems to think the same. The three of us make our way cautiously down to join the group that has gathered at the edge of the road. Any food that was able to be salvaged is rationed out among the survivors. Those with any competency in medicine tend to the wounded and make-shift beds have been set up for the patients in the most critical condition. Few words are exchanged outside of what is necessary for a sense of organization throughout the tiny camp and everyone is reasonably disheartened.

Jyn, Taiyo, and I line up for our small portion of hard bread and watery soup. The man serving it has one arm in a sling made of torn cloth but he offers us a smile regardless. We sit near the edge of the camp where we eat in silence, devouring our meals. Once she finished, Taiyo stands up, heading off to offer her help to those in need. A young Halfblood woman with pale green hair and strange birthmarks not unlike the spots on a fawn's coat makes her way over to inform Jyn that his ankle isn't nearly as broken as he thought it was.

"Are you sure?" Jyn questions her for the third time.

She smiles kindly. "Yes. You must have twisted it but I assure you, it isn't a major injury."

He sighs, finally inclined to believe her. "Thank the gods. Walking is the only way we have to get home."

"Are you not from here?" she asks, brushing her hands off on her skirt.

Jyn shakes his head. "No, we came from Elview for the festivals. Just unfortunate timing. He's not even from Akelia."

"Really?" The woman turns to me. "Where are travelling from?"

I swallow nervously. "Iolleria. We both live in Elview now, though."

"I hope you have a chance to see the nicer parts of our fair kingdom, then," she says, smiling. "I'm sure you've seen it but the Order's cathedral in Elview is by far one of the most stunning places in Alkelia."

"Do you go to Elview often?" Jyn asks her.

The woman nods. "Of course. I work for the Order as a healer so I did some of my training there. It's a lovely city, really, but I grew up here at the Black Tower."

Jyn and I exchange a nervous look. If she works for the Order, we can't afford to mess up our story with her around.

"I'm sorry," Jyn says. "It must be horrible to see your home destroyed like this."

She only shrugs. "The Order is resilient. We will not fall so easily. You are both Halfbloods; you know that this cannot be our end."

I try to smile. "Of course. I wish you luck, then."

Ordinarily, I would be wishing her luck with the revival of the Order. Now, I mean to wish her luck surviving the storm that is still yet to come.

"Thank you." She bows her head. "My husband and I mean to move to Elview once this is over so perhaps we will be seeing you around."

Someone calls for her and the woman gathers up her skirts, waving at us over her shoulder as she hurries back to the camp.

"Strange . . ." Jyn says.

"What's strange?" I ask.

He shrugs. "She still thinks the Order is good."

"She works for them."

Jyn gives me a tired look. "*I* work for them. *Kellin* works for them. Same with Taiyo. It's strange to hear people talk about the Order as they're still heroes now that we know they aren't."

I nod. "Well, it's a secret for a reason, right? I'm guessing no one saw that it was the Inquisitors who set the city on fire and they would never admit to it. The entire kingdom would turn against both the Order and Xethos if they knew the truth, don't you think?"

"Either that or they would burn whoever told them," Jyn grumbles. "Which I think is the more likely option. And the reason why we haven't told anyone else."

"An unfortunately good point," I admit.

Jyn stands up, stretching his arms over his head. He slings his half-empty quiver over his shoulder and runs his fingers through his dirty hair. "I'm going to go see if I can help," he says. "Water is useful in times like this."

"Okay. I don't think there's much I can do but I'll come."

We find Taiyo telling stories to a handful of children who stare up at her with wide eyes, transfixed by the tales she weaves. I find myself just as mystified as the children as she illustrates, with nothing more than words, a hero who fights on dragon-back in an epic battle. Jyn wanders off to help fill a basin with drinking water. I've learned that his magic allows him to create and manipulate water, either in the form of a pool or as a powerful blast.

" . . . and so the hero was victorious," Taiyo says, delivering the finale of her story. "With the villain defeated, the hero and his dragon returned to their village to live happily ever after."

A child with beautiful, iridescent wings raises her hand. She can't be more than six or seven but her eyes hold wisdom behind her years. "Why was the villain so mean?"

Taiyo smiles kindly. "Because he was the villain. That was his role."

"But wasn't he somebody too?" the girl asks. "Don't the bad guys want something too? Maybe he needed a hug and then everything would have been okay."

"Some people are mean because they want something, yes," Taiyo tells the little girl. "But there are some people who just want others to hurt."

The girl frowns. "That's not very nice."

"No, but that's just the way things are." I can tell Taiyo is trying to make this easier for the poor child to understand but it's not entirely a simple concept. "Think about the people who burnt your home. They only wanted to make your lives hard. The best thing you can do is to continue to be happy and never let them get you down, okay?"

"Okay . . ." The girl's wings flutter and she sits up a little straighter. "I'm going to be a hero just like the one in the story! And I'll never let the bad guys win!"

Taiyo laughs. "Okay. That sounds like a very good plan."

The girl jumps up and, wings buzzing, she takes off running. One of the others leaps up as well, shouting that he's going to be a hero as well, as runs after her. I step aside to avoid being trampled as they all go dashing past, tackling each other to the ground and falling into a heap of giggling limbs. Smiling, I walk over to Taiyo. She stands up, brushing the dirt off her skirts and stretching out her stiff limbs.

"That was quite the story," I tell her.

"Thanks. My father used to tell it to me when I was little." Not meeting my eyes, she smiles as if she's remembered something.

"Where is he now?" I ask.

"Dead," she says plainly.

"Oh . . ." My eyes go wide. "I'm so sorry. I didn't realize."

She shrugs. "It's okay. That was a long time ago."

I only nod, unsure of what to say next.

The more time I spend here the more I realize how many people are just like me. Taiyo, just like me, lost her parents to something she could not stop. All around us, children are without their parents, crying out for a mother and father who will never open their eyes. Ash coats everything in a thick layer of grey and reminds me of the fire that tore apart my home. My heart aches for those who lost someone to the destruction or to the Order.

Looking around, I realize that it is not the kingdom that is evil. There is nothing cruel or twisted about these people. There is only honest, pure innocence in the hearts of the children who must now call the ruins of the Black City their home. Even the woman who spoke to us of the Order and their resilience is not evil. She only wanted to serve her kingdom and her family. None of these people want to cause harm to those who have fallen but nor could they protect them.

This is a kingdom of kind people who can do nothing to stop the darkness that encroaches around them.

19

KANE

KELLIN

It takes three days to get to Ridgewatch. Three days and every second of it feels like torture. I can't help but think about what waits for us in the city since I haven't exactly been there in a while, and the last time wasn't entirely sunshine and rainbows. Not that the sun ever shines there anyway. My mother doesn't speak to me for the entire trip while everyone else basically treats me like I'm some random stranger who's decided to join them. We arrive at the castle just outside of Ridgewatch on the evening of the third day, just as the snow starts to fall.

The castle isn't much of a castle, more of a manor really, yet it's still called Clearwater Castle, named after the family that has lived here for generations. The Clearwaters are part of the King's Council in the North, making them important enough to have their home so near the capital, but in my opinion, every Clearwater is just an ass with a fancy title and some gold. In the snow, the castle is glowing with light, but it doesn't look warm or inviting; the place is worse than the Underworld itself.

No gardens surround the castle—it's pointless to have a garden in a place where it never stops snowing—but a small forest for hunting lies just behind the expansive grey and gold stone building. I shiver at the sight of it, dreading whatever might happen next. Until now, I've never had to pay attention to politics or royalty. I've now been launched into the unknown land of the exact thing I was trying to escape. The snow makes it look more like some other world compared to Elview or even the Black City.

In Elview, it only snows in the winter, but here it never stops, even now in the middle of summer. While in Elview it's always raining, which is far better than the snow, it would be nice to see the sun every once in a while. I've heard the coast of Iolleria is all beaches and sun, but Iolleria seems a million miles away and I'm stuck here in the cold instead.

Thinking about Iolleria reminds me of Senika. The strange, beautiful sailor who appeared in my life as if by magic. When I left them three days ago, Senika tried to come with me but there was never any hope of that happening. Hopefully, by now he's all back in Elview or at least close. Elview is safer for him than Ridgewatch or the Black City.

Once we're all inside, I'm told dinner will happen in two hours. Someone tries to take Fenix to the kennels with the hunting dogs, but one look from me makes them leave her alone. If I'm going to survive this place, I'll need Fenix. The two of us spend time wandering the halls until we find ourselves in a room I never thought I would see again.

It hasn't changed, of course, the chambers fit for a prince. There's still the same massive, canopied bed in the middle of the room, with dark blue curtains tied back and that tall wood wardrobe against the wall. The windows hide behind dark drapes, but I know the view outside the glass. The city skyline stretches outward, the Kane family's castle at its centre. A bookshelf once stacked with books now sits empty next to the door leading to the bathroom and next to the wardrobe is a tall mirror with a golden frame. There are no lamps in the room. To be expected, since no one has lived here for years.

This room used to be mine. As I run my fingers along the mantle over the fireplace, I remember all the nights I lay in that bed and all the days spent sitting by the window with a book or some toys. It's so strange to be back here after all this time to find everything just as I left it. The only difference is all the dust. And how empty and cold the room feels, all filled with silence. It's like a tomb. As I stand silently in the room, I feel as if I've stepped into someplace that was never meant to be disturbed, a grave for the child my mother thinks she lost.

My boots are silent on the soft carpet as I walk over to push back the curtains. The view is as I predicted. The city of Ridewatch is a thousand tiny distant lights. The towering castle sits empty. It could be mine, and it will be unless I do something fast.

Shaking my head, I put the thoughts of kings out of my head. There's no point in thinking about that. Right now, I have other things to worry about, such as getting out of this place and away from all these damn people. Everyone here hates me, yet for some reason they expect me to be here. I just want to go home to the cathedral. At least there I have people who know to leave me alone, even if it's because they're afraid of me or whatever.

I turn to leave but stop when I see my reflection in the gilded mirror. Dark shadows under my lifeless eyes make me look far more exhausted than I really am. My skin looks ghost-like in the dark. My hair is a wild mess, still filled with ash even though we left the city days ago, and my bangs refuse to stay out of my eyes. The jagged scar across my nose matches the fainter one cutting through my eyebrow, just over my right eye. If you ignore the scars and the ears and those golden eyes, there's nothing special about my face; I'm not particularly attractive but not necessarily unattractive either. I don't exactly have anything else remarkable about me. Just normal.

My eyes are the only thing beautiful about me. They glow when I use my power, brighter when I use more of it, but I'm nearly always using some amount of it. Now, they shine just enough to be noticeable without being obnoxious. I've been told that my eyes are creepy, like something from another world, and that I always look angry because of it.

Dirt and ash cover my clothing from days of travelling and the fire, but I don't have anything else to wear so it works for now. I have a long black jacket that reaches down to my ankles, black pants and a white shirt that is closer to grey now. My tall boots have bits of armour built into them as well as a bit of a heel so I can pretend I'm a little taller. Under my jacket, I wear metal arm guards but no other armour. It tends to slow me down in battle and isn't exactly practical for everyday things. There's a dagger sheathed on my leg and several more in my jacket and on my belt plus my spear across my back—my own personal arsenal. A pocket watch on a slim silver chain connects to my corset, but I'm honestly surprised it hasn't shattered into a thousand pieces yet.

Fenix bumps her head against my hand, making a small sound that very clearly means she wants attention. I scratch her ears and give her a smile that feels almost sad. She has never been here before, nor has she met most of the people, which I suppose is making her nervous. Now that we're here, though, I will need to find some food for her. It's unlikely anyone else will remember she's even here, and they definitely won't let her into the dining hall. Aristocrats are so boring.

With a final look around, I step back into the hallway and carefully close the door. Compared to my room, the hall feels so alive. Oil lamps cast bright light over the walls and I breath a sigh of relief to be freed from the ghostly stillness of the room on the other side of the door.

"There you are, Your Highness." The voice is so sudden it makes me jump. I look down the hallway to see a dainty-looking servant girl wearing a plain cream-coloured dress. "I have been instructed to help you prepare for dinner."

I look down at my clothing. "I can't I just go like this?"

She shakes her head. "Lady Clearwater wishes for you to appear . . . sophisticated, she said."

Of course, my mother said that. She's obsessed with image and looking better than everyone else. Naturally, her children must look flawless as well. If given the choice between listening to her and pulling all my feathers out one by one, I'd rather be crushed to death by a meteor. "I don't really care what she said. I'm not wearing whatever stupid outfit she has for me."

There's nothing wrong with how I dress, I know that, it's just that she has made a hobby of scrutinizing every detail of everything I do, no matter what I've done. I only see her once a year but she always manages to pick out every problem she has with me in that short amount of time. Sure, I tend to wear the same thing just about every day, but not everyone has the luxury of having a different outfit for each hour of the day without ever repeating a single item.

"Your Highness, I would greatly recommend it," the girl advises relentlessly. No doubt she was told to spare me no kindness. "I'm sorry to say that you do look rather like you've been through hell."

That does it. I sigh and let her drag me off to *look sophisticated*, partly because I don't have the energy to argue anymore and partly because I don't want to be covered with this damn ash for yet another day. The girl turns out to be quite nice, but I suspect it's only because she's been told not to make me angry, which makes it insulting. By the time dinner comes around, I don't look like I've nearly died, been in a fire, and travelled for three days. There's no more ash in my hair or dirt on my hands. The only casualty is that they don't let me wear my normal clothing and insist I wear a proper suit instead. Apparently, Lord Clearwater doesn't like his guests having weapons at the dinner table. But I manage to negotiate my way into bringing a dagger because even dinner is dangerous around here.

When I arrive in the dining hall, the table is already half full with my mother and her husband sitting at the end, deep in whispered conversation. Elias and his sister, Lilian, are next to them, both looking like the perfect children they are expected to be. Further down the table, the final member of my least favourite family is Rorik, his nose in a book even at dinner. The rest of the table is mainly other Clearwater aunts and uncles or brothers and sisters; even Robert's father, who must be about a thousand years old, has arrived for the occasion.

The only empty seat I can find is right across from Elias and Lilian which means I have the pleasure of talking to them for the next few hours. As soon as I sit down, both of them fall silent and look over at me, worried expressions on their faces.

"What are you doing here?" Elias demands.

I roll my eyes, words dripping with sarcasm. "Our wonderful mother had the grand idea of bringing me up here just for this. And how pleased I am to be here."

Lilian smiles nervously. "Yes, how nice it is to have all of us here again."

Elias laughs. "This is ridiculous. Just look at him, they would never make *him* sovereign. They would have more luck with a pig ruling the North."

"Oh, that's not true," Lilian says. "Pigs are far more stupid than any human."

The golden-haired prince turns his icy eyes back to me. "Halfbloods aren't human. Not by a long shot. Look, he's just some freak who's crawled up from Gosritaan claiming he deserves to be here. But you could never rule the North."

Every part of me wants to either punch him in that perfect face of his or stand up and walk out of here and never come back. But I just shrug, trying to at least appear calm. "I don't want to be king anyway. If you want the crown I'm not going to stop you. And I'm not from Gosritaan, I'm your brother."

From the anger sparking in his eyes, I'm guessing I said something I wasn't supposed to, but that's all I ever do. Elias hates having any connection to me. "You . . . when I'm king, the first thing I'll do is ban you from ever setting foot in the North ever again."

"You don't have to exile me, Elias. If it were up to me, I would be back in Elview, far, far away from you *bastard*."

Before he has a chance to respond, the doors to the kitchen open, and out march a stream of servants carrying plates stacked high with every kind of food anyone could ever imagine. There is enough food here to feed an army—carrots, potatoes, pork, bread, beans, eggs, plus a thousand different sauces and soups and even a whole roasted pig. I end up with a plate with more food piled on it than I could eat in a week yet there's still hardly any empty space on the table with how many dishes there are.

Once everyone has food, Lord Clearwater stands up, tapping a knife against his plate to get everyone's attention. "Welcome, welcome. It is such an honour to have you all gathered here this evening, even if we are here in light of the death of our king. He was a good man, and an honourable one as well, but his time has passed and now we welcome a new king to the throne of the North. In seven days, the coronation will be held and tomorrow we will be attending the funeral. But tonight we must celebrate the life of the man who now heads to the Afterlife. We are here to celebrate all the good that came from his rule but also from him as a friend or acquaintance. Now, I promised I wouldn't be taking too much time with this. So, let the feast begin!"

The next few hours are a blur of noise as people attempt to converse across the table. Servants hurry in and out of the room, carrying empty dishes and replacing them with new ones. At some point, wine is poured, and it doesn't stop, flowing infinitely from the gold in the royal coffers. I hardly touch my food even though it looks amazing. I haven't eaten a proper meal in days, only travel food and whatever we could buy in the city, but my appetite seems to have taken a vacation. Thankfully, Elias and Lilian don't try to talk to me again, and I don't know the other people sitting near me, so I don't have to talk to anyone. No one gets yelled at, but I also feel rather awkward being the only one sitting in silence.

Eventually, people stand and dance to music that doesn't exist, pushing chairs away to make more room. Still, I sit there alone, swirling the cup of wine someone was stupid enough to give me while staring at my plate. I wish they would have let me bring Fenix, but I was told no animals are allowed at dinner so she had to be left in the small guest room they gave us. I could have stayed in my old room but I would never be able to sleep in that place.

The whole ordeal of dinner is rather unbearable. I want nothing more than to go back to Elview. Even if I had to walk all the way there it would be better than this. At least Elview has people I actually like.

I find myself wondering if Senika, Jyn, and Taiyo made it back safely or if they stayed in the Black City longer. Maybe they ended up dead at the side of the road, killed by Inquisitors or bandits. Maybe they made it back to Elview and are trying to figure out what to do next. Now that I think about it, that whole thing was a terrible idea. We really should have stayed in Elview. Or maybe this is all some weird dream, and soon I'll wake up in the cathedral before the festival and the party and Xethos and all this will just go away.

But I know it isn't a dream. Dreams are never this long or detailed and the ordeal of the past few days makes all far too much sense to be a dream anyway. If it was a dream, I could do whatever I wanted.

I shrink down into my chair, hunching my shoulders and lowering my head in hopes of simply vanishing from this horrible place. There isn't a single person here who cares about me or even slightly less than hates me. It's driving me crazy. If I had even one ally here, I might have a chance of getting out, but there is no escape from a place like this, with highly trained guards at every door. Even with all my training, the security here makes me feel like I am just one kid in the middle of it all. Besides, even if I could escape, they would likely drag me right back here just to kick me out again after they hand the throne to Elias. I am just a pawn here, a way to formally put their favourite son on the throne since they need all of us here to properly "choose" a king.

Desperately, I reach out for the spirits in my mind, unsure if I can even talk to them. I can sense them, as always, but I've never tried to speak to them first before. Yet as soon as I reach out, I hear Airadyne's voice in my head, more like words written in my mind than her real voice.

We cannot help you, child. She speaks to me before I even get to ask anything.

There must be something you can do, I think, wondering if she can hear all my thoughts. *Can't you at least tell me how to get out of here?*

We do not concern ourselves with mortal affairs. Airadyne says sternly. I can sense her tone without really hearing her voice. *Especially not this.*

Why? There's so much you could do.

If we meddle too much, you humans will never learn, she explains. *You are like small children, naive and foolish and never learning your lesson. We stay out of things so you learn to depend only on yourselves.*

And just like that, she's gone. I can feel the emptiness the instant she leaves, a void left by her missing presence. It makes me wonder if she has been lurking in my mind this whole time. Only then do I notice how I've been sitting with my elbows on the table and my head in my hands like I'm trying to block out the sound of the room. I quickly sit upright and shove my hands under my legs like they might try to do something without my consent.

Suddenly, the door crashes open and the entire room turns to see a wild-eyed man standing there, clearly not a guest in the castle. His clothing is white with snow, but he isn't wearing a jacket and looks minutes away from freezing to death. Twisted, broken horns curl up from his wild hair and his eyes are wide and crazed.

"The Halfblood Heir has returned!" he shouts. "He's come to free us all!" With wide, grey eyes he scans the room frantically until he finds me in the crowd. "Look! Our saviour, come to free us all from this mortal prison."

The man bursts out into maniacal laughter as the guards grab him, shoving him out the door. They drag him away, and all the while he shouts of a saviour come to end his suffering, a hero he assumes must be me. But I am no hero, all I want is to save the lives of those who cannot save themselves. That doesn't include random crazies like this man. His laughter echoes down the hallway and waves of murmured concerns pass through the dining room, accompanied by fearful glances in my direction. Robert Clearwater hurries out the door after the guards with a terrified look on his face.

"Are you feeling well?" Elias asks tauntingly once the man is gone. "Perhaps you should go rest, it would be a shame if the future crown were to fall ill."

"I'm fine," I snap.

"Certain? I can always inform Mother that you will be unable to attend the council meeting in five days." He smiles slyly, hinting at something I can't quite understand.

I shake my head. "Unless you want to be the one unable to attend, don't talk to me."

He laughs, but there's a hint of nervousness underneath the teasing. "I'm not afraid of you, Kellin. You have no power here."

Narrowing my glowing eyes, I ask, "Are you sure you aren't afraid?"

At some point late into the night, Elenore and Robert leave, signalling the end of the dinner—and my time to finally be free from this place. I wait a few minutes after they leave, so it doesn't look like I'm just trying to get away as soon as possible, but that turns out to be a bad idea.

"Hey. Kid." I look up to see a tall man with a thick red beard standing beside my chair. "You're Elenore's bastard, right?"

I nod and grumble, wanting to leave and not talk more. "Yeah. What do you want?"

"Nothin'. I just saw you sittin' here alone and thought I'd ask why," The man says with a casual shrug.

"That's not your business." I stand and head for the door. The last thing I want is another awkward conversation with someone I don't know. "I'm leaving now, anyway."

He chuckles. "Hey, I just wanted to ask some questions. I mean, being a Halfblood and all, well, people can't help but be curious. So

I was wonderin', if you're really from Gosritaan, what are you planin' to do here?"

I spin around and glare at him, but it's rather hard to intimidate someone a foot taller than you. Just about everyone is taller than me. "If you're gonna ask stupid questions, don't bother me with them. I am not from the Underworld, I am from right here in Alkelia. Got it?"

"Yeah, that's a good joke, kid, but it's not very funny anymore. Listen, all you gotta do is tell me what's up and I'll leave you alone." This conversation went downhill so fast, it basically went off a cliff.

"Would you leave me alone if you knew what I can do?" My hand hovers over the handle of my knife, but I'm praying I don't have to use it.

"Magic don't scare me, little guy. C'mon, I'm not gonna hurt you, I just wanna know." This man must be so drunk he's forgotten how to use his brain. No sane person ever talks to me like this. "They sayin' you'll be king, so I gotta know my king, don't I?"

"*Fututus et mori in igni.* If one more word comes out of your stupid mouth, I'll cut your tongue out." If you can't intimidate someone, threats work great too.

The man laughs. "Heh, that's a good one." Then it seems to hit him that I wasn't speaking Alkelian. "Wait, what'd you say?"

"Fuck off and die in a fire, old man. I'm not answering your idiotic questions and I'm not in a very good mood so you'd be wise to leave me alone." Pushing open the tall double doors, I step into the hall and let them slam in his face.

Compared to the noisy dining hall, it's silent here, even with the spirits in my head. For some reason, tonight I'm far more aware of them—of every whisper—and it's driving me crazy. They're so loud. It's like the festival all over again, but it's been weeks since then and there's no cure for loud spirits. There have been times when I've thought I'm just crazy and none of them are real, mere voices in my head. Tonight, they're the only thing on my mind. That and the silver-haired Halfblood sailor I left behind three days ago.

20

RETURN

SENIKA

We take the long route back to Elview. None of us want to pass through the forest again so we travel along the road this time. Our horses are either dead or missing in the fire so we have to walk the whole way, which is far, far worse than riding. The first part of the journey is spent on the back of a merchant's wagon, but when we reach Alicante, we continue on while he stays in the city. Alicante is one of the most beautiful cities I've ever seen, made entirely of glass towers and picturesque houses that make me wish we could stay longer. But Jyn and Taiyo both seem eager to get home, and I can tell there's a lecture from the Captain waiting for me. We travel slowly, only hiking for a few hours each day before stopping to rest. None of us talk much.

On the third night past Alicante, we camp near the steep bank of the Slash. Taiyo taught me how to light a fire on the first night of our trip back, so I help her build one under the cover of one of the few trees nearby. Here, the river bank isn't much of a bank, more of a cliff that drops off suddenly. I'm tempted to make a barrier out of rocks so no one falls into the rushing water. The late summer nights are beautiful, with skies so clear I can see stars I never knew were there. We're so far away from everything. The only light comes from the moon, the stars, and our fire. I know it's the same sky I used to sit under back home, but it seems so different now. Here, no city lights dim the brightness of those stars.

So much has changed since I left Iolleria, but I still sit under the same sky with the same stars, even in a different kingdom—if a nation without a proper king to rule it can be called a kingdom. Up until about six months ago, I hardly left home outside of my dad's boat trips to other towns or cities along the coast. He often helped transport goods across the kingdom, and as soon as I was old enough, I started to go with him. The war changed all of that.

When Dad went off to fight, it was just me and Mum left at home to wait for his return. A year later, there was no word of him until the day his crew arrived back with his boat in shambles and no captain. My mum was heartbroken, but less than two months later, I was sent off to fight as well. That's the only reason I know how to use a sword, how to fight. There's no way I could ever be as good as Kellin, though; I saw the way he fought back in the city. I never want to end up on the wrong side of his blade. I trained for almost ten months, but as soon as the first battle came, I knew I couldn't do it.

If there's anything I regret, it's that. I abandoned everything and ran back to Isondale instead of fighting while the people I had trained beside died and still are dying. Once I got back, however, I only kept running. I ran until I stumbled my way right into another war, another kingdom ruled by death. Even Gendry, my best friend, couldn't stop me.

A strange feeling of sadness washes over me thinking about Gendry. I left him behind too, though in Elview, not Isondale. Gendry, Kira, Emaya and their crew are the only ones who know I'm not dead and now even they don't know where I've gone. When I get back, I have to find them as soon as possible and explain everything. If there's going to be war here—which does look possible from what I've seen—they should get out as fast while they still can.

"So who's taking the first watch?" Jyn finally breaks the long silence that has taken over our tiny group.

I yawn but nod. "I can do it."

Taiyo smiles slyly—she often reminds me of a fox, especially when she smiles like that. "Excellent. I'll be asleep then. If you need something, don't ask me."

With that, she rolls over, unconscious in seconds. Taiyo hasn't offered to stay up and take watch the entire trip. Only once did I dare to ask her to do it, and she refused, claiming that wasn't her job. She's spent the past week complaining about the weather, the trees, the damn wind. I think I'm starting to hate her.

Jyn, on the other hand, doesn't seem to know *how* to complain. All this time, it doesn't matter what happens, he just keeps going. It's far better than the rest of us can do, but also a little strange. From what I've gathered, Jyn and Kellin are best friends, but I don't think Jyn really *cares*. When Kellin stormed out of the library, Jyn didn't do anything, only sighed and said it would be okay, which is how I ended up being the one to follow that cat into the middle of nowhere when she came racing back to the Tower. And how I ended up being the only one who knows Kellin almost killed himself that night. Maybe Kellin isn't the one he cares about, but rather someone or something else.

"Then I'll get some sleep too." Jyn lies down, facing the cliff.

"Hey, there's something I've been wondering, actually," I say quickly. "What's the deal with Kellin's family?"

For a moment, I think Jyn might already be asleep; he doesn't look at me or say anything. Then he sighs and flips onto his back to look up at the sky. "I'm not entirely sure. And I'm probably the one who knows the most about him. All I know is his mom isn't exactly a good person. Like, at all. She hates him and every other Halfblood even if she pretends otherwise in public. I would say ask him yourself but we both know how that would end." He shakes his head. "He would rather act like nothing ever happened than tell people about it. I think it still hurts him to think about it."

"I tried asking him," I say. "He's about as talkative as a locked drawer. Do you know what she did to him?"

Jyn picks at a loose thread in his tunic. "I can only guess, but I'd say it's years of abuse he's hiding under that mask. If you feel like asking, you probably have the best chance of any of us at learning anything. He trusts you, I think."

We fall silent after that, and soon Jyn is asleep, leaving me to watch the fire burn and wonder what strange sort of world I've gotten myself into.

I never asked to be a Halfblood, none of us did, but in my case, I was born like this. Most people are "chosen" at some point in their lives, yet no spirit ever appeared to tell me I was special. My mother was a Halfblood and my father had no magic of any kind, which makes me a weird, rare hybrid that shouldn't exist. Under most circumstances, Halfbloods can't have kids, but it seems like my mother was the exception, and I am the one left somewhere in between being a Halfblood and not. Sure, I have magic, something people dream of having, but I never wanted any of it. I want to be normal.

When I was about thirteen, Dad had the idea of an eyepatch, something I could use to hide my eye. My eyes are silver and the left one has a butterfly in place of a pupil. Those eyes, among other things, mark me as different. I have hair that looks like an old man's, but I'm only seventeen. Once, I dyed my hair with red dye, only succeeding in looking stupid. Not that I look *bad* with red hair. I did a truly horrible job that didn't go away for months. I'm never trying that again. So I'm stuck with white hair and silver eyes and powers I don't want. And now I'm in the last place anyone with any sort of magic wants to end up.

Yet even here, in this miserable excuse for a kingdom, I managed to find something worthwhile. People that aren't what I had expected, people who aren't total idiots who conquer everything in sight. I was always taught that every Alkelian was a meathead who only cared about themself and glory—but what else is there to know about an empire founded on the principle of victory?

I sigh and lay down in the grass, yawning. Not for the first time, I wish I could be out at sea. When you're raised on the ocean, it's hard to get away from it even when you need to get as far from everything around it as you possibly can. There's something about floating along on the open sea that can't compare to the trees and hills of Alkelia. Everything here feels so dull and dreary and drained of colour; it never stops raining and when it does, it's all foggy and that's equally as miserable. I wouldn't be surprised if even the hottest summer days had rain to accompany them. Then again, it's summer now even if it is almost over.

The next morning we're back on the road shortly after sunrise. We don't have much to pack up so we just put out the fire before setting off toward the city once again. Jyn tells me there's another small city called Blueport between here and Elview where we can hopefully stop to get some food and a night of proper sleep, but none of us have any idea how far we are from there. Like every other day, the sky is thick with clouds. Except today, it's actually raining. Only a drizzle, but still enough to feel despairing.

By midday, we can see the city in the distance. It looks just like any other port city I've been to—if I ignore the walls around it, that is. Every place here has those walls, built of stone that surround entire cities. A few times, we passed towns too small for people to waste their time building walls or even putting on maps, but for the most part, every single city has them. Elview has two; one to separate the royal and military part of the city from the rest and one that protects it all from the world.

This city has different walls, though. Soldiers patrol their ramparts, and at the gates, anyone who enters is questioned intensely by a group of guards led by a man with a scarred face and broadsword in his hand. We join the small line of people waiting to enter the city. The tension in the air is almost suffocating.

The scarred man lets a group of travellers in and then stops a woman on a horse, telling her to dismount before promptly ordering one of his men to empty her saddlebags. She stands nervously near the gate, eyes flickering toward the city and then back at the road, while he asks her where she's coming from and what her business is.

"I'm coming from Rivers," She explains in a small voice, tugging the hood of her cloak lower. "M-my sister lives in South Cross and I was headed to . . . to help her. Her son is sick, you see, and she hasn't got the money or time to help him alone."

"Is that how it is?" The man sneers. "Your sister's kid a Halfblood, too, I s'pose?"

The woman draws a sharp breath. "N-no, I don't know what you mean . . ."

Suddenly, the man reaches out and yanks her hood back, revealing two pale horns poking out from her wild, blue curls. Gasping, the woman reaches for her hood but it's far too late; everyone has already seen. The man laughs. "Would ya' look at that? Girl's a freak. I could have ya' locked up for that, princess."

"Let's just get out of here," Jyn whispers.

Taiyo shakes her head. "We're out of food, Jyn, and none of us want to spend another night

"Please, I—I didn't do anything wrong," The Halfblood girl pleads desperately. "I just need to get to my family. Please."

"Well, I can't let ya' do that, girlie. But there are other things you could do that could ah, let ya' past." The man smiles a smile full of yellowed teeth that makes the woman cringe.

That's it, I can't do this. I step forward, placing myself between the man and the Halfblood woman. "Leave her alone."

The man turns his dark gaze to me. "Ah, stay outta this, kid. This is between me and the lady."

"And it looks like she doesn't want a part in it," I retort, trying to defuse the encounter as calmly as I can. "Look, if you just leave her alone and let us pass, we can all get on with our day."

He just laughs and looks me up and down. "Yer a Halfblood freak as well, and yer friend too. I ain't lettin' monsters like you run around my city unchecked. Besides, ya got weapons on ya, don't ya?"

I put my hand on my sword, closing my eyes briefly to keep myself from launching this bastard into the stars. "Sir, none of us want trouble. You just have to leave her alone."

Behind him, the other guards are starting to get nervous, watching with hands hovering near their weapons while the rest of the people waiting in line whisper, probably deciding whether or not to get out of here. Just when I start to prepare for the worst, the man waves his hand dismissively, clearly tired of this situation and seeing the attention drawn to us. I doubt this man would keep his job if his boss knew this is how he went about protecting the city. It always works. Make a scene, draw attention, and people stop whatever misbehaviour they're up to; things like this don't work if everyone knows.

"Fine," The man says shortly. "Get out of here. I don't care."

He turns his back and the Halfblood woman hurriedly takes back the reins of her horse, rushing into the city. I nod to the guard, muttering a few words of thanks even though he doesn't hear nor care, then the group of us are past the walls. The line behind us keeps moving forward.

The city of Blueport is as I expected, cramped and smelling of fish like every other port city in the world. The difference is that this one has a strange stuffy feeling to it, like everyone here is holding their breath and waiting for something inevitable to happen. The streets are quiet, and the few people we do see look at us like we're criminals. Everywhere, soldiers patrol and watch everything. With this much security, it would be impossible for anything to go wrong, but they all act like it's already happened. Whatever "it" might be. The man at the gate could have easily arrested us yet he let us in regardless, perhaps knowing that if we were trouble, his friends in here would get us. It almost makes me wonder if they're looking for someone—or something—in particular.

"Thank you," the Halfblood woman says tentatively.

I hadn't even noticed she was still here; I thought she would have taken off the second she was free. "It's nothing. I couldn't let him do that to you."

She smiles gratefully. "Well, us Halfbloods have to stick together, you know." She pauses for a moment before speaking in a more confident tone. "My name is Rose. If you ever happen to be passing through South Cross, my door is open to all in need."

"Oh, thanks. My name is—agh."

Jyn grabs my arm and cuts me off. "Thanks, but we have to get going."

"I'll see you around then!" Rose calls after us as Jyn drags me down the road.

"Hey, what's up with you?" I ask as I yank my arm free, slightly upset that he interrupted our conversation like that.

"We don't have time for small talk. Let's find a place to stay then get out of here as soon as morning comes."

"I think we have time to help people, Jyn." I raise my eyebrow at him, a look that is far less effective with only one eye, but I think he gets the idea.

"And what if she's an Inquisitor? What if you gave us away to our enemies? They could have spies everywhere. You have no idea what the Order is capable of, Senika."

I'll admit, this place creeps me out. Like, a lot. It's all shadowy and silent but I'd rather have people I know here than live in a world of strangers. Besides, there was nothing dangerous or shifty about the woman. Sure, she might have been lying about why she was going to South Cross. Most people lie about their names when running away—unless they're stupid—but she was just scared and alone. And here I was thinking Jyn trusted people.

But I also think he's right about one thing. I don't know anything about the Order. In Iolleria, we rarely hear of other nations, but sometimes when I hung out near the docks, I heard whispers or rumours about Alkelia or Anro or Isher, the kingdoms across the bay. Sometimes, I heard of Halfbloods escaping from Alkelia and how the Order would take in Halfbloods in need. This seems like it was a rather secret operation but it still surprised me to hear what's actually happening since the Order was always portrayed as heroic. Now, I think that was by design; if they look perfect and people believe in them, they can get away with a lot more. I can only imagine how the people of this country would react, especially after seeing how Kellin reacted.

No one would believe their heroes are killers.

We find our way to a tavern near the edge of the city that seems pretty empty and manage to get three rooms for cheap but we hardly have enough coin for food. We try to haggle for a room with three beds but the woman at the counter insists that the only rooms they have available have single beds and that we must split up. Since none of us have the energy—or money—to bargain any further, we eventually give up and accept the three rooms plus food before finding a table in the corner where we can hide. The three of us devour the cheapest meals we could buy, tucked into a corner, without hardly a word to share between us. A barmaid passes by our table, not bothering to offer us drinks even if we couldn't afford them. The food is fine—edible, but far from outstanding—and with our meagre budget, we didn't get enough to truly qualify as a full meal. I finish and want to all but run out of the room to escape the strange looks people keep giving us. Part of me wonders if it's because Jyn and I are Halfbloods.

Jyn tucks his empty coin purse into his pocket.

"We'll make it to Elview tomorrow, right?" I ask, worriedly.

Jyn shrugs. "Unless we run into trouble between here and there, we should be there just after nightfall if we leave early tomorrow morning."

"Finally." Taiyo sighs. "I've had enough of this travel thing for a lifetime. Once we're back there, I am never leaving the city again."

"I can't say I blame you," I say. "I'm going to go to sleep."

"Okay, good night," Jyn says. "Our rooms should all be in the same hall so we won't be far if anyone needs anything."

I nod. "Right. And we should get going pretty early tomorrow so we can make it to Elview in good time. Plus, I don't want to spend any more time here than we need." I add the last part as quietly as I can, leaning forward so they can hear my words.

Taiyo stifles a laugh. "Agreed."

As I step into my room, a horrible feeling of doubt takes over. There's something horribly *wrong* with this city that none of us can seem to shake. That guard, when we first arrived, gave me a bad impression of this place, that's for sure, but it's more than that. None of the people seem to want to talk to us. The handful of folks in the main room downstairs watched us like hawks. Even the woman behind the counter only spoke to us as much as she had to, no more; just enough to ask how many rooms and how much food we need.

The sun vanishes below the horizon a few hours later and the city becomes even stranger. The buzz of the city fades, leaving behind only the roaring of the river. From my window, I have a great view of the river and the harbour where the boats dock for the night. I can see the lights of South Cross, the other riverside city, like a million tiny fireflies past the dark river. Past the city walls, the road is empty but still winds through the countryside, following the river until it reaches Elview somewhere past what I can see.

Just as I'm nearly asleep, there's a knock on my door and suddenly I've never been more awake. I try to lay still for a moment, listening for anything that might give away who could be at my door this late. There's another knock. I stand up, grabbing my eyepatch and tying it behind my head before yanking on my boots and tiptoeing over. The person knocks again, more impatient this time.

"Open this door." A gruff voice I don't recognize comes from the other side. "You have five seconds to let me in or I'll open it myself."

I grab my sword from where I left it on a chair near the window but don't draw it just yet, silently praying I don't have to use it. "Who's there?"

"You have five seconds," the voice repeats. "I will not ask again."

Sighing, I walk over to the door. "And I'm not opening it until you tell me what you want. Sorry, I'm not in the habit of letting strangers into my bedroom."

Something slams into the door and I flinch. It's unfortunate that rotting wood doesn't hold very well when it's attacked. There's some muttering outside, then they hit the door again, shaking its frame and splintering its hinges. I look around, desperate for some sort of escape plan. If Jyn and Taiyo were here, I would just say climb out the window, but I have no idea where they are. I can't leave without them.

"Yeah, yeah. I'm coming." With shaking hands, I unlock the door to see a massive man with a thick beard and shoulders so broad he fills the entire doorframe. Next to him, I feel tiny, and I'm not exactly short.

"There you go," the giant man grumbles. "You're coming with us, kid."

Drawing my sword, I stare at him. "No way. Not until you tell me what's going on."

"I'm from the Order," he huffs. "You and your two friends are wanted by Storm."

"And you expect me to go with you? No thanks." My heart is pounding, wondering what the Order would want from me. Did someone call them here to kill us? Jyn and I are both Halfbloods, and after the scene we caused arriving here, it wouldn't surprise me much if someone wanted us dead.

He sighs, exasperated. "I wasn't giving you a choice. Now come on."

Then he turns and walks away, leaving me very few options but to follow him. So I do.

I don't know what they want from us. Along with the big man, there are six others, five of them dressed in armour while the sixth wears priest-like robes. It makes me wonder why they need seven people to find three kids. They don't treat us like prisoners, luckily, giving us horses and letting us ride freely. However, they did drag us out of the inn in the middle of the night to get back to Elview seemingly as fast as possible. We ride right through the night, and by the time the sun rises, the city itself is visible, aglow with morning sunlight.

We're dragged through the city and straight to the imposing cathedral with far more towers and spikes than necessary. I've been here before, of course, yet it never fails to impress me with those carefully carved stones and elegantly dark architecture, its towers reaching up to touch the grey clouds with rigid spires of grey stone. It reminds me of mountains or an ancient building constructed in another era. There's nothing like it in Iolleria, and even from the outside, it's stunning.

Waiting for us in the entryway beneath the high, arched ceiling is a tall man with white hair and a face that looks carved from stone, old and unmovable yet wise and sharp. He wears the red and silver robes I have learned to associate with the Order, yet his clothes are far more dignified and elegant than the others present here with refined tailoring and intricate embroidery. At the sight of us, he folds his hands behind his back and lifts his chin slightly.

"You have arrived," he observes in a voice just as cold and disinterested as his face would imply. "I was expecting to see Kane here as well, not some sailor, Lukas."

The giant man bows his head. "We could not find the missing knight, Your Honour."

"Hmm." the white-haired man hums thoughtfully before turning those icy eyes to me. He leans forward, his eyes level with mine. "I don't suppose you have any information for me?"

I shake my head. "Uh, no, I don't even know what you're talking about."

"Your new friend, Kellin Kane," he says. "However, I am aware that you do not know anything of this kingdom and its people. Ser Kane was taken by his mother, that is what you will tell me, and she has taken him to the North." He straightens, still speaking with frightening authority. "We have no business in the decision of kings. As such, we will only wait until he returns. Leave us, child of Isondale, and we will call on you when need be."

"That's it?" I ask. "You aren't going demand more information?"

His gaze is as cold and unfeeling as stone when he tells me, "I can see your thoughts, sailor, therefore I have no need for asking questions. As I said, there is nothing we can do without interfering with the Northern royalty. Now go."

I turn and walk back out the heavy wooden doors, mystified by the cathedral and the Order and the man who read my mind.

Once I'm outside, however, it doesn't take me long to realize that I have no idea how to get down to the harbour from here. You would think that someone who drags you from bed to another city might have the sense to at least show you how to get where you've been told to go. But apparently, the Order doesn't much like helping people, despite their whole existence revolving around helping Halfbloods who they now kill. I start down the road, hoping I might be able to see the harbour from somewhere.

All around, the streets are busy with people hurrying to start their day, setting up their shops and heading off to wherever they need to be. The smell of freshly baked bread wafts through the street as I pass a bakery, reminding me of Mum back home, a million miles away and all alone. She runs a tiny bakery in the front of our house that her father owned when she was a kid, so the house was always full of pastries and bread and all sorts of other delicacies. There were always people stopping past to buy something or just to talk, but the door was always open either way. Sometimes, I would come home to find she'd invited half the neighbourhood and a dozen people none of us know over for lunch. The kitchen was always packed with people we knew and sometimes people I'd never seen before.

Here and there, people exchange gossip for the day, catching up on who did what and who's left town and who's new. They all talk in Alkelian, so I don't understand all of it, but it's enough to catch snippets of conversation. I grew up speaking Iollerian, but a lot of people back home spoke Alkelian as well. With the number of travellers I met, it was worth learning the language as well. Eventually, I wound up using both languages just as often. It's the perfect language to have learned before ending up here.

After walking for a while, I spot the glimmer of water between two houses and head in that direction, thankful to finally have an idea of where I'm going. It turns out, however, that I picked the exact wrong route. I wind through a labyrinth of houses, alleyways, and side streets before I find myself standing at the opposite end of the docks from where I need to be. Regardless, I know where I'm going now, so it's easy to follow the wooden walkways to the tall masts of the *Vanquisher*, a ship I could recognize anywhere. It stands out amongst the Alkelian and Anroish boats, carved in the extravagant Iollerian style with its name painted in gold along the bow.

As I approach, I spot several of the crew standing around on the docks amongst the wooden boxes and crates we brought here, talking in Iollerian. For a moment, I hesitate. I went missing for more than a week, what happens now that I'm back? Thankfully, that question is answered before I spend too much time standing there like an idiot.

"Senika!" Captain Kira Aliver herself notices me and walks down the gangplank, talking far louder than necessary. "There you are! We were wondering if you ditched us."

I smile. "I wouldn't ditch, Captain. I was just . . ." I trail off. What *was* I doing and how do I explain it to her?

"Ah, it doesn't matter." She puts her arm around my shoulders and leads me back to the ship. "We have you back now. Are you hungry? Let's get you something to eat, how about that?"

As we board the ship, Gendry, with his frizzy red hair and bright blue eyes looks over at us with a wide grin on his face, showing off the gap in his front teeth. "Hey, would you look who's back? We missed you, Sen."

"Hello, Gendry," I say, returning that joyful smile. After everything that's happened, it's amazing to be back here. "Good to see you again."

Kira sits me down at the table set up near the mast, shooing away two others who were sitting there drinking, then calls for someone to bring up some food from down below. She plunks down on the bench across from me and Gendry, watching me eat. It's a little strange, but I can't blame her after I vanished for so long.

After wolfing down a meal of bread and vegetables and fresh fish, I push my plate aside and then ask, "Aren't you going to ask where I was?"

The Captain shrugs, stretching her arms above her head. "Nah, I figure you knew what you were doing and had it under control. If you want to tell us, though, I can't say I'm not curious. And you know I'm a sucker for a good adventure."

Emerging from down below, Emaya Aliver, Gendry's other mom, says, "Oh don't pressure him into that, Kira. If he doesn't want to say what happened, he doesn't have to."

Emaya kisses the Captain on the cheek and Kira huffs. "Yeah, and I suppose you aren't interested in whatever it was he did?"

"That's not what I said, love." Emaya turns to me. "It's good to see you again, Senika. I knew you would show up back here at some point."

I smile. "Well, I couldn't just leave you guys after all this time."

"I wish you'd taken me with you," Gendry complains. "I don't even know where you were but it's probably better than here."

My smile falters a little. "I wouldn't count on that. It wasn't exactly a vacation."

Of course, that only makes Kira more interested. "Oh-ho, well *now* you've got me. So, tell us, where were you?"

If it were anyone else, this would feel like an interrogation, a buff pirate lady demanding to know where I was, but I just laugh. "I don't think you'd believe me even if I did tell you."

"We aren't that stupid," Gendry points out, elbowing me in the shoulder. "Try it."

I sigh before explaining, "I heard from someone here that the Order has been killing Halfbloods. Full-on murder-everyone-they-see kind of thing. Me and him and another Halfblood, plus some girl who I don't really know, went to the Black Tower to see if it was true. It's . . . very much true. They burned down the entire city and killed most of the people there."

"Damn," Kira curses. Her tone is far more serious now, all the jokes from before completely gone. "I mean, shit . . . kid, that's not good.

Not good at all. So, what did you do? I guess you didn't come running right back here."

I shake my head. "Not really. That guy turned out to be the bastard of a princess or whatever and his mother came to bring him back home to make him rule the North. I don't really understand that part. So me and the other two were heading back here and we got caught by the Order and apparently, they all work for those jerks so they brought us back here. But for some reason, they told me to just leave. And . . . now I'm here."

Kira nods and Emaya gives me a pitying look while Gendry stares at a knot in the wood of the table. "So . . ." Kira says. "When do we get to meet him?"

"Uh, what?" I can't find a better way to reply.

She rolls her eyes. "The Halfblood who took you away from us. You know, the mysterious foreign lover?"

I shake my head, flustered. "No, no, no. It isn't like that, Kira. He's all the way in the North anyway and he probably won't be coming back for a while."

It occurs to me then that I might never see Kellin again. He will likely be up North dealing with his weird family for a lot longer than we'll be able to stay here. And even if he did come back, I don't really think he would want to see me of all people.

Emaya smacks Kira's arm. "Shush, you know you shouldn't say things like that. Implying that they're in love. I bet they hardly know each other."

"Well, I mean . . ." I start. "We've known each other for less than a month. That's not nearly enough time to really know someone, but it's definitely not like that."

The past few weeks have felt like a lifetime and in some ways, it feels like I've known Kellin for a lot longer than that. And yet I know I want to know him better.

Kira shakes her head. "Fine, fine. But one day I do have to meet this guy." She stands up and heads for the stairs that lead below deck. "I've got to go take care of some things now but I promise I'll hear more about this later, okay?"

"I should get back to work as well," Emaya says. "Senika, you take all the time you need to rest and if you need anything just let us know and we'll see what we can do. But Gendry, I do need you to finish stitching the sail. You're the only one here who can do it decently, and it has to be fixed before we set off again."

"Can't I talk to Senika for a bit longer?" he asks.

"Gendry, you'll have plenty of time for talk later but we could be setting sail tomorrow, for all I know," she reasons, shaking her head and ruffling his hair gently. "You know how your mother can be."

I end up helping him fix the sail, even though Emaya urged me not to, and I only stab my finger with a needle six times. Dinner comes, consisting of an array of fish and fresh bread and some vegetables someone picked up from a market. With pirates, dinner is rarely uneventful. It always ends up a party, and tonight some of the crew pull out instruments and start playing some horrible song, but it gets people dancing and laughing. Exhausted, I leave early, but even in the tiny cabin I share with Gendry below deck, I can hear the music and the laughter.

At some point late into the night, long after the party ends, I wake up coughing. I sit up frantically, stumbling out of bed and trying not to wake Gendry who is fast asleep, lying sideways across his bed. In the narrow hallway, I lean against the wall, struggling to breathe. I cough again and this time I taste blood in my mouth. My hands are shaking as I push my sweaty hair away from my forehead. When the coughing finally stops, I slide my back down the wall to sit on the hard wooden floor, still breathing hard.

I close my eyes and hang my head. This happens sometimes, mostly when I'm too active or when there's a lot of dust, but also occasionally it happens without reason. I've been sick for as long as I can remember, apparently from the smoke from when my village was burned down or something, but it never gets any better. In fact, it's only gotten worse lately, another reason why I can't fight. The second a battle starts, my lungs can't handle the strain and there's nothing I can do. Doctors have tried to help me, to fix this and make me better but nothing helps. Halfbloods are meant to have some level of increased self-healing, but that doesn't fix irreversible damage from so many years ago.

Coughing again, I wipe the blood off my lips. Fifteen years. That's how long I have left to live. In fifteen years, I'll be thirty-two. That puts me halfway through my life at seventeen. And I'm not going to spend what little time I have left fighting.

21

—◆○◆—

KING OF THE NORTH

KELLIN

For a proper decision to be made, all heirs, legitimate or otherwise, need to be present for the election. Elias, Lilian, Rorik and I thus all have the same claim to the throne. I'm the oldest, so tradition says I am to be King of the North. I'm not sure why Elenore would say I will be King after she's spent years making it painfully clear that Elias will be King, not me. After all, I'm the one they all said they would rather see dead than here in Ridgewatch again.

But what happens when the oldest heir is a bastard who's been cast out by everyone in the kingdom? It's never happened before, as far as anyone remembers, so we're going off our own rules now, it looks like.

I don't think Elenore wants me to rule the North; no one does. She likely wants me here so it can be official when she hands Elias the crown. Our whole lives, he has been her favourite. He's the one people fawn over and want to talk to. He's the proper son with a normal family. I'm the outcast no one wants around.

So there isn't any reason to not have completely removed me from the inheritance. They all hate me, and certainly, no one wants me to rule a quarter of the kingdom, but I guess it's the same thing as my mother acting like everything is perfectly normal in public and then turning around and making my life miserable the second no one is looking. These people like masks, the kind they can hide behind when it's convenient, removing them when it isn't. They play games they call politics. Lying and cheating.

I can wear a mask too. And if that's a game they want to play, I can play. But sooner or later they better know I'm playing by *my* rules.

The sun will rise soon, marking the day of the funeral and the start of the discussions of Kings and Queens. Here's the worst part about being made to rule this stupid kingdom: they'll make me marry some lady who doesn't love me and who I could never love. It seems like a simple thing, but there is no way they can make me get married. In the Order, they forbid anyone from getting married, saying we serve a god and cannot afford distractions such as love. Other things like too much partying and drinking aren't allowed either, but love always seemed like the strangest one to me.

I stare out over the city of Ridgewatch, the view blurred by snow and the dull light of early morning. My breath forms clouds in the air but from where I sit on the balcony, I am sheltered from the snowfall. The spirits seem restless tonight, desperate to drag up things better off forgotten. I gave up on sleep hours ago when I realized they wouldn't shut up.

Sometimes, I can block them out by forcing my attention to another source. Cold air, rain on my skin, pain. But tonight, none of my strategies are working and nothing I do stops my mind from spiralling further.

Snow will always remind me of that night, of blood and feathers and cold eating away at my bones. I can practically hear her voice still, telling me I'm a failure, that I could never be her child. That I'm a demon, come to destroy them all.

But I'm not.

Am I?

When I close my eyes, all I can see is that snow, red with blood and feathers drifting to the ground all around her feet. Every detail is sharp, even after all this time. The cold, the pain, everything. The sound of her footsteps in the doorway, the echo as the door slammed shut behind her. She locked me away from everything I had ever known.

But that wasn't the only time she was like that.

There was one night when I found her bedroom door slightly open, and inside I could hear her crying. I thought I could help, but the second she saw me, her eyes were as unfeeling as stone. She slammed the door in my face. She shut me out a thousand times. It was stupid. *I* was stupid to think I could ever be what she wanted me to be.

I remember so many days filled with shouting and anger, but I thought every kid was yelled at. So I put up with it. I put up with it when she hit me and yelled at me, even when I had to curl up and hide from everything. Yet there is so much more I don't remember. I've heard minds can block out traumatic events to protect a person, but I still remember the worst of it.

I remember how she treated Elias like the sun in her sky.

At night, I would lie awake, shivering at the thought of what would happen when day arrived, but in my dreams, at least I found happiness. They were always dreams of my mother and my father together, even though I never knew him. And Elias was there too, except we were the best of friends.

But eventually, I knew it could never be that way.

At some point, I started dreaming of being alone. It would be just me, wandering alone through a forest or a field without having to worry about what people thought of me. Those dreams were an escape, along with the books from the library when I could get my hands on one. From a young age, I would spend hours reading, losing myself in tales of adventurers and magic and heroes, people who could save others.

In some ways, it was easier then. I could escape into a book or a dream but now even my dreams are haunted by the horrible parts of this world. Those dreams aren't kind like the ones I had as a kid, they are filled with death and pain and sorrow, not happiness and love and peace. But things like happiness and love aren't meant for people like me. I deserve none of them, not being who I am, not in this world. This is a world that I have never belonged to, it's a world where kindness is an expectation and love is demanded but I do not know either. There is no escape from any of it.

I can still picture it all perfectly. I see blood covering my hand, dripping to the polished floor as pain rips through my arm. Again, a flash of light reflected off a silver blade. Her voice echoes in my mind, speaking like she always does, spitting out my name like it's poison.

"Shut up," I tell the voices in my head. "Stop saying those things. *Faex.* Just shut up."

They're all going to die. It's all your fault.

"No, they aren't. I don't know what you're talking about."

The spirits laugh, talking in a voice that is at once many and one. *You know. They will die because of you. All of them.*

"Who? Who's going to die?"

Everyone. Dead butterflies.

Another image flashes behind my eyes. The ruins of old buildings with the wind howling through them. In the air float the broken bodies of a thousand tiny, silver butterflies.

"No. No, he isn't going to die. Leave me alone."

You will see. They will die. Fallen snow, oceans dry, broken stones.

More pictures. Fenix, dead in a pool of blood on the floor of a stone building. Jyn, with an arrow through his heart, lying on the forest floor. Taiyo, her body crushed under piles of rock and burned so badly I hardly recognize her. Safiya, the Kyrani princess, her head on a stake outside a ruined palace. The cathedral sits in ruins and rubble while the rest of the city beneath it is destroyed and uninhabited. Somewhere a forest burns red hot, the flames leaving a scar of charred earth behind them. The sun is swallowed by a curtain of darkness over a city I don't recognize while monsters crawl from cracks in the dry ground to devour everything in their path. A thousand deaths accompanied by utter destruction flash before my eyes.

"Nothing will happen. Leave me alone." I curse the voices in Old Alkelian. "*Solum relinquatis.*"

The voices just laugh again. *You will see. One day.*

Those same images flicker in my mind, again and again, so fast I can hardly tell one from another, accompanied by the wicked laughter of the spirits and the roar of the wind. In the middle of it all, I see my face, eyes burning gold. Scarlet blood splatters across my pale cheeks.

"Shut up!" I shout, digging my nails into my hair and hugging my knees to my chest.

The pictures flash brighter and the wind grows deafening until I think I might really go insane. In the middle of it all, I hear a voice that seems vaguely familiar telling someone named Wolf to stop, that this isn't necessary. I don't understand any of it so I just grit my teeth and shut my eyes. All at once, just as it reaches its worst, it's all gone. Just as fast as it appeared, the images and that sound of the wind and the spirit's voices vanish.

I'm alone on the balcony again.

Gripping the handle of my knife so hard I think it might break, I glance around frantically in case something else happens.

There's nothing. I'm alone as always.

I slump back against the wall, exhausted as the sun rises over the city of Ridgewatch. It looks beautiful, but it's impossible to forget how this city's people threw me out. Putting away my knife, I close my eyes and take a deep breath, pressing the palms of my hands into my eyes and trying to forget the world.

I slip my hand into my pocket, reaching for the warm metal of the coin Senika gave me. Perhaps I should have simply thrown it away, tossed it into the flames of the burning city or the wild waters of the river. But as I stare at the words engraved on its surface, I don't regret keeping it. The words are not in a language I know but I can guess their meaning to be something about protection and warding off evil or bad luck. I can picture the smile on his face when he pressed the coin into my hand, how he said it was to protect me, and I recall how I had nearly turned it down. Now I realize why he gave it to me.

He wished to protect me—but perhaps I'm the one the world needs protecting from.

The next day is the funeral. It's the death of a king and possibly the last of the Kane family, so they've gone all out, decorating the castle and the city in the Kane colours of blue and gold, as well as white. The main funeral service is held in the chapel of Gweneyra, goddess of winter, outside the castle. For a eulogy, a priest rambles on and on about how the deceased will dine in her frozen halls forever in the afterlife. Since it's the funeral of a king, only the nobility has been allowed to attend, all of them dressed in white silk and furs. I'm forced to sit with the rest of the royals, all of them the perfect image of Northern nobility, whereas I fit in just about as well as a wolf in a herd of sheep. I slouch in my seat, restless and tired and wishing I could sleep for several days until the whole nonsense of kings and queens and whatever else is over with and I can go home.

There's yet another fancy dinner after the funeral, this time held in the castle ballroom crowded with all the Northern nobility possible. I spend the night standing awkwardly in the corner while everyone else pretends I don't exist. At a certain point, I stopped caring whether people noticed I was there because even if they see me, they're all far too cowardly to actually say anything. I watch Elias at the head table, smiling and chatting with anyone around, the perfect image of a prince. Would I have been like him if I weren't a Halfblood?

When it becomes acceptably late, I disappear out of the castle and step into the dark, snowy courtyard out front. A fleet of carriages belonging to various houses sit parked and waiting for their turn to head back home. Ours waits right in front of the steps sweeping up to the castle.

"Where's the rest of the family?" the driver says upon seeing me.

"Inside. I'm leaving early." I stuff my hands into the pockets of my jacket, praying he won't make this difficult.

He eyes me suspiciously. "I was instructed not to leave without Lord Clearwater."

"Look, I just want to get out of here and go to bed. Why do people always have to make things so hard for me?" I sigh. It's too cold out here to be standing around talking, and I'm really not in the mood for arguing today.

Thankfully, the man nods toward the carriage door. "Alright, get in. I'll take you back to the manor, but I don't like going against orders."

I shrug as I climb into the carriage. "If anyone asks, you can say I threatened you; they'll believe it."

After a long ride through the bumpy, icy streets and out to the Clearwater Castle, I drag myself up the stairs to my room and faceplant on the bed. Fenix meows a greeting and after a moment I hear her start to get up, shaking her fur and making the spikes all down her back rattle together. She plods over and then jumps up onto the bed which creaks in protest at her weight.

I roll onto my back to look up at the massive cat. "You're so lucky, you can just stay here and sleep all day and night."

Fenix chirps and rubs her chin on my face, getting at least a ton of fur in my mouth. "Hey, you didn't need to do that." I sputter. "Yes, I know you're cute, you don't need to rub it in my face. Literally."

I stand up, yanking my jacket off and throwing it onto the floor near the door. They gave me new, fancy clothing for the funeral—a horrible, pristine white suit and a fur-lined jacket far more comfortable than I'd like to admit. The wardrobe is empty of anything a reasonable person would ever wear. I stuff the ugly suit into the bottom, digging around for something without frills or ruffles. Eventually, I give up and flop back into bed, asleep before my head reaches the pillow.

The next evening, we all gather once again for dinner at the castle, this time in an impressive banquet room with a high, arched ceiling. There's a glorious painting across the ceiling of the goddess Gweneyra of the winter riding a white stag and spreading winter wherever she travels. Delicate snowflakes shimmer in the light of the gold chandeliers. Two long tables sit parallel to each other down the room with a third table for royalty at the end of the grand room. Every seat in the room is occupied by a noble in sparkling white diamonds and silk. Servants in plain white suits serve platters of exquisite-looking food, filling the entire room with the aroma of oranges, chicken, herbs and a dozen other smells I couldn't even name. I sit near the end of the royal table right next to little Rorik. His book's been pried out of his hands for today. Further down, Elenore talks and laughs with some pretty highborn lady I've never seen before. At her side, Robert smiles and listens to their conversation without adding much, like the pitiful lapdog he is. Meanwhile, Elias flirts with some girl who clearly wants nothing but his title while he seems completely enamoured with her. I roll my eyes. Doesn't she realize he's betrothed?

"Pardon me," a small, nervous voice says from next to me and I turn to see a woman with shining pearls in her blond hair smiling at me. "Could you pass the—oh." She stops speaking the instant she realizes who she has spoken to, her eyes suddenly wide and scared. Apparently, she forgot to check who she was seated beside. "I—I'm sorry, I didn't mean to bother you."

I grin and place the butter on the table in front of her without knowing if that was really what she was asking for. "No, don't apologize. I promise I won't hurt you."

Her face turns pink and she turns away from me, ducking behind her lace fan. "Well . . . you see, they always talk about the monstrous Halfblood bastard of Lady Clearwater. They're only rumours but . . . well one can't be too careful, I suppose."

Tilting my head to one side, I ask her. "And how true do the rumours seem to you?"

"I cannot say. It's hardly polite to judge someone so quickly."

"I couldn't agree more, m'lady," I reply kindly before downing the rest of the wine in my glass. "However, it's unwise to believe someone to be other than how their reputation portrays them."

Before she can respond, I stand up, tapping a spoon against the side of my wine glass. In seconds, the crowded room falls silent, all eyes on me. I stare back at them, about to open my mouth to speak when they start talking.

"What's he doing here?" Someone whispers rather unsubtly.

"Are we in danger?" A lady gasps.

"Hey, someone get this freak out of here!" a third person shouts and it's quickly followed by others who evidently all want me gone.

I sigh. Without thinking, I step up onto the table and kick a plate onto the floor where it shatters. Silence falls once again. As I look out at them, I find satisfaction in the mixture of confusion, fury, and dread upon the faces of the gathered crowd. I stand out among the mourners in white even more than usual, with my dark suit and the cape fastened around my shoulders with a silver chain. The pattern of silver gems and thread forms the distinct shape of wings, each feather outlined in shining diamonds. The rings on my hands glitter silver along with the feather-shaped buttons on my jacket and boots. At the sight of the cape, I watch my mother's face wrinkle in fury—and possibly humiliation. The only hint of white is the ribbon at the end of my long braid. Unfaltering, I force myself to hold my chin higher and clench my shaking hands into fists at my sides.

"Listen. You all want me gone, so I'll make this fast." I hold my arms out at my side, speaking loud enough for them all to hear me. "I am Kellin Kane, the bastard of Elenore Clearwater." I turn to face my mother and see her face turn a delightful shade of red at the blunt confirmation of her affair with a man she could never marry. "But I am not meant to be king. In fact, I would much rather get out of here and never return until the day every one of you is sleeping six feet under. Therefore I withdraw my claim from the throne. I want nothing to do with this damned place."

"Then you can leave." Elenore stands, her hands placed on the table sternly. "And I swear, if you ever dare to show your face here again, I will personally end you."

I grin wolfishly. "I would like to see you try."

"You can't just leave!" Elias shouts. "Mother, the law requires all heirs to be present for a new king to be properly chosen. He *must* stay or my reign will never be true. Make him stay!"

Elenore's icy gaze never leaves me. "Kellin Kane is no longer a part of this family. He has withdrawn his claim to the throne so he is no longer needed here. Elias will be king"

"Mother—" Elias starts to protest again but Elenore whirls around, silencing him.

"Enough," she snaps. "No Halfblood has any place here, Elias, regardless of their blood. No Halfblood will ever call themself king so long as I breathe. I will have this monster's head if he dares set foot here again, I promise you that."

"My lady." An old man stands up to object "Mr. Kane is your son and a high-ranking member of the Order. It would be unwise to threaten someone of such a status."

Elenore's face only grows increasingly furious. "That . . . *monster* is not my son. He has not set foot in the North in more than eight years; he abandoned me and my family and as such I will treat him as I wish. And as we all know, Halfbloods are nothing but inhuman and cruel *demons* who should not, under any circumstance, be allowed to hold the power he holds as a member of the Order. It's a joke of an organization that should be removed from power immediately."

The man holds up a thin, wrinkled hand. "My lady, please. We are gathered here to acknowledge each of the heirs to the throne. If any of them wishes to withdraw, they are permitted to do so without threats, blackmail, or pressure. Regardless of your views. Mr. Kane is well within his rights here."

"My views?" Elenore raises her voice, shrill and high-pitched in her venomous anger. "Halfbloods are a blite upon the world but you seem to have forgotten that. He is a monster! I am protecting our kingdom!"

"Hey, I don't want anything to do with you either, bitch," I snap. "Now, I'll be leaving and never coming back." I turn to address the old man. "And it's Ser Kane to you."

The man just stares at me, astounded. My mother grits her teeth and nods. "Yes, I have no doubt you are eager to return to whichever hole of hell you came from. Be gone, demon."

I jump down from the table and walk down the aisle between the two long tables. Everyone watches me with wide eyes, no doubt expecting me to do something crazy or dangerous. I wouldn't be surprised if they thought I wanted nothing but to steal the throne from Elias. But truly, I can't wait to be free of this place. Besides, I have more important matters to attend to—such as saving the world. As I walk, not a single person dares to make even the smallest of sounds, my polished shoes on the smooth, marble floor the only noise to interrupt the silence.

And only when the tall doors fall shut behind me do I finally allow myself to breathe.

It takes about forty-five minutes to get back to Clearwater castle on horseback which means within an hour of leaving Ridgewatch, I'm tiptoeing down to the kitchen to steal some food. I push open the door, and the smell of baked bread, roasted vegetables, and cooked pork hits me, even though no food is currently being cooked in the kitchens. The room is like every other room in this castle, just the way I remember it. As I walk over to the cupboards that take up most of the wall to the left of the door, my eyes land on the back door.

I nearly trip over my own feet.

My breath catches in my throat and I freeze. It's just a door really, but the last time I saw it, I was on the other side, watching it lock me out of my own home.

I rip my eyes away and focus on my task. From here, it's about an eight-day ride to Elview, but that's only if I follow the roads and travel only during the day. Every part of me wants to get as far away from this place as fast as I possibly can, and I don't intend to ever set foot in the North ever again. Besides, it won't stay summer for much longer, and that means the North will be even colder, especially at night. The best way to keep warm is to keep moving.

Ignoring the door behind me, I open the cupboard and start shoving food into the saddlebag in my hand. Fenix lifts her head and tries to steal a bag of flour, but I grab it before she makes a mess all over the floor. Not that I would mind giving these people more problems to deal with. I would just rather sneak out than cause a disaster on my way.

As I slip back up the narrow staircase, it feels like the walls are closing in on me. I lower my head and pull up the fur-lined hood of my cloak, wishing I could shrink inside of it. It almost makes me sad that I can't bring the winged cape with me, but it turns out that much steel and diamonds are far too heavy to be very practical. I've abandoned it for my regular clothes with the addition of the fur cloak. Fenix slinks up the stairs next to me, and I place my hand on her head, forcing myself to look forward and keep walking. Somehow each breath seems more difficult than the last. My boots feel leaden, making it hard to walk.

When I reach the door at the top of the stairs, I reach for the doorknob, but my hand shakes so badly, I can't open it. I close my eyes. Blood, crimson on the white snow, is all I can see. Even inside the castle, the cold creeps into my bones and makes everything hurt so bad I can't move an inch. I remember the way it burned my lungs as I lay there, freezing, barely even alive and unable to do anything about it.

That's the thing I hate the most, being helpless, being trapped and hurt with no way out and no way to fight. I learnt to fight so there would never be a day when I would be helpless ever again so long as I can stay alive. Even now, my fingers curl around the cool handle of one of my daggers. I can still keep fighting.

But there is no way to fight the ghosts of the past.

My eyes snap open and I shove the door open, slamming it shut behind me so hard I think it might break the wooden frame. Fenix yelps as I almost catch her tail in the door.

"Sorry," I mutter. "Let's get out of here."

Every second I spend in this place drains me of life and reminds me of the past that will never go away. It's like swimming while wearing steel around your ankles, not enough to drown you all at once but just enough that if you don't make it to shore before you get tired, you might just fade away into nothing. Each step I take out of here is weighed down by steel, each step harder than the one before. The dark ocean that is this castle threatens to swallow me up.

So I think about the shore, the other side of the water. Elview, my home even if there isn't much more there for me than here. Senika and Jyn, even Taiyo, the few people who don't manage to hate me just for existing.

There's also the matter of the quest we set out on. This whole detour up north has been an inconvenience and we're running low on time already. Who knows how many Halfbloods have fallen before Xethos's Inquisitors while I've been away.

I peek cautiously into the hall around the corner, dreading that someone might see me and raise an alarm. The corridor is deserted but I spot an old compass on display in a glass case. A small plaque gives a short explanation of its significance that I don't read is nailed into the wooden base. I approach the table where the case rests and find that no lock prevents me from opening it. Smirking, I open the case. A compass will help should I get lost or sidetracked. I tuck it into my pocket, glancing over my shoulder once more before continuing on.

As I approach the corner to the grand entrance hall, I hear voices. They're speaking softly, but the words echo across the walls and arched room nonetheless. I duck back around the corner, pressing my back against the green wall and praying they didn't see me.

"... this is for the good of the realm," one voice says. A man's voice, although not one I recognize. "With those bastards dead, Alkelia will prosper and none will stand in our way."

"Naturally," the second person responds, regal and likely highborn. "I believe our fair kingdom has been infested by those beasts for too long now. They may call themselves heroes but Xethos knows they are nothing more than pests. And to use their own against them? Genius, I say."

"So you understand, my lady," the first voice replies. "I say the sooner we rid ourselves of those nasty Halfbloods, the better."

The woman gasps. "You dare to speak their name? In these halls, my lord!"

"I don't fear them." The man sounds exasperated. "If you shy away from the name of your enemy, you are a coward."

"I suppose... But how can we be certain they are not watching our every move? They could be lurking in the shadows right now, waiting to infect our children with that awful, awful disease. I say they are something to be feared."

Her companion sighs. "You have a mother's heart, my lady. I understand that you wish to protect your children. And that is a noble wish, considering they are yet to be born."

"Only a few weeks now . . ."

The pair vanishes out of earshot, their voices fading down the hallway. I frown, waiting in my hiding spot until I can be certain that they are gone. From the sound of it, they both know about Xethos killing Halfbloods, and they spoke of it like common knowledge. If everyone here knows what's happening, I only need to escape more quickly. I yank my hood up over my head and place my hand on Fenix's back as I rush toward the tall doors, throwing them open as if breaking free from prison.

But when I step outside into the fading twilight, it's snowing. I shudder, pausing on the front steps of the castle and taking a moment to steel myself before stepping out into the snow. The cobblestone driveway is covered in a thin dusty layer that crunches under my boots and blows around in all directions, carried by a soft yet cold wind. I pull my hood down further over my eyes until I can barely see anything more than the ground beneath my feet and Fenix's paws padding along beside me.

Outside the stables, I push my hood back just enough to make sure I'm in the right place. A snowflake lands on my nose; I flinch, but it doesn't hurt.

Of course, it doesn't, idiot. I think to myself. *It's just snow and snow can't hurt you.*

But my gloved hands are shaking as I saddle a horse, fumbling with the clasps and buckles of the saddlebag. I tie my spear across the back of the saddle, half-hidden under the saddlebags since it's too awkward to ride with it across my back under my thick cloak. The horse seems nervous to see Fenix, but the cat just dances around in the light snow, more than happy to ignore the horse.

I swing into the saddle and take off, headed far, far away. This place is a prison but now I am free. This time, it is on my own accord.

22

More Beautiful Than the Stars

Kellin

I manage to cut off an extra two days on the trip back to Elview by abandoning the road and cutting across the plains between Ridgewatch and a little town called Odessa then heading straight south to Elview from there. Thankfully, the compass I found still works, otherwise, we would have wasted days running in circles on those plains before I realized we weren't going anywhere.

Several times, I think someone might be following me, soldiers from the North ensuring I keep my promise and leave most likely. The smoke from their fire is like a beacon drawing my attention to their location each night and occasionally, I catch a glimpse of riders on the horizon.

It's late in the afternoon of the sixth day that I ride through the gates of Elview, more relived than I ever thought possible to be back here. A handful of greyish clouds threaten to dump rain on the people walking the streets. The air is full of the smell that always comes with a storm, but it's not enough to hide the bright blue sky. The city has calmed down since the Assembly and fallen back into the normal flow of life, people milling about in closing markets and shutting down their shops for the day. Still, heads turn at the sight of me, a Halfblood riding through the city with a giant, white cat beside me, and a few people even change their direction to avoid me. The bells of the cathedral announce the fifth hour of the afternoon, ringing seventeen times before falling silent again. People pause to count those chimes, listening carefully for them to end so they can continue their various conversations.

The first place I go is the docks where I locate the Iollerian pirate ship easily. Tonight the harbour is quiet and nearly empty of boats, much unlike the last time I was here. It occurs to me as I guide my skittish horse across the creaking wooden dock that I'm not sure why I've even come here instead of going right to the cathedral. That is, until I spot the grand ship named *Vanquisher* is sitting alone and looking rather deserted without a single person visible on the deck. Sitting on a wooden crate beside the ship, Senika is the only person nearby. Apart from the handful of sailors and merchants wandering the docks, the two of us are the only ones around.

The sun is setting, bathing the world in shades of pink and orange and creating long shadows across the dock. In the orange light, Senika's silvery hair looks almost the same colour, and his angular features appear far more sharp and dramatic. Something about him seems strangely beautiful with the sun setting behind him, outlined in pink and orange like the fiery halo of some god or the light of a star, burning bright and brilliant. He doesn't notice me standing there, occupied with sorting through several tattered maps laid out in his lap, until Fenix bounds over to greet him happily. For a moment, he looks at her confused before glancing up to see me walking toward him. I let out a relieved breath I didn't know I was holding.

"You're here." His face lights up with a brilliant grin and he immediately sets aside the pile of old maps. "I thought you would be stuck being King or whatever."

I shrug. "Yeah, I don't think I'll have to worry about that for a very long time. I came right here, but I thought you might have left already."

"What's that supposed to mean?" Senika asks.

"Ah, well you had mentioned that you might be leaving Alkelia soon," I explain. "But you're still here."

He nods. "The Captain is a bit unpredictable, but I think she needs a place to hide out for a while so it doesn't seem like we'll be gone too soon."

"Oh."

"Honestly I could use a while to chill out, too," he continues, ignoring my rather unhelpful comment. "After all that's happened, I mean."

"Did anything happen on the way back here?" I ask, worried.

He pauses momentarily. "Yeah . . . I mean, the Order found us in Blueport. They were looking for you, I think. It sounds like you're kind of important here. You should talk to Jyn, by the way, it seemed like something was bothering him last I saw him."

I shrug. "I guess . . . Did they mention anything about the city, though?"

"No, nothing. But it was Inquisitors we fought so they must know something. Can you ask someone? Surely there was someone who ordered the attack to happen."

"I'll see what I can do but there isn't much I can ask without looking suspicious." Looking up at the tall masts of the ship, I observe, "There's no one around, what have you even been doing this whole time?"

He holds up the maps. "Figuring out where to go next. I tried to explore the city a bit but I keep getting lost and there hasn't really been anyone to show me around."

"I could . . . I could show you the city," I say. "Maybe tomorrow?"

For a moment, I think he might laugh and say that's a ridiculous idea and we have better things to be doing but instead he smiles. "Sure, that sounds great."

"Hey, Senika!" A voice calls from on the boat and a boy with bright, curly red hair appears leaning over the side. "Where did you put those maps?"

"They're right here, don't freak out." Senika holds up the maps and the other boy starts down the gangplank toward us. Fenix meows at him, her tail flicking cheerfully through the air. She wanders over to see him and sniffs his hands like she can't figure out who he is.

"Did we gain a new crewmate?" he asks upon seeing me.

"No, it's Kellin," Senika says, sparing me from the awkwardness of introducing myself. "He's a friend. Um, Kellin this is Gendry, he's the Captain's son."

"I happen to have heard of you." The red-haired pirate grins. "You're the mysterious Halfblood who took Senika to that city place."

Glancing over at Senika, I can't help but wonder what he said about me. ". . . I have never heard of you."

Gendry gives Senika a wilted look. "I've been your friend for all these years and you couldn't even mention my name?"

"Sorry, we had other things to do." Senika shrugs.

Raising an eyebrow skeptically, Gendry asks, "Yeah, like what? I take a few guesses."

Senika's face turns bright red, and I narrow my eyes at the two of them, considering what that might mean. The sun has nearly vanished fully below the horizon and it's starting to darken, a few faint stars visible in the purple of the sky. Clouds are gathering into a potential storm, and I don't want to get caught out in the rain. Besides, I do need to return to the cathedral and explain myself.

"I should go now," I tell them. "I'll see you tomorrow, Butterfly."

"Okay, see you." He almost sounds sad to see me go.

As I walk away, Gendry asks, "What's going on tomorrow?"

Senika responds with silence.

I reach the cathedral just as it starts to rain, the sky dark and cloudy without a moon or stars visible anywhere. As I walk up the shadowy steps, I look at the twisted spires and sharp angles of the cathedral and sigh at the comforting familiarity of it all. Yet, ever since I learned the truth, it doesn't feel the same. In the carvings on the door, all I can see is Xethos, the god who is tearing our kingdom apart from the inside. Now that I know what the Order has been doing all this time, I wonder how I could have been so blind to how its power was built on the blood of others. Enemies of Alkelia.

There are images of Xethos's triumphs during the War of the Gods 600 years ago carved into the door and painted throughout the walls of the cathedral along with a hundred other battles, all of them won by a god I now realize isn't actually great as the legends make him out to be. In all the time I've spent with the Order, I never could have thought any of us were serving a murderer bold enough to kill his own people.

The inside of the cathedral is dark and quiet. Just about everyone has left for the day or gone to bed. A man sits in the pews facing the extravagant gilded pulpit with his head bowed, the words of his prayers too soft to hear. He doesn't look up as Fenix and I slip through the door and across the entryway to the stairs. I walk quietly, careful not to wake anyone as I sneak through the halls. Seconds after I close my door behind me, someone knocks on the wood.

I freeze. If Storm finds out I know the truth, he'll kill me. But it is impossible to keep secrets from someone who can read my mind.

"Kellin?" I let out a breath at the sound of Jyn's voice on the other side. "Is that you?"

I open the door to see him standing there with a worried look on his face. "Yeah, I'm here."

"Gods, I thought I'd never see you again. You have no idea how great it is to see you."

"And you have no idea how good it is to be back here," I say. "That place is . . ."

I don't have to finish the sentence. Jyn nods. "I know. But you're back now and we do need to figure out what our next step is."

"Nothing," I say with finality. "For now, I mean. We can figure it out in a few days, but right now I need to sleep."

He nods but hesitates before speaking again. "Your mother, what did she want?"

"My uncle is dead," I reply bluntly. "Elias will be crowned King of the North in a few days. They needed me there so they could rub in the fact that no one wants me there."

Both of us are silent for a long time then Jyn sighs. "As long as it's all good, I guess."

I expect Jyn to make some joke or do something to take my mind off it, but he doesn't say anything else. Just like Senika said, there has to be something wrong.

"Jyn, what happened?" I ask.

He doesn't meet my eyes, glancing at the floor instead. "When we got back here, Storm demanded to know where you were like he thought you were dead. He even sent a group to drag us back here from Blueport in the middle of the night."

Like he thought I was dead? That only makes sense if he knew where we were and what happened there. Someone could have told him we were there after the order had been given to burn the city, and he didn't want his perfect prodigy dead. When Jyn and Taiyo returned, he would have expected me to be with them, so he naturally assumed I'm dead.

Not across the kingdom with a mother who wants me dead.

"We all made it, though," I point out. "With the connections he has, he must have known where I was."

"That's what I thought too, but from how he acted, it sure didn't seem like it. You should go talk to him tomorrow, though, since we don't know what kind of information he might have."

I yawn. "Not tomorrow, I have plans. I'll go the day after."

Finally, Jyn laughs. "Plans? What kind of plans?" Shrugging, I just tell him, "Nothing too desperate, but I can't miss it."

The next morning arrives full of sunlight, the city alive with noise as people hurry about their days. There isn't a single cloud in the sky after last night's rain. Everything feels bright and happy—unusual for a city where it rains nearly all the time. It's already afternoon by the time I get to the harbour because I didn't feel like waking up early today. Senika and his friend Gendry are sitting on the dock arguing about something. Just like yesterday, they're apparently the only ones here.

"What are you doing?" I ask as I approach.

"Kellin, this is . . . sacrilege or something!" Senika cries. "*He* thinks the sea is green, not blue."

"Is that . . . important?" I question.

"Well, yes of course. The sea is clearly blue." He points at the water and then points west instead, likely realizing the river isn't the sea.

"I didn't say it wasn't blue," Gendry clarifies. "I said it *can be* green."

I consider this for a moment. "He's right, it can be both. Blue and green."

Senika throws his hands into the air. "You're ganging up on me. You were meant to agree with me, Kellin."

Shaking my head, I say, "I don't understand how that can be sacrilege. It has nothing to do with the gods. Oceno is the god of the sea, does that have anything to do with it?"

"Is your head made of stones?" He stands up, collecting his sword belt and strapping it around his hips. "Never mind, where are we going?"

"Uh, where do you want to go?" I haven't the slightest clue where he might want to go even though I've lived here for years.

Gendry smiles mischievously. "Mom was right, you are—"

Senika kicks him in the leg. "No, she wasn't. Shut up."

Gendry switches to a language I assume is Iollerian to ask something then smiles and Senika answers, slightly angrier. The two of them argue for a while then Senika frowns and seems to give up.

"Okay, let's go now." He grabs my arm and drags me away from the ship.

I pry my arm out of his grasp, uncomfortable. "What was that about?"

"It was nothing. Gendry's been my friend for a long time and he's one of only a few people who know that I . . ." He trails off as if he almost said something he shouldn't have, shaking his head.

Today, he left behind his jacket, revealing a red gemstone pendant I hadn't noticed before sparking at the base of his pale throat. He's left the collar of his shirt undone, leaving the line of his collarbone and a sliver of his pale chest exposed. The butterfly tattoo on his neck is more visible too, exposing the fine details inked with a careful hand across the perfect wings to mimic his own butterflies. He wears an earring with a tiny, delicate silver butterfly hanging from a short chain, making me wonder how I didn't realize his power when we first met, considering even the hilt of his sword bears a butterfly.

We end up walking up near the castle to a place called Silverwood Park, where a tangle of paths winds through a small forest of trees with silvery-white bark, hence the name. There are a few ponds of clear—and very much blue—water, and we walk past a group of kids feeding ducks near one of them.

"How long have you lived here?" Senika asks.

"Five years," I say, watching a bird perched up on the branches of a tree. "Before that, I lived in the Black City too."

"You didn't live with your family?" He sounds surprised, but I guess he doesn't know anything about my life.

I shake my head and try to make my words sound casual. "I did until I was nine but then I joined the Order, so I've lived with them for most of my life."

"What's the Order like? I mean I know kind of what they do, but what's it like to grow up with them?"

"You ask so many questions."

"Sorry. How else am I supposed to get to know you?"

"Why do you need to know me?" I say. "Aren't you leaving soon anyway? After that, we'll never see each other again."

"Oh." The word sounds sad, like he didn't realize we only have a short amount of time together. "I guess so."

We walk in silence for a while until he adds, "Would it be strange if I said I would miss you?"

"No."

"No? We barely know each other. Isn't it strange to miss someone you don't know?"

I shake my head. "I don't think so. Sure, we might not know each other very well, but if you want to know someone, maybe you can be sad you never got that chance. And that's kind of like missing someone."

"I guess," he says thoughtfully. "I wish I could stay here longer."

"Why are you here anyway? Other than the whole running away."

He sighs, laughing a little. "The Captain is in trouble with the government and needed a place to get away from them. It's nothing new, she's always up to something."

"What did she do?" I inquire.

"No idea." He shrugs. "Stole something maybe, but if she goes back and they find out she helped me, she'll be charged for assisting a deserter, and I'll be dragged back to the war front."

"She sounds like a strange person."

Senika laughs. "That would be an understatement. Captain Kira is one of the greatest sailors out there, and also an excellent thief and pirate. She's kind of like another mom to me. Her and Emaya."

"Who's Emaya?" Now I'm the one asking too many questions.

"Captain Kira's wife, Gendry's other mom."

I blink, surprised at this. "I thought that was illegal in Iolleria. You know, um . . ."

"Yeah, it is, but no one says no to Kira." There's almost a sad undertone to his words.

"Your family seems nice," I observe, even though it's likely he already knows.

"But they aren't my real family, you know."

I shrug. "You're here with them aren't you? And you just said they're like family. I'm no expert in family, but they seem like family to me."

He stays quiet for a moment then smiles. "If that's how this works, then I've got an awful strange family. Three of them are pirates, one's a baker and the other is a soldier."

To my surprise, I find myself smiling at him, at the way he smiles, at the light in his eye. Senika has a way of living that makes the world feel easier. When I'm with him, the weight of it all vanishes, if only for a moment. I know it sounds strange. A single person can't change my world. But somehow, when here with Senika, I am happy. Usually, I would hate anyone trying to befriend me—they always have ulterior motives. With Senika, there isn't a single part of me that can hate or distrust him.

This is so stupid. In all honesty, it is. How can one boy flip my whole life upside down just by being here?

We spend most of the day wandering aimlessly through the markets of the city, stopping occasionally to admire the scenery or step into a store. Thankfully, he doesn't drag me into another random dance in the streets, but it doesn't feel much like I'm showing him the city with the number of times he yanks me off to somewhere else. We get plenty of strange looks, two Halfbloods, one of us a pirate, but he never seems to mind, so I ignore them. Soon, all that matters is Senika.

For a long time, we talk about everything and nothing all at once. I learned his favourite colour is blue, like the sea, and that he loves the rain on warm summer nights. He enjoys watching the sunset and taking long walks by the sea. He likes the smell of fresh bread because it reminds him of his mother and long talks late at night remind him of his father. We talk all afternoon, but I could listen to him forever.

When the sun has set, we start back to the harbour. On the way there, we pass close to the wall that separates the rich from the poor. On one side, the neighbourhoods are clean and well-kept whereas the other side of the wall is all dirty streets and buildings that no one has bothered to take care of. We stand on the wide, carefully swept street surrounded by beautiful houses and colourful gardens. A tree grows close to the wall, children often climb the tree to get to its top. It's a tiny corner of the city other people never seem to know about, which makes it the perfect spot to run away to.

"Wait, one more thing." I grab the sleeve of Senika's shirt, dragging him over to the tree.

"What are we doing?" he asks.

Instead of answering, I jump up and pull myself onto the lowest branch. When I've perched myself in the tree, I look down.

Senika laughs. "Tree climbing? Really?"

"Come on, just trust me." I reach down to help him up but in a flash of light he shifts and I'm surrounded by butterflies. A moment later, he reappears sitting on the wall with a smile on his face. I roll my eyes and complain, "That's cheating."

"It's not cheating, I just have an advantage." He shrugs as if it was nothing.

I climb to the highest branch, all too aware that he watches every move I make, and when I reach the top, he reaches out his hand. For a brief moment, I hesitate to take it, but when I do, he pulls me up to the top of the wall. The feeling of his skin on mine is strange—warm, but also discomforting. My face feels hot.

From here, we can see nearly all of Elview. The houses stretch out forever, each one like a tiny light beneath the castle and the cathedral ruling over it all. The stone walls encase the city protectively. The sky is perfectly clear with the setting sun casting long shadows and bathing the city in the last of its rays. Three moons rise on the opposite side of the sky.

"This is amazing." Senika sighs.

"You asked to see the city, so here it is, Butterfly." I stand beside him looking out at the scene before us, hands in my pockets.

He smiles. "Turns out you're a pretty good tour guide. I wish I could show you Isondale."

"Isondale?" I look at him sideways. "That's in Iolleria, and I can't get there very easily."

"Well, I know it's in Iolleria. And I wish you could come back with me." He looks up at me, not a hint of joking in his eye.

I shake my head. "My home is Alkelia, as terrible as it is."

"I know. We both have our separate lives in separate places to get back to."

It hurts to think that so soon he will be gone and my life will go back to normal. All I wanted for so long was normal, but now that he's here, I don't want to let him go even if it's the only future ahead of us. This is only temporary, just a sliver of joy in an endless road of loneliness and pain where there is no Senika. He must return home and I have debts to pay to the Order. That is, if either of us survives Xethos.

"You could stay here," I say, the words surprising even me.

Senika looks out at the darkening city. "There is nothing here but death, Kellin. You must realize there is no light in this place. It's slowly tearing itself apart, and soon it will all come crumbling down. One day, there won't be anything here for you to hold onto."

If you're here it's worth it, I think. But I can't say that out loud. He won't miss me when he's gone, not really. I will just keep going with whatever resembles life here. I sit next to him on the wall, our feet dangling over the edge, over the tiled roofs of houses down below. For a long time, neither of us says anything. We sit in perfect silence as the sun sets behind us and the moons rise over Elview.

The light of the moon and the stars are dim compared to that of the sun, and there are more shadows at night. But even now, Senika is beautiful. Here, he seems to shine, silver and white against the black of the night like a star. I have never thought about someone as I do about him, and it makes me worry. If someone finds out, both of us will face consequences. But if he's leaving anyway, what's the harm in one night of peace?

"If I could come to Iolleria, I would," I tell him, breaking the long silence.

"Why do you want to stay here?" Senika asks in response. "What's here that matters so much?"

I shrug. "Nothing. The Order saved my life so I guess I owe them that. Besides, Halfbloods are dying pointlessly and I need to do something about that before I go anywhere."

"That's heroic of you." he says.

Shaking my head, I insist, "I'm not a hero, Senika, I'm just . . . a monster. If I weren't a Halfblood, if I didn't have this terrible power, then I might be a hero, but that's not how it is. I can't be anyone's saviour until I can prove I'm not the monster they think I am."

"You think you need to be perfect." It sounds more like a statement than a question.

"Doesn't everyone? Don't we all wish we were good?"

He shakes his head. "No one can be perfect, Kellin. We're all just messy and flawed in beautiful ways."

"That's not true, Butterfly. There are people who can do everything, people who are smart and kind and strong, and I can never be one of them." I shift my gaze from his face to look at the rooftops below us.

"Who told you that?"

The question catches me off guard. "What?"

"Someone must have convinced you that you can't be beautiful or kind or heroic. So who was it? Because I know they lied."

I don't reply for a while, calculating what to say next, and when I do speak, it's in a soft, quiet voice. "In the North, people believe that Halfbloods are monsters from Gosritaan. It's something they've believed in for so long, no one can change their mind. I was very young when the spirits chose me, but even still, my mother hated me with her whole being. They all saw me as a curse taking root in their family, but I didn't understand why. My mother . . . she was the only one who would say those horrible things to my face; everyone else was too scared I would curse them as I had cursed our family."

I stop, looking over at Senika, worried I said too much.

Instead of the hatred I have grown so used to, I find sadness and concern. "She was wrong. She must be, because you have never seemed like a monster to me. Anyone who would dare to call their own child a monster is evil to their very bones."

"And what if she was right? What if I am a curse or a demon?"

He shrugs. "Then I'm wrong. But there is nothing right about what she did."

For once, I actually believe those words from another person. There is no sign to indicate he's lying, and every part of me wants to believe what he says is true. Because if it isn't, then I'll be believing in the wrong person.

"It feels like you're the first person to believe me," I whisper.

"Well, you aren't lying so I see no reason not to. Besides, you aren't a monster."

Then without thinking, I reach out and take his hand, intertwining our fingers. Neither of us says anything, and I don't look at his face, scared I did something wrong. Before I can let go and run away, he leans his head on my shoulder.

My heart skips a beat while my breath catches, stuck in my throat.

I don't mind his head on my shoulder; in fact, I treasure it. His eyes, closed. Me, too scared to even breathe. He's still holding my hand, and I'm certain I'm blushing red, terrified and ecstatic at the same time.

And at that moment, even if it is just for a moment, all that matters is the boy who can turn into butterflies shining brighter than the stars above. All the death and destruction, all the blood and pain, it all fades away until my world is only what's right in front of me. Senika, the partly human sailor who has the ability to change lives without even realizing it. The boy, more beautiful than the stars and more perfect than anyone else, with his tattoo and eyepatch and silver eyes.

If I could stay here forever, I would.

23

THE WAY OF FATE

SENIKA

Five days pass before we all find ourselves together again, this time in the library of the cathedral. It's a massive space, filled with rows and rows of tall wooden bookshelves and precarious stacks of books that look ready to tip over at any moment. Dusty windows let in rays of dim light and illuminate the dust drifting through the air. It has the feel of a place that's been neglected for too long, like a cave filled with lost treasures or an abandoned house with secrets around every corner. I just hope those secrets aren't as terrible as I think they are.

We've settled ourselves in a dim corner, surrounded by yet more books that Kellin claimed might help us but I'm not sure how. Kellin's cat, Fenix, is sleeping with her head in his lap on the floor since he decided to pick a spot without a single chair. Jyn sits with his back against one of the shelves, flipping through a dusty old tome that looks ready to crumble into bits, and Taiyo stands nearby, sorting through a book whose pages have all fallen out. It feels the same as back in the Black Tower but with much less yelling and knife-throwing.

"Oh gods, I'm late aren't I?" I look up to see a Kyrani girl with dark skin and her hair tied into a thousand tiny braids. Her outfit screams nobility, blue and gold silks adorned with extravagant gold accessories including golden beads braided into her hair.

"Who are you?" I ask without thinking.

The girl smiles. "I am Safiya, Princess of Kyran. You must be Senika, I have heard of you from the others and I can't say how delighted I am to meet you."

I glance over at them, Taiyo glaring at the princess, Jyn setting aside his book and Kellin promptly ignoring her. "Yeah, nice to meet you. Do you know . . . like all the things?"

She laughs politely. "Yes, I have been informed of the great danger of this kingdom. It is a horrible peril and I cannot put in words just how disastrous it is so I will help in any way I can."

"What is our plan anyway?" Jyn asks, turning his attention to Kellin who doesn't bother to look up.

"We need to take down the Order," Kellin says with the same casual tone as someone saying we need to buy more bread. "And the only way to do that is to get rid of Xethos."

"Sounds simple enough," Taiyo says sarcastically. "Why don't you go catch one of the moons in a jar while you're at it?"

Kellin glares at her. "I know it isn't simple, Taiyo. Which is why we are here."

She shakes her head, unconvinced. "Reading books will help us destroy one of the most powerful organizations in the world, if not *the* most powerful? You really have lost your mind."

He holds up the book in his hand. "Books about Xethos. About the War of Gods and Doriak's attempts to destroy Morsevdon. They all talk about Xethos in battle, one of them has to explain some weakness of his."

"These are all ancient." Taiyo sighs.

Taiyo's skepticism confuses me; I think Kellin's plan makes perfect sense.

But she adds, "If they do say anything, it might not be true anymore. The Order has had centuries to perfect their methods and Xethos has had even longer."

"That's not entirely true," Jyn interjects. "As far as we know, they haven't been . . . doing this for very long, maybe only a few months or years, and it's completely different from what they did before, so they might have no idea what they're doing."

Pointing at Jyn, Kellin's eyes light up. "Exactly. But if it turns out this has happened before, then maybe we can find some record of that."

Safiya nods. "I see. So by finding our enemy's weakness, we can go for that rather than hoping we don't hit a brick wall."

"I don't think gods have weaknesses," Taiyo interrupts, ever the pessimist. "And even if he did, it's probably impossible to exploit."

Kellin taps his forehead knowingly. "Everyone is afraid of something, Taiyo. Only the dead are an exception."

Of course. Fear is something even gods aren't immune to. All we need to do is find what he's scared of and we've won. There's only one problem.

"How do we make him afraid?" I ask.

Kellin and Jyn both laugh. "That's what I do, butterfly." Kellin grins at me, a bit of an insane look in his gold eyes. "I can look in people's minds and make them afraid, as long as they're afraid of something. And everyone is afraid."

That makes more sense than it should. I remember the way Alyssa screamed when Kellin attacked her, so much more terrified than she would have been otherwise. He had nearly attacked her before right when we arrived, and all she did was smile. But if the second time he was in her head, she could have been seeing so much more than just a knife. It's a power he can use at any time without anyone knowing—if it weren't for his glowing eyes.

"Oh," is all I say.

"So what do we do?" Taiyo asks. "Break into the Crystal Palace, get in his mind, and threaten him until he says he won't kill anyone else?"

Kellin nods. "Pretty much. And don't say I'm stupid, I already know."

Safiya smiles. "I could get us into the Palace without having to, you know, break in. As long as everyone is fine with pretending to be attending a party."

"What kind of party are you thinking exactly?" Taiyo wonders.

"Well . . . As you may know, I am to marry Elias Clearwater in two week's time," Safiya explains. "One week from now, he will be here for the official wedding announcement. From what I have heard, it will be quite the party, but it will also give a perfect reason for us to be there. Kellin will be expected anyway since it is his family." I don't miss the way Kellin grimaces at the word family. "Jyn can get in with him, and as for you two, you can be my personal guests."

"How do we know Xethos will be there?" Taiyo never seems to run out of questions.

Safiya shrugs. "I expect since it is a union between two kingdoms he will attend, if only for a while. And if he does not, well, we will be in the Palace anyway. Security will be focused on the party itself, not Xethos."

"It can't be that easy," Kellin marvels. "I mean, once we're in, how do we get out of the party? And then how do we find Xethos? A big group of us is too obvious so we would have to split up, but Safiya would be expected to be at the center of attention all night."

"I will stay at the party and serve as a distraction, then," Safiya compromises. "That should give you time to sneak out."

"Then we find Xethos and end this *faex*." Kellin is grinning wickedly and I can almost see the plan forming in his mind. He's amazing, really, to have convinced himself that he is anything other than perfect. "But I think he has some way to block my magic and it could come down to a fight in which case we have no chance. Catch him by surprise and we might stand a chance. So who's in?"

Jyn raises his hand without hesitation, and Taiyo does the same a second later. I look around and try to find some excuse to not launch ourselves into certain death but in the end, I just shake my head and say, "Why not? Let's do this, I suppose."

Preparations begin immediately. Safiya sets to work finding fancy clothing to serve as disguises while Taiyo gathers as much information about the party from the other servants as she can. A few days later, invitations arrive for Kellin and Jyn. True to her word, Safiya manages to get Taiyo and me invited as well. Kellin spends most of his time holed up in the library with those books, searching for any weakness or fear Xethos might have, but time is running out. He hasn't found anything of much use as far as the rest of us can tell. Taiyo even sneaks into the Palace one day to see what she can learn about the layout and places Xethos frequents. She learns that the party will be held in a ballroom overlooking the gardens on the north side of the castle, which is unfortunately far across the complex from the throne room where he seems to spend most of his time.

Three days before the party, Elias Clearwater and the rest of the procession of Northerners arrive. We all watch as they wind their way up to the castle where Xethos himself is waiting to welcome the newly crowned King of the North. Only Kellin stays behind, saying he would rather gouge his eyes out than see them any more than necessary. Safiya watches Elias in sombre silence, dread in her dark eyes, before she slips away to greet him herself. It's clear she wants nothing to do with Elias or Alkelia if she can stay out of it, so I can't understand why she doesn't flee. I suppose being royalty comes with burdens I never expected.

The night before the party, I find Kellin still hiding in the library, nose buried in a leather-bound book. He obviously hasn't slept properly in days with dark circles under his eyes, his voice tired and strained. Sitting under the same window as always, he hasn't bothered to light a lamp, just reading by the light of the three full moons with his eyes glowing faintly in the dark. Just like every other time I've come by, Fenix is sitting by his side, a faithful companion even now when doom seems only hours away. He looks small, almost fragile, here all alone in the dark.

"Kellin?" I speak softly, but my voice still sounds too loud in the perfectly still quiet of the library. "You should go sleep."

He shakes his head. "No, I haven't found anything. I need to keep looking."

"You're going to be exhausted by tomorrow if you stay up," I say. "If you don't have the strength for this, we can't make it happen. We will fail, and thousands will die."

"People will die if I don't go to sleep?" He raises one eyebrow like I said something incredibly stupid. "That sounds like a threat, Butterfly."

I shake my head. "No, not directly, but if we can't pull this off tomorrow, Xethos and the Order will stay in power and our knowledge of them will be exposed. We could die, but we won't be the only ones."

"All the more important that I learn his weakness then," he points out. "I can sleep in the morning or when this is done but now I need an answer."

Sitting on the floor in front of him, I reach out and take the book from his hands. "As long as you can get in his head tomorrow, we can win. And for that, you need your energy. Half-asleep Kellin won't be able to help us nearly as much as awake Kellin can."

He opens his mouth to protest but doesn't say anything. Instead, he leans forward and wraps his arms around me in an awkward hug, his head against my shoulder, eyes closed. I remember a night so long ago when he told me not to touch him, to stay away from him as if my life depended on it. And yet here he is, half asleep in my arms and definitely not telling me to go away. For a moment, I don't know what to do, scared he might leave. But he doesn't, so I hug him back carefully.

"Senika?" he whispers. "I don't want you to go."

I sigh. The Captain has started talking about leaving, going home to Iolleria, and then I will have to choose between my home and Kellin. Ever since I left, I've thought of nothing but going back to the life I used to have, yet now I want nothing more than to stay right here. But I can't stay, I know that. Leaving home and abandoning everything I ever had was the wrong decision, and there's no way to turn back now. At the very least, I owe Mum an explanation. She shouldn't have to think her only child is dead.

I don't want to let him go, I want to stay here with him forever, in a world where no one can hurt us and we can live carefree forever. I don't want to forget him, the soldier who appeared out of nowhere to drag me into this mess. So for now, I hold him close, his arms around my waist and his head on my shoulder.

"Tell me you won't leave, Butterfly," he whispers into my shirt when I don't answer right away, practically begging. "Please."

"I'm not going anywhere," I lie, even though every part of me wants it to be true.

On the morning of the party, I sit on the deck of the ship with Gendry. Kira and Emaya went off to meet with some merchant, and the rest of the crew left on their own adventures for the day, leaving the two of us to watch the ship. I can't seem to stop moving today, restless and fidgety, glancing at the time on the clock tower nearby every two minutes.

"You're plotting something," Gendry observes. He's laying on his back, watching me pace upside down.

"I'm not plotting anything," I tell him. We both speak in Iollerian, foregoing the sharp, jagged-sounding Alkelian language.

"You're definitely plotting. Does it have something to do with him?" He doesn't have to say who "he" is. I talk about Kellin so much, he's practically a permanent part of our conversations.

I consider lying again, but I know how dangerous the upcoming party might be—that I might not return tonight. "We're going to do something incredibly stupid, something that could be straight-up suicide. And if we fail, thousands of people could die, including us."

Gendry flips onto his stomach, holding up one hand. "Hold on. First, can you stop pacing, it's hard to look at you like that. Second, who exactly is 'we' here 'cause I'm guessing it's more than just you two. And third, does it have to do with fighting any gods?"

Sighing, I stop moving and stand awkwardly in the middle of the empty deck with my hands in my pockets. "*We* are me, Kellin and three of his friends. Two of them are the ones who came to the Black Tower with us, the third is a princess from Kyran who is meant to marry the King of the North. And yes, fighting gods is exactly what the plan is."

Gendry groans. "Yup, you're screwed. But how exactly are you going to make this happen?"

"By attending a party," I say just to see how ridiculous it sounds.

He blinks. "You're going to kill a god with a party?"

"Well we aren't going to kill him, we can't do that, just . . . threaten him with fear. And the party is just the way into the Crystal Palace."

"And whose idea was this?"

"Kellin's, mostly."

Gendry stands up, brushing his hands on his pants like they're covered in something. "Right, well I best go tell him not to kill my best friend."

I grab his arm. "I'm not going to die, I swear." It's a lie; that's not something I can promise. "And if I get close, Kellin won't let me die. He won't."

He stares at me, quiet for a moment. Then, "You love him don't you?"

The words are barely more than a whisper but somehow they seem so much louder.

I don't love Kellin, I can't. And yet . . . I love the way he says my name and how he calls me Butterfly. I love how he held my hand that night on the wall, I love how he hugged me like the world was ending just last night. I love his smile when he's up to something, I love that sly look in his eyes when he knows something, I love his feathers even if he thinks they make him a monster, I love that he refuses to cut his hair and I love the scars on his slender hands.

But I don't love him.

"No, that's ridiculous," I say.

Gendry gives me a doubtful look. "And the sea is *purple*. I've heard about nothing but him for weeks now. You look at him like he's the most amazing thing you've ever seen. But soon you'll have to leave and you won't ever see him again, you know that better than anyone. You don't love him? You're the one with a stone head if that's what you think, Senika."

Then he disappears below deck, the door falling shut behind him and leaving me to wonder what this world has come to. Gendry has been my best friend for nearly my whole life; he knows me better than anyone, sometimes even better than I do. But he has to be wrong. In no world can I stay with Kellin, so even if I *did* love him—which I don't—it wouldn't last, and we would both be heartbroken when it fell apart. I said I would stay, and I knew it was a lie before the words even left my mouth but now I wish more than ever for a chance to stay.

When I shift, my vision blurs, splitting into a thousand fragmented perspectives, and my body tingles and then goes numb. In the blink of an eye, a thousand silver butterflies replace my human body. It took me years to get used to the feeling of shifting and even longer to shift so easily, but now it comes just as simple as breathing. The feeling of flying high over the world, nearly invisible if not for the sun glinting off my thousands of wings, is almost intoxicating. I take off, leaving the ship far below and vanishing high above the city. From here, I can see everything from a thousand different angles, each of my butterflies spreading out over the city while all headed for the same place. I don't have a plan of where to go, but as soon as I'm in the air, it's like my wings have a mind of their own. The Crystal Palace.

The Palace glows white and gold in the sunlight, the sky a flawless blue background to the impressive towers and sparkling windows. Guards stand at every entrance, some Halfbloods wearing the red and silver Order uniforms. I've flown past here a hundred times since we made our plan, careful to stay out of sight in case someone figured out what I was doing. By now, all the pieces of our plan are in place and ready for tonight.

All any of us can do now is hope the party goes as it should.

24

MASQUERADE

KELLIN

When night arrives, I pile into a carriage with Jyn, praying this party won't go as horrible as the last one. We had to leave Fenix behind tonight since I was worried she might get hurt or draw too much attention. Our goal is to be as inconspicuous as possible and having a snowcat with us isn't particularly helpful. We arrive right on time and join the trail of people heading into the castle, all dressed in extravagant gowns and suits. It's a masquerade, so everyone is wearing masks to hide their faces, my own covering only my eyes and depicting an owl made of steel feathers.

As we enter the ballroom, I scan the room for Senika, searching for that now-familiar silver hair. I don't know when he and Taiyo might arrive or what they'll be wearing, only that they will be here. Safiya stands across the room, talking to my mother, both dressed in fur-adorned gowns. People crowd the room, some dancing to the music played by a small string band, others hanging near the tables of food, and still more floating about conversing with just about anyone they can.

There are guards at the main entrance and undoubtedly others are blending in with the crowd like we are. None of them stand near the doors to the garden, thankfully leaving us a more than convenient escape. It all seems a little too easy.

"This isn't going to work," I mumble to Jyn.

"It'll be fine. We just need to find a chance to get out of here," he whispers back from under his grey mask.

"Where are Senika and Taiyo?" I ask, still watching the doors for either of them to show up. "They should be here by now, shouldn't they?"

He shakes his head. "Just hold on, they'll be here soon."

We head toward the glass doors leading onto the balcony that wraps around the entire ballroom over the gardens. I swipe a glass of champagne from a masked servant, hoping to look casual even though my mind is alert and my body buzzes with adrenaline. Next to me, I doubt Jyn is doing any better, fidgeting with the dull grey buttons on the sleeves of his coat and frequently adjusting his mask as if it's the most irritating thing he's ever worn.

"Stop freaking out," I tell him.

"You're telling me that?" He smiles. "Try calming down yourself first."

"They're all here," I nod toward where the Clearwater family stands across the room, Safiya's hand on Elias's arm. "Every single one of them is right there."

"Pretend you don't know them." It's a suggestion he's made before, to just imagine they aren't even there, that they don't exist. "Just focus on what we have to do."

I look up at him, clutching the stem of my glass so tight I think it might shatter. "That really doesn't improve anything, you know. We are about to do the most dangerous thing we've ever even thought of."

Nodding nervously, Jyn says, "Yeah, it's fucking terrifying."

And then we both laugh because we know this is stupid, that we could die tonight, that possibly not a single person here will make it out of here. If we mess up, the guards will lock down the palace until every person who aided us is captured and brought to justice. This is treason after all.

I feel exposed without the familiar weight of my weapons, but bringing weapons would be drawing attention to ourselves. Being Halfbloods does enough of that. This whole thing makes me feel rather like an assassin sent to kill some high-ranking guest; it just so happens that the target is an unkillable god and I'm just a kid with magic.

A flash of silver catches my eye. Finally, I spot Senika standing beside the stairs. He's wearing a white tailcoat with white pants and a pale mask covering the left side of his face in place of the eyepatch. White, the colour of death, and everything he wears tonight. His usually messy hair is brushed back from his face and tucked behind his pointed ears. Amidst the sea of colour, he stands out shockingly, turning heads just by being there dressed for a funeral. Across the room, our eyes meet, but he barely reacts while I stand there frozen. By walking down the stairs, he cast a spell that rooted me in place.

I force myself to turn away, ignoring him like I would any other person here.

"I guess we know where *he* is, then," Jyn says, clearly just as shocked as everyone else. "Now we wait for Taiyo."

Nearly an hour passes; she doesn't appear. Jyn keeps checking the time, muttering "she should be here, she should be here," but she never shows up. Across the room, Safiya is doing everything she can to keep Elias's attention elsewhere in an attempt to delay the announcement that will hopefully shift the crowd's focus enough to allow us to slip out. I turn my back to the room to avoid staring at Senika and looking like a fool but I quickly realize that staring at a wall isn't much more helpful. Yet, I don't do anything about it.

"What's going on? She's meant to be here." Jyn looks at the clock for the thousandth time.

"She will be here." I grit my teeth, praying she didn't give up on us after all. "She has to be eventually."

"Safiya won't be able to distract them much longer. We can wait but I doubt—oh . . ." Jyn's voice trails off, and I turn to look at him, but then I see what he's looking at.

Taiyo stands at the top of the stairs dressed in a yellow gown with a long, shimmering cape that trails behind her from her shoulder. The neckline of the dress dips far lower than is acceptable at a party like this and the fabric shows off her elegant figure perfectly, gathering at her hips before spilling to the ground like a waterfall. Glitter covers her bare shoulders and arms, making her glow in the light of the chandeliers. Covering the top half of her face is a golden mask moulded perfectly to her face that hides the scar cutting across her eye, the one I know she hates so much. Her red-brown hair is twisted up onto the top of her head, a handful of curls tumbling down to frame her face. Compared to the girl I'm used to seeing, this Taiyo is almost unrecognizable. Both Jyn and I stare at her as she sweeps down the stairs to join the party.

"She's here," I whisper to Jyn as if the way the room fell silent for the second time tonight wasn't enough of an indication.

"Thanks, I noticed," he replies in a hushed voice.

A moment later I ask, "When should we make our move?"

Jyn casts a final look out at the party. "Whenever you're ready."

With a brisk nod, I turn away and melt into the crowd of people. I head for the doors but wind my way through, passing by the dancers at the center of the party and staying far from my family. When I reach the doors, I look behind me, meeting Senika's eyes again before I disappear into the gardens beyond the glass door. The cool night air hits me like a wave, a sharp change from the heat of the ballroom. Behind me, I hear the click of a spoon against a glass and Safiya begins her speech, words inaudible from outside. Tonight, the sky and the stars are hidden by dark clouds, an ominous sign. I hope they aren't a clue as to what lies ahead of us. I wait at the bottom of the stairs leading into the garden, shivering without a jacket in the cold.

Less than five minutes later, I hear the door open again and Senika appears. Up close, I can see the tiny diamonds on every button of his jacket and the silver patterns embroidered around the collar and hem. He even wears several silver rings on his fingers, one of them inlaid with a perfect white gem that glitters in the light escaping from the glass doors.

"I guess you like to make an entrance," I say with a smile.

He shrugs. "Not on purpose. Safiya said it could work to buy you some time if anything goes wrong. But if blending in was the goal, you missed that mark too."

I feel my face turn red, and suddenly I'm very glad it's so dark. I chose to wear something I can fight in, just in case it came to that—comfortable boots, a plain black shirt and pants. The remarkable parts of my outfit I know I'll have to lose before we find Xethos. A half cape shaped like a dark wing is fastened on my shoulder with an extravagant silver clasp, and on one arm I wear a fancy but rather ineffective arm guard forming sleek feathers. I chose to wear my usual corset with the silver chain of my watch attached to it, and my hair is half done up in a ponytail, tied with a black ribbon, while the rest falls down my back.

"I'll stand out no matter what I wear," I point out. "Did you see if the others were headed this way?" I add after a moment.

"No, but I'm sure they'll be here soon," he says.

As if on cue, Jyn comes around the corner, likely having exited from a different door to seem less suspicious. He glances over his shoulder to make sure no one followed him. "Taiyo should be here soon. We should get ready to move."

Beside the stairs and underneath some bushes, we find the spot where Taiyo stashed our weapons earlier today. I had been reluctant to hand over my spear but there wasn't really another way to get weapons into the castle since we couldn't bring them to the party. Jyn's bow, along with a quiver of arrows fletched with grey feathers, hides there too next to Senika's silver sword. I unclasp my cape and let it fall to the ground, leaving it there in a pile of fabric. As we gather our weapons, Taiyo hurries down the stairs to meet us.

"There, we're all out." She smiles beneath her gold mask. "I didn't mean to be late, but we're all here now, so it isn't much of a problem."

"You look amazing," Jyn tells her, nearly breathless.

She tucks a stray piece of hair behind her ear. "It's nothing much. Honestly."

"We better get moving," I interrupt. "We don't have much time."

Jyn nods. "Right, what's the plan?"

I point at him. "You and I will head to the throne room. Senika and Taiyo, you two search the other places you found." I hand Senika a tiny flash bomb I stole from the armoury at the cathedral. "If you find anything, set that off and we'll find you."

"What about you?" he asks, tucking the bomb into his pocket.

"As soon as we find him, I'll end this," I assure him, although I'm not very confident in this plan. There are too many unknowns, and so far it's all been much, much easier than it should have been. We got in and out of the ballroom without arising any suspicions, and now all we need to do is locate Xethos since he didn't show up at the party.

Unless we left too soon.

"Then we get out of here before anyone figures us out," Senika adds.

I hesitate. Honestly, I hadn't planned an escape; there's no way we make it out of here alive. "Right. I'll see you on the other side, butterfly."

We part ways, Jyn and I heading through the gardens toward the throne room while Senika and Taiyo head toward the east wing to start their search as well. My palms are sweaty, and I keep looking behind us to make sure we aren't being followed, but every time, it's just the empty garden. I tell myself to relax, that everything will work out, yet as hard as I try, I can't shake the feeling that we won't succeed.

When we near the throne room, we find a door leading into the castle and slip inside to find ourselves in a bedroom. It's dark, but I can see the shape of a massive bed and a chair in front of a fireplace. The room is vacant and cold, but it still feels like we've intruded on someone's personal space.

Jyn pauses, looking behind us and making sure the hall is empty.

"Come on, we need to keep moving." It feels like we're so close but I can't feel anyone nearby, which is unsettling.

"Yeah, I'm coming," he says hesitantly.

At that moment, two guards appear from around the corner. One of them shouts, alerting anyone else nearby that we're here. Both are dressed in gold armour that nearly glows under the light of the glass chandelier and marks them as Xethos's personal guards. I curse under my breath, tightening my grip on my spear and preparing for a fight.

"Freeze!" the second guard shouts. "You are not to be in this wing; we have grounds to arrest you."

"As soon as they get close," Jyn whispers, "you get out of here. Find Xethos and end this. I can keep these guys occupied until the others get here."

This catches me off guard. "What? No, I can't go in there alone. And I'm not leaving you here, either."

But it's far too late to come up with any better plan. The guards are already drawing close, and both of their swords are drawn. "We'll give you one chance," one of them orders. "Lay down your weapons and put your hands above your head."

"Sorry," I retort. "I can't do that."

Jyn's arrow sticks into the wall directly behind their heads, and he instantly notches another, ready to fire. I lunge forward, stabbing at the gap in one of their helmets, right at his eyes. The man deflects with his sword but leaves his side wide open. I spin my weapon to smash the spiked end of it into his knee. He stumbles and catches himself against the wall but I'm on him again before he can recover. I pin him there with my forearm across his chest, yank the helmet off his head, and punch him square in the nose, my rings breaking his skin and leaving rivulets of crimson running down his face.

"Run!" Jyn shouts. I glance over my shoulder to see him slashing at the other guard with the blades on one end of his bow.

I yank off my mask and smack the guard across the face again with its metal, beak-like nosepiece. The man slumps to the ground, half unconscious when I release him, but I don't wait around. Instead, I turn and sprint away, leaving Jyn to fight alone and praying this works out.

25

OF CATS AND SUNLIGHT

FENIX

I lay on my back, soaking up the sunlight streaming through the window. Eyes closed, I stretch myself out, flicking my tail happily. Next to me, The Kid is busy doing something and ignoring me, but I don't mind much as long as he's here. There are stacks of musty-smelling books everywhere and the air is filled with dust that makes me sneeze. A while ago, the other one, the new one with silver hair, and the fancy one came by to say something, but The Kid didn't want to leave.

At the sound of flapping wings outside the open window, I look up to see a bird perched on the branch of the tree just beyond my reach. I chirp at it, telling it to stay out of here. The Kid reaches over and pats my head, saying something in his human language. I can never understand what he says, but sometimes I understand the meaning by the tone of his voice.

He looks away from me when another one, the person who reminds me of sunlight, enters the room. She says something to him and he nods, saying something else in a tired voice then Sunlight replies and leaves again. It's been like that for a few days, The Kid hiding in the book room while every once and a while one of the other ones will come and find him. Sometimes we leave with the other one, but mostly we just stay here.

I think something is changing with him. There are new ones around, and we spend less time with the scary one or outside in the air. The one who comes the most is the star one who smells like the sea and bugs all at once and The Kid seems to like it the best when he comes to find us until Star starts telling him to do things he doesn't want to do. The blue one also visits a lot, mostly to help with looking at the musty books The Kid seems to like so much. Something is off about The Blue One, a certain smell that tells me something isn't right, close to the smell of fear—but something else as well.

I stand up, stretch, then lay down with my chin on The Kid's arm, blinking at him intently. He says something, tapping my nose with one finger then goes back to looking at the books, turning the old pages every once and a while.

He doesn't move again for a long time, so I stay there next to him. But all of a sudden, when I'm nearly asleep, he stands up, throwing the book he was so interested in onto the floor. He says something that sounds angry, so I meow back and he smiles a little bit, bending down to pet my ears again. If he knows I can't understand him, he doesn't show it, just talking away in incoherent noises. Then he walks over to the door and I bounce after him, out into the cold hall of the stoney building.

26

DOWNFALL

KELLIN

The doors of the throne room are made of solid gold. My heart pounds, frantic after the fight, and it feels surreal to be standing here even if Xethos might not be in there. But someone is on the other side of this door, and whoever it is, they're afraid.

I brace myself, preparing for whatever lies beyond, then shove the doors open. Sure enough, Xethos stands before his throne, but to my surprise, my mother stands beside him, her hands tied behind her back. She's blindfolded as well, clearly not here by her own choice. The second I enter the room, I instinctively reach for both their minds, trying to gain some power over them. I see Elenore's fear of dying, of losing her power and dignity, but I can't see anything in Xethos's mind. It's like smashing into a brick wall face first.

I gasp and stumble, sudden pain erupting behind my eyes.

"Ah, there you are," Xethos says as the doors slam shut behind me. "We were starting to wonder when you arrive."

"You knew I was coming?" I stare at the two of them, only slightly horrified.

"Of course," Xethos grins wickedly. "I have expected this day for a long time."

"I won't turn around and pretend this isn't happening," I growl, pointing my spear toward Xethos. "You can't just kill the ones *you* created to protect your people. Now let her go, and maybe I won't tear this whole place down."

The god just laughs. "I created Halfbloods, I can get rid of them. You are nothing but an annoyance, Kellin Kane, I will do what I want and you will perish alongside all your silly friends. And it starts with her."

He turns to where my mother stands blindfolded near the dias. She tilts her head at the sound of his approach but doesn't say anything. I watch in horror as Xethos draws his glowing sword and leans toward her.

"I think"—he speaks as if he is making a very important decision—"that this is the woman who caused you all this pain. You do remember how she tried to kill you? So if that happens to be the case, then *why* would you want me to spare her? I will give you one chance, bastard. Take your blade and kill her, end her life now and put an end to all your suffering. If you can do this one thing, I will show you mercy."

I stand frozen and shocked. Kill her? I can't do that. Sure, she abused me, tried to kill me and abandoned me, but for some reason, I can't make myself move, to lift my blade and kill my own mother. If I kill her, I will be a murderer—a far, far worse fate than letting her live. It would prove that I am a monster.

My head spins, and for a moment the world feels far away and distant. There's something about Xethos that's different from the last time I met him. Just being here is exhausting. It's the same feeling as when I use my power too much, even though I've hardly used it since arriving at the party. I wipe sweat from my brow and push my hair out of my face, wishing I had thought to tie it up earlier.

Then my mother says something I know I should have expected. "Don't do it, fool. My life is worth far more than yours."

Her words make Xethos grin. "Listen to her. Surely this makes you angry, surely you want to kill her. I know you are capable of this, you have killed before. Now do it!" He yanks the blindfold away from her face, revealing her terrified eyes.

Hesitantly, I step forward, gritting my teeth and lifting my spear. I can kill her. All I have to do is this one act, then maybe my own death won't be quite so painful. It should be easy. But it isn't. And before long, I've spent too much time thinking and it's far too late.

Xethos spins his sword in his hand and stabs it straight through my mother's stomach. Her eyes go wide and blood drips from her mouth, a small gasp escaping her lips. I watch her fall to the ground, red blood pooling beneath her.

Xethos laughs again.

I rush forward, abandoning my spear on the ground and reaching out for my mother. Her breath is ragged and painful. I'm helpless. If I can't save her, what good is there in continuing to fight? I am not a hero; I am a monster.

"You're useless . . ." she mutters, quiet yet stern. "Should've . . . killed you . . . while I could."

I stare at her as her eyes turn glassy and her body goes still. A single tear creeps down my cheek. I shouldn't be sad; she never cared if I lived or died. *She* was the monster. Even now, her last words voiced regret that I ever lived. Still . . . I wish I could have been strong enough to save her. I stagger to my feet, reaching for my spear again.

"You should be thanking me," Xethos says. "After all, she was the source of all the pain you've ever felt. And now . . ." He spreads his hands wide. "Now you are free. Only when humans are free, do they know who they really are. Perhaps I will give you one more chance. In fact, I will offer you a contract. You can stay and work for me, my perfect soldier. I could give you everything you could ever want if you just do what I ask of you. You may find that in time, the killing will become easy."

"You are a monster." My voice is so calm and cold, it scares even me. "I will *never* bow to you."

The whole plan has gone out the window. Even if I wanted to, I can't get in his head. So it was a worthless plan anyway.

"I would like to see you try, mortal. I am a *god* and you are no more than a tiny, insignificant insect to me. The life of a mortal means nothing to me but I will admit you have been a pest that I must be rid of."

"I might not be able to kill you, but I can try." I step forward, knowing this could be the end of all this right here. "And if I can't do it maybe I can start something and someone else can be stronger and more worthy of this than me."

The god glares at me, eyes like embers. "No mortal can kill me. I am the god of victory, I will never lose, I *cannot* lose. You are a fool to think you can do anything."

I laugh, realizing how completely strange and almost hilarious our conversation is. "I've spent my whole life being told I'm a fool. All they talk about is how useless and strange I am. It means nothing anymore. All of it, it's pointless."

Suddenly, I stumble again, the world spinning around me. Faintly, I hear Xethos chuckle, mocking me in one way or another, probably calling me weak. But all sound fades to a distant hum. I reach out, grasping for anything I can use against him but cold washes over me when I find nothing.

Of all things in this world, Xethos isn't afraid of any of them.

Mind spinning, I stagger and fall to one knee, catching myself before I faceplant on the marble floor. There's a sudden buzzing in my ear and it takes a moment before I even notice just how exhausted I am. Just being in the presence of a god is excruciating. My body is hot and cold all at once, and time moves at a strange pace, making it hard to breathe.

"What's wrong?" Xethos distantly taunts me, sounding miles away. "Can't live up to the threats? What a shame . . ."

With a bang, the world snaps back to normal. I turn my head to see the doors of the massive hall thrown open with Senika and Jyn standing in the doorway. Jyn is bleeding from a gash in his arm, but he still holds his bow tightly. Senika looks like he just got dragged through the ocean and then across a field of rocks, dripping all over the floor with his clothing torn and bloody from a hundred tiny cuts. My eyes go wide when I see them. They weren't supposed to come after me or even know where I am. But of course, Jyn *would* follow me as quickly as possible.

"Kellin!" Senika calls out, rushing over to where I kneel on the ground. He stands beside me protectively and glares at Xethos. In his hand, the edge of his sword is bloody. "What did you do to him?"

"Wait," Jyn says. "What happened here?" When I look at him, I see his gaze is fixed on the body of my mother, dead in a pool of her own blood that stains the smooth, polished floor crimson.

"He killed her," I explain cooly, still stunned and feeling detached from the world in front of me. "He killed her, he killed her and . . . I couldn't save her, I should have saved her. Useless. *Occidit eam.*"

"You are weak." Xethos smirks, folding his hands behind his back. He watches the three of us with a condescending gaze. "These *friends* of yours will only slow you down. Be rid of them. Join me, and I can show you true power."

"Let's get out of here," Senika says, reaching out to me. "Before it's too late."

"No," I force myself to get to my feet and repeat the same words, numb. "He *killed* her. He killed them all. And *I'm* going to kill *him*."

In the blink of an eye, I dart forward, past Senika and straight toward Xethos. He throws his sword up in front of him, blocking my spear at the last second. My vision tunnels in on him, and I barely catch my balance from the first attack before I lash out again. Sword a brilliant arc of light, Xethos is a step ahead of me no matter what I do. Each step I take, he matches, and every time I strike, he blocks perfectly. I duck under his sword and stab at his leg, only to be met by the very same sword yet again. I leap back to avoid being skewered. He slashes at my shoulder and I stumble as I step to the side. Seeing that brief moment where I falter, the god feints a blow at my side but switches at the last second to knock my legs out from under me. I nearly lose my grip on my spear as I fall to the ground and roll a few feet away from him.

Between laboured breaths, I watch Xethos approach me with slow, careful steps, the tip of his sword trailing on the floor, causing sparks to leap from where it scratches the stones. When he stops, he raises his sword, preparing to kill me once and for all. I close my eyes, ready for the end but it never comes.

Xethos grunts in pain. I look up to see an arrow protruding from his shoulder. Jyn stands across the room, arm still drawn back.

"Okay, *now* we go." Senika appears beside me, grabbing my arm and yanking me to my feet. I trip over my shoes and he barely catches me from falling again.

Jyn throws open the heavy doors and I'm dragged out into the hall. Time seems to skip forward and suddenly we stand in the street outside of the castle. The air is shockingly cold, but it seems to clear my head a little. Darkness has closed in around the city, covering it in the thick blanket of night. Everything seems so quiet compared to inside the palace. A cold wind ruffles my hair, carrying the scent of the sea with it. When we reach the road winding down from the steps of the palace to the city, Jyn stops and looks around.

"We should wait here," he says, sitting down at the side of the empty road. "Safiya and Taiyo will be here soon."

I walk over to him and point out, "You're hurt."

He shrugs. "It's not that bad, only a scratch. I'll be fine."

"You should do something about it."

"I'll be fine."

"Jyn, you're bleeding all over the road, stop saying you're fine and let me help," I insist. "How difficult does this need to be?"

He looks at me with sad eyes and then sighs. "Fine."

I crouch beside him to look at the cut across his upper arm, which is definitely more than just a scratch. "It's from a knife," I observe. "What happened?"

"There were more guards," he says, looking at the road instead of at me. "We had to fight to get to you."

I shake my head. "You didn't need to come after me, I was doing alright on my own."

"Kellin, what did he try to make you do?"

I stand up and turn away, wanting to avoid this conversation but he grabs my arm.

"Hey, Kellin. I'm sorry."

"Sorry for what? For making me leave you to die? For letting me come here? Or maybe for him killing my mother? Or it is something else? There's a lot to apologize for, Jyn, so don't bother trying." I yank my arm away from him, walk to the stone barrier that separates the road from the cliff, and stare down at the dark river far below.

After all that has happened, the night seems too peaceful. I can't relax. We're still too close to Xethos, but neither Senika nor Jyn looks ready to leave. My whole body is on fire, like I'm still caught up in that fight, and I don't think I can sit still. I try to relax, closing my eyes and standing very still, but I quickly realize relaxing isn't something I can do right now. So I walk over to where Senika is standing further down the road.

"What are you doing?" I ask, staring into the darkness that he seems so fixated with.

"Taiyo said she would find Safiya and then come right here, but they aren't here yet." He doesn't look at me when he speaks.

"Then we should wait for them." I glance over my shoulder at the castle up the hill. "They'll be here. They'll be here."

"He killed her."

I look at Senika in shock.

"That's what you kept saying," he adds. "I thought you hated her."

I look at the ground, clenching my hands into fists. "I know. She . . . I should be *happy* but for some reason, I'm just mad. And sad," I admit. Hastily, I wipe the tears from my eyes.

"Kellin." He turns to look at me.

I hope he can't see me crying in the dark but I know he can from the gentleness of his voice.

"She was your mother, it's normal to be sad. You're allowed to cry."

I shake my head frantically. "No, you don't know what happened. She . . . she abandoned me. She wanted me to die. She tried to *kill* me, Butterfly. I shouldn't be sad. All her existence ever brought was pain, I *can't* cry for her."

Then just like that, the tears all come at once until my vision blurs and I'm standing there in the middle of the road leading up to the palace sobbing. Senika reaches out and pulls me into a hug and I just let him hold me there while he whispers my name over and over and over. And in my head, the voices constantly murmur, never ceasing. Tonight under the stars, they seem louder and more cruel than usual in a chorus of hurt and sorrow that echoes my own pain.

And the whole time the same words float through my mind. I couldn't save her, I couldn't save her, I couldn't save her.

I am a monster.

27

ALONE

KELLIN

I wake up alone with sunlight streaming in through the open window. The curtains blow gently in the breeze. Near the window, Fenix is still peacefully asleep with her tail wrapped around her paws. It occasionally flicks her nose. Any other morning, the scene would make me smile, but now I can't get the events of yesterday out of my head.

I stand up to close to the window. Even though the sky is bright blue, dark storm clouds rise on the horizon. From here, the castle is visible, a collection of gold and white towers that loom over the city. It's meant to be beautiful, but I can only think about why it still stands. Because a tyrant rules.

This kingdom is built on blood.

My memory of last night is blurry, as if someone erased all the fine details from my brain. Yet I can clearly see my mother dead on a marble floor, her blood red against the white stone. I remember how it felt like that sword hit me instead. I was the one dying, not her. Maybe I should have died there, maybe I should have died many times many years ago. But for some reason, I'm still standing on my feet while others fall at the hand of a god I cannot stop. I'm watching the world burn around me.

Fenix yawns as I step around her to collapse back into bed, burying my head under the pillow and wishing for a redo on the past month and a half. Instead, I just lay there for hours as the sun creeps higher into the sky and the clouds draw closer and closer. At some point, Fenix curls up beside me with her head next to mine and falls asleep. I close my eyes and try to sleep, to just disappear from this horrible world, but it never comes. Instead, I lay there nearly all day until, finally, there's a knock at my door.

I don't get up to answer it. If it's Jyn, he won't even bother waiting for me to open the door. It wouldn't be anyone else, so I just lay there. If it is Jyn, I don't want to hear what he has to say. But the door never opens.

"Kellin?" To my surprise, it's Senika's voice I hear. "Can I come in?"

I don't answer, but the door opens anyway. Not really wanting to talk, I close my eyes and pretend to be asleep.

"Kellin," Senika says. "How long are you going to stay in bed?"

I roll over and glare at him. "Why are you here?"

He shrugs. "I don't really know. I guess . . . I wanted to see if you're okay."

"Is that a rhetorical question?"

"Well, no not really."

"I couldn't save her," I whisper, almost scared of how he might react. "How can I think I could be any good if I can't even save one person?"

But he just nods and tells me, "It's not your fault. There are some things we can never hope to control."

I turn away from him and mumble, "I just want to be alone."

"Okay, I'll go then."

Just as I hear him start to leave, I say, "If you want . . . you can stay."

"Are you sure? I can go if you want to be alone." Even as he says it, I know he won't go. Instead, he steps through the piles of clutter—mostly books and clothing—on my floor to sit next to me on the bed.

"When you said you would stay . . . the other day . . ." I say, slowly. "That was a lie, wasn't it?"

He doesn't answer for a long time. Then: "You know I have to go home eventually. I can't stay here. I'm sorry."

"You should go then," I say, even if I want him to stay more than anything else. "I . . . I think it would be better for you to go. You'll just get hurt if you stay here."

"No that's not why I need to leave. I need to get back to Mum and . . . I need to fix the mess I made by running away."

I roll over to look at him. "You say that like it's your fault. Which it isn't. You didn't want to fight, so you left. You needed time, so you found a way to get that time."

He shakes his head. "No, I shouldn't have run away at all. I was a coward. I need to go make that right again."

I nod. "So go. And once this is all over, I will come to find you, I promise. If I survive."

"I don't want to leave in the middle of this," he protests.

"Then don't. Go whenever you feel is right and I'll find you one day."

With a small sigh, he smiles slightly. "You sure know how to be convincing. So fine, when the Captain wants to go, I will go with her, but only as long as you swear you will find me again one day."

"If I survive," I add.

"No, you have to make it out alive. Otherwise, I'm staying here and making sure you live, okay?"

I raise my eyebrow. "So if I say I won't survive, you'll stay? Well, in that case, I won't be making it out of there, butterfly."

Senika laughs and it makes me smile to see him happy. "I would rather you didn't die, whether I'm here or not. That way I can show you Iolleria and you can get out of here."

"Then one day I'll find you again."

"Kellin . . . ?" He says nervously and shifts his gaze to the floor. "I don't think I have very much time."

"What does that mean?" I narrow my eyes in confusion.

"You know my home was burned down when I was young." The tone of his voice is distant, almost as if he is telling me something that happened to someone else. "The smoke damaged my lungs, and they think I have fifteen years left to live at best. I was the only one to survive but I'm still going to die."

"No," I blurt immediately without knowing what I can do about this. "You can't die."

"Fifteen years," he repeats, tears welling in his eyes. "That's all I have left, Kellin."

Death doesn't scare me. Not my own death, at least. But when it's someone else facing that fate, I have to change it. Those Halfbloods Xethos killed all deserved to live—or at least a chance. Senika deserves a chance too. He doesn't deserve to die young after living his whole life sick and waiting for death to take him; that's far too unfair. I can't allow it. But here I am again. Another person is going to die while I am unable to prevent it.

For a while, neither of us says anything, but I don't mind. I like having him here, even if it is only for a short time, even if one day I will have to stop pretending this can last. It isn't awkward to sit here in silence. It's rather comfortable. Words don't need to be spoken. Rain falls outside, and I drift in and out of sleep, still exhausted from last night.

At some point, I wake up to Senika asleep beside me, rain pounding on the roof. The world is quiet and far away; I don't have the strength to hate it. I watch him lying there next to Fenix, both of them fast asleep and deep in dreams. Fenix is taking up far more of the bed than she should be allowed to, sandwiched between us. Senika looks like an angel, perhaps descended for a while to rest here, and I reach out to brush a bit of hair out of his face, my fingers grazing his skin to make sure he's real. I never used to believe a person could be as beautiful and kind. I never had a reason to believe it.

But I was wrong.

And, somehow, that perfect angel chose me. He chose to be here, and he wants to stay. He chose to be here, even knowing what I can do, how much I can hurt him. Somehow, he wants to stay.

I wish I could capture this moment in a bottle and keep it forever.

"You know monsters don't care about people?" The question catches me off guard, but he doesn't even open his eye to look at me.

"Wha . . . ? I thought you were asleep."

He smiles. "I was, but now I'm not. It's true, though. Monsters are incapable of caring of loving anyone; it's what makes them monsters. They feel no sympathy. They don't know kindness. That's how I know you aren't a monster—you are none of those things. You want to save people, and you care when they die. You don't want to hurt anyone. You protect them instead, even if it tears you apart."

A single tear drips down my cheek. "But I can't save them. I could care more than anyone has ever cared, and I still won't ever be strong enough to do anything about it." My voice is hardly more than a whisper. "You can't say those things and not know anything that's happened."

"You don't have to tell me." He takes my hand carefully in his and examines the scars across my skin. "There is enough of the story right here for me to know that someone hurt you badly enough that you can't even talk about it. But if you want to tell me, I will listen. Promise. And I do mean it, that's a promise I can keep."

"It's better to not talk about it. Then I can pretend it didn't happen, it's easier that way."

He nods. "I know but . . . you should know that you don't have to be perfect."

"Everyone else is perfect," I say, but what I really want to say is that he's perfect.

"Not all of us."

I close my eyes and don't say anything for a long time. It feels strange to have let another person in like this, to not push him away like everyone else and instead to ask him to stay here. But if he leaves, I will be alone. Truly alone again. Jyn won't be there this time. I will only have myself.

"What do we do?" I ask. "Our plan failed, and now Xethos knows everything. What happens next?"

"I don't know," Senika admits. "You really couldn't find anything to use against him?"

I shake my head, sitting up to hug my knees to my chest. "It was terrible. His head was just . . . empty. There's nothing Xethos is afraid of. I can't do anything."

He asks, "Isn't that impossible? Didn't you say the only ones who don't feel fear are the dead?"

And that changes everything. I said it myself, even gods aren't immune to fear, but the dead are. The only way for Xethos to have no fear is if he's dead. It sounds impossible, but if there were a necromancer strong enough, they could resurrect him. They could rule all of Alkelia through him.

I stare at Senika. "You are a genius."

"Uh, thanks, but I don't follow." He stares back at me, confusion clear on his face.

"Xethos is dead," I say blankly.

He stares at me for a moment longer, waiting for a real explanation. "You do realize that makes no sense at all, right?"

"If the dead feel no fear, that's the only way Xethos could completely block out my power. Unless he has some kind of magic-blocking ability that's never been heard of, but that would be ridiculous. When I looked in his mind, I couldn't see anything at all, not even a tiny little fear of heights. He has to be completely immune to fear, and the only way to do that is to die."

Senika waves his hands in front of his face. "Wait, wait, wait. Slow down. We literally saw him *last night*. If he's dead, he's the best-looking corpse I've ever seen."

I frown. "Are you saying he's hot?"

He laughs, smiling and shaking his head. "No, but that's not the point. How can he be dead and still, you know, *walk*?"

"Necromancy."

The door slams open so fast, it nearly falls off its hinges.

"What have you done?" The High Priest stands in the doorway of my room, eyes burning with fury.

I scramble to my feet reaching for the nearest weapon—my spear, leaning against the wall. Fenix looks up, bleary-eyed, at Storm.

He crosses the room in a few long strides, blood-red robes swishing at his feet. "First, you vanish and I learn that you went off to *The Black Tower*, of all places. And now, I find out that you *attacked* Xethos. I could have you hung for any number of crimes."

"What's going on?" Senika asks, still sitting on the edge of my bed. He glances between Storm and me.

"Truthfully, you should hang with him, foreigner." Storm's ice-cold gaze turns to Senika. "An attack against our god is a crime worthy of death but your crimes are far greater, Kane. I can't count how many times I've let you get away with these tricks of yours but I swear, this is the end for you."

"So you knew all along, then?" I ask. I reach for his mind, praying that I can keep him talking long enough to break down the steel walls that defend his consciousness. "You knew he was killing Halfbloods?"

"I don't see why it matters if I did. Kellin Kane, you are under arrest for treason, heresy, trespassing, murder, theft and insurrection." He steps aside and armed guards flood into the room.

Fenix leaps at them, fangs bared. Cursing under my breath, I grab Senika's arm. Before they can reach us, I turn and leap through the window, arms raised to protect my face and glass shattering around me. A blinding flash of light surrounds me as Senika's body explodes into a hundred tiny butterflies.

The arched roof of the entryway rushes up toward me, more than a story below the window. I try to roll when I land but my feet skid on the slopped tiles and I catch my balance seconds before I fall. From above, I hear Storm shouting for someone to stop us. Senika's butterflies surround me, light glancing off each of their wings. I nod and swing my legs over the edge of the roof, holding onto the shingles as I dangle two stories above the road. I barely manage to find a foothold in the gap between two stones before my fingers slip. My fingers are bloody and aching by the time I reach the bottom, dropping the last two feet to the ground.

I stumble, catching myself before I faceplant on the road. My ankle protests when I try to put weight on it. Fragments of glass have embedded themselves in my arms, thankfully lodged in my arm guards rather than my skin. Senika reappears beside me, looking dazed.

"You're insane," he observes.

I shrug. "Yeah, but I got us out." Glancing back up at the broken window, I add, "Now, we better get out of here before they catch up."

People quickly move aside, clearing the way for us. I almost want to tell them to act as if we aren't here. The extra attention will only point the Order in our direction. I walk as fast as I can, limping slightly. Storm won't hesitate to send people after us and soon, the entire city will be crawling with people who want us rotting in prison. We have to get away as fast as we can.

"What about Fenix?" Senika asks, hurrying to keep up with me as we wind through the labyrinthine streets.

"She'll catch up," I tell him. "She always does."

But that's only if Storm lets her escape the cathedral. As far as I know, he can't read the minds of animals but it doesn't take a mind reader to know that Fenix will follow me. Nearly her whole life, Fenix has followed me, never far from my side, and our lives are intrinsically intertwined. I can only imagine how Storm would dare to use that against us.

I turn into a narrow alleyway, leaning on the wall. My ankle is screaming at me but we have to keep moving unless we want to get caught. Closing my eyes, I calm my breathing and scan the area for a mind I recognize. The spirits echo my worries in voices that ebb and flow like the tide. Thankfully, I can't sense any fear that points to the presence of the Order here. We're safe for now but that won't last long.

"Are you okay?" Senika asks. I open my eyes to see him leaning against the wall across from me, a concerned look on his face.

I nod. "Yeah. My ankle hurts from that jump but I should be fine."

He glances out at the busy street, making sure no one has caught up to us yet. "What do we do now?"

"Hide, I suppose. And strike as soon as we can. But for now, we need to wait for Fenix."

Senika nods, glancing at me before turning back to watch the people passing by. Still, I can't sense anyone searching for us but it won't be long before Storm finds us. I tip my head back to look up at the sliver of sky visible between the buildings. Those clouds have nearly covered the sun and any blue sky that remained.

"Something about this doesn't feel right," I say after a moment. Senika looks at me, waiting for me to elaborate. "I mean, Xethos said he was expecting me last night."

"What are you saying?" he asks.

"Somehow, he knew we were coming and had time to prepare for that. I saw my mother at the party, but by the time we got to the throne room, she was there too, which means sometime after we left, he captured her in hopes she could be used as leverage against me. He knew exactly what to expect."

He used Elenore against us and somehow it worked. I can't get it out of my head; the fact that she died while I stood there uselessly, the fact that the one person I should hate more than anyone is the person I was forced to watch die and the one I couldn't save.

"You mean there's a spy," he says, practically reading my mind.

I nod. "Exactly. Someone has betrayed us."

28

THE TALE OF STONEGATE

TAIYO

My name is Taiyo Stone and I am a traitor.

Yes, the Taiyo you knew until now wouldn't dream of betraying her friends, but that is only part of the story. But we all have our share of secrets, don't we?

So here's the truth: I had no choice.

I remember it like yesterday. My father was a Lord, ruling over a small section of land just outside the border of Alkelia. He, along with his forebearers, was proud to have withstood the conquests of the god of victory. When I was very young, perhaps only five or six, Xethos and his army tore that city apart until all that remained was a pile of ash and a little girl. I had hidden away in a secret stone passage underneath the castle where I was to wait until my mother found me so we could escape together.

But she never came.

I waited all through the night, praying someone would come. But eventually, silence fell outside. I knew no one would come. Prying the heavy door open, I found my mother dead and burned so badly, I hardly recognized her. I knew what it meant; she had been so close.

We almost made it out. The screams outside the door had belonged to her.

That's when I was found. A tall man with piercing blue eyes and white hair found me kneeling in the ashes, sobbing and all alone. He was kind and told me I was safe now, that he would take me somewhere no one could hurt me. And the person he took me to was none other than Xethos himself. I was taken back to Alkelia under the pretense of "mercy," but I would hardly call it that. At first, they thought I was a spy or had some kind of valuable information. Uncountable days and nights I spent in the dungeon of his palace, tortured until I could hardly make sense of the world. When it became clear I, a mere child, knew nothing, he was merciful, handing me over to the Order, saying they could take care of me. But it didn't take me long to realize reality—because I wasn't a Halfblood, they didn't want me there. So even though I started off training like all the others, as they grew up and got stronger, I was left behind; merely a maid tasked with cleaning up after them.

By the time I was fourteen, I found irrelevance came with its benefits. They saw me as a useless, pathetic girl and that was something I could use against them. I started gathering information, things I could use as leverage to send this forsaken kingdom tumbling down. But then something happened that I didn't plan for. I stumbled upon information regarding Halfbloods slaughtered by Xethos and his precious Order. Naturally, I was curious and went to Xethos to learn more.

He said my hatred for the Halfbloods could help him. All I needed to do was report what I learned from the Order and he would let me live. At first, I believed I could get out of it, that somehow I could find something to bring down the Order and escape from Xethos's clutches, but it wasn't long until I realized he controlled every part of my life. He gave me no choice but to remain as his spy in the Order, slowly tearing it apart from the inside until there would be nothing left. And I let him use me. I let him think I served only him, feeding him information on the inner workings of the Order and watching his Halfbloods slaughter each other.

The second unexpected thing happened later that year under the name of Kellin Kane. I was fourteen, he was twelve, both of us trapped in separate ways. He had the power I could only dream of and ways to break this system I needed. So I got closer. I hated him for being a Halfblood, another monster under the control of the Order. Another enemy. But he was useful. Through him, I could gather more information than I knew what to do with, and when I overheard him talking to Jyn about his discovery of Xethos killing Halfbloods, it only got better. If they thought I was on their side, they would tell me exactly what they knew. I wouldn't have to lift a finger. I could simply watch as it all fell apart.

But I had to trick Xethos too, which wasn't as easy. He thought I was spying for him, and Kellin thought I fought alongside him, but I never liked either of them. Xethos was the one I had to escape.

It was easier than expected.

Once I told Xethos I would accompany Kellin to the Black Tower, I had him convinced I would simply turn the foolish boy over without a second thought. So that's what I did. I informed Xethos of every move the Halfblood trio made and let him tear apart their lives while I slipped into the background again. Kellin was far too confident that I wouldn't betray him. I hadn't after five years, after all. So while he was busy worrying about things more important than a single maid, I was able to do as I pleased.

So technically speaking, I never betrayed anyone. I was never on anyone's side; there was nothing to betray. They just thought I couldn't possibly be good enough to hurt them. But if that's what they think, I can't wait to see their faces when they learn the truth.

It's amazing how easily people will trust you if you can be no one.

The truth is that Halfbloods must fall along with Alkelia. They are the monsters who fuel the kingdom's ability to crush all who oppose them. Xethos will destroy them and, in turn, his precious kingdom will crumble.

Perhaps you, Dear Reader, will choose not to believe the truth. I have built everything on a web of lies. This could merely be another lie. I am someone who has spent my life twisting an illusion of a helpless girl to hide behind. But if you want to believe anything, believe this.

Kellin Kane is a heretic who will tear apart this world.

The day after the party that went horribly wrong for everyone but me, I am busy folding laundry in the old, crypt-like rooms under the cathedral. This place is a maze of stone tunnels, each of the long and winding corridors lined with servants' quarters. It isn't a place for true Halfblood members of the Order, and yet Jyn is here.

He's out of breath when he comes flying around the corner with Fenix just behind him. It's rare to see the cat without her master.

"Taiyo!" Jyn skids to a halt in the doorway, not stopping to catch his breath. "I think something happened to Kellin. Storm's all in a panic. Fenix came to get me but I can't find Kellin. We have to go find him before Storm does."

Fenix gently takes his pant leg in her teeth, trying to drag him away. Of course, something did happen. Storm was on orders from Xethos to arrest both Kellin and Senika. By now, both of them should be locked up tight with a death sentence on their pretty little heads. I had intended to let them expose the Order and watch it be the first stone to fall but they've got too close to killing Xethos.

"What?" I ask. "Do you think he did something?"

If Storm is in a panic, surely something went wrong.

Jyn shrugs. "I have no idea. Storm is sending out soldiers to search the streets and there are rumours of a criminal on the loose. After last night, it makes sense for them to arrest Kellin."

"And what about Senika? Have you heard anything from him?"

"No." He shakes his head, exasperated. "We have to find them, Taiyo."

Again, Fenix yanks at Jyn's leg, grumbling.

"Follow the cat, I suppose." I gesture at Fenix.

Jyn nods and Fenix takes off down the hall again. I frown, glancing at my half-finished work before following them.

29

TRAITOR

KELLIN

I'm headed back to the cathedral, the place I just barely escaped from. This time, my goal is vastly different. If someone betrayed us, it has to be someone who was with us the entire time.

Someone who knew our plans.

That leaves only three people: Jyn, Taiyo and Safiya.

I find it unlikely for Senika to be the one working against me.

It's possible Safiya only let u use the party to get close to Xethos in hopes that he would capture us right then. It would also make sense for the traitor to be someone who arrived here just before this ordeal began.

However, for them to be an effective spy, they would have to be part of every part of our plans. Someone we trust and can gain access to every detail of our plans. A newcomer like Safiya doesn't have access to the kind of knowledge that a seasoned member of the Order would. Then again, an effective spy would have fabricated everything we know about her.

"What are you planning?" Senika asks.

"I'm going to find whoever betrayed us." I storm through the streets, not bothering to apologize to the people I cut off as I go.

"Shouldn't we think this through before we do anything reckless?" He makes a good point but I doubt there's time to sit around and make plans.

Up ahead, a commotion breaks out, voices rising with anger. I falter, instantly dreading that the Order has found us. The street is packed and we won't be able to make an escape quickly enough if they really are here.

The crisis is averted when Fenix bursts out of the crowd, bounding toward me with her tail high. I rush over to her, kneeling in the middle of the road to check for any wounds she may have acquired since we were separated. She licks my face, purring. Once I'm certain she's okay, I throw my arms around her, burying my face in her thick white fur.

"Kellin!"

Looking up, I see Jyn hurrying toward me as well, pushing people aside. Taiyo appears behind him, holding her skirts to avoid tripping over them. Both of them look nervous.

Placing my hand on Fenix's head, I stand up to address them. "What happened?"

I almost say I'm glad they're alright before I remember that either of them could be actively feeding information to Xethos.

Jyn shakes his head, looking me up and down. "We should be asking you that. The cathedral is in chaos, Storm is panicking, and the Order is up in arms. What did you do?"

Glancing over my shoulder at Senika, I sigh. "I believe one of you should have the answer to that. Who wants to explain themself first?"

"What are you talking about?" Jyn asks. "Why would we—"

"One of you betrayed us, Jyn," I say bluntly. "If it's you, just admit it."

His eyes widen. "Kellin, you can't just accuse us of that. We're your *friends*. You can't think we would ever betray you."

"You have no idea what I would think," I say.

"Took you long enough." Taiyo examines her nails. Her voice is uncharacteristically cold.

I narrow my eyes at her, reaching into her mind for anything I can use against her. "I knew it. You're working with Xethos, aren't you? You never wanted to help us."

She smirks, her grin full of malice like this is all a joke. "So? What are you going to do?"

I walk over to her slowly, stopping to stand just a couple of feet away. For a second, neither of us even dares to breathe. Then I punch her square in the jaw. She stumbles backward and barely avoids falling over completely.

Taiyo laughs. "So you think violence can save you, then."

In response, I kick her in the shin with my thick-soled boots. "I'm going to make sure no one can ever fall into your damn trap ever again."

I grab her by the collar to keep her from falling when I slam my knee into her stomach. My eyes glow; power rushes through my veins. Her terror fuels me like dry wood on a fire. Perhaps once I might have shown mercy toward her, but now I don't feel anything at all. Taiyo was someone I trusted. I was horribly wrong.

"You are nothing but a filthy traitor. You lied. You will learn the price to pay for that."

Just as I raise my fist again, drawing on the fear in her mind, there's a hand on my shoulder. I glance behind me to see Jyn standing there. Part of me wants to turn around and punch him too for what he said the other night but I can't bring myself to be angry with him.

"Don't," he says. "If you hurt her, you are no better than any of them."

"I don't need to be better," I tell him coldly. "I just need to win."

But I lower my arm and let go of Taiyo's shirt, allowing her to crumple to the ground. Jyn releases his grip as well, but he doesn't move. A troubled look fills his face as he examines the two of us.

"And how will beating her up help you win?" he asks. "Revenge won't do anything, Kellin."

I don't say a word for a long time, digging my nails into the palms of my hands and glaring at Taiyo. Then I whisper, "Why did you do it? I thought you cared about us. I thought you were my friend."

"Then you were mistaken." She smiles again, touching the red mark on her cheek where I hit her. "Would I be able to convince you I didn't have a choice?"

"There's always a choice," I say, fuming. "You work for Xethos, don't you? And you have this whole time, ever since the start. That's how you got into the Order without being a Halfblood. That's how you always know what everyone is up to. But there's more to that story."

She looks down at her hands. "I never wanted to work for him, but—"

"I don't care," I interrupt. "Save your story for someone foolish enough to give you another chance. You are a traitor and a liar. I will make sure you never mess with anyone again and you will not ruin my plans. *Iuro.*"

I spin around and start to leave but Jyn grabs my wrist.

"Wait," he says. "If Xethos knows everything, we need to be careful."

"Uh, guys . . ." Senika starts but is ignored.

"I don't *care* what Xethos knows," I hiss at Jyn. "I have to end this before it goes any further."

"You would have killed Taiyo," he points out. "How is that helping anyone?"

"She betrayed us. She is the enemy, Jyn," I remind him. "Her actions could have killed us all." I try to yank my arm free but he refuses to let go. "Fuck. Let go of me."

"Not until you tell me you won't kill anyone." He grabs my other arm too, trapping me. "You're scaring me, okay? I don't want you or anyone else to get hurt. The city is crawling with soldiers trying to put you in chains. We need to lay low for a while or someone is going to die and it won't be Xethos."

"Guys!" Senika is still trying to get our attention.

"Let go of me, Jyn," I warn. "I still have things I need to do."

He shakes his head. "I've seen what you can do, Kellin, and I know I can't stop you, but I want you to realize that what you're doing is dangerous."

Fenix tugs at the bottom of my coat, yowling angrily. I disregard her, too furious to see reason.

Still trying to free myself, I protest, "No one is going to die. I just have to end this."

"Really? So you'd just beat them up until they can't fight back then keep moving? Because I'm pretty sure that's what you would have done to Taiyo just now."

"Will someone listen to me?" Senika shouts.

Both of us turn to look at him, shocked at the sudden anger in his voice. Clearly pleased with herself, Fenix lets go of my coat. She sits, meowing sternly.

Running his fingers through his hair, he sighs. "Look, if you would stop arguing, you would notice that Taiyo is gone and the cathedral is on fire. We don't have *time* to make enemies among ourselves, okay?"

Horrified, I look around, searching for Taiyo but the only sign that she was ever here is the blood on the cobblestones. Spinning around, I see the flames curling up around the cathedral, smoke rising into the sky. Jyn lets go of me, thoughts occupied by more important things now. I curse under my breath and watch as our home burns.

"We have to do something," I announce.

Senika throws his hands up in the air. "That's what I was trying to say."

"No." Jyn shakes his head. "No, Kellin, we have to run. There's nothing we can do now."

I ignore him and take off running down the street, shoving through the crowds that gathered around us. Fenix sprints past me like a bolt of white and purple lightning aimed at the cathedral. My ankle screams but I push the pain out of my mind, running as if my life depends on it and terrified that this is out of my hands.

Mere minutes later, I slam to a halt at the base of the steps leading up to the cathedral. Smoke fills the air and flames have consumed most of the building but still, people stumble out through the doors. I cover my mouth with my sleeve, coughing. A man in the red and silver robes of the Order staggers past me, covered in ash.

I intercept him and demand, "Is anyone else in there?"

"I . . . I think so but—" He breaks off, coughing. "It's no use. It's all lost."

He hobbles past me and I let him go.

Before I can make a decision, Fenix bolts past me.

I shout her name but my voice is lost in the roar of the fire. Glancing over my shoulder, I see Jyn and Senika making their way through the crowd. Cursing under my breath, I make my decision, knowing it could be my last.

I follow Fenix into the flames, my eyes burning from the smoke-filled air. The wooden doors have been reduced to ash and much of the wooden framework of the building is collapsing but the stone walls still hold. Fire devours everything, obstructing my vision as I search for Fenix. I pull the collar of my shirt over my mouth and nose, pushing forward.

Everything appears grey and faded through the thick smoke, making it impossible to know if the shapes before me are people or parts of the building. The spirits scream for me to get out, blocking out all other noise. I push deeper into the room, stepping over broken pews, and ignore all my instincts saying I have to save myself.

But I can't leave Fenix here.

Finally, I find her at the foot of the great statue near the end of the hall. Her fur is grey with ash and something is clasped between her teeth. As I approach her, I realize that she holds the tattered robes of a person. She yanks at them, attempting to pull them out of the quickly crumbling building.

"Fenix—" I cough, my voice lost.

She blinks up at me with wide violet eyes and tugs at the person's robes once more. When I try to pry the fabric from her jaw, I finally recognize the face of the person and stop.

It's High Priest Storm.

The last thing I see before the world is consumed by fire and ash is Fenix, standing over the limp body of the man who ruined my life.

30

A Different Problem

Airadyne

"This was not supposed to happen."

Airadyne paces restlessly through the air. All around her, reality shimmers like a curtain has been drawn over it, fading it to shades of grey. Her white hair floats on an invisible wind and her dress swirls around her ankles like water.

"But it did," Wolf says, smiling as much as a plumb of smoke can. "Is this not what you always tell me, Airadyne? Are you not the one who tells me to remain calm, that this is all in the hands of fate?"

"That is different, Wolf," she says, whirling around to face him. Behind her, rain has begun to fall over the cathedral quenching the flames and washing away the blood that coats the stones. "I am patient but now this is moving far faster than I had anticipated. He will soon know that our hero approaches."

Wolf laughs, a low, growling sound like a vicious animal. "You worry he is not ready."

"I do not. A hero is ready whether they know it or not."

"But you do worry."

Airadyne does not answer for a long time. She watches the world with pale eyes that have seen kingdoms rise and fall. She has given guidance to heroes that have now passed to legend, she has stood beside kings and she has advised the greatest armies this world has ever seen. She serves no god but rather time itself. Her duty is to ensure the continuation of reality and that the world of Morsevdon never fails.

Airadyne does not worry for the safety of mere mortals—their life passes in the blink of an eye to her. Life is trivial to one who cannot die. She knows that they must die as all mortal beings must so she guides her heroes through their insignificant lives in an attempt to make those few years they walk this plane of reality mean something. The heroes she leads are only tools to her but still, Airadyne worries for this one.

"I worry that it will not be enough," she says to Wolf. "I worry that despite all our efforts, this world will soon run out of time. I do not wish for their lives to be lost in vain."

She looks out at the remains of the cathedral. Bodies lie there, broken, bloody, and burned. To her, this building meant nothing. But to the kingdom known as Alkelia, it was a symbol of hope and light, a towering masterpiece constructed in honour of their greatest hero, Ophiele. She fears the one who brought its destruction has also brought the destruction of his kingdom.

"This is more than a few *humans*," Wolf snarls. "You know how little their lives mean, Airadyne. Do not waste your time waiting for them to be *ready*."

But something in Airadyne has changed. She has watched this hero of hers since he was a child. She has weighed his actions and deliberated his strength. She has seen him suffer and each time he falls, she watches him rise. It was she who felt in her very core that he was the one worthy enough to be her hero, even when Wolf insisted that she wasted her time. Since her creation, she has sworn that mortal lives shall be nothing but a means to an end. Insignificant.

Yet she has watched this one grow. She has watched him live. And now she sees that he has never been insignificant.

"I have watched him all his life," she says. "This one is more, Wolf. He will mean something. This world will change because of him."

Wolf growls and shifts impatiently but he knows better than to argue with her. He is her only companion, after all. Airadyne smiles.

Human lives are far more complex than she could ever know. She never cared for her heroes; she would choose them, tell them what they need to know, and then she would be done. But for this one—this single mortal who will change this world—she will be there always. She will be there when he falls, she will be there to cry with him, she will be there when he is victorious. And she will be there when he lives.

31

RUINS OF ANOTHER LIFE

KELLIN

I come to amidst a world of rain and shattered stone. The sky is black but I can't tell if it's because of the rain or if night has fallen. Fragmented pillars and broken walls jut into the sky like the jagged teeth of a monster. The fires have been put out by the rain that pounds down unrelenting at what remains of the world.

I lay there and let the rain wash away the ash and dust that covers everything. I'm floating in a world that doesn't exist, a dream or illusion. It will fade as all dreams do eventually. Until then, I remain unmoving, surrounded by death and destruction caused by a force I could not stop. Amidst the ruins of another life, I wait for the dream to end and for reality to take me back once more.

I close my eyes, drifting in incomprehensible darkness.

"Kellin?"

The voice comes from the end of an endless tunnel, altered by the distance. The buzz of rain against the stones accompanies it.

"Please wake up."

Vaguely, I register pain. Like needles under my skin, it stabs and burns.

"Kellin, you need to wake up."

I open my eyes and the world comes crashing down on me.

Tears well in my eyes as the pain threatens to pull me under again. The rain on my face is sharply cold and very, very real. Senika's face comes into focus at the edge of my vision, his hair soaked and ash streaked across his pale skin.

Slowly, I sit up, grimacing.

"Where is everyone?" I ask.

Senika hesitates. "They left. Taiyo went to Xethos, I think. Jyn . . . said he needed some time. I don't know where he went."

The rain-scented air is a relief after the smoke but I still find it hard to breathe.

My hands are slick with blood. My own, this time, from where tiny rocks have embedded themselves in my skin. It covers my clothing, leaking from cuts and gashes formed by debris sent flying in the explosion.

There is blood on the stones too. Scarlet blood spilled from the bodies of people I may have known. Those bodies lie scattered through the destruction, broken and twisted and unrecognizable. All around, I see the phantom shapes of what used to sit here; the towering cathedral, perfect even in all the darkness surrounding it in my memory.

In the ruins, I see the red robes of High Priest Storm soaked nearly black by rain and by blood and clinging to his broken body as he lies as still as the stones around him. Dead. A sharp laugh bubbles up inside me. I don't feel sad to see him gone; in fact, of all people, he might be one I truly wished dead.

I open my mouth to speak to Senika but freeze when I spot a flash of white among the grey stone and the black night. Fenix lies perfectly still in the rain and my heart nearly stops when I see the red staining her fur. I drag myself onto my hands and knees, crawling to her side, but she isn't moving, her purple eyes glassy and dim. I reach for her, whispering her name, but she is too far away. The world blurs and tilts as I struggle to find my next breath.

The tears finally break through, tumbling down my cheeks. I cling to handfuls of Fenix's fur, begging her to wake up. But I know it's impossible.

I look around me at the ruins of the cathedral. I'm kneeling just past what used to be the grand entrance with its towering domed ceiling and massive stained glass windows with rain pouring down around me. Now pillars lie in pieces across the cracked marble floors and only part of the spiral staircase stands. Just hours ago, this place was filled with the members of the Order as they went along with their normal nightly activities but now all that remains is death and destruction in the silence of the night. My clothing sticks to my body, drenched in freezing rain, and my hair falls in front of my face in a sodden, dark curtain. I shiver in the cold, wrapping my arms around myself.

For a long time, I stay there, rain soaking into my bones and tears streaking down my face. The spirits are laughing at me. I can hear them at the edge of my conscience, whispering to each other as if I can't hear them. It feels like my heart is being ripped from my chest like someone reached in and pulled it out with their bare hand. But it is no wound that causes this pain; it is their words.

Finally, I look back over my shoulder, terrified that no one will be there. Instead, I see Senika standing in the rain, with his white hair plastered to his forehead. "Senika," I whisper, briefly thinking he might leave as well.

He pushes his wet hair out of his eyes and walks toward me. When he crouches down in front of me, I tense and close my eyes, thinking he might try to hurt me.

"I'm so sorry." His voice is grief-stricken and sorrowful. "I know you were just trying to help."

"Maybe you don't know me," I whisper, numb. "I wanted them dead and now they are. I couldn't kill Xethos and now it's only getting worse."

"Maybe I don't." He places his hand on my shoulder and I suck in a sharp breath. "I haven't known you for very long, but I know you have a good heart. You aren't cruel or mean, you simply want someone to understand you. But killing won't make anyone understand. All that can do is make them see you as a monster."

I look up at him. "They're right, Senika. I *am* a monster. You can't see it, but it's true. Death and destruction follow everywhere I go."

I want to run away and hide like I always have but instead I collapse against his chest, exhausted. He pauses for a fraction of a second before wrapping his arms around me.

"They're wrong. All of them. I don't know why, but some people choose to only see the bad in people. What they see in you is someone who refuses to follow the rules and lashes out and destroys things when he's angry. But there's always another side to every story. Your whole life has been spent trying to hide from things other people can't imagine because you're the only one who can. You aren't a monster, you're hurt."

"Stop," I say. The next words hurt, but there's no other way. "Don't say anything. Just go, I'm dangerous and you'll only get hurt by staying here. Please, just go. Leave me here."

"No."

"... What?"

He shakes his head. "I'm not leaving you. Never. I can't abandon you."

"Butterfly, I don't want to hurt you. I could *kill* you if you stay."

"It'd be worth it."

"No, it fucking wouldn't!" I yell. "I'm a *monster* and murderer, I'll just kill you along with everyone else! Go away, Senika. It's for your own good."

I don't know what to expect from him but some part of me hopes he might stay. But if he stays, he could die. If he left he would be safe. I am protecting him by telling him to go far, far away. The further the better, really, even if it hurts both of us. This way he will be safe.

"I love you." Those words make me freeze. Love? No one loves me. He must be lying. He has to be. Hesitantly, he pauses and takes a deep breath.

I stare at him, dismayed.

"This is really strange," he says, "and you might not believe me but I think I love you. I love you more than anything in this world."

For a moment I blink the rain and tears from my eyes, wondering if this dream will be over soon, but in the end, I know it's all real. It's real, and I don't want to wake up, because both of us are dying anyway. But I'm tired, and the world feels distant and strange. Without thinking, I kiss him. My fingers grab the collar of his shirt, yanking him toward me. At the last second, I hesitate, and it turns into just the faintest brush of my lips on his.

My heart beats frantically. It doesn't last long but for just a moment, it's like nothing else in the world matters, only the fireworks that suddenly go off in my heart and the boy with hair like starlight.

Then I pull away, shattering the brief moment. His eyes go wide. He starts to say something but I put my hand over his mouth, shaking my head.

"Shush, no more talking." I lean my head against his shoulder again and close my eyes. My hand falls back to the cold stones limply. "I'm so fucking tired. Let me sleep."

He shakes my shoulder, but my eyelids feel heavy and I don't want to move. "Kellin. Don't fall asleep here, we still need to get away from here. You can't sleep yet. Hey. Come on."

But it's too late. My eyes fall shut and I let myself vanish into a deep, peaceful sleep. The lingering feel of his lips on mine fills my mind completely.

32

Truth

Kellin

I wake up in a dark room. My body is heavy, immovable as stone.
I lie still with my eyes closed, listening to learn where I might be.
Mostly, it's just quiet, but I can hear the faint ripple of waves against
wood and whispers of voices above me, perhaps on the second floor
of wherever I am. Finally, I force my eyes open and blink away the
darkness.

It's a small, narrow room with curved, wooden walls and no windows, like a cabin under a boat. The only light comes from the gap
under the door at the far end of the room, but on the table beside the
bed where I lay is a lamp with no light in it. I turn my head and see
another bed on the other side of the space, which is small enough that
the aisle between the beds is barely wide enough to walk down. The
other bed is empty, but the sheets look messy and very much slept in.
I reach for where Fenix usually sleeps next to me, but she isn't there.

Some part of me feels like I should cry for her death or find someone
to blame, but no tears arrive. The only one to blame is me. I couldn't
save her or even stop her from running into the fire. It's my own fault
she is dead, yet there is nothing I can do to make up for it, no one to

apologize to or even yell at. I wish there was something someone could do to reverse it. Instead, all I can do is lie here and try to find some way to live without her.

My head pounds, but I force myself to get up, knowing I need to know where I am. As soon as I move, my whole body starts to hurt again, and I notice my hands and arms have been carefully wrapped in bandages. As soon as I stand, I stumble and nearly faceplant on the floor, the entire world tilting dangerously. I reach the door and push it open to see a narrow hallway lined with doors. There are no lights, so I tiptoe carefully down the hall in the dim light. I find the stairs at the end of the hallway and slowly make my way up.

I pause at the top, looking around at the scene in front of me. It's night time; bright stars fill the sky, surrounding a shining sliver of a moon. I shiver in the autumn air cold without my jacket. The mast of the ship reaches high up to brush the constellations, the white sails bright against the dark sky. Near the front of the ship, two figures sit around a wooden box converted into a table playing a game of cards. The ship is tied to the docks and it takes me a moment to recognize it as the one Senika came here on. One of the people playing cards is fidgeting with the corner of one card more than he is playing and I recognize the way the pale light reflects off his starlight hair. It's such a normal scene, just two people playing cards on the deck of a ship but the game looks more like a distraction from something else than for fun. The floorboards creak under my feet and Senika looks up and then abandons the game to rush over to me, nearly tripping over a pile of rope in his hurry

"Kellin," he says with a relieved sigh. "You should be resting. Why are you here?"

I frown. "You should be resting too. It's the middle of the night. Where are we anyway?"

"On the ship. We needed somewhere to go and this was the only place I could think of where we could be safe." I nod but don't say anything. He looks me up and down then throws his arms around me, crushing all the air out of my lungs. "I'm so glad you're alright."

I try to remove myself from his arms. "I can't breathe. Also, my whole body hurts, please stop it."

"Senika!" The other person on the deck yells at him. "Do you plan on introducing your little lover here or do I get to guess who he is?"

Scowling, Senika answers, "It's not like that, Kira." Then he looks over at me and asks, "Right?"

I shrug, which somehow manages to hurt my shoulders. "I don't know. Why would you ask me?"

Almost laughing, he gives me a strange look. "Oh, I have no idea, why *would* I ask you, Kellin?"

The woman at the front of the ship laughs. "You two are hilarious." She walks over and extends her hand to me. "The name's Captain Kira Aliver and *this* beautiful ship happens to be mine. Senika is an honourary crewmate and a friend so I don't mind having you here too."

I stare at her hand. The captain is far taller than me, with long fiery red hair, and she's dressed in a long red coat with a sleek rapier sheathed at her hip. She wears high heels that look like they might break my ankles if I wore them, but she walks with long, confident strides. There's something intimidating but friendly about her. She's confident without being arrogant and loud without being annoying or threatening.

When I don't do anything for a few seconds too long she grins. "Shy? That's alright, I know Senika likes you for a reason."

"Um, yeah," I stammer, unreasonably nervous. "I'm, uh, Kellin." I consider adding the part about being in the Order, but now the entire city is looking for me, that might not be my greatest idea.

She laughs again. "Of course! You're the kid they're saying is more powerful than Opheile herself."

Suddenly, every word I've ever known escapes my brain and I wave my hands around like an idiot. "I—what … Opheile? No … that—ah. Wait. No, not true. I am not."

The captain gives me an amused look but before she can say anything more, Senika interrupts. "Kellin, why don't you go back to bed? You need to be resting, and there isn't much to do here anyway."

He grabs me by the shoulders and steers me toward the stairs again. I almost trip over a loose floorboard and stumble down a few steps before Senika grabs my hand.

"Are you trying to get rid of me?" I ask, wondering if perhaps there's a reason why he decided to interrupt the conversation.

"Don't fall," he says, purposely ignoring my question. "It'd hurt an awful lot to fall down these stairs."

I smirk. "You say that like you have experience."

"Okay, maybe I do," he admits. "It's still not a good idea."

We walk in silence until we reach the door of the small cabin at the end of the ship. I hesitate in the doorway. "Butterfly?"

"Yeah?" I can hardly see him in the dimly lit room.

"Why didn't you go with the others?"

"Because that would mean leaving you behind. And I don't want to ever do that."

Neither of us says anything for a long while before I ask, "Don't you think it's just dangerous to be with me? I mean, I destroyed the cathedral and I killed people. Jyn, Safiya, and Taiyo, maybe they're right about staying away. Plus you hardly know me."

In the dark, he shakes his head. "No. You can't think like that. No one ever survives this world if they lose faith in themselves. You have to remember that no matter what happens, you are right. Even if no one believes you, believe in yourself."

Smiling sadly, I reply, "I am my only ally sometimes."

"But now you have me." He brushes a stray piece of hair out of my face and grins.

I glare at him and push his hand away. "Yeah, I guess I do. And that's better than other times."

We stand in silence for a while, which somehow manages to not be awkward, before he announces, "The captain wants to leave soon and go back to Iolleria. Her crew thinks that's the best decision as well. I was . . ." He stops and sighs heavily. "I'm thinking about going with them."

"Okay," I speak slowly, unsure of what he wants to hear. "Then you should go. It's your home and there isn't much here for you. You should go with the crew."

"You think I'm leaving just like that?" He laughs. "I was going to ask if you wanted to come with me."

"Oh . . ." I look at the floor, thinking for a moment before I meet his eyes again. "I can't leave here yet. I need to finish what I've started before I go away. It's best if you leave before you get hurt."

He shakes his head and stubbornly argues, "No, I'm not leaving without you. If you're staying, so am I. Don't try to convince me otherwise."

I sigh and give him a mischievous smirk. "I'm not going to be able to get you to leave. But if you stay, know that things aren't going to be pretty here. Once you let me leave this boat, I am going to kill Xethos. Or . . . whoever is controlling him."

"I'm staying with you, Kellin," he insists. "Maybe one day I'll go back home but for now I'm staying here."

Nodding slowly, I don't say anything for a long time. "Senika, last night . . . did you mean what you said?" I finally ask in a serious voice.

Senika doesn't respond for a long time. "Of course I meant it. Kellin, I meant every word I said there and I . . ." He looks at the ground, his voice suddenly seeming almost sad.

"I love you." I must be out of my mind to say that out loud. There's no way this is real, and even if it is, we can't be in love. It'll only make it harder for him to walk away. One day, he will leave like everyone else, and if this is how it is, it will only be worse. After all, everyone seems to go eventually. Even Jyn, who I thought would be here forever, has turned his back on me.

And if I love him it will only hurt more when he does go.

Yet I now realize I might have loved him the first time I saw him. If that's true, I've loved him for every second in between. Because he is the one who cares, the one who is willing to stay with me even knowing what I can do and what I have done. He is the one who will love me even if I am a monster. For that, I will love him as long as I live.

I shake my head frantically. "No. I'm sorry. Please just . . . forget about this whole mess."

Forget I kissed him, forget he loves me, forget that he said he would never leave. Forget it all. We have to.

When I start to walk away, he catches my arm. "I won't. I don't care what you say, I won't leave you here and I won't forget this happened. I promise you that."

"You would stay even though you know I'm a monster?"

"No, I would stay because I know you aren't a monster."

I frown. "Well, you can't deny that I've done some terrible things."

"This world doesn't like you very much, does it?"

It takes me a long time to answer. The sound of waves against the side of the ship seems louder than before, but it's the only noise filling the darkness. The silence that fills the space between us is so complete, I can almost hear his heartbeat, my own heart beating faster with every passing second. A cold breeze blows down the hallway from the open door at the top of the stairs, calm and gentle and still smelling of rain. For a brief second, I let my eyelids flutter shut, taking a deep breath of the cool air before speaking again.

"I used to have wings," I whisper, almost afraid to say it and break that perfect quiet.

"What?"

Eyes fixed on the floor, I explain quietly, "I had wings. People always told me those wings made me . . . less than human, just like my magic, but I liked them. When I was nine, my mother tried to kill me. I was always a monster to her and . . . I guess eventually it seemed true enough, so I believed her even though I used to think she was a liar."

"I'm so sorry," he mutters.

"Don't say that. It won't fix anything," I reply, brushing away tears. After all this time, he's the first person I've really told, and even thinking of it hurts.

"You don't deserve that. She should be the one apologizing."

"She's dead, Butterfly. I watched her die. And even after all she did, I wish she lived."

He shakes his head. "We can't change the past, not a single part of it, so don't start regretting what's already come and gone."

"She always said . . . I was a curse, a demon who had replaced her son. I hated her more than anything and all I wanted was to get away but she controlled everything. In the North, Halfbloods are hated by just about everyone . . . I knew that, but I still wanted her to love me.

And I hate myself for ever thinking she could love someone like me. You are . . . the first person I have ever told this to."

"She was wrong, Kellin." Senika takes my hand, holding it gently as if I might shatter. "You are not a monster, and you deserve to be loved more than anyone else. That's why I won't leave you. Because I love you and nothing can convince me that you are any kind of demon. And I am honoured to be the one to know."

I don't know how to respond to that. I want to believe he's lying, that none of it is true. Because if it's the truth, I was wrong. But all I can ever be is a monster. My power is the kind that can and will tear everything apart, the kind that is better suited for being a villain and the kind that anyone would want to get rid of.

"Love is dangerous," I say. "I might not even survive the next few days, much less many years after that. And even if I did, staying with me will only bring more trouble for you."

He shrugs. "You realize that I'm going to die too? At best, I have fifteen years. At worst, I might not wake up tomorrow. If we're both doomed, why not do it together?"

I pause to consider this. It's true, both of us are practically already dead with only a few people to care when we do die but for some reason, I've decided that his presence will only lead to him dying. I want to protect him from myself, but I can't bear the thought of being alone again. Now, after so long, I think I've found someone who will stay, but I'm too afraid to get close in case he leaves in the end.

"Let's go do this, then." I grin.

In the dream, I'm on a beach. The waves crash gently against the soft, white sand while the setting sun turns the whole world pink and

yellow and orange. My feet are bare and the sand is hot on my skin. On my back are two marvellous black-feathered wings, just like they used to be, in place of the messy scars I've grown accustomed to. As I walk, I stretch them out behind me, loving the feel of the breeze ruffling my feathers and how perfectly whole I am with them. In the distance, a wooden house painted blue perches on a cliff to overlook the water. Across the sand, Senika stands with the sea washing over his feet and his back turned to me.

I walk over to where he waits for me. In the light of the sun, his pale hair looks more gold than silver and his skin glows. He turns to look at me and his eyes light up, a smile spreading across his face. Here, he isn't wearing his eyepatch like usual; instead, he has one silver eye while the other is a brilliant shade of blue.

He holds out one hand, reaching toward me, and I take it without hesitation. When he speaks, I don't hear his words, only watch his lips move, but I understand what he means and I nod. In a small flash of light, he shifts, and I'm surrounded by butterflies that flash pink and orange and yellow in the sunlight.

Then, the sun isn't setting but rather rising over us to bring in a new dawn. I extend my hands up to the sky and reach for the butterflies that dance around me, careless of the harm I can bring to them. But here, the boy who lay dying in the snow, the boy who lost everything over and over, and the boy who could never be loved are all gone. Here, I am Kellin Kane.

And I am not a monster.

33

SAFE

SENIKA

The sun is already high in the sky by the time I make it to the cathedral, half-hidden by clouds. It's been days since I last stood here, and everything has changed so much since then. Still, people are picking through the ruins, trying to salvage anything they can. From what I've heard, there were twenty people injured and another dozen or so killed, including High Priest Eldric Storm. The massive, wooden doors, with their intricately carved designs are now nothing more than splinters. The incredible stained glass window behind the pulpit is fragments of colour, broken and shattered across the crumbling stones. The place feels like a graveyard, silent and ghostly even as several people search the ruins carefully. The dead have been buried by now and many of the wounded are being treated in various places across the city, but their blood still stains the stones red even after all the rain.

I stand near the remains of one of the pillars, still trying to process the events of that night. Jyn and Taiyo were Kellin's closest—and perhaps, only—friends but they still left him. Kellin has watched his world fall apart over and over, death forever looming over his shoulder. Fenix is gone, along with any home he ever knew. I wish I could turn back the clock and make sure it never happened. I know that's wrong; he doesn't need anyone's pity. But the least I can do is not abandon him.

When I told Kira I was going to stay here, she only nodded solemnly and said she would be staying too, then. I guess she and Emaya both figured out rather quickly what was going on and decided we wouldn't be getting away with this alone. In fact, Emaya told me it was their responsibility to keep me safe since they were the ones who helped me escape Iolleria. The two of them even made me swear I would go back once this was over and talk to Mum. Gendry claims it would be boring on the ship without me, so I am therefore obliged to stick around and stay alive.

"Are you part of the cleanup crew, kid?"

I look up to see a burly man with an impressive moustache standing with his arms crossed before me. I shrug. "Not really. I can help, though."

The man narrows his eyes upon hearing my accent. "You're Iollerian. What are you doing here at a time like this?"

I shrug and casually brush off the question, hating that I have to lie. "I'm just here for a few days. Bad timing is all."

"Whatever, you don't need to tell your story." He waves toward where the door should be. "Get out, then. We aren't allowed to have random people hanging around here until the investigation is over."

"Investigation?" I ask. "You mean they don't know what happened here?"

"Look, we've all got a lot on our plates right now and I don't have time to deal with your questions. If you want to bother someone, go to the castle and speak with the investigation team," the man says.

I nod and reluctantly start to walk away, then I pause and ask, "Will they rebuild it?"

"Eventually they'll have to. The cathedral was a symbol of the Order and a place for the people of the city to gather." He looks me up and down before adding, "Hey, you're a Halfblood, aren't you? Did you have something to do with the Order?"

I shake my head. "No. Someone I know was hurt here." It's the best explanation I can give without exposing my real involvement with this place, especially with the entire city looking for Kellin. Xethos instantly revealed that there was someone trying to kill him and, although he didn't give any names, he blamed the destruction of the cathedral on Kellin.

"Sorry to hear that, kid." The man shakes his head. "It's an awful thing that happened the other day. I hope your friend gets better."

Nodding again, I say, "Yeah, and the bastard that hurt him will die."

I mean exactly what I say, but to him, it means something quite different. He shakes his head disapprovingly. "That might be a little extreme, but whatever works for you. Take care, kid."

The man turns and walks back to where he was working, saying something to another worker on the way. I start to leave as well but stop when I almost step on something. Bending down to pick it up, I see that it's a thick book with a weathered leather cover and golden writing I don't understand scrawled across it. When I run my fingers across the yellowed pages, dust flies into the air and the pages all but crumble under my touch. It's a miracle this survived the fire. Glancing around to make sure no one sees me, I grab the book and open it to a random page.

Staring back at me is a drawing of a face, twisted and monstrous like something from a nightmare but born of charcoal lines and dark shadows. It looks almost human except for the crooked horns and snake eyes. There are dark circles under those eyes as they stare into my soul, and the thing's mouth is open, exposing rows and rows of jagged, saw-like teeth with a forked tongue that seems far too long. I stare at the drawing and the notes scribbled in the margins around it, dazed, before snapping the book shut.

I look over my shoulder again and then open to the same page—carefully, as if it might leap out and attack me. The monster is like nothing I've seen before, something not of this world, accompanied by sharp writing I don't recognize. The book gives me a bad feeling. Closing it again, I hurry away before anyone can see me taking it. If they caught me stealing from the crime scene, they might think I'm an accomplice. Which isn't entirely wrong, but I would rather not get arrested.

The morning after the disaster, I went back to the cathedral, mostly to find what had been lost in our hurry to get away but also to see what had happened in the daylight. At the time, there was no one around, just me wandering through the ruins of so many lives. Standing there, I didn't understand how someone could even do that and perhaps for a moment, I thought it must have been the work of demons.

When I get back to the ship, Kellin is sitting near the bow, impatiently tying knots in a length of rope. He's frowning at it as if it offended him somehow, and his injured hands work slowly, shaking slightly. The bandages are red with blood. There's no one else on deck, and part of me is amazed Emaya even let him get out of bed, much less sit up here alone. Knowing Kellin, however, I know he's glad to be free from her endless worrying.

After the cathedral fell, soldiers from the Order have been patrolling the streets more frequently in search of the criminals Storm was meant to bring in as well as whoever started the fire. We don't know if they know the face of the person they're hunting but Kellin and I stay below deck each time they pass regardless. This brief escape from the stifling rooms down there must be heavenly for him.

"You look like you're planning to murder that rope," I say without thinking. I instantly regret saying it.

He flinches, hurt. "I'm not going to murder anyone."

"Right. Sorry." I sit across from him, examining the dozens of knots tied in the rope. "What are you doing anyway?"

"Tying knots," he says shortly.

"Is there a reason to be tying knots in a rope?" I ask.

"Not really. I just didn't have anything else to do." He finally looks up at me. "Do you know there isn't a single book on this whole boat?"

I think for a moment. "That . . . doesn't surprise me. Can you speak Iollerian?"

He gives me a confused look. "No? What does that have to do with books?"

"I don't know. I'm just thinking, you know if you come to Iolleria you'll have to learn at least a little bit."

Leaning forward a bit, he says, "You'll have to teach me then."

"I'm probably a bad teacher, but I guess I can try," I say. "You do know some other language, what is it?"

He shrugs and returns to tying knots. "The Old Tongue, the God's Langauge, Old Alkelian. It has many names and not many to speak it."

"So how do you know it?" I wonder.

"I . . . mostly taught myself." He pauses to consider me then looks back at the rope. "After I joined the Order, a lot of people still didn't want me there. They knew I was a prince of the part of the kingdom that hates Halfbloods the most so they assumed I was just like everyone else there and because of that, they pushed me away. That's why I don't tell people about who I am. When I was . . . eleven, it got really bad. I was alone and no one cared so I tried to . . ." He holds up his hand and points to where his tattoos are hidden under the bandages. I understand what he means without him saying it fully. "After that,

I tried to distract myself I guess. Learning something complicated seemed like a good way to do that. But it's pretty similar to regular Alkelian, so it wasn't that hard at all."

I almost apologize but when I remember what he said last night, I stop myself. "You learned a forgotten language by yourself? That's . . . amazing, actually. Most people would learn an instrument or . . . knit."

He shrugs. "I can play the piano. I taught myself that too."

"Really? Next, you're going to say you're a professional . . . I don't know, horse-rider."

"Oh, I am."

"You're joking," I say.

He snickers, almost humourlessly. "Yeah. But I did learn to play the piano. Mostly, I spent my time learning to fight. If I knew how to fight, I would never be helpless. That's what I thought, at least."

"So is there a reason you picked the most complicated weapon around?" I inquire curiously.

He glances over to where his spear rests next to him. It's got a massive scratch through the blue-painted runes near the blade but I managed to save it from the ruins of the cathedral before anyone else got ahold of it. Not that they could do much with it anyway; it's made of rune steel, a kind of metal that somehow burns anyone who isn't a Halfblood. Even I'm not immune to that.

"Not really," he says. "It's just more fun. That was also when I met Fenix."

"She was really important to you, then," I say softly. "I'm sorry."

He shrugs then looks up to meet my gaze. "You don't have to apologize. It feels like I'm the one who killed her. I kind of . . . I hate myself for what I did. She saved my life, and this is what happens."

"But it wasn't your fault. We can't always be in control, right?"

"So then it's just my luck I happened to be there when a dozen people and the cat that saved my life all died, isn't it?" he says bitterly. "When I was alone, it was her and Jyn who came to me, but now they're both gone and I don't know what to do without them."

With the heightened security throughout the city, we haven't been able to look for Jyn and it doesn't appear that he's tried to find us either. Kellin's jumped to the conclusion that his friend abandoned him, even though I've told him a dozen times that Jyn will come back.

"So maybe this is how you know you don't need them anymore. Sometimes . . . I think the gods do things just to test us, they take away the people we love and turn them against us but they also give us others who can help us when everything else is gone. I don't know how much it means, but now you have me and I promise I'll do what I can."

He stares back at me, somewhat astounded. "You . . . you would do that? I mean, you know what I can do yet you would still stay here with me. You are truly amazing, Butterfly."

"I guess I just don't want to see you hurt. I mean, I love you and I'll do everything I can to see you smile," I tell him.

". . . No one has ever said these things before," he whispers, as if he's afraid to say it. "No one has ever been like you."

"Well then they're missing out, aren't they? And I am happy to be the first." I smile and push the book toward him. "I found something at the cathedral, by the way. Not sure if it means anything, but I brought it anyway."

When he sees the book, his eyes go wide. "That's . . . I found that in the library weeks ago. Taiyo said something about it being in the language of the dead."

"It's from the Deadlands?" I ask. "I thought everything from there was destroyed centuries ago."

He shrugs, picking up the book and flipping through it cautiously. "I thought so too, but this writing is like nothing I've seen before. So unless you can come up with a better explanation, that's all we got."

Noticing the streaks of blood his fingers leave on the pages, I reach out and grab his hand carefully. "Wait, you're hurting your hands."

He looks down at his bandaged fingers like he just noticed the blood. "I'm fine."

I shake my head. "You had a hundred tiny pieces of rock embedded in your skin, that is very much not fine. And now you're going to get blood all over everything."

He pulls his hand away slowly. "Butterfly. I'm *fine*. Stop worrying about me, okay?"

I start to protest then sigh. "I just don't want you to get hurt."

"I know, but you're going to be all wrinkly by the time you're twenty if you keep worrying."

After that, I can't take him seriously anymore and I burst out laughing. "I'm not worrying *that* much. I just—" I break off, coughing and covering my mouth with the back of my hand. The smoke from the fire took a toll on me.

"Senika?" Kellin tentatively places his hand on my shoulder. "Are you okay?"

I wave him away, suddenly exhausted. "I'm fine, just tired."

"I don't believe you," he says, skeptically.

"Trust me, I'm fine," I pause then add, "We both need to stop saying that."

He shrugs, awkwardly taking back his hand. "Probably."

I smile but don't say anything. It's almost funny how the two of us came to be together; two kids with more problems than either can count and yet we're both here, regardless of all that could go wrong. He thinks he's a monster, but all I see is a kid who grew up too fast, without a choice of what would happen next. He never had a chance to be a kid. Both of us are still so young, and I think it's unfair he's suffered so much. Yet through it all, he manages to stay standing and keep fighting, even if it gets him killed, and that makes him braver than anyone I've ever known.

"Kellin!" I look up to see Emaya rushing through the door from below deck, her curly hair sticking up in all directions. "I thought I told you to rest and this doesn't look like resting. Come here, you need to go back to bed."

He groans. "I don't want to."

"Well, that hardly matters." She gestures for him to go back downstairs. "If you keep messing around up here you won't get better, now will you?"

Casting me a reluctant glance, he allows her to usher him to the stairs. "Fine, but only as long as I have to."

"Yes, yes." Emaya turns to me, pointing sternly. "And Senika, no nonsense. He needs sleep, not you keeping him up."

"How am I keeping him awake?" I protest, scrambling to my feet and hiding the book behind my back.

Emaya glares at me. "You know exactly what you do, Senika."

"What did I do?" I ask, slightly offended.

"Oh shush, you should be resting too." She practically drags Kellin down the stairs without giving me time to answer, the door falling shut behind them.

Ever since I brought Kellin here, Emaya has been all over him like a cat with a kitten, constantly watching him and making sure he doesn't get into trouble or hurt himself again. I don't think he really minds having someone watch over him like that, but I've also been a victim of Emaya's relentless care-taking, and I know he isn't eager to have someone bugging him all the time. The rest of the crew, however, just treats him like one of their own, leaving him be but never pushing him away. I've tried to tell Kira to at least let him walk around on the docks, but she's convinced a single step off this boat will result in his arrest. Both of us have been restless these past few days and any moment of peace is quite welcome.

He was a mess after I brought him here from the cathedral's ruins, muttering about how he ruined everything and that he's a monster, a demon, a curse. At night, he wakes up feverish and screaming from things unseen to anyone other than him. He thinks he's going insane, but despite the sharp, angry mask he wears, he just wants to be loved—almost like a little kid.

"How long are you going to stare at the door?" Gendry's voice snaps me out of my thoughts. He speaks in Iollerian, staring at me from near the gangplank.

"I wasn't staring at anything," I respond.

"Yes, you were." He drops the box he had been carrying with a thud. "I bet you were dreaming about him."

"I don't know what you're talking about."

Gendry laughs. "Yeah right. Did he kiss you or something?"

I shake my head. "No, I've told you before, it's not like that." I feel bad lying to him but if I admit the truth, he might never leave me alone.

"Uh-huh. You like him," He cranes his neck to look at the book that I'm doing a very poor job of hiding from him. "What do you have by the way?"

"Also nothing," I say. "Where have you been all day?"

"Since everything is nothing today, I've been doing nothing," he shoots back.

"I hate you."

He grins. "You couldn't live without me."

"I bet I could."

"We should go swimming."

"That is the most random thing we could possibly do right now," I reply.

He shrugs. "Do you have a reason not to?"

"Yeah, I'm going to have a nap."

I start down the stairs and Gendry calls, "Emaya's gonna kill you!"

Rolling my eyes, I let the door slam shut behind me. Emaya might have told me to leave Kellin alone but Gendry knows that soon, Kellin will just get up and leave. None of us will be able to do anything to stop him, even me. When that happens, I know I'll be going along with him. Emaya will lecture me for weeks about how dangerous that is and how we should be more careful.

Sure enough, two days later, I wake up to someone shaking my shoulder. I sit up and blink, disoriented until my eyes adjust to the dark cabin. Standing beside my bed, Kellin is fully dressed with his spear across his back and his hair tied back. His golden eyes glow faintly like a cat.

"You're going to think I'm crazy," he says in a hushed voice.

"Right . . . we've been through this, you aren't crazy," I remind him. "Are you okay? Did something happen?"

He shakes his head. "I have stupid ideas and I know exactly what everyone is afraid of, which sounds pretty crazy to me."

"Being different isn't crazy," I point out, not for the first time.

"You're afraid of being a coward. And of disappointing people who love you," he says bluntly. "Also fire. And I'm not disappointed in you."

I pause, taken aback by having all that set out in front of me so plainly. "Where were you going with this? What's your idea for the night?"

"I'm going to kill Xethos," he says far too casually. "Again."

"You're right that, does sound insane. Can I come?" I ask without hesitation.

"Well, I thought it was obvious I wouldn't be going alone," he whispers. "I'm going to find Jyn, too. And . . . Taiyo. The spirits told me where they're staying."

Sometimes, he does say things I don't understand, like when he talks about the spirits who speak to him. I've heard of Halfbloods communicating with spirits before, but most Halfbloods in Iolleria get shipped off to fight. It isn't a very common thing in the first place, so I knew very few others. "So where do we need to go?"

"Just the castle. They're with Safiya. And unfortunately, Elias has stuck around too. Besides, it's time to end this before anyone else dies. I need to make sure Xethos can't come back ever again. He's ruined too much."

Nodding, I climb out of bed and start getting ready. "Perfect. Let's go fight a god."

34

STONES...

KELLIN

I avoid the cathedral on the way to the castle, even though the fastest route is right past it. But I can't face the reality of what I did. I know it makes me weak, unable to face my own mistakes, yet going there will make it seem all too real. The past week has been terrible without Fenix, and I'm trying to continue without her, but the space next to me where she used to walk is painfully empty. The kind pirate lady called Emaya took care of me, treating the wounds on my hands, arms, and back while never asking a single question. I'm thankful for that. But now I wish I had a chance to thank her before I threw myself into certain death once again.

We move quickly through the shadowy streets, adrenaline already pulsing through my veins as I start to formulate a plan in my mind. Senika agreed to join me without hesitation, but I doubt Jyn will do the same. In all honesty, I expected Senika to leave a long time ago, to realize how terrible I am and run away from danger but I'm glad he's still here.

As we approach the towering castle, my heart pounds faster and I instinctively take inventory of my weapons—my spear, plus four knives. My hands are shaking as my fingers fumble with the clasp on one of my armguards, restless and anxious. Senika reaches out and silently takes my hand in his, forcing me to stop fidgeting. The tiny gesture feels almost illegal. No one should be able to offer such comfort with just a touch. I glance over at him, but he just smiles reassuringly.

The castle towers over us, bright and magnificent as always, but now it looks like the gates of doom. Once the doors close behind us, there will be no turning back. There are two guards at the front entrance, both looking half-asleep from a long, boring shift in the middle of the night. I walk straight up to them, not bothering to hide or disguise myself.

"Halt!" one of them calls, lurching to attention when they see me.

I disregard the command and stalk up the steps to them. The second guard moves to block my path and I stop walking inches from his face. He tries to hit me so I block and knock him out with a punch to the jaw that sends needles of pain through my hand. When the man who spoke first steps up, I draw a knife, spinning it in my hands. He starts to draw his sword but I knock him off-balance by jabbing my knee into his gut and slamming him into the wall next to the door, holding the blade to his throat.

"Where can I find Xethos?" I hiss. The man's breath smells of liquor, but I lean closer, using my full weight to trap him against the wall.

He shakes his head, a stupid idea that causes my knife to draw blood and he squeaks. "T-throne room. Please . . . don't hurt me."

I release him and he falls to the ground, stunned. "I try not to make a habit of killing."

Leaving him there, I heave open the door and step inside with Senika just behind me. The bandages on my hand make my grip on my knife feel strange, but I don't sheath it, knowing I will need it soon. I start down the corridor then pause and turn to look at Senika.

"We might not survive this," I begin. "So I kind of want to say . . . you aren't a disappointment. To me, you are the most beautiful person in this world and I will love you until the day I die. Which could be today. You are more beautiful than the stars and you are the only person who doesn't think I'm crazy or a monster or stupid or something. You're brave and kind and smart and *so fucking perfect* and I wouldn't have survived the past month without you, Butterfly, so thanks, I guess, and, and . . . Gods, I don't know what I'm saying."

He stares at me and I realize it's kind of dumb to do this now. Then he grins. "You're definitely stupid. And reckless and a genius and courageous and wild and I love all of that about you. But please don't say you'll die here, because I don't know how I ever lived without knowing that the whole time you were here and I never knew it."

I grin, grabbing his hand and turning back down the corridor. "Now let's go do the stupidest thing either of us has thought of."

As we near the throne room, it occurs to me that the castle is far too quiet. The silence in the castle is unnerving after all the noisy parties I've attended here. The halls are lit, but not a single sound comes from any of the rooms along the hall. Our footsteps are loud enough to give us away if the sound of my heart pounding in my chest doesn't do that first. In my head, the muttering spirits offset the quiet by taking turns taunting me in faint voices. Every step brings us closer to death or victory.

Tonight is the night that will change all of Alkelia. All of Morse-vdon, even.

We round the corner and enter the hallway to the throne room lies. I clutch my spear in shaking hands and Senika draws his sword, the soft scrape of metal on metal echoing too loudly in my ears. The gilded doors are just as imposing as the last time I was here, except now they're thrown open as if to welcome guests inside. I sneak over to the entrance and my head spins, not-so-kindly informing me that Xethos is there along with three others.

A long wooden table has been placed in the centre of the room, set for six like Xethos is preparing for a dinner party. Candles in golden holders light up the space, sending flickering shadows across the gold walls and reflecting off the plates and cutlery on the table. Xethos himself is seated at the head of the table on his gold throne, dressed in shining armour, likely made of pure gold like the rest of the room. His face looks strained, eyes wild and cheeks hollow in sharp contrast to the last time I saw him. Next to him, Taiyo is dressed in gold as well, her sparkling skirts swirling around her feet as she paces impatiently. Jyn and Safiya are seated at the table too, both tied up and blindfolded. The scene looks like some sick twist on a nice party although it is somewhat lacking in atmosphere.

"What the fuck is this?" I demand, storming into the room.

Xethos stands, holding out his arms with a welcoming grin. "There they are. We were starting to wonder when the stars of the show would make an appearance. You know, you're little friends and I here have been very patiently waiting."

"Let them go," I warn him. "Or I swear, I will murder you."

"And here I was thinking you hated them. But it looks like I was wrong because look, here you are, playing the hero again."

"Kellin?" Jyn sounds scared, turning his head and searching for me.

"What's our plan here exactly?" Senika mutters from behind me.

"We put that bastard back in his grave," I whisper before I start toward Xethos. But Taiyo steps in front of me, crossing her arms in front of her calmly. "Stay out of my way," I say evenly.

"I can't let you hurt him," There's a cold, dark look in her green eyes that reminds me of icy water in a calm but chilling lake. "If only because you want him dead. He is useful to me."

Xethos laughs, striding over to place a gloved hand on Taiyo's shoulder. "It would seem someone knows the meaning of loyalty and obedience. What a good child."

Taiyo grits her teeth but doesn't interrupt him, turning her gaze to the ground.

"You see," Xethos adds, "she has been my perfect servant for many years."

"Why do you keep killing them?" I demand. "Halfbloods have been an inconvenience before, so what's the use in all this killing?"

For a moment, the god just stares in disbelief before bursting out in laughter again. "Mortal stupidity never ceases to amuse. Do you truly not know? Halfbloods were born from the blood of demons, gods, and humans—a true miracle, really. But alas, only one-third holds true strength, while the rest makes you weak and impure. It was Ophiele who hid this from you, which was wise, but if you knew, perhaps you would fall onto your blades to purge the weakness from this world. And despite their pathetic power, Halfbloods are the only thing that stands in the way of this world crumbling to ash."

I stare at him. "Are you done? You know, I hate talkative people."

Taiyo screams, and Xethos stumbles backward as freezing water dumps on the two of them. Near the table, Jyn flexes his wrist, testing his strength before sending a blast of water into Taiyo's face. Senika grins and then sets to work freeing Safiya, who throws her arms around him gratefully the instant she's free. As soon as he regains his footing, Xethos raises his hand. With a flick of his wrist, he sends Jyn slamming into the table.

"Jyn!" I shout, racing past Xethos to where Jyn lies in a crumpled heap on the floor.

"You little *Halfbloods* keep getting in my way," Xethos growls. "Why can't you just stay out of my way?"

The entire room changes. The air feels heavy, like running with water up to my waist, and my head spins as nausea washes over me. I stumble and fall to my knees, barely avoiding a beam of light that shoots past my head without explanation. Glancing over my shoulder, I see Xethos's eyes have turned pure black, dark cracks spiderwebbing from the corners of his eyes and inky tears dripping down his face. Golden energy no longer surrounds him. Instead, darkness fills the air. His bright armour chips away, revealing black underneath. But his whole body still glows darkly as he walks toward me, footsteps like thunder.

I reach for my power, trying to find anything to defend myself with. Instead of the normal pull of magic, I find nothing. It's like our last fight, except now there's nothing there at all, not even the fear of the others in the room. Even the constant buzz of spirits in my head is muted and far away. My stomach drops and horror fills my insides instead, the all-consuming fear of helplessness leaving me paralyzed.

"You see, you are weak." Even his voice is different, rough and without mercy. A long black and gold sword takes shape in his hands, a dark parody of the one I'd seen before. "My mission is to cleanse this world of all those unworthy of living here, those who will not bow before the true god. You Halfbloods always think you have a right to do as you please just because you have power, but that power makes you arrogant. Arrogance makes you *weak*."

"Bullshit," I snap. "I don't even know who you are."

This new god grins wickedly, extending a claw-like hand toward me. "I am Eris, Lord of Shadows. I am but a servant of Doriak. I am here to prepare your world for his return. Xethos was merely a puppet in my plan."

Eris. Lord of Shadows and god of the dead. One of two gods exiled to Gosritaan for their attempted destruction of Morsevdon. The patron god of necromancers. Of course.

"Kellin!" Someone calls out my name in a familiar voice, but it takes a moment for me to locate Senika. My mind feels foggy and full of clouds rather than a brain, making it hard to focus on anything, much less comprehend what's happening. When I finally see him, it's like looking through a nearly opaque curtain, only part of the world visible.

"Senika?" My voice sounds too small so I shout his name again. "Senika!"

The toe of a steel boot slams into my stomach, causing me to sprawl onto my back uselessly.

"You care about them," the dark god observes. "To care for another is to allow yourself a weakness. I can help with that. I can remove that weakness."

I struggle onto my hands and knees, watching him turn on Senika. Jyn still lies unconscious nearby and Safiya hides under the table while Taiyo watches, stunned and soaking wet from farther away. The god who was Xethos points his sword at Senika, slashing it through the air and causing a blade of light to cut through the space just above Senika's head where it scorches the wall across the throne room. The room shakes, raining bits of broken stone down from the roof onto us. I stagger to my feet, my head pounding and foggy.

A flash of light surrounds Senika, but he doesn't shift, instead collapsing to the ground, coughing painfully. His fear washes over me, filling the room like smoke as he tries to drag himself to his feet.

With shaking hands, he reaches for his sword, but Eris kicks it away, knocking it just out of Senika's reach.

"A Shifter who can't shift." The god grins maliciously. "How pathetic."

The air crackles with unfathomable energy as Eris raises his own sword, poised to strike. Golden light and black shadows combine, twisting around his blade like snakes. Senika coughs blood, his hands curling into fists.

He's going to kill him. I realize in horror.

In my head, a single spirit cackles. *Dead butterflies.*

Reaching for my spear, I race forward, gathering all the strength I can muster to leap in front of Eris. His sword comes down in a black arc, golden light flickering along its edge. I make it there a split second before it's too late. The crash of metal on metal is deafening, a sound that echoes through the entire room as our blades cross.

For a moment, Eris hesitates, taken aback. Then his void-like eyes narrow. He tries to shove me back with his sword scraping the shaft of my spear. I almost lose my footing, stumbling back a few inches. Out of the corner of my eye, I see Senika's hand reach for his sword as he crawls out of the way. A tiny flicker of my power is back, just enough to sense fear but not enough to do anything with it. My feet slip on the marble floor.

I just need to hold on long enough to buy time for my power to return.

"What have you done?" I growl. "How is this possible?"

Eris's sword suddenly vanishes and he steps backward, causing me to stumble forward and fall to the floor. "A simple magic block," he says calmly. "With something so easy, I can make you all useless. Isn't it bizarre how weak you all are?"

He raises his sword again, slashing it through the air and sending a volley of light rays toward me. None of them hit me, but when they strike the floor, they leave behind scorch marks. I try to stand, vision doubling as the world blurs. I almost fall on my face. Eris sends a second round of light arrows, but this time one of them burns the feathers on my ear, slicing through strands of my hair.

Eris laughs. "Look, you are pathetic creatures. Yet you are called the guardians of this world. I pity those who think they are protected by you weaklings. Soon, this world will fall, and the true saviour will rise once again."

"*Si me interrogas, potes te ipsum ire, monstrum nefandum.*" I curse him under my breath in Old Alkelian. "You sound like an idiot. There is no saviour of this world, and it certainly won't be you or whatever demon you're trying to bring to life."

"Oh shut up, would you?" With a dismissive wave of his hand, a bolt of light shoots toward me, colliding with the stone wall mere inches from my head. "You are becoming a nuisance, Halfblood."

"Then kill me."

Behind him, Senika kneels on the floor, staring at his blood-soaked hands. He looks up, terror plain on his face when he meets my eyes. Eris seems to have forgotten him, but the god still has a firm hold on all of our magic. Jyn is still unconscious and Safiya has no experience with battle or magic of any kind. We have absolutely no chance of winning this, not unless I change something fast.

"Gladly," The god's voice is cold like ice and completely devoid of mercy.

Instantly, a hundred more bolts of light rain down on me. Some of them hit their mark, tearing my clothing and drawing blood across my body. One of them hits my armguard with a hiss, melting the metal. A second wave follows quickly after the first, a thousand tiny needles raining down at his command. I fall to my knees, spear falling from my fingers as blood drips from a thousand burning cuts. I don't need to survive this; I just need to buy enough time for Senika to finish the fight.

That's how long it takes me to realize that we're no longer fighting a dead man.

Even if Eris is using Xethos's body as a tool, his mind is still in control. That's all I need. I reach for my power but instantly hit a wall, nausea making me feel lightheaded again. When I try to stand, Eris raises his hand, summoning a bolt of light that hovers beside his head for a moment.

"Stay down," he hisses, launching the bolt at me.

My body feels weak, like all the strength is being sucked out of it, draining me of all capability to fight back. Each cut burns like a fire that runs along my body, scorching me to my very bones. I reach for a knife—like it would do any good—but my bloody fingers grip the handle weakly. And just as I accept that here is where I die, Taiyo steps in front of me.

35

... TO MY GLASS HOUSE

KELLIN

The bolt of light hits Taiyo square in the chest, and she stumbles backward. I shout her name, but I don't hear my voice as I lunge toward her, catching her before her body hits the ground. I fall to my knees. Her dress is bloody and ruined where the bolt hit her, the tiny gems sowed into her bodice melted into her skin. The flesh beneath it burns black and bloody, a ruined mess worse than anything I've ever seen. She looks at me with fear and sadness in her eyes along with regret I didn't think she could ever feel.

"Kellin . . ." Her voice is quiet and broken, a whisper in the roar of battle. "I'm sorry . . . This world cannot fall to him."

"What are you talking about?" I ask, unsure of what to do. There is nothing I can do to save her now, only watch as she dies. "Why . . . Why would you do this?"

"He is worse than you . . ." She takes in a shaky breath but ends up coughing blood instead. "I must save us . . . I have . . . to . . . stop them . . ."

Then she's gone. Dead in my arms. I stare at her blank eyes for a long moment, astonished and frozen in place. Then my gaze shifts back to

Eris. His expression is just as shocked as mine, but he quickly snaps back to that cold neutrality.

But his guard lowered just long enough to be useful.

I can feel my power returning, strength rushing back into my body and the cacophony of noise in my head surging in to replace the horrible silence. Without hesitation, I reach into Eris's mind, seeing not emptiness like before, but a world where all are happy with the exception of him. His greatest fear is far too simple, too easy after all the time spent searching.

As soon as I find it, Eris freezes.

"It's you," he mutters. "It shouldn't be you."

I reach for my spear, gathering all my power at my fingertips, heedless of the consequences. "I don't know what you're talking about."

"The one who will stop us, the one who will destroy or save this world." He stares at me, horrified. "You are not like the others. You are the one with the power to change everything. It is simple fate."

"Frankly, I don't care about fate," I coldly inform him, coldly. "But I do care about the people you've killed, and for that, I will destroy you."

In the blink of an eye, I dash forward, slamming a wall of wind into his chest that sends him flying as fear fills his mind. I tighten my grip on my spear, and as soon as he regains his footing, only slightly thrown off from my attack on his mind, I'm behind him. He whirls, sword reappearing in his hand, but it's too slow. My blade cuts through his armour like it's butter. There's a thud as his severed hand hits the floor, smoking while the armour melts and turns to dust. His half-formed sword falls to the ground next to it, and he staggers backward, off-balance and wounded. The dark cracks around his eyes glow gold as a blot of light shoots toward me. It hits my side but I don't falter, slashing forward again and again. I've gained the upper hand now, and I won't back down. Eris steps backward, blocking his blows with one arm as he attempts to gather his strength again. My unrelenting attacks strike his dark armour, sending sparks leaping into the air. The fresh wound in my side burns—I force myself to ignore it, to keep moving even now.

Eris leaps backward, using the fraction of time he gains for himself to form a helmet over his head just before my spear smashes into the side of it, creating thin cracks. The narrow eye slits of the helmet mean there is no way for me to hurt him. So I turn on his mind, hammering at the vulnerability of fear. With each hit, I dig deeper into his mind, reaching for more and letting it fuel every move I make.

Wind spirals around us, pushing Eris back and tearing at my clothes like fingers. The world vanishes, melting away until only our battle remains. My vision tunnels in on him, red with fury. The spirits in my head scream louder. All other noise becomes irrelevant. Their words no longer matter to me, white noise to accompany the rage. I let myself lose control of my power, allowing it to run mad in his mind, torturing him enough to drive any man insane, while a hurricane of wind howls through the room and turns it upside down.

He is not the right one.

Be patient, Wolf.

I have waited long enough. There must be a mistake.

He is the one. We will see soon enough.

No, you are wrong. He is not the saviour, he is the destroyer.

Destroyer. That word makes me hesitate. Those two voices came out of nowhere—louder than the rest, the only ones that matter. I snap back to myself, seeing Eris before me, left helpless with shattered armour and no weapons. The end is within my sight. This rush of power is amazing, allowing me to do anything with just a thought. But soon it won't be so easy. The wind blows around us, yanking my hair free from its ponytail and billowing my jacket out behind me. I know my golden eyes burn hot enough to rival the light of the sun. All the world's power sits at my fingertips.

I kick him to the ground then reach out and yank the helmet off Eris's head, tossing it to the side to look at his face. The dark cracks have spread across his whole face like he's about to crumble into pieces. Instead of anger, his black eyes hold defeat. It's strange to see the face of Xethos so ruined, but stranger still is the sight of the God of Victory kneeling at my feet.

"You are a fool to think you can take this world for your own," I say, my voice strangely quiet among the voices of the spirits in my mind. "If you try this again, I swear I will hunt you down and kill you properly, Lord of Shadows."

"Killing a puppet will do nothing to stop me. In the end, even your power cannot compare to that of the First God," Eris replies. "To him, you and I are both weak."

Destroy his heart. A spirit says, probably testing me. *Destroy it and end this.*

"Next time, I'll bring an army," I promise. "Next time, I will destroy you and your First God. *Iuro.*"

Eris laughs. "You swear it? Do you think you can kill him? You are *nothing* compared to him. You could kill him a thousand times and never have enough power to even injure him."

"Then I'll bring every army this world has to offer. But you will not win this," I warn. "And I cannot lose."

Destroy his heart. The spirit commands again.

And I obey.

I gather all my strength into my next hit, slashing upward and shattering what remains of his armour and leaving his chest exposed and vulnerable. The very air swirls around me, winding around the shaft of my spear as I strike straight through his heart. Blood sprays onto my clothing, staining my shirt red. Eris's hand grabs my spear, as if trying to yank it out to save himself, but it's useless. The cracks in his face glow gold then his flesh crumbles, skin peeling off to reveal nothingness behind it as his body turns to dust. His grip slackens then his arm falls limp to his side before all his armour clatters to the ground, surrounded by ash and dust. The wind picks up some of the dust, blowing it away until I reel my power back in, stopping it completely.

Instantly, I stumble, drained. My vision flickers black around the edges and I blink frantically to keep myself awake. The hole in my side flares, as if I'm repeatedly stabbed with a flaming sword. I fall to one knee, unable to stay on my feet.

Silver butterflies fill the air and Senika materializes in front of me. His face is paler than normal, exhaustion visible in his silver-blue eye. There's blood on his shirt.

"Kellin! Are you okay? You're hurt." He grabs me by the shoulders, sending needles of pain through my body.

I nod slowly, strangely disoriented. "I'm okay, I'm okay. We did it."

"No," He shakes his head. "*You* did it. That was incredible, I didn't know you could do anything like that."

"Neither did I," I mutter, reaching up to brush his hair out of his eyes. Using so much of my power like that is making me feel drunk. "You're beautiful, butterfly. Can I kiss you?"

"You sound insane." He gives me a small smile.

"I'm fine, shut up," I whisper. I kiss him, tasting blood on his lips. Then I lean my head against his chest, closing my eyes and breathing hard.

"Okay, you do know you're bleeding all over the place right?" he asks. "You're acting like you're drunk." He takes my face in his hands to make me look at him.

I shake my head. "I'm fine. We need to get Jyn and Safiya out of here. They're hurt . . ."

"So are you," he insists. "And this castle looks ready to collapse at any minute. So let's hurry up and get out of here. Can you walk?"

Nodding, I stand up on shaky legs, limping over to where Jyn lies unconscious on the floor. "I'm fine," I mutter. "Don't worry about me."

I slowly make my way over to Jyn, shaking his shoulder gently when I kneel next to him. His green hair has turned grey from all the dust in the air, and blood leaks from a wide gash on his forehead. All around him, the dishes from the dinner table have fallen and shattered, leaving behind nothing but fragments of white and blue porcelain. I shake his shoulder again when he doesn't wake up at first. This time, he stirs, opening his eyes to look at me.

"What happened?" Jyn mumbles, taking in the destroyed throne room.

"We're getting out of here," I tell him, not wanting to recount everything.

"Is Xethos dead?"

I shrug. "I'll explain later."

Standing, I help him to his feet before turning to leave. Senika manages to pull Safiya out from where she had hidden under the table, but the princess is shaking and terrified, tears streaking her cheeks. When we reach the door, I pause.

"Wait, there's one more thing." I turn and walk back to where Taiyo's body lies, still and cold as stone. "We can't leave her here."

Jyn hobbles over, favouring one leg. "I can carry her. We can bury her in the Order cemetery and have a pretty funeral. She would like that." He whispers the last part as he bends down, collecting her body in his arms.

Safiya places a hand on Jyn's arm, walking with him to the door. I watch them go, wondering what we do now. Dust rains down from the cracked ceiling, turning the world grey and muting all its other colours. Outside the tall windows, the faint greyish light of dawn is starting to creep over the horizon, finally allowing light into the world again. I stand in the pool of light created by one of the windows and look out at the river beyond. The window is broken. Jagged bits of glass around the inside of its gilded frame shine in the dim light of dawn.

"Kellin?" Senika walks over to stand next to me. "Are you coming?"

I nod. "Yeah. I just . . . need to catch my breath."

"Okay. I'll stay with you," he says.

The world feels distant and fuzzy like I'm watching it from behind someone else's eyes. My head pounds painfully. Strangely enough, the spirits have gone completely silent, not a single whisper remaining in my mind. I hadn't expected to see the sunrise today; in fact, I hadn't expected to see it ever again. Tonight was meant to be the night I died.

"Butterfly?" I whisper. "Can we run away now?"

He takes my hand. "Gladly. I would go anywhere with you."

I smile at him, just happy that he's still here. "Let's go to Iolleria. That sounds nice. We should buy a house by the sea and live there forever. Just you and me. I would like that."

"We can go wherever you want."

When he kisses me, it feels as strange and far away as the rest of the world. I run my fingers through his hair, turning it red with blood. He doesn't notice the blood, doesn't notice my shaking hands or bloody clothing. But there are tears in his eyes as he looks at me and takes both my hands, holding them carefully to his chest. I kiss him again desperately with tears running down my face, not wanting to disappear.

"I'm sorry, Butterfly," I whisper, my body feeling weak and fading. "I'm so sorry."

The world fades to black with the finality I had always expected from death, simple and complete darkness.

36

To Save a Hero

Airadyne

The spirit watches the Halfblood who lies unconscious in the bed, his mind tormented by nightmares he cannot escape, his body unable to rise. Beside him, the one who calls himself Senika sits, unwilling to sleep while his lover battles with death. Airadyne watches calmly, for this is the fate she foresaw long ago. He will push himself near the brink of death to fight for the cause she gave him, the cause of saving lives, but each time he will shatter the heart of the one who loves him. This Airadyne had not predicted. In the prophecy told to her, the boy fights alone until he finds the others, yet she cannot determine who the others it speaks of may be.

Through the years, she has seen many who may fight this battle in her name. There was the hero Ophiele, the Halfblood who fought alongside Xethos himself in the first battle against Gosritaan. Then came a knight from Isher who could have held back the tides of monsters alone, as the prophecy said. The warlord of the True North could have done it, and so could the necromancer, if he had not turned his back on the spirits. The kitsune who lost her voice or the dragon rider who rewrote the laws of this world could both be powerful enough, but Airadyne thinks perhaps only time will tell.

For now, her hero is this child who has lost everything but still fights for those he does not know. She thinks he is strong enough, yet repeatedly she has been told he will fail her. His mind will break—his body will give out—but she holds faith that she can make him be the one.

Still, she worries for the pair of lovers. One will die, she knows, one or perhaps both, for not all heroes can be allowed to live. And when that day comes, she will mourn with whomever remains. For the death of a hero is always a tragedy, no matter if she knew them or not. As she watches them now, it is easy for her to imagine her chosen one dying where he lies. But the battle is not yet over.

He cannot fail her now.

"Airadyne." Wolf appears next to her, a cloud of smoke in the partial reality they float in. "How long will you watch them?"

"For as long as I must," Airadyne replies assuredly.

"And if he dies?" The smoky spirit questions her. "What will you do then?"

Airadyne smiles beneath the white mask that covers her eyes. "Then I will simply find another. There are always more heroes, my dear friend."

"And if they all fail you?" Wolf asks.

"Then it is I who has failed them," she says calmly. "For if they die, it is me who has not prepared the right ones for this battle. But I am certain there will be one who can win this fight for us."

"Yes, there must be one," Wolf agrees for once. "But even you cannot know all. Perhaps this battle is not ours to win."

Airadyne shakes her head. "No. There will be a hero who can win. There must be."

She leans down, space bending around her to let her reach through the side of the ship. Holding one pale, slender hand over the sleeping hero's face she gathers her strength and wills him to rise. At first, he does not stir, remaining still and unaware of her presence. Then, at last, his eyes slowly open and meet the eyes of his lover, relief flooding those golden eyes.

Airadyne smiles, her job done.

She retreats from the mortal realm once again.

37

Alive Again

Kellin

Through the dark fog, I hear someone talking in a hushed voice. The voice is a familiar one, soft and gentle with an accent reminiscent of a song. Someone else answers the first voice, clearly trying to comfort them. Then I glimpse someone sitting next to my bed, dim light filling the room around them. Between it all, there are flashes of pain, fever dreams and uneasy sleep in a strange, unending cycle. A soft, distant conversation is followed by pain like fire tearing my body apart.

Then—inexplicable dreams of the sea, the sky, and a boy with wings.

I slip back into the comfortable blackness. It's like watching the world from far, far away.

After what feels like an eternity, a solid image of reality manages to take shape. Stranger terror catches me and I bolt upright but collapse back onto the mattress when pain courses through my body, gasping for breath.

"It's okay, you can rest." Senika's voice is quiet as he brushes my hair out of my face, his fingers cold against my hot skin. "You're safe now."

He looks like he's from another dream, his hair sticking up in every direction and his butterfly tattoo glowing faintly in the lamplight. He isn't wearing his eyepatch and somehow my mind finds it normal that his left eye has a silver and white butterfly in place of an iris. I reach up to touch his face, tracing from his eye down his cheekbone.

"Butterfly," I whisper, my voice raspy from disuse.

"I'm here." He touches my hand, a soft brush of his skin on mine that makes my whole body ache. "How are you?"

"Everything hurts." I groan. It's certainly true. Every inch of my body is on fire, and I feel rather like I've been run over by a stampede of horses. "What happened?"

He touches the back of his hand to my forehead, measuring my temperature. "The best name I have for it is overload. You used too much power at once. I've seen it happen to soldiers in Iolleria during a battle. They get too caught up in it and forget to control their power and end up in worse states than their enemy. I don't know much about it, but this proves how dangerous it is."

"Ugh, I feel like I've died and come back to life."

"Well, you got close. You've slept for four days straight, and for the first day or so, no one could get near you without your magic attacking them," he explains grimly. "From what Emaya's said, you're lucky to be alive."

I close my eyes for a moment. The voices of the spirits are strangely absent again today leaving my head silent and empty. "I was meant to die," I whisper.

"Please, please never do that again," Senika pleads. "I'd really like for you to stay alive."

I nod. "Yeah . . . I'll try."

We sit in silence for a while, neither of us sure of what there is to be said. I hold his hand even though it hurts. From the sound of it, we're back on the ship but it's quiet, not a single sound coming from the deck above or the other cabins below. The waves crashing gently against the side of the boat are comforting now, a constant sound that anchors me to the real world. It's hard to tell what time of day it might be, but the world is so silent. Even the usual busyness of the docks is gone.

"Where are Jyn and Safiya?" I ask after a long time. I nearly ask about Taiyo and Fenix too, but I stop myself. There were so many times Fenix was next to me. I just expect her to be there.

"Safiya has been caught up in politics lately," he tells me. "She called off the marriage and claimed Alkelia is too dangerous, but I guess there's still a lot to deal with. Jyn has been resting mostly, but people are trying to regroup the Order so I guess he's been busy with that. Even after everything, they still see the Order as a symbol of peace."

"And you? Are you okay?"

He pauses for a moment, unsure of how to answer. "I've been waiting for you, Kira and Emaya said we won't leave until you're better and if you decide to come . . . they would be more than happy to have you."

I frown. "That's not what I asked. You look like you haven't slept in days."

Again, he doesn't answer right away. "I was worried you wouldn't wake up. I thought I lost you." There are tears in his eyes when he speaks. "Emaya did everything she could but . . . she said you might be beyond our help. I was scared."

I try to sit up again, reaching to comfort him but my side screams in pain and I have to stop. "Hey, I woke up, didn't I? We both made it out alive, even if we are a bit broken."

He nods, leaning forward to kiss my forehead. "I know. But I never want to lose you."

"*Memento mori*," I whisper. "We all die, Butterfly. It's just a matter of when."

After that, it's another day before I can properly eat—two before I can get out of bed, though not for very long. Senika stays with me the entire time and refuses to sleep until he can't possibly stay awake any longer. The battle took a toll on him too. He keeps coughing but insists he's fine even when the pain is visible in his eyes. Sometimes, I try to ask him what happened but he just brushes me away, saying he's fine, that he'll be alright. Mostly, he just frets about my injuries, the thousand tiny cuts across my body and the angry burn just above my hip.

On the second night, I woke to him asleep in the chair next to me, snoring softly with the lamp still burning dimly next to him. If he knew I was awake, he would be panicking that he fell asleep when he should have been taking care of me. I watch him sleep until I drift off as well, caught up in dreams of silent snow and black feathers.

Three days after I first awoke, I finally have the strength to walk up the stairs to the deck. It's nearly raining, so there isn't much to see. Most of the crew are avoiding the gloomy weather in the cabins below deck. However, Kira, Gendry, and Emaya are sitting around the table near the mast, playing a quiet game of cards. At the sound of the door opening, all three of them immediately turn to look at Senika and me.

"So you are alive," Kira observes with a bright smile. "It's good to see you, kid."

Emaya frowns and shakes her head. "I said you should rest more, did I not?"

"It's boring down there," I reason, out of breath just from walking up the stairs. Every step makes my body scream in pain, and when my loose shirt brushes the wound in my side, another hundred needles stab into my skin through the thick bandages.

I take an unsteady step toward the table, leaning on Senika to avoid falling over. He wouldn't let me walk on my own, and to be honest, I don't think I could have made it up those stairs otherwise.

"That was awfully brave of you," Kira says. "Not just anyone could go toe to toe with a god like that, much less the Lord of Shadows." I look at her, startled, but she laughs and adds, "Don't worry, Senika filled us in on everything. You're lucky to be alive, kid."

"Alive but certainly not well," Emaya points out. "You shouldn't be walking around like this. You could hurt yourself more."

I shrug, which doesn't help at all. "Yeah . . . thank you, by the way. For taking care of me. You too, butterfly."

Kira gives Emaya a meaningful look and then says, "We wouldn't leave you to die like that. Your friends back there, they sound like shitty friends."

Emaya smacks the captain in the arm. "*Kira*! Don't say that, the poor kid almost died."

"What? It's true; they left him at the first chance they could find."

Clicking her tongue, Emaya turns her attention back to me. "Do you need anything? I can get you something to eat. Jakob has made the most wonderful soup, I'm sure you simply must try it."

Time passes quickly with them, meaningless conversations and jokes filling the deck with laughter and smiles. I don't say much, sitting next to Senika and listening to the banter between them. The conversation switches from Iollerian to Alkelian every other sentence, making it hard for me to keep up, but I catch the meaning of most of it. True to Emaya's word, the soup is quite good, but I don't finish it, worried I might vomit it all back up later. When it starts to rain, we all hurry back inside to our cabins. I'm exhausted by then, ready to fall asleep on my feet and hurting all over.

After a short nap, Senika and I find a deck of cards and play a handful of games in our cabin, betting random objects like shoes or bits of dust on the cards spread out across one of the beds. He wins most of the games, earning my jacket, my left boot, one knife, the handful of coins we found through the room, and a kiss. I win a hat borrowed—or stolen—from Kira and Senika's jacket. Both of which are much too big for me.

"You look like a pirate." Senika laughs. "A very small pirate."

I kick his leg with my bare foot. "Shut up, it's not that big." The hat keeps slipping down over my eyes, preventing me from seeing, but I just push it back up. "I think you sabotaged me by betting this thing."

He grins. "You've figured out my strategy. It's your turn though."

"Fine, I'm betting this stupid hat." I lean forward and place it on his head. "I want nothing to do with it anymore."

Trying not to laugh, he shows me his cards. "Good, because I just won."

I throw my cards at his face. "Ah, screw you. You cheated."

"How could I cheat?" He pretends to sound offended but does a poor job of hiding his smile. "You're just bad at this."

"I've never played before, stupid," I remind him. "Therefore you had an advantage. Which is cheating."

He stares at me for a few seconds and I glare back before we both burst out laughing. I feel ridiculous sitting here with one shoe and an ill-fitting jacket, but it's better than the past few days when I've done nothing but sleep or lay in bed. Almost instantly, I double over in pain, clutching my side and he starts coughing, both of us reminded of our situation.

"Ugh, bad idea," I groan.

"Yup, no more laughing. We have to be very serious," he says, sitting up straighter and lifting his chin. "This is a highly serious game between two dignified people."

I roll my eyes. "Yes, I feel very dignified with my one shoe."

"Well, maybe you aren't dignified, but I certainly am," He adjusts the lopsided hat on his head, nearly knocking it right off.

"Butterfly, you have three shoes. That isn't very dignified," I point out.

"Maybe you're a shoe thief for stealing one from me."

I sputter. "*I'm* the shoe thief? As I recall, *you* are the one who cheated and stole my shoe. And my jacket and my money and my knife."

"It's called skill."

"And I refuse to accept that. So you cheated."

He smiles at me again. "I am so glad you're alive."

I shrug. "Only barely. And I can't do much in the state I'm in."

"Barely is better than not at all," he says. "I would much rather have an alive Kellin than a dead Kellin."

"Are you trying to distract me?"

"Yes. It's working."

I shake my head. "It's not working. You're still a cheater."

He kisses me softly on the mouth. "How about now? Are you distracted yet?"

"I—" I hold up one hand. "Yes, I do believe that worked."

"Mission accomplished then." He places his remaining cards face up on the bed. "I'm kind of done with this anyway. And you have nothing left to bet."

"Because you stole it all," I grumble, gathering up all the cards and stacking them neatly.

"No, I didn't steal anything. You lost, so please never take up gambling."

The next day it rains again, but this time we don't stay inside. Today, we walk through the rain, up the hill and down the winding roads of Elview to the graveyard. We pass through the tall iron gates and follow the path past rows and rows of stone grave markers. Tall trees with sweeping branches line the way, protecting parts of the path from the rain with their thick leaves. Both Senika and I walk in silence, almost afraid to disrupt the eerie quiet of this place. In my hand, I carry a bunch of white flowers we bought on the way here, pale petals now dripping with rainwater. Far from the gate, in a spot that overlooks the river with the castle out of view, an open grave waits.

Jyn and Safiya are both dressed in white, standing near the gravestone and examining the words carved into it. Neither Senika nor I could find anything white to wear, so we both came dressed as normal but now it makes me feel a little sad. There's a woman there too, dressed in the simple robes of a priest, coloured white for death with a veil covering her face completely. The three of them all look up at our arrival.

"You made it," Jyn says by way of greeting. "It's good to see you."

"We wouldn't miss it," I tell him.

In the open grave lies a coffin carved of dark oak wood with gold around its edges and a plaque with the name Taiyo Stone on it. The gravestone has her name as well with the date and an Old Alkelian saying underneath, highlighted in gold writing. It's a grave made for royalty, with money straight from the coffers of King Elias himself.

"*In pulverem revertimer*," I whisper. It's something the grave of every Halfblood bares, a sign to the gods and a morbid reminder that this is the fate of all of us. Seeing it written under Taiyo's name is strange; she wasn't a Halfblood, yet she earned it nonetheless.

The priestess raises her hands and starts to sing the song of death. Its words are Old Alkelian, haunting and sorrowful, and I've never heard someone sing it so well. Each note is filled with grief and mourning for a girl she never knew. Around her hands, the priestess uses magic to create illusions depicting the story of life, a baby born to a loving mother and father, a child growing up and becoming an adult, falling in love and having children of their own before finally, the last image of a single flower on a grave fades away. From the grave of the first, a flower slowly blooms, flourishing under the sun in the last notes of the song. Each picture is formed of gold threads that shift and change, melting away to allow another to replace it before they all vanish in golden flecks that dissipate in the rain.

When it ends, the priestess waves her hand. The dirt around the edges of the grave shifts, falling in over the wood coffin until the last of the oak disappears underneath it. The priestess gestures to the grave again, this time conjuring the image of a girl sleeping under the ground. The details of her face are exactly like Taiyo's, her eyes closed in quiet slumber, and her hands are folded across her chest, holding a bouquet of golden flowers.

"*In pulverem revertimer, sed de cinere resurgemus,*" the priestess whispers. She finishes, folding her hands behind her back.

I brush away tears I hadn't noticed before and step forward to place the flowers next to the head of the sleeping girl. Jyn also offers flowers, blue and yellow rather than traditional white. The defiance of those flowers makes me smile because Taiyo would never wear white to a funeral.

No one says anything for a long time. We stand in the rain watching the illusion of the sleeping girl until the priestess nods solemnly and takes her leave. Safiya leaves quietly a moment later, walking silently down the path. Before he goes, Senika places a hand on my shoulder and I reach out to brush my fingers against his as he turns and walks away.

"You know," Jyn intones, breaking the quiet in a soft voice. "She would have liked this. She would have liked to be remembered, even if it's like this."

I nod. "I hope she didn't hate me in the end."

He doesn't answer for so long that I start to think he didn't hear me. "I wish she didn't have to die. I wish death wasn't the end."

I look down at the ground. The illusion of the sleeping girl has nearly vanished, only a faint outline remaining in gold. "Me too."

Jyn turns to leave but only makes it a few steps before facing me again. "Kellin?" He waits for me to look up before continuing. "I'm sorry. I shouldn't have left you. I shouldn't have done a lot of things. I was kind of a shitty friend, honestly. So I understand if you can't forgive me but I can't live as your enemy."

It takes me a long time to answer. Of course, I agree. I hate him for some of the things he did but I refuse to be enemies. Jyn has always been my friend and I can hardly imagine what my life would be like if we never met. So I say, "I forgive you. You were really, *really* shitty but I've been shitty to you and you've always forgiven it. We've always turned out on the same side, Jyn."

He tries to smile but it fades, clouded by the circumstances. "Thank you. I– I'm glad I know you, Kellin."

I don't reply.

After that, Jyn leaves too. I watch him walk away but I stay in the graveyard for a long time afterward. Sitting in the wet grass next to the grave, I watch the river flow past the city. It isn't raining hard, but it's a cold, half-frozen autumn rain that chills me to the bone. Yet, I stay until the sun breaks through the dark clouds. By the time I stand to leave, I'm frozen and soaked to the bone, but I don't hurry away. I pause in front of the grave, silent tears running down my face, before walking away.

It feels like walking away from my own life, but so much has changed. I don't know what my life is anymore. Everything I knew has fallen apart; Fenix and Taiyo are dead, the cathedral is gone, the Order is in ruins and all of Alkelia is lost without their god. But at the same time, I have something I never dreamed of.

I have Senika—and I have a way out of here.

For the first time in many, many years, I can see light in the darkness. For once, I might have a chance.

"*In pulverem revertimur, sed de cinere resurgemus,*" I whisper as I go.

To dust, we return, but from death comes life.

38

◆―○―◆

To a New Dawn

Kellin

"The Order will be reformed," Jyn informs me on the fourth day after Taiyo's funeral. "The remaining members from around the kingdom have been gathering and they've—I've been attending the meetings too but mostly out of curiosity—been trying to reestablish ourselves. They want to divide the leadership amongst a council, rather than having one man who rules everything."

I nod. "Seems reasonable."

We sit on the deck of the *Vanquisher*, watching yet another rainstorm roll over the horizon. Emaya has hardly let me leave the ship in four days, but thankfully Jyn has come by to fill me in on what I've missed lately. It's almost been two weeks since the battle with Eris, but I'm still injured and weak. I'm not eager to go anywhere.

"They've requested for me to sit on the council," he adds. "It would take some work but I think I could get you a place there too. There are a few others as well but I heard Alyssa might be one of them."

Without hesitation, I shake my head. "No. I don't want anything to do with the Order anymore. After all this, I can't see them as heroes."

"Yeah," Jyn nods. "I think I'm going to take the offer but it seems like a lot of responsibility. I just can't walk away after all this time. Plus, this could be my chance to make things better for future generations."

I look out at the water, nodding. The harbour is mostly empty. The majority of ships left quickly after the supposed death of Xethos, but a few remain moored at the docks. From the sound of it, the rest of the city is equally deserted, with most of the people having left in case another catastrophe occurs. Otherwise, they're simply hiding away in their homes. I can't blame people for leaving. With the chaos filling the city lately, even the bravest warriors are on edge. Most of them don't know the truth behind the fall of Xethos but I understand their fear for their safety after such an event. No god has died in nearly 600 years, after all, and no one knows what to expect. Of course, I know that it's over but I still find myself looking over my shoulder and watching the docks for anything out of the ordinary.

Soldiers still patrol the streets although, with the Order scattered, there isn't much organization behind them. Most of the nobility seem desperate to regain control but even they appear lost and clueless, fumbling as they attempt to govern themselves without a god to do it for them. My face decorates wanted posters across the city, along with an extensive list of crimes that grows ever more absurd. As before, I hardly leave the boat although I can't find much of a reason to do such a thing.

"Will Safiya go back to Kyran?" I ask.

Jyn shrugs. "I guess so. She talks about it all the time. I think she really misses it."

"It's home," I say. "Everyone misses their home when they leave."

"What will you do?" he inquires. "I heard the captain talking about going back to Iolleria soon, but will you go with them?"

I sigh. "Maybe. I think it would be best to get out of here for a while. Once people learn what I did, I won't have many allies here anymore. Not that someone with a criminal record as long as mine has many allies to start with. I know Senika wants to go home too, so I think I might go with him."

Jyn gives me a crooked smile. "So you and him, huh? Good for you."

Shrugging, I say, "I thought he was just going to leave, and it would be pointless, but now I think we have a chance."

"You should go," he says decidedly. "You have a shot at happiness and you deserve to take it. Go with him."

I nod. "I think I might."

That night, I lie awake staring at the low ceiling of the tiny cabin. I had that dream again, the one of the snow and the red blood and the feathers floating to the ground. The same dream that's haunted me for years. Darkness fills the cabin and shadows line the walls but I don't want to light the lamp to chase them away in case I wake up Senika. He fell asleep with his clothes still on, too tired to take them off. When I got here, he was shivering, so I gave him my jacket as well but I doubt that helped much.

"Are you ever going to sleep?" Senika rolls over to look at me, apparently not asleep at all.

I let out a long breath. "I had a dream."

He nods sleepily. "You were crying. Are you okay?"

"I'm fine, I guess. It's nothing unusual. Just . . . nightmares."

"She really hurt you, didn't she?" he asks quietly, as if he's afraid of the words.

I don't answer for a very long time, letting silence fill the room until I say, "She was cruel to me, but I used to think that if I changed—if I became the person she wanted me to be—she wouldn't hate me anymore. But . . . no matter what I did, I would always be the villain to her. A monster who replaced her child."

"If I told you you're perfect, you wouldn't believe me, would you?"

"Probably not."

"No matter what she did to you, I will always love you. You will always be perfect to me." He reaches out, fingers extended, but we're too far apart for him to reach me.

"I don't know how I survived without you, Butterfly. Actually, you have saved my life a total of . . . three times, so I *really* wouldn't have survived without you."

He narrows his eyes thoughtfully, that strange left eye catching my attention as always. It's beautiful, like someone trapped a silver butterfly inside his eye and framed it with his white eyelashes. "I can think of two times. When was the third?"

"You saved me by simply arriving in my life."

"If love was a poetry contest, you would win every time." He groans

"If you honestly think I know how to do this whole love thing, you are horribly wrong."

"Then maybe you're a poet."

I snort. "I am definitely not a poet either."

"I think you're a lot of things you don't want to give yourself credit for."

Those words somehow leave me with nothing to say, so I just look at him, waiting for him to continue.

"Now as much as I would like to stay up and talk, I am exhausted, and if you don't sleep, Emaya will be on your ass all day tomorrow." He sighs.

I roll my eyes. "Fine, fine. Good night, Butterfly."

"Good night, my love."

Three days later, the *Vanquisher* prepares to set off. The sun shines over Elview, a rare but welcome sight at this time of year. Under it, the city is bright and alive, but the space where the cathedral used to stand still feels wrong, a ruin of fallen stone and broken glass where a masterpiece once stood.

For the first time since the fire, I walk through the remains of my home. I came here alone but the ghosts of those who once walked over these stones accompany me with each step I take. Most of the broken stones and shattered glass has been pushed into piles that will soon be removed for the construction of the new cathedral. The beautiful stained glass, stunning paintings, and masterful statues have been reduced to ash and dust, indistinguishable from the stones that once made up the floors and walls. If I didn't know better, I would never guess that such a structure ever stood here.

I reach the edge of the cliff, overlooking the river. There used to be a gorgeous, peaceful courtyard here, flowers growing beside it and lanterns to light it at night. Now all that remains is the charred remains of posts that once held up the roof over the space.

I look at the small clay urn in my hands. It has no decoration or adornments because the outside matters very little in comparison to its precious contents. I find myself holding my breath when I open it. The pale ashes inside the urn have nothing remarkable about them at first but that makes this no easier.

These are Fenix's ashes.

This is all that remains of my best friend.

She was all I had for so long, my anchor to this world when everything felt lost. We grew up together. We ran, slept, fought, and cried together. Fenix was a part of me that I can't erase so, in a way, we died together too. She will forever be part of my soul.

Still, I can't think of anything to say as I let her ashes fall into the river a hundred feet below me. There are no words for death, not when our bond went beyond any spoken language. I watch the ashes vanish into the water, hardly aware of my own tears. Once the last of them have fallen, I let the urn fall from my limp fingers and shatter on the stones. I don't pick up the broken fragments.

My tears flow freely as I walk away. There are only two words on my tongue as I leave everything I used to know behind.

"Goodbye, Fenix."

Later, I stand on the docks with Jyn, Safiya, and Senika. Behind us, the crew of the *Vanquisher* rushes about, white sails high as they hurry around. Kira stands near the wheel, shouting orders while they work. All around, laughter fills the air. It's been two weeks since we killed Xethos, and in those two weeks, the world feels completely changed.

"I guess this is goodbye, then," Jyn remarks.

"For now," I promise. "I'll come back one day."

He nods. "You better."

"You'll be okay here?" I ask.

"Probably." He shrugs. "It's going to be weird without you here."

"I don't think a lot of people want me here," I say. "You know, now that the entire kingdom wants me dead. Besides, I think I need to get away for a bit."

"And if you ever need a place to stay, I will personally make certain that Kyran's gates are always open," Safiya adds with a kind smile.

Jyn turns to Senika. "You better take care of him. Make sure he doesn't cause too much trouble. I do kind of want to see him alive again."

Senika laughs. "I can't make any promises, but I'll do my best."

"I'm not going to die," I remind them, scowling.

From up on the boat, Gendry yells, "If you're coming, get over here already!"

Turning around, Senika shouts back in Iollerian and then says to the rest of us, "We should get going."

I nod, glad to be gone but sad I might never come back. "I guess . . . we're leaving now. I'll see you again eventually, I promise."

Jyn smiles sadly. "I'll miss you in the meantime."

"I expect nothing less. Oh, and one more thing. I think you should stay with the Order. You can do good things there."

"I—yeah." Jyn looks shocked, his smile fading for a moment before returning as he assures me, "Yeah, I'll do that. I can't imagine leaving them."

As the ship sets sail, I stand on the deck and look back at Jyn and Safiya down below. They both wave, and I wave back. When we glide off into the open water, wind fills our sails and the whole world stretches out in front of us. I stand at the edge of the ship for a long time after the two of them disappear from my view, becoming tiny spots on the dock then nothing at all. The wind ruffles my hair, whipping it into my face and obscuring my view but it also pushes us forward, to Iolleria. Senika stands next to me, watching silently until the cliffs are all there is to see.

"I've never been out of Alkelia," I admit.

"Then I have a lot to show you." He grins. "Just wait until we get to Isondale, you'll love it. There are so many good places to eat and a festival that will happen soon. We can go to the sea and I'll show you the Old Castle. It's going to be perfect."

"I can't wait." I step closer to him and reach for his hand.

"Will you miss Elview?" Senika asks.

"Not sure," I say. "Maybe. I might go back one day, but for now, I need to get away."

"So your solution is to run away to another kingdom?" There's a skeptical lilt to his voice.

"With you though," I say. "And I don't think this really counts as running away."

"Good, because if we both made a habit of running to other kingdoms to escape our problems, we would never get anything done."

I elbow him in the ribs. "I never ran from the problem, I just beat it up."

He shrugs. "Well, I don't know if that's much better."

"When we get to Isondale," I say after a brief silence. "What will you do?"

"I don't know," He admits with a sigh. "I guess I'll go home and tell Mum what I did. I'll introduce you to her, and we can go from there."

There's a smile on his face when he speaks, like he's imagining a perfect future. It's strange to be here after spending my whole life thinking I would be trapped in the hell called Alkelia with no one who cared. Now, I am free. I'm leaving Alkelia.

I have Senika.

"Let's start with getting there safe and staying alive," I say.

"Ah yes, that sounds like an excellent beginning." He agrees with a bright grin.

And when he smiles, I smile back.

EPILOGUE: GHOSTS

VENDETTA

"You nearly killed him."

Eris shrugs. "I had not expected him to reveal himself so soon. But he is strong; he will live. He must."

"We lost our most valuable asset," I say. "Without Alkelia under our control, this could be much harder."

"You will figure it out. You always do."

Only when the door falls shut behind the Lord of Shadows do I allow myself to relax. Just when I found the Halfblood who is meant to destroy this world, the very same kid attacks Eris's pawn in Alkelia and nearly kills himself in the process. I turn to the crystal ball on the table, yanking the white cover back over it. Then I pick up a stack of books, brushing dust off their pages and returning them to their rightful places on the shelves lining the room.

The room has no roof, only crumbling walls and a wonderful view of the sky that makes me glad it never rains here. If it did, the books would be ruined. The walls are hidden behind rows and rows of crowded bookshelves, all of them housing dust old tomes containing wisdom thought to be lost centuries ago. This is the Library of Camiah, a city destroyed by the gods when they sealed the Gates of Gosritaan. The people who once lived here are nothing more than bones and dust. Their killers rule this world without worry.

One day, I will see the death of the gods. One day, they will die, and all those dead because of them will have peace. Even Eris, the god I have served for many decades, will die alongside them. Because he is a killer, and killers cannot live in the world I will create.

"He uses you as a pawn." The voice behind me is startling, cold and vacant.

"He will die, Zegreus," I say.

The man sweeps across the room, his feet hovering inches over the ground. Zegreus is a ghost, the first one I ever raised, but he is also my teacher. He claims to be a necromancer who was killed during the destruction of Camiah. Whether or not that's true, he has taught me to raise the dead in order for me to become indispensable to Eris. Necromancers can stop aging, but Zegreus is a frail old man with a wispy beard and pale, wrinkled skin, turned translucent in his present ghostly state.

"Vendetta, I worry that you grow too bold," the ghost frets. "The Lord of Shadows is determined to bring Doriak back to this world and there is little that can prevent him from reaching his goal. If the boy falls into his hands, he will be unstoppable. You know this."

"Which is why I need to act fast." I drop the books on top of one of the many stacks. "If I can kill him, even just banish him, I can do the same to the others. This world will be freed from its constraints."

"Vendetta. Do not forget where you came from."

A long time ago, I was a boy from the Serpent Isles. I was just another kid from a village, a boy with a name long forgotten. I had friends and a family, all of them forgotten just like I am. But the storm took them all. A storm was brought by the Goddess of Wind, Esyn in her anger at Oceno, God of the Sea. It was Eris who found me and saw my talent for necromancy, although I cannot say how. More time than I can count has passed since then, but time means nothing when it cannot change anything.

He brought me here to Camiah, saying I was to be his perfect tool to achieve the greatness of destroying this world. Perhaps he saw my anger toward the gods because he didn't try to get close to me, simply allowing me to learn of my powers alone while he watched the world for his chance to act. He was waiting for the child with the power to destroy or save this world, but the child was never born.

It was simply by accident that Zegreus was raised once more. I was wandering through the dark crypts under the castle, searching for any indication of magic and sure enough, Zegreus appeared before me, a ghost offering to teach me all I needed to know. It took half a century for me to grow strong enough to truly raise the dead. Zegreus asked me to give him a real body, but his had been lost many years before I even came here. But I could build us an army of unkillable soldiers. When Eris asked me to raise Xethos from the dead, I didn't think I could do it, much less allow Eris to have partial control of the body along with the dead god. But I did it, I raised a god from the dead.

It was a few months later that we discovered the Halfblood idiot learning of our plans in Alkelia. A Halfblood who couldn't be more than a pest. We planned to simply play a few games and then snuff him out, but plans don't always work out. Only when the fool revealed himself to "Xethos" did we see the truth.

He was the one the prophecies spoke of.

Eris nearly killed the Halfblood but another saved him. I didn't have to intercept, but I made certain Eris wouldn't let it happen again.

"Yeah. I haven't forgotten," I say to Zegreus. "I've only grown impatient."

ACKNOWLEDGMENTS

This book is the product of many late nights reading fantasy novels, hours when I should have been doing homework and a tiny spark of an idea that grew over many, many years. It came into being due to the endless patience of my friends, *Lord of the Rings* nights with my Dad and all the money dedicated to my book-buy sprees. Although each of these may feel like small things, to me, they mean the world.

I would first like to thank all my friends for their undying love and support but most of all, I need to thank Talia Boehnisch. You put up with my endless questions, nagging and self-doubt yet you were still the first to read *Whispers of Gods and Ghosts* and as if that wasn't enough, this beautiful cover art is the product of your time and effort. The amount of gratitude I have for you is completely unquantifiable in any sort of terms.

To Chloe Milne, thank you for the many, many times you listened to my very long-winded explanations and rants as well as for your amazing support, excitement and encouragement.

To Amelia Cook and Caroline McLeod thank you for tolerating my persistence to read my book and for never doubting me even when I nearly hit delete on this entire project. Your support is forever appreciated and welcome. Know that I could not have done this without you.

Thank you (again) to my incredible editor and mentor, Chris Tavenor. The excitement you've shown for my work is something I once could only dream of. Every second you dedicated to this project means the world to me.

The next ones are in no particular order since that would be impossible to determine among these fabulous people. To my uncle, John Carswell for reading and editing and giving whole-hearted encouragement. To my grandma for gifting me the book that first got me into reading. All my teachers but especially my fourth and seventh-grade teachers, Mr. and Mrs. Presesky, for first telling me to write and for continuing to tell me to keep going. If I could, I would thank you in person although you might not even know what you did.

Thank you to the amazing Coralie Moss for reaching out to offer advice and introduce me to the self-publishing process.

To my cats, Raven, Rico and Spot for being the best listeners a writer could ask for. My best friend Raven, you inspired Fenix so, although you may be oblivious, this couldn't have been done without you.

Thank you Mum and Dad for always pushing me to improve and to never give up on my dreams even when everything feels impossible. Without all of you, this would not have happened and I am eternally grateful to each and every one of the people who helped me, even if you don't think you did much.

Finally, I want to thank all the writers out there. *Whispers of Gods and Ghosts* is the product of many, many years spent reading and creating worlds in my head. This would not have been possible without the authors who were brave enough to put their work into the world for tiny-me to discover and fall in love with.

And to all those still hoping to publish, especially young writers, never give up, hold onto your dreams and remember that the closer

you are to achieving something great, the more you will doubt yourself.

About Author

Rain Carswell lives in Banff, Canada where they were born and raised and have been writing since fourth grade. They live with two black cats who have been nothing but good luck. Their time is spent writing fantasy novels, daydreaming and stressing over school. This is their first novel.